Mountain Rescue: The Ascent

Sky Croft

*Yellow Rose Books
by Regal Crest*

Texas

Copyright © 2013 by Sky Croft

All rights reserved. No part of this publication may be reproduced, transmitted in any form or by any means, electronic or mechanical, including photocopy, recording, or any information storage and retrieval system, without permission in writing from the publisher. The characters, incidents and dialogue herein are fictional and any resemblance to actual events or persons, living or dead, is purely coincidental.

ISBN 978-1-61929-098-3

First Printing 2013

9 8 7 6 5 4 3 2 1

Cover design by Donna Pawlowski

Published by:

Regal Crest Enterprises, LLC
229 Sheridan Loop
Belton, TX 76513

Find us on the World Wide Web at
http://www.regalcrest.biz

Printed in the United States of America

Acknowledgments

A big thanks to my brother-in-law, Andy, for imparting his knowledge on the world of climbing, and for allowing me to tag along so I could experience it for myself. His computer savvy is also greatly appreciated—thank you for all your assistance (particularly designing my website) and support you've given over the years.

A special thanks to my family, who have always been supportive of my writing. This book would've never been published without their words of encouragement, or their unwavering belief in me. For that, and for many other things, I am deeply grateful. Thank you will never be enough.

For my beloved Grandma, the nicest woman I've ever met.

Chapter One

THE DARKNESS SLID down the mountainside, covering the lone figure like a shroud. She stood on the cliff edge, her tied-back hair blowing wildly.

Some people would think that she was overconfident, cocky, or even mad for standing in her somewhat precarious position. But those people didn't know Kelly Saber. Not only was Saber an expert climber, she was part of an elite Mountain Rescue team, hence why she stood on an outcrop of rock in the freezing rain, as night fell around her.

Her shoulders shook as a shiver ran through her. The harsh wind blew savagely against her tall slender form and she hopped up and down for a moment, trying to return some much needed warmth to her body.

Damn UK, she thought. *Does it ever stop raining?* And worse still, she was in the Scottish Highlands, where the locals joked, 'If it's not raining, it's about too, and if it's not about too, it already is.'

Clear blue eyes scanned the horizon intently, searching for the rescue helicopter. In one hand she clutched an unlit signal flare. Saber would need every second the flare could give her to attract the chopper. Visibility was poor and getting worse by the minute.

The team had been out for hours, searching for three lost hikers. They found them huddled just below the summit. The men had reached the peak, but on their way back down, the sudden rain made the rocks slippery. One of the men had stumbled, trapping his leg between two rocks as he fell. The stones, much harder than his flesh, didn't give way, but his ankle did. It snapped.

The hikers were sensible enough to file a route plan at the Mountain Rescue station beforehand and when they hadn't returned within their given time frame, it'd been relatively easy for the rescue team to find them.

Saber's ears pricked up at the sound of rotors in the distance. She thought the sound came from her left, but she couldn't see any search lights.

Her hand itched to strike the flare, but she waited impatiently. With her free hand she wiped her eyes, trying to clear them of the rain.

The whirring of the helicopter's blades drew nearer, and at last she was able to pick out the lights. It edged slowly toward her, its beam distorted by the downpour.

Once Saber was sure that the helicopter was in a position to see her, she struck the flare. It lit on the first try, causing light and smoke to emerge quickly. Holding the flare above her, she waved it left, then right, breaking through the darkness with an orange glow.

The helicopter's beam staggered in her direction.

With her other hand she pulled out a VHF radio. She pressed the button, pausing for a moment before speaking into the transceiver. "Doug, chopper's here. ETA?"

Static was heard on the other end before Doug said, "Fifteen minutes."

Saber silently cursed, she thought they would have been closer by now. "Okay, I'll lead the bird to you, meet you halfway."

It went quiet for a few seconds. "I'd appreciate that, Saber."

Another voice came through. "Yes. Thanks a lot."

She recognised Coop's tone instantly and smiled in response. Stanley Cooper was the eldest of the group at forty-six, and that was probably the reason why he was so polite. He had impeccable manners, and was one of the few men left who were naturally chivalrous. Saber was fiercely independent and it had taken her a while to get used to his ways, thinking at first that he was being condescending. Now, she loved him like a brother.

"You're welcome, Coop. Rest those old bones." She smirked.

"You just thank your lucky stars you were born a woman!" he said, the banter settling like a comfortable blanket between them. They both shared a wicked sense of humor, and that was what had first drawn them to each other.

Saber chuckled, shaking her head. "Stop whining and get moving."

The light finally landed on her. She threw down the flare, which faded and went out. As the search light illuminated her, she pointed with the radio, indicating she was going to take them to the rest of the team.

The helicopter pilot, Stuart Masterton, had worked with their Mountain Rescue team on many occasions, and Saber knew that he would understand what she was doing. If Stuart had needed clarification he could have spoken to her over the radio.

As Saber started to walk forward, the crewman working the searchlight moved it slightly so that it was just ahead of her, illuminating the way. She gave a thumbs up.

She climbed down from the outcrop of rock. When her feet landed on even ground, she quickened her pace, breaking into a slow jog. After several minutes she held her hand out to the right, veering off in that direction. The light remained with her, bathing everything in a surreal grey color.

She knew that the helicopter was fitted with advanced all-weather search and navigation equipment, but she had decided to make their job a little bit easier by presenting herself in clear view. The Sea King could find her team themselves, although they would have difficulty extracting them from where she had left them. She'd originally intended for the team to meet her here, but they were still a way off, so now she was leading the chopper up to a piece of open ground, where both teams would appreciate the lack of obstacles in their way.

Scrambling up some rocks, the wind carried voices to her, coming from above. She continued her ascent, nimbly moving from rock to boulder with ease born out of years of practice. She was grateful for the light though, knowing that it wouldn't be fun in the dark. In fact it would be damn perilous.

It took her a few more minutes to reach the top. When she did, the ground in front of her levelled out—she was on the trail. The rest of the team would be coming along this path any moment now. She crossed to a boulder and sat down. Facing the helicopter, she pointed to their left. The light moved that way, leaving her in the dark.

About one hundred metres away were seven men, four carrying a stretcher, one on the stretcher, and two ambling tiredly behind. The four men were maneuvring the stretcher expertly between two large boulders when the light hit them. The two men, the hikers who had been rescued, waved frantically at the helicopter.

Douglas McIntyre, the leader of the rescue team, kept everyone moving forward until the ground flattened and there was nothing to obstruct them.

"Jesus, Saber!" Rich said when he spotted her looming out of the darkness. His hand darted dramatically to his chest, the other busy holding the stretcher. "Almost gave me a friggin' heart attack."

"So what are you whining for? Almost doesn't count."

"Ha ha."

"Right, put him down," Doug said. Following his lead, the stretcher was carefully placed on the ground.

Stuart's voice crackled over the airwaves. "You ready for the winch?"

Doug retrieved the radio from his belt. "Send it down."

A mechanical whirring was heard overhead as the winch operator sent down the winch man. The rescue team all rechecked that their corner of the stretcher was secure, before attaching the necessary equipment allowing the winch to take hold. All the bindings came together in the center, and when the winch man landed, he fastened the hook into place.

"Take her up," the winch man said.

The wire's grating noise was evident as the winch pulled the injured man up toward the chopper. Once in, the stretcher was set down and fastened in place, then the winch descended again for the others.

"Who's next?"

Doug indicated the two shaking hikers.

The winch man crossed to the nearest hiker, and quickly fastened him to his own harness. He put the hook into place and they were both hoisted skyward. Once everyone was onboard, the door slid shut and Stuart flew them all toward the nearest hospital.

SYDNEY GREENWOOD WAS looking forward to the end of her

shift. She had already worked a double, and was now running purely on coffee. Glancing at her watch, she smiled, five minutes to go. Just enough time to finish the notes she was working on.

The Accident and Emergency doors suddenly swung open, and in came her next patient.

Stepping forward, she sighed to herself. Someone else could have easily handled it. She wasn't the only doctor in the hospital. Although she told herself this frequently, it was in her nature to help people—even when she was sleep-deprived.

Sydney grabbed a nearby gurney and pushed it toward the new arrivals. "Put him on here," she said.

The four people carrying the stretcher were all identically dressed in black trousers and red and black coats. They didn't hesitate and carried the man over to her, placing him professionally on the gurney.

Sydney recognised the clothes instantly, knowing them to be Mountain Rescue. The only contrast in their attire was that each person wore a different color helmet.

"What happened?" Sydney asked. The rain-covered person next to her moved away, giving her room to work. She glanced up to thank the man, surprised when she found herself looking at a woman—and a beautiful woman at that. Intense blue eyes captured her green eyes as she gave the woman a grateful nod. The tall, good-looking stranger tipped her head in acknowledgement, stepping back farther still.

Across the stretcher, a bearded man spoke up, "This is Steven Knight. Mountaineering accident. His ankle's broken."

Sydney turned her attention back to the patient on the stretcher, taking out a small torch and shining it into his eyes. "Hi, Steven. My name's Dr. Greenwood. Follow the light for me." She watched his pupils for a moment. "How long has he been out in this weather?"

"About nine hours. Half of that in the rain. Downpours have been on and off all day."

Sydney signalled a couple of nearby nurses, who took the gurney from the rescue team and wheeled it down the white, clinically cold corridor. Another nurse came over to escort the remaining two rescued hikers, who were visibly shaking, to cubicles, where they could get out of their wet clothes and be carefully monitored.

"Thanks a lot guys," Steven shouted back.

"You're welcome," an older man said.

Sydney then regarded the rest of the group, addressing the bearded man who she assumed to be in charge, "Are you or any of your team injured?"

"No. Thanks for your help, Doctor. I'll come and collect the stretcher later." He moved toward the door.

"You should still be examined," Sydney said, walking directly into his path so the man had no choice but to stop. "How long have you been out in this weather?"

"This was a quick one, believe me." He tried to go around Sydney, but she was having none of it.

She peered up at him, not the slightest bit intimidated by his much taller frame. "How long?"

His lips twitched in amusement, though his facial hair helped to conceal it. "Three hours or so. It was straightforward."

Sydney looked the team over, all were dripping wet. Their Mountain Rescue gear was waterproof, but she knew that against the harsh mountain conditions the cold could still penetrate. Her eyes landed on a young man wearing a silver helmet, with the word *Rich* emblazoned on the front. She assumed that was his name, and not some monetary declaration. "His lips are going blue."

The leader turned sharply, clearly wanting to see for himself.

"Rich, is it?" At his nod, Sydney said, "Let's get you checked out."

"I'm fine." Rich didn't give her a chance to say anything further, pushing through the team and heading for the exit.

The blue-eyed beauty got in his way. "Rich, go get checked over."

Rich frowned, his annoyance showing. "No way, I'm not having you guys goading me for the next three months."

Sydney caught the woman's gaze, silently appealing to her.

Moments passed, then a relenting sigh. "Fine, we'll all get the once over." The woman shook her head, seemingly at herself, before glancing to the team leader, who nodded his acceptance.

Sydney smiled broadly. "Great. Follow me."

SABER SAT IN the cubicle waiting her turn to be seen. What had gotten into her? She could be at home right now, in her own bed, a cup of hot chocolate in her hands. Instead, she was sitting on a horribly firm mattress in a hospital, and she hated hospitals. She was cold, tired, and hungry, and in a foul temper as she had no-one else to blame but herself for the current situation. *I never could say no to a pretty face.*

She had stripped out of her mountain gear, and was left in a pair of black combats and a red microfiber fleece. Her walking boots were tucked under the bed, covered with mud. Her helmet, backpack, and wet clothes were alongside them. Long legs were curled underneath her, and a blanket was draped over her shoulders.

Saber's hand supported her right elbow, taking the weight off her shoulder. The cold weather had caused it to stiffen up, the old injury still bothering her. Her mind drifted for a few moments, unpleasant memories surfacing.

She was startled when a warm hand touched her forearm. She hadn't heard anyone enter through the screening curtain.

Saber straightened instantly, her eyes refocusing to find a woman standing in front of her. It was the pretty blonde doctor she'd met outside in the hallway. Dr. Greenwood, if she remembered correctly.

The doctor was slim, petite, and her short hair accentuated her natural good looks.

She was also watching Saber intently. Saber had no clue as to how long the doctor had been standing there, receiving no response, or even basic recognition from her. Only the doctor's touch had brought a reaction, and Saber could easily guess what the doctor was thinking. Had she simply been lost in her thoughts, or was there something more sinister going on? Perhaps she'd taken a knock to the head while out on the rescue?

"Are you all right?"

Saber nodded, somewhat bashfully. "Sorry, I was just thinking."

Dr. Greenwood clearly wasn't convinced, for she retrieved a small light from her breast pocket. As she raised it, however, a hand stopped her.

Saber felt a connection when they touched. A shiver coursed through her, although it was anything but unpleasant. Their eyes locked for an immeasurable moment, and Saber just knew that whatever she was feeling, the doctor was feeling too.

Dr. Greenwood cleared her throat, as if caught between embarrassment and...something Saber couldn't yet determine.

Saber returned her hand to its previous position. She shook her head slightly, trying to remember what she'd intended to say. "I'm fine. I didn't hear you that's all. I was distracted."

"Humor me." Dr. Greenwood lifted the light again, looking pleased when no protest came forth. Saber stayed absolutely still while her pupils were examined. "That's fine."

"Told you," Saber said, smiling to soften the words. "You're a stubborn one, aren't you?" That was twice now the doctor hadn't taken no for an answer.

Dr. Greenwood smirked as she put the light back into her white lab coat. "You have to be in this line of work."

"I bet."

Dr. Greenwood studied her, taking in her posture with a frown. "I thought you said you weren't hurt?"

Saber's forehead creased in confusion. "I'm not."

The doctor indicated her arm, which was once again being supported by her hand.

"Oh, no. I'm all right." Saber immediately removed her hand, moving her arm around to prove it. "See?"

Dr. Greenwood let the matter drop. "Okay, if you say so."

"How's Rich doing?" Saber changed the conversation. There was nothing the doctor could do for her shoulder anyway.

"His temperature's coming back up."

"Great. When can we go?" Saber was unable to keep the enthusiasm out of her voice. She edged forward on the bed.

"Gee, everyone I treat asks that same question. Do I smell or something?" Dr. Greenwood joked good-naturedly.

Saber chuckled. "No, I just don't like hospitals."

"Who does?"

"Good point." Saber shrugged out of the blanket, laying it next to her. She was eager to leave.

"An hour or so. Depends on his progress." Her head tilted in thought. "How did you get here?"

An hour? Jesus, the things I get myself into. She was starving, and suspected the time would be spent hunting for a vending machine. "Chopper."

"Thought so, how are you going to get home?"

"We'll get a taxi," Saber said, surprised by her consideration.

"For five people?" she asked doubtfully. "You'll be a bit squashed."

"Try spending the night in a tiny cave with them. We're used to tight spaces. Either that or we'll get two."

"Where do you live?"

"Shirebridge."

"I'm finished with my shift for tonight. I'll give you guys a lift," Dr. Greenwood offered.

"I couldn't ask you to do that." Saber wondered if the doctor was this kind to all her patients. Although her work with the Mountain Rescue Service often brought her to the hospital, she had never seen this woman before. She definitely would've remembered.

"You didn't." At her hesitation, Dr. Greenwood said, "My car's big enough."

Saber smiled at that. "Is it out of your way?"

"No, I live there."

Dark eyebrows shot up. She knew everyone in the village. It was a very small community. People referred to it as a village, but it was really a hamlet, and it was even small by that standard.

Dr. Greenwood continued, seemingly amused by her expression, "I'm just in the process of moving actually. I'm hoping to finish this weekend."

"Are you the one who bought Sanders' old place?" Saber asked.

"I don't know." She went quiet, as if trying to think of a way to describe her new home. "It's on the edge of the village, set back from the stream."

Saber nodded. "That's it. You picked a great house." In her opinion, it was the best in the village.

"Thanks. Needs a bit of work though."

"You should speak to Doug about that, the guy with the beard. He's the local handyman."

The doctor flashed a grin. "Thanks, I will. I'm Sydney Greenwood by the way." She held out her hand.

Saber gripped it lightly, but gave a firm shake. "Kelly Saber."

"YOU WEREN'T KIDDING about your car!" Saber said as she

examined the black Range Rover. "Sport V8. Nice." She clambered into the front passenger seat.

"I see I'm not the only one who's into cars," Sydney said, surprised.

Saber returned the smile. "Guilty. But good luck trying to educate these guys," she thrust her thumb toward the backseat, "because they don't know the difference between a Porsche and a Skoda."

Sydney laughed.

"Hey!" Rich squealed in outrage. "I know what a Porsche looks like."

"As long as it gets me from A to B, I don't care what it looks like," Doug said, fastening the seat belt around his large frame.

Both women rolled their eyes at each other.

Sydney started the engine and waited for the boot to close. Three men who she'd learned were Doug, Rich, and Jeff, sat in the back seat. Coop was farther back again, the boot having ample space. In fact, out of everyone he had the most room, even after all the wet clothes, helmets, and backpacks had been piled in beside him.

As the boot was closed, Sydney said, "I thought if I was living in a little country village way out in the sticks, I should have the car for it."

"That was your excuse, huh?" Saber teased, running a hand over the black leather interior.

Sydney narrowed her eyes. "I thought it was pretty good." She pulled out of the parking space and onto the road. She liked driving at this time of night, as there wasn't much traffic around.

Saber held up two scuffed palms in mock defence. "I didn't say it wasn't."

"So, Sydney, you need a hand moving in this weekend? Or do you have a fella to help you?" Coop asked.

"No, I haven't got anyone. My family lives a good few hours away." She glanced in the rear-view mirror at Coop. "I would really appreciate some help."

"Consider it done. Me and Saber will be over first thing Saturday, how's that?"

"That would be great."

Saber nodded easily. "Sure, no problem. What about the rest of you guys?"

"I'm in," Doug said.

"I'll have to check with the wife, but I don't see why not," Jeff added.

"Count me in, too," Rich spoke up from the middle seat. "Hey, afterward we could take Syd over to the Café." He leaned forward, playfully punching Saber in the shoulder. "You can cook your special."

"We're trying to welcome the woman, not scare her off," Saber joked.

"Yeah, yeah." Rich looked to Sydney. "Wait till you try her breakfasts!"

Sydney smiled. "You're a chef?"

"Yep. I work at the Café."

"She's the best cook in the village." Rich drummed his fingers repetitively against the side of Saber's seat.

"Excluding Marty, I'm the only cook in the village," Saber said wryly.

Rich hit her again, harder this time. "She's just being modest."

Sydney's grin faded as she saw Saber's imperceptible flinch. Her training as a doctor made her much more observant than most people. *So she has hurt her shoulder. Now who's stubborn?* She made a mental note to bring the subject up later, knowing now wasn't the time.

"Fine, we can take Syd to the café," Saber said. "You guys can show her around the place while I cook."

"Yes!" Rich drew the word out, as he settled back in his seat.

"Sounds good," Sydney said, driving the 4x4 toward her new home.

Chapter Two

WHEN SATURDAY FINALLY arrived, Sydney had managed to catch up on her sleep, and she was excited to be moving the last of her stuff in.

A knock on the door caught her off guard and she put down her coffee. She looked at the clock—9:00 a.m. She crossed to the window. Coop did indeed mean first thing, both he and Saber were outside.

Sydney opened the door, her eyes widening when they landed on Saber. Her long black hair was flowing freely around her shoulders, and her blue jeans and white T-shirt highlighted every curve of her well-toned body. The woman was breathtaking.

They looked at each other for a long moment before Coop cleared his throat.

"Sorry, come in." Sydney moved aside, trying to ignore the amusement on Coop's face. "Thanks very much for coming."

"It's no bother," he said instantly. "We're glad to help, aren't we, Saber?"

Saber nodded mutely. Seeing where her eyes were, Sydney glanced down at herself. She was dressed casually: green khaki's and a brown T-shirt. "It's quite different from my hospital persona, I know."

Saber looked somewhat abashed. "Sorry, the contrast just caught me by surprise." She tilted her head thoughtfully. "I like it."

Sydney smiled.

"The others are coming by at noon, so that should give us enough time to make a trip to your old place, come back, and start unpacking," Coop said. "What do you think?"

"I'm glad you're organised," Sydney said, as she put on her running shoes, bending to fasten the laces. She tied them in double knots, not wanting them to come undone. It would be just her luck to trip while carrying a box full of breakable ornaments.

"Right then, I'll follow you two in my car."

"Are you sure, Coop?" Saber asked. "I assumed we'd all be going together."

"I'm not letting you near my car. I've seen you drive!" Coop joked.

Sydney giggled as she stood back up.

"If you like your car in one piece, you'll do the same."

"Noted," Sydney said, pretending to be serious. She retrieved her coat off the peg, but didn't put it on. She hung it over her forearm. It looked nice outside, and she wasn't the slightest bit cold.

"Hey!" Saber said. "I'm a good driver."

"I'm sure you'd win a crash derby," Coop teased.

Saber smiled. "What's the prize money like?"

"Not enough to buy you a new car."

Sydney snatched up her car keys from a nearby shelf, and then pointed warningly at Saber. "You, keep away."

Saber started to laugh. "Aw, Coop, I really wanted to drive that car!" He dodged as she playfully swiped at his arm.

They all stepped out of the house and Sydney locked the door. "You sure you don't mind travelling alone? You can come with us." She walked down the porch steps and onto the drive, heading toward the detached double garage.

"Nah, this way we can bring twice as much back. It'll be quicker. Besides, it'll allow you two to get to know each other better." Coop threw Saber a mischievous wink.

"Okay, try to keep up."

"SO HOW LONG have you and Coop been together?" Sydney asked, after a few minutes driving.

"I came to the village when I was sixteen, so eighteen years," Saber said easily. "He's the best guy I've ever met."

"It's nice that you get on so well." Sydney switched on the air-conditioning to cool the car down.

"He's my best friend. Actually, he's more than that."

"I figured that part." Sydney smiled. "I'm not that dense."

"What do you mean?"

Sydney looked across to her passenger, brow creasing. "Well, that you guys are a couple."

Saber burst out laughing. She fiddled with the vents for a moment, directing the fresh breeze on to her face. "Is that what you think?"

"Yes. You just said you'd been together for eighteen years."

"I didn't realise you meant together, together!" Saber sniggered. "Ew. I mean no offence to Coop, but he's like my brother. That's what I was going to say, he's more than my best friend, he's like a brother to me."

"Oh, I see. My mistake."

"Plus, he's a bloke, which really doesn't do it for me." Saber replayed what Sydney had said. "So apparently, you are that dense." She grinned at Sydney's insulted expression, and their laughter mixed together as the car rambled through the countryside.

An hour later they reached the biggest town in the area—Gransford. It contained the hospital where Sydney worked, several shops, a post office, and a supermarket.

"How come you're moving from here?" Saber asked, as Sydney parked the car. "It's a lot farther to get to work."

Sydney got out of the vehicle and locked it. "It is, but I don't mind the commute. Besides, here's not rural enough for me. I've had my eye on Shirebridge for a while now. It seems like it has a nice little community."

"It does," Saber said. "They're good people. Some are a bit odd," she smiled, "but they're friendly. You'll fit right in."

Sydney looked as if she didn't know whether to be flattered or insulted. "Thanks. I think." She walked toward a detached house that was near the hospital. "I'll miss being able to pop home for lunch though."

"Yeah. I bet that was handy." Saber fell into step beside her. "Marge will love you."

"This is me." Sydney indicated the building. "Marge?"

"Nice," Saber said, examining the house's profile. "My boss. She owns the café." Affection shone clearly through in her voice. "She gave me my first job."

"Is that so? Does that mean you've always worked at the café?"

"Mm. I used to work tables before I became the chef," Saber said, while she waited for the front door to be opened.

It swung wide, and Sydney stepped inside, bending down to pick up a handful of miscellaneous items off the floor. "I thought I'd re-routed all my mail." She flicked through the letters. "All junk."

Coop jogged up to the door, joining them. Sydney greeted him, as Saber moved aside so he could enter.

"It's all boxed. Most of it's in the living room." Sydney led them down the now empty hallway.

Saber chuckled upon spotting the large mound of boxes. "Good thing you brought your own car, Coop."

"Err, yeah."

"You should've seen it before," Sydney said good-naturedly. "This isn't even half."

"Now I'm realising why you have no one to help you, Syd, they've died from overexertion!" Laughter met Coop's words. "You think I'm joking?"

THE THOUGHT DIDN'T strike Sydney again until she watched Coop pick up one of the boxes and leave the room. *God, I am dense. She's got an injured shoulder, and I'm asking her to carry boxes for me? Way to treat a woman right, Syd.*

Saber crouched, selecting one of the heavier boxes.

Sydney quickly stepped up beside her. "I'll take that, it's full of books." At Saber's curious look, she said, "It's very heavy."

"So?" Ebony hair shook as Saber chuckled. "Don't worry, I've got it." She straightened, bringing the box with her effortlessly.

Sydney watched her closely for a reaction, a wince, grimace, anything. She got nothing. *I must've been mistaken.* "So I see." She glanced at her impressive arm muscles and swallowed. Saber was extremely well-toned, but still maintained her femininity. The biceps flexed a little, and she looked up into Saber's smirking face.

"Did you forget what I do in my free time?"

Sydney was embarrassed at being caught. "Umm, no. I just...I've never seen a woman as fit as you, and I've seen a lot of women."

Saber regarded her suggestively. "Oh really?"

"Yes and..." Sydney groaned, realising what she'd said. Turning bright red, she covered her face with her hands.

"Well, well, well. It just goes to show you can't judge a book by its cover."

Sydney scowled at her. "What I meant was, as a doctor, I've seen a lot of women."

"Hey." Saber shrugged nonchalantly. "You don't have to explain yourself to me."

Sydney giggled. "I was giving you a compliment. Next time, I'll keep my thoughts to myself."

"Okay, Okay, I'm sorry." Blue eyes dropped to Sydney's figure, giving her a slow once over. "You should look in a mirror. You're not so bad yourself."

It took a moment for Sydney's overloaded brain to catch up with the conversation after seeing Saber look at her like that. She flushed again, and was sure that any second now her face was actually going to explode. "Thanks," she finally mumbled.

Saber sauntered out of the living room and into the hall. "You're cute when you blush," she shouted back.

The inferno in Sydney's cheeks increased. She was relieved that Saber had left the room, as she knew that she wore the goofiest grin.

ONCE THE LAST box was loaded into the car, Sydney shut the boot. Saber immediately started for the passenger side, so she playfully asked, "Where do you think you're going?"

Saber looked at her in surprise. "I thought that was all of it?"

"It is." Sydney waved at Coop as he drove past them, his car also laden with boxes. She was pleased that he'd suggested taking two cars, since they'd only just managed to fit everything in.

Saber came back over, her confusion evident.

Sydney waited until Saber was stood directly in front of her. "Close your eyes." A single dark eyebrow rose in response. "Close your eyes or you don't get your surprise." The eyebrow disappeared into Saber's hairline. Sydney chuckled mischievously, but Saber's eyes remained wide open. "Please?" She stuck out her bottom lip.

Saber sighed. "You're a dirty fighter." Her eyes shut without further argument.

"Hold out your hands."

Two strong hands with long elegant fingers were placed in front of Sydney, palms up. A jingle was heard as she pulled out an item from her pocket, placing it gently in the offered hands. She let her touch linger for a few moments longer than was needed, simply enjoying the warmth. "Open."

A surprised, but genuinely delighted expression crossed Saber's face when her gaze landed on the car keys. "Really?"

Sydney nodded, enchanted by her response.

Saber excitedly bounced on the balls of her feet, drawing a further chuckle from Sydney.

"Go on." Sydney tipped her head to the driver's door.

Saber, it seemed, didn't need to be told twice. As she passed Sydney, she squeezed her shoulder.

Sydney was taken aback by how comfortable she felt around Saber, and had to keep reminding herself that she hadn't known her for very long. She got into the car and looked across at Saber, who was standing in the doorway, frowning. She broke into laughter when she realised the reason why—the seat position.

"How do you drive that close? I can't even get in!"

Sydney leaned over, pressing a button on the side of the driver's seat. It started to slide back. "I'm a lot smaller than you, Sabe."

"Sabe?" Saber tilted her head, as if pondering her new, shortened name. "I like that." She gestured to the moving seat. "You're smaller, but you're not a dwarf."

Sydney scoffed. "I need it to be that close."

Saber waited for the seat to come to a halt at its full extension. "That's better."

"You can't possibly need that much space!"

Saber climbed in, her long legs filling the footwell easily. She started to adjust the mirrors.

Sydney shook her head disbelievingly. "Your legs are longer than I thought."

"Hmm, thinking about my legs were you? I'm starting to worry about you, Syd," Saber joked.

Sydney smiled, but to her annoyance, color still stained her cheeks.

Saber twisted in the seat, facing Sydney. "Then as a doctor, I need your help."

Sydney grew serious, her mind reeling at the sudden change in topic. "What's up?"

"I'm suddenly jealous of my legs, what can I do to stop that? I think amputation is a bit extreme, but...Ow!" Saber grinned as Sydney slapped her thigh.

Sydney laughed loudly. "You're impossible."

"Hey, I'm being serious." Saber couldn't keep a straight face, despite her obvious attempt. She was slapped again, and more laughter followed. "God, I thought I was butch. Ouch."

"Get driving before I change my mind," Sydney said, pointing at the road ahead.

"Bossy, too," Saber said with a smirk. "All right, I'm going." She started the engine and pulled away. "Did I mention that I've only ever driven automatics?" She smoothly changed the gears, and then peeked over to the passenger seat.

Sydney gave her an amused look. "Do you ever stop?"

"Do you want me to?"

Sydney shook her head. "Nope."

"Quit complaining then."

Green eyes narrowed, feigning outrage. "Watch the road."

"Yes, ma'am." Saber's attention returned to the road for a few seconds before she glanced back.

They grinned at each other.

"WHAT MADE YOU change your mind?" Saber asked from the driver's seat. She glanced at the clock, realising that they would make it back to Sydney's house with twenty minutes to spare before the rest of the guys showed up.

"Huh?" Sydney was gazing out the window, watching the scenery pass by. The surrounding countryside was beautiful, and the shining sun in the clear blue sky only enhanced the view. She regarded Saber.

"What changed your mind? About me driving the car?"

Sydney shook her head. "I didn't change my mind, I was always going to let you drive it."

"Really?"

"Yes. As soon as I realised you were a fellow car enthusiast. I was just teasing you."

Saber navigated the 4x4 around a bend, and the sunlight hit them full on. She put the visor down to shield her eyes.

Sydney did the same, but because she was that much shorter it didn't have much effect. She straightened to get those few extra inches, and she stopped squinting when her eyes reached the shade.

Saber found the whole thing entertaining, although she didn't let on. She knew some people were sensitive about their height. She, herself, had been teased at school because of her height. It hadn't gone on for very long though, a fist to the guy's jaw soon stopped his comments. "I thought for sure Coop had put you off."

"No, he was just messing about. Besides, even if he'd been serious I wouldn't have listened."

Saber raised a questioning brow, but her eyes remained on the road. "How come?"

"Okay, let me go over what I know about you. You save lives — not even for a living, you do it for free, on your own time, because it's the right thing to do. From my experience that type of person isn't reckless, in fact, in my opinion, they're incredibly heroic and wouldn't endanger anyone." She took a breath. "So naturally, I didn't think twice about letting you drive my car."

It was Saber's turn to blush. She cleared her throat self-consciously. "Thank you."

"You're welcome." Sydney paused for a moment. "Sabe?"

Saber shifted as she turned her head. She was growing quite fond of her new shortened name, especially the way it sounded on the other woman's lips. "Syd?" Saber abbreviated her name too, drawing the word out.

Sydney smiled cheekily. "You're cute when you blush."

Saber burst out laughing as her gaze went back to the road. "Touché."

"Sabe?"

"Yeah?"

"Open her up."

Saber glanced over, a grin emerging. "Finally, a woman after my own heart." Her foot hit the accelerator.

COOP ARRIVED AT Shirebridge a few minutes behind them. They were starting to unload the boot when he jogged over. "How did you get in front of me?"

"We did a little off-roading." Saber held up the car keys, waving them in his face. "It's a hell of a car to drive."

Coop smirked. "What did you do to earn that? Did you use those big blue eyes on her?"

"You'll never know, old-timer."

"I'll get the door." Sydney tucked a box under one arm and held out a hand.

Noticing that Sydney's car keys also had the house key attached, Saber passed them over before picking up a box herself. She then watched Sydney cross to the porch. She had a cute walk. And an even cuter...

"Ahem." Coop loudly cleared his throat, interrupting her thoughts. He made a show of following where Saber's gaze had been. "She's nice, huh?"

"Yeah, she is."

"Gorgeous, too." Coop nudged her teasingly. Saber merely looked at him. "Don't give me that! I saw where your eyes were!" He jostled her again.

Saber's mouth quirked. "Are you going to just stand there all day, or are you going to help?" She started to walk toward the house.

He instantly picked up a box and quickly moved to her side. "Happy now? You know, you'd make a fine looking couple."

"Cut it out, Coop," Saber said, in a warning tone.

"You would. Imagine the little one's you two would have. What with your eyes and her blonde hair. Wow."

Saber suddenly drew to an abrupt halt, a condescending expression forming. "I hate to break this to you, Coop, but we're both women, there's something missing that stops that process." Her nose scrunched up. "Thank God."

Coop laughed, his gentle brown eyes twinkling. "I know that, but I'm sure Rich would be glad to step in. We all know how he feels about you."

"If you don't cut it out, I'll tell Sydney you think she's gorgeous."

Silence greeted her.

"Thank you."

COOP RAN A hand through his short-cropped red hair, stopping to scratch his head as he did so. "I'm done in." He yawned as he slouched on Sydney's brown sofa.

Saber glanced up at him from her seat on the floor. The furniture was in, but she preferred to sit here, her back resting against a wall. "Me, too, but at least Syd's got everything now."

Coop nodded. "She picked a lovely house." Humor crept into his tone. "Looks to me like you and her share good taste."

"Mm, I love this place," Saber said quietly.

"I know you do. It's been your dream to live here since I first met you." Coop sighed at her wistful expression. "I wish you had let me lend you the money."

A firm shake of her head. "No way, I wouldn't have been able to pay you back in a million years, not on my wages."

"I could've just given it to you."

"No you couldn't. I wouldn't have accepted it."

"You and your stubborn pride." He shook his head in disapproval. "In my day, women were grateful for gifts."

"I am grateful for the offer. But that doesn't mean I could accept it. Dreams are overrated anyway," she said, to convince herself as much as Coop.

"Women." A confused look appeared on his impish face. "Just when I think I've got you figured out..." He shook his head again.

Saber crossed her legs. "I've always supported myself, Coop, you know that. I'm not going to change the habit of a lifetime now, am I?"

"Pride," he repeated.

A grin creased her face. "It's why you love me."

"No, I love you despite that," Coop said, smiling. "It's a darn close call though!"

Saber's eyes filled up, and she smiled softly. He was the only family she had. Her parents were still alive but she had stopped thinking of them as family a long time ago. She looked away, embarrassed.

Coop remained silent, giving her a moment.

Sydney entered the room, carrying a tray filled with three glasses and three cans of lemonade.

"Has the old place changed much?" Coop asked, as he took a glass and can from Sydney. With a smile, he thanked her courteously.

Saber consciously pulled herself together as she glanced around, her eyes scanning the sitting room and the attached dining room. The room was large—being both long and wide, but despite that, it managed to maintain a nice homey feel. She ran a hand over the wall, not surprised to find the old fashioned wallpaper still there. "No, it hasn't changed at all."

Sydney walked over to Saber and handed her an ice cold can, followed by a glass.

"Thanks," Saber said. "When I first came here, I used to do some odd jobs for Sanders, the guy who used to live here."

"I'll give you a tour later and you can see if anything's different."

"I'd like that."

"I'll have to decorate this room first. I can't stand the wallpaper." Sydney gave the dark stripy print a distasteful glance.

Saber chuckled. "Sanders did have unusual taste."

Sydney nodded, crossing to the remaining sofa. "You can say that again." She regarded Saber with an amused expression. "I have seats you know."

Coop almost choked on his drink. Laughing, he faced Sydney. "I've been trying for years to get her to sit on my furniture."

"I like the floor," Saber said simply.

"The sofa's not that uncomfortable!" Sydney's words drew another round of laughter from Coop.

"Don't take it personally," he said. "She just hates chairs, even her own. She'd prefer to sit on the floor."

When Sydney looked to her for confirmation, Saber nodded. "It's true. I only bought a sofa in my place for other people to sit on. I hardly use it."

Coop covered his mouth politely when he yawned, stretching his legs out in front of him.

"Here." Sydney put down her drink and went to Coop. She bent over and pressed a button on the side of the couch. A low electronic sound was heard, as the seat shifted backward and a foot came out to prop up Coop's feet. "It's a recliner." Glancing at a wide-eyed Coop, she indicated the button. He leaned forward and examined it. "This one takes you up, this one down." Finished with the brief tutorial, Sydney headed back to her seat. "Make yourself comfortable."

Coop smiled brightly as he played with it, laying flat. "You could sleep on here." Making himself upright again, he released the button, leaving his feet up. He seemed impressed. "I've gotta get me one of these."

"It is pretty good," Saber said.

"You could try it, you know if you weren't sitting on the floor."

Sydney raised a questioning brow. "How come you prefer it?"

"As a kid, I spent most of my time outside, either walking or climbing. I guess I just got used to the hard ground." She shrugged, looking back and forth between them. "It's not that odd."

"It is!" Coop and Sydney blurted simultaneously. They chuckled.

Saber shook her head. "It's not."

Sydney took a long drink. "What about in a restaurant?"

"I sit on a chair like everybody else. The same at work, or when I'm in public." Saber became droll. "I don't think Marge would appreciate it, hygiene in the kitchen and all that."

Sydney's green eyes grew wide, as if an awful thought had occurred to her. "Please tell me you sleep in a bed?"

Saber grinned wickedly. "Wouldn't you like to know?"

Sydney colored slightly. She looked to Coop for an answer, while putting her nearly empty glass down onto the table.

"How would I know?" he said, sounding mortified.

"I guess I'll just have to wait and see." Sydney poured the rest of the can into the cup, filling it to the brim.

Saber could tell from Sydney's expression that the words had simply been spoken without thinking, and it hadn't even occurred to her how they might be taken. Still, she couldn't help but tease. "Someone's confident!"

Once again, Sydney blushed, turning so red she resembled a beetroot. She grabbed a nearby cushion and buried her face into it.

Coop was embarrassed also, but he joined in with Saber's laughter. After a few moments, Sydney did too.

"THAT'S THE CAFÉ there." Rich earnestly pointed to a small building at the dead center of the village.

Sydney nodded, her stomach rumbling as she walked toward it. She looked over her shoulder, through the group, her eyes searching for Saber. The woman was at the back, wedged between Coop and Doug. Doug was the only one in the group of equal height to Saber, but he was a lot broader than she was.

It had been a long day, but finally everything was set up. The team had been kind enough to help her put the furniture where she wanted it, so now her house actually felt lived in.

Sydney had also spoken in depth to Doug about the changes she wanted to make to the house. Doug was obviously good at his job, and had given her a few suggestions that she wouldn't have even thought of, stating that he and his workmates would be happy to help. She'd been surprised to learn who his workmates were. Doug ran a small business, Jeff was the carpenter, and Rich was his handyman. She wondered if the team spent any time apart. She found herself somewhat jealous of the group's dynamic though, they all seemed to get on really well. She would love to have friends like these.

Sydney returned her attention to Rich. "You were telling me before about the food, what's best?"

Jeff fell into step next to her and answered her question. "The steak." Jeff's name was actually Duncan Jeffries, but he was nicknamed Jeff. Over half of the group were referred to by their surnames: Saber, Jeff, and Coop.

Sydney noticed that he was the same height as her. "God, it's nice not to have to look up to see you. I was getting a sore neck."

Jeff snickered. "Yeah, I know exactly what you mean."

"The steak's the best, huh?" she asked, examining the man. Jeff was the quietest of the group, only speaking when he had something specific to add. He had an undemanding presence about him, and Sydney found herself instantly liking him. His hazel eyes lit up whenever he discussed either his wife, Julia, or his son, Brian. Jeff was a very slender man, but clearly had a wiry strength about him. Moving her oak cupboard had proved that. His face was narrow and thin, he looked almost gaunt, and his short brown hair and clean shaven face didn't help matters.

"No way!" Rich said, from the other side of Sydney. "The breakfast's the best."

Sydney couldn't help but smile at the enthusiasm in Rich's voice. He looked to be only a couple of years younger than herself, but if that was true he was very immature for his age. She did not doubt that he was the youngest member on the team.

"Steak," Jeff repeated. "Well at least that's my preference, I'm sure you can make up your own mind."

"From what Rich has told me, I can't go wrong." Sydney's stomach grumbled loudly. "I could eat a horse."

"That's good, too," Jeff joked.

"It would be if Saber cooked it." Rich glanced back to the woman. "She's incredible."

Sydney caught Jeff rolling his eyes. He'd obviously heard this conversation before. More than once. *Uh oh, someone's got a crush. At least he's got good taste.* She tried changing the subject. "I bet you've got some interesting stories to tell, being part of a Mountain Rescue team."

"Have we ever!" Rich dragged his gaze away from Saber, and tracked to Sydney's face. "We've got hundreds."

"I'd like to hear some."

"Okay. One time we got called out to rescue this farmer who got stranded on the mountainside with his flock, and..." Rich was distracted by Jeff, who was shaking his head strongly. "What?"

"She doesn't want to hear that one."

Rich frowned. "Why not? It's funny."

"It was disgusting." Coop came alongside them. "Sydney's a lady. Don't you dare finish that story. It was bad enough that Saber had to see it."

Rich laughed instantaneously. "I remember the look on your face. I wish I'd had a camera."

Coop glared at him, not looking the slightest bit amused. "I think that was the only person I was ever reluctant to save."

His words surprised Sydney. "Why? What did he do?"

Rich opened his mouth to reply, but Coop cut him off. "Richard Powell, don't you dare!" he said sternly. "You're forgetting your manners, boy."

"Oh, come on, Coop, she's a doctor for Christ's sake. She's seen all sorts."

"Watch your language. Besides that is not the point," he said. "I think it says a lot about you, when that's the first story you think of."

Rich scowled, looking decidedly unhappy.

"We're about to have our lunch. I don't think she'd be able to enjoy her food if you continue," Jeff added.

Coop flashed white teeth at him, clearly glad of the support. Jeff quietly dipped his head in response.

There was a long silence, and Sydney began to wish that she'd never asked the question in the first place.

"What about the time with the wildcat?" Coop said.

Rich's floppy light brown hair covered his eyes as he stared at the ground, sulking moodily.

"You tell it, Rich," Coop continued. "You're the best one at telling stories. You've got a good memory and remember all the details."

Rich looked up at the unexpected compliment.

"Wow, a wildcat?" Sydney tried to encourage him. It was already apparent to her that Rich and Coop were complete opposites, and she wondered if their age difference was the cause: Rich being the youngest, and Coop being the eldest on the team.

"Go on, son," Coop said.

"All right." Rich cleared his throat, pushing wavy hair behind an ear. "We were out on a regular route check." He explained to Sydney, "You see, we have to check the paths, make sure they're clear, that sort of thing." He gave Coop a fleeting glance.

Coop clapped a hand on his back. "Good man."

Rich's spirits seemed to pick up, and he carried on telling his story with regained enthusiasm.

Sydney caught Coop's eye and he winked at her. She smiled at him. He had considerable charm and seemed to be a genuinely nice guy with, from what she had just seen, flawless manners. Sydney respected him for that, even if they were a bit dated. She could see why Saber was so fond of the man.

AS IT WAS mid-afternoon by the time they went for lunch the café was nearly empty, which meant they easily found a table.

Sydney was extremely relieved by this as the few other people that were in the café kept giving her curious looks. She couldn't blame them. In such a small community where everyone knew everybody else it was big news when someone new arrived.

Rich led the way to a large table, and slid along the seat until he was at the end.

Coop gestured for Sydney to precede him. She did so, and he followed, filling that side of the table. Doug sat opposite Rich, then Jeff, which left the remaining seat free for Saber.

Saber didn't sit down. "What would you like to drink?" she asked Sydney. "We've got tea, coffee, coke, orange or apple juice, milk, water, wine, spirits, and beer."

Sydney was surprised at the last three on the list, and it must have shown on her face.

Saber grinned. "We're also the pub."

"Small village," Doug said, his lips curling upward.

Sure enough, when Sydney glanced around, she saw barstools sitting directly under the counter. Otherwise it looked like a regular café. It was decorated in pale shades of cream and burgundy, and she found it pleasing to the eye. The long counter was positioned in the center, at the back of the room, and behind that was a doorway that led to the kitchen. It was deceptively spacious given its appearance from the outside.

"Apple juice, please."

Saber nodded and walked off.

Sydney was wondering why Saber hadn't asked anyone else, when she noticed the woman grabbing a few glasses off a nearby shelf, setting them down on the counter. She realised that Saber already knew what the men would want.

Saber opened the silver vertical fridge and removed two bottles of beer. After she'd filled the glasses with the other drinks, Coop got up and helpfully carried them back to the table. As Saber cracked the lids off the beer, a towel whipped through the doorway behind her and caught her squarely on the backside.

"Yow!" Saber jumped, almost spilling the beer. She whirled around to face the culprit, finding a tiny woman in her mid-fifties glaring at her.

"What are you doing?" the woman asked, waddling forward. Her brown eyes narrowed as her plump form advanced.

"Marge, I'm helping," Saber said. "I'm getting drinks for that lot." She waved her hand toward the corner of the room.

"It's your day off," Marge said, in an exasperated tone. "I'll do it."

"I'm going to rustle up something for them to eat."

"You're going to cook as well!" Marge tutted. "They are so fussy, why won't Marty do? I ought to give them bread and butter." She caught sight of the extra addition at the table. "Is that your new friend?"

Saber nodded. "Come on over, I'll introduce you."

Marge wiped her hands on the apron that hung from her waist, then she shuffled after Saber. "Pretty little thing." She ran a hand through her hair, as if to try and tidy it as they neared the table.

"Hi, Marge," Coop greeted politely. "How are you today?"

"I'm fine, thank you."

"Sydney, this is Marge Westbrooke. Marge, this is Sydney Greenwood." Saber multitasked, introducing them while also handing Rich and Jeff their beers.

"Nice to meet you." Sydney returned the café owner's warm smile. Marge had brown hair, which was speckled with grey, and a friendly face with mischievous eyes.

"That's a nice house you've got there, Doctor." At Sydney's quizzical look, Marge tipped her head upward. "She's told me all about you."

AFTER ENDLESS DISCUSSION they still hadn't decided what to eat, and the debate abruptly ended when Saber held up a hand. "Syd, are you a vegetarian?"

Sydney shook her head.

"Right, then I'll do what I usually do to keep everyone happy." With that, Saber simply disappeared off into the kitchen.

Before Sydney could ask what that meant, Doug started to speak, automatically taking charge of the conversation. She recognised that he was a natural born leader, and the others in the team appeared more than happy for him to do so. Sydney knew that sometimes, being the leader meant a certain distance was placed between them and the rest of the group, but it didn't seem to be the case here.

Doug was strong, powerfully built, and ruggedly handsome. He leaned forward and rested his muscular forearms on the table, fixing her with a direct stare. His brown facial hair twitched as he said, "So, Sydney, what made you become a doctor?"

Sydney took a drink of her apple juice, enjoying the sweet tang. "Same reason I expect you joined Mountain Rescue."

"You like to climb?" Doug teased.

Sydney smiled. "To help people," she said. "But you're right, I do like to climb."

Rich's disbelief was evident. "You're a climber? A *rock* climber? Like us?"

"Mm-hmm. I don't get to climb as much as I'd like to though."

"That'll change now you're living here," Coop said with certainty. "If you want, we could show you the routes, some of the best climbs?"

Sydney nodded emphatically. "I would really like that."

"I bet Saber would too," Coop said. "There's quite a few around this area."

"You got your own gear?" Rich asked skeptically. "Stickies and harness?"

"Of course." Sydney's temple creased. All serious climbers had their own equipment, shoes and a harness were the most basic items that a climber needed.

"What grade do you climb at?" Rich pressed her for information. At Sydney's brief hesitation, a smug look plastered itself on to his face.

Clarity hit her, his questions suddenly making sense. "Oh, I see. You think I'm a gear freak."

"Gear freak?" Coop sounded puzzled.

Doug scratched his beard. "Someone who collects the parts but doesn't use them, just so they can impress people by saying that they climb."

"I usually climb at about 5C or 6A," Sydney said. "One of my favorites is the Old Man of Stoer."

It went quiet for an instant, then Doug and Jeff started to laugh.

Coop clapped a hand gently against Sydney's back, clearly pleased that she'd put Rich in his place.

Rich just sat there, as if stunned into silence.

"I'm impressed," Doug said. "Gear freak my ass!"

"A doctor and an expert climber? Who are you, Superwoman?" Rich looked at her with newfound respect. "Mind, I shouldn't be surprised, look at those arms!" He squeezed her bicep a couple of times.

Sydney felt her cheeks heat as all eyes were directed to her biceps.

"Nice muscle tone...Superwoman." Doug grinned impishly. "I think I hear a nickname calling."

Sydney's eyes widened. "No, no. Syd's fine thanks."

THE TIME FLEW while they were waiting for lunch. Before they knew it, Saber was carrying out huge plates from the kitchen. She placed two down, which were overflowing with steak, gammon, sausages, and bacon.

Marge carried over a bowl full of mashed potatoes and another full of vegetables.

Saber retrieved the final plate, this one a mix of roast potatoes and Yorkshire pudding.

"Is this all for us?" Sydney wondered aloud.

"This is Saber's specialty." Rich rubbed his hands together earnestly. "Everything you could possibly want."

Marge came back with a gravy boat and various sauces. She put them down and pointed to Saber, then at the end seat. "You. Sit."

Saber chuckled, but did as ordered.

Delicious smells wafted up from the table. "This looks great," Sydney said. "You really didn't have to go to so much trouble."

"I know, but I wanted to. We are celebrating after all." Saber smiled.

"We are?"

Saber gestured at Coop, who graciously took over, raising his glass and waiting until everyone copied him. "To our new friend. May she find happiness here in her new home."

"Welcome to the village," Doug added.

Sydney was grinning from ear to ear. "Aw, thanks you guys." She held up her own glass. "And thanks to Saber, for preparing this wonderful meal."

"Saber," the men toasted, tipping their glasses to her.

Sydney took a drink, noticing Saber's blue eyes sparkling across at her.

"Let's eat," Rich said, and the whole team dug in at once.

Sydney was slightly taken aback, not yet comfortable enough to just join in. Coop kindly passed her a plate, making sure that she got what she wanted. He waited patiently, offering them to her one by one. She gave him a grateful look.

"Like rabid dogs, aren't they?" he said humorously.

No one protested — they were all too busy eating.

Sydney chuckled as she glanced around the table, finding Coop's description to be quite accurate. She was surprised to find three different types of steak: rare, medium, and well-done, and she was struck by how thoughtful Saber was, providing something for everyone's tastes. She concentrated on her own meal for a few moments, enjoying every bite that she took. Understanding now why Rich had raved about it so. She let out a happy sound as she ate, giving the cook a thumbs up. The food was delicious, but she enjoyed the smile Saber gave her even more.

"Told you," Rich mumbled around a mouthful.

After the meal that Sydney described as 'Ambrosia,' they went for a leisurely stroll through Shirebridge.

The first time Sydney had entered the village, marked by the wooden gate with the bright green name etched into it, she'd realised that she was somewhere special.

She'd stepped out of her car and simply stared. Leaning back against the gate, she'd looked down at the valley in front of her, mountains encasing the tiny village on all sides. Flowing down from the mountain directly ahead of her was a waterfall. It ran into a wide stream that wound its way through the countryside. At the center of the valley was the village, and the stream gurgled right past the dozen buildings there. On one side of the stream, behind the houses, was a large forest that came to a halt near the foot of the mountain.

The houses were old-fashioned but beautiful, the wooden beams that appeared between the grey stone adding both strength and character. The houses were dotted around on both sides of the stream, and two narrow bridges at each end of the village allowed access to either side.

Sydney would have been happy living in any house there. They were all unique in some way, but one in particular had caught her eye. A large house sat at the very end of the village, just after the bridge. It was set back from the stream and had complete privacy.

As the road into Shirebridge was a dead end, she realised that the village would have very few visitors. The other road that led through the mountains veered off on top of the hill, just before the gated sign.

As they walked along, Sydney was drawn out of her memories when Jeff spoke up from beside her. "That's mine there." He pointed across the stream to a smart looking house with a swing hanging from a tree in the garden.

Sydney's eyes grew wide in admiration. "Your garden's incredible. I've never seen anything like it."

"Thanks. Julia's a keen gardener."

"I can tell. Is that a pond?"

"Yes. It's two-tiered so a waterfall comes down, you can't see it from this angle," Jeff said. "It attracts the wildlife."

"I bet you get all sorts of animals around here?"

"We do. And what's great is, if you put out the right food, they'll come to you. Your back garden's great anyway, 'cause there's nothing between you and the forest, and your front goes straight down to the stream."

Sydney had to smile, these people knew more about her house than she did. "What did Sanders do?" She knew the old man had died, but was curious as to what his link was with the team. They'd clearly spent a lot of time at his house.

"Sanders ran the business that I now have," Doug said. "He trained me. When he retired, I took over from him. He was a dear friend."

"And a good man," Coop said.

"Shame about his taste in décor." Rich's face scrunched up.

"Tell me about it," Sydney muttered flatly, drawing laughter from both Doug and Rich.

"You'll soon get the place sorted," Saber said, speaking for the first time since leaving the café. She was alongside Coop, a few steps behind the rest of the team.

"Let's hope she's got better taste!" Coop teased.

Sydney nodded in agreement. "Let's hope."

"You're forgetting the reclining sofas, Coop," Saber said.

"Good point, she's got great taste."

Sydney shook her head, smiling at Coop's expression. "If they go missing, I'll know where to look." She pointed, and he gestured to himself innocently.

"She's got you pegged." Saber bumped Coop with her shoulder and he stopped walking.

Both women stopped too, allowing the three men in front to put some distance between them. Sydney liked the others a lot, but Saber and Coop were already her favorite—they just clicked.

"Oh I see, this is how it's going to be, huh? Two against one?" Coop rubbed his shoulder, as if trying to feign an injury. "I'm in so much trouble."

Sydney smiled.

"I hear you've climbed Stoer?" Saber said.

Sydney nodded at her before turning her attention to Coop. "Telling stories about me, were you?"

Coop didn't deny it. "Yep."

Looking back to Saber, Sydney continued, "Coop's gonna show me some of the climbs around here, you game?"

Saber grinned. "Absolutely."

"What about tomorrow?" Coop shrugged his broad shoulders at Saber's questioning glance. "We can make a day of it. We'll take you up Bracken Groove on Scar Peak." He pointed behind the café. "That mountain there."

"Scar Peak? Sound's delightful."

Coop snorted in amusement.

Saber indicated the mountain behind Sydney's house. "That's The Water Tower."

Sydney spotted the waterfall there. "At least it's aptly named." She gestured over the stream toward the last. "And that one?"

"Toppling Crag," Coop said.

"Okay." Sydney eagerly nodded. "I'll hunt out my stuff tonight."

Saber tipped her head. "I'll bring lunch."

"You most certainly will not!" Sydney said.

Saber blinked, clearly taken aback. "My food's not that bad."

Sydney scoffed. "Hardly." She placed a hand on Saber's upper arm, enjoying the contact. "You cooked today. And it was amazing. The least I can do is prepare a packed lunch for us tomorrow."

"Oh." Saber smiled. "All right."

"What do you like?" Sydney reluctantly removed her hand.

"We're not picky, are we, Coop?" She continued at his headshake, "Whatever you've got is fine."

"That makes things easy."

"I would offer to make lunch, but the mountainside's a really bad place to get food poisoning," Coop said matter-of-factly.

Sydney laughed abruptly. "You can't be that bad?"

Saber pushed a dark lock of hair behind her ear. "Trust me, he is."

Coop held up a hand. "See."

"Although to be fair, Coop, you can warm up soup."

He nodded enthusiastically. "You're right, I can." Turning to Sydney, he said, "Any time you fancy soup, I'm your guy."

Chapter Three

SABER WAS CLIMBING up a sheer rock face, leading the climb. Sydney and Coop were waiting below, watching her in awe. Coop was expertly guiding the rope through his belay, which attached to his harness.

"Christ!" Sydney said as she watched Saber climb out from beneath an overhang. Saber swung a long leg up, twisting herself to reach for the next hold. Completing the move, her body was vertical once again. The approach itself wasn't unusual, but the speed she did it was.

The lead climber was the person at most risk. If they fell they could drop quite a distance and relied on their equipment to stop them from hitting the ground. If they were fortunate they'd come away bruised, if not and their gear came out, they could suffer serious injury or worse. Unfortunately, those were the dangers of climbing.

"Sorry, Coop." Sydney remembered that he didn't like profanity. When Coop let out an unexpected chuckle, she tore her eyes from Saber and looked at him.

"She's amazing, isn't she?"

He read my mind, Sydney thought.

"It's plastered all over your face," he said dryly. "Don't be embarrassed, I think she's amazing too."

Sydney smiled. "Yes, she is." She followed his gaze upward when the rope stopped moving, surprised to find that Saber had already reached the top, and was waving down at them.

"That was nothing," Coop said seriously.

"Are you kidding? She's the best I've ever seen, she's…" Sydney couldn't even think of an appropriate word.

"A monkey?"

Sydney giggled. "Maybe in a former life."

"Saber's the best climber on the team, she's crucial when time's of the essence. Which is pretty much always."

"How can you call that nothing?"

"You haven't seen anything yet." A wide grin crossed his face as Sydney's eyebrows hiked up.

"Are you guys gonna join me, or are you just gonna stand there and talk?" Saber's voice came through both radios clearly.

One was clipped on to Coop's harness, the other to Sydney's. Saber had brought an extra radio along for her to use for the day.

"You go next," Coop said.

Saber's strong tones were heard again. "You're missing a hell of a view."

Sydney raised the radio to her lips, the short rope that tied it to her harness allowing for the extension. "I take it patience isn't one of your virtues?" she queried, after holding the button in for a moment like Saber had shown her. Beside her, Coop snorted.

"Shut up, Coop," Saber said instantly, drawing startled looks from them both. She was too high up to hear that.

Sydney began to laugh. "Boy, does she know you." She fastened herself to the rope, using the figure-eight loop.

Coop joined in with her laughter, while giving her knot a quick inspection. She was more than capable, but waited patiently, a good climber always checked and double-checked. She rolled her shoulders to loosen them, and flexed her fingers a few times before reaching around her back and dipping her hands into the black chalk bag. Her fingertips came out white. The chalk would help her grip the rock.

"Okay. I'm set," Sydney said into the radio. She felt the rope being taken in. It pulled taught against her, then slackened slightly, allowing her room to move.

"Climb when you're ready."

"Climbing now."

SABER WAS SITTING at the top of the climb, firmly secured. The equipment would keep her in place if either she or one of the others fell. She was currently belaying Sydney, and as she watched, she was impressed by the smaller woman's form. Sydney pulled herself higher, and Saber took in the excess slack.

Sydney stopped when she reached the last stretch of the climb. Holding on to the rock with one hand, she pushed into her chalk bag with the other. If Sydney were to fall, she wouldn't drop to the last piece of protection like the lead-climber would, she was secured from above.

Grinning up at Saber, she bent her hand back and forth, clearly trying to slacken the muscles in her forearm. "I'm afraid I'm not as quick as you."

"It's not a race," Saber said, raising her voice slightly so Sydney could hear. "You're doing fine."

Sydney switched her hold, shaking out the other hand. Looking behind, she took in the view.

Saber did the same. She could see right across the valley, Shirebridge nestled in between the three mountains. The clear turquoise sky contrasted sharply against the darker shades of the peaks, and she simply admired it for a moment. "Beautiful, isn't it?"

Green eyes rose to Saber's face, and held there as if mesmerized. "It certainly is."

Sydney's expression left Saber in no doubt that she was referring to her, and she smiled brightly.

Her energy seemingly renewed, Sydney continued her ascent.

SYDNEY PLONKED HERSELF down next to Saber, so they were sitting side by side. "Phew." She wiped a bead of sweat from her temple. "That was great."

Saber picked up the quickdraw beside her, and reached for Sydney's harness. She clipped the karabiner on and twisted the screw gate closed.

Sydney followed the rope that she was now attached to, surprised to see it already secured. "When did you rig that?"

Pale blue eyes looked up from their task, mere inches from Sydney's face. "When you two were chatting."

"Productive, aren't we?" she teased, very conscious of the hands at her waist.

A small smile. "Habit." Saber untied the other rope. "You've gotta be five steps ahead when you're on a rescue."

Sydney nodded, understanding completely. Her own job was like that.

Saber coiled the rope and shouted a warning down to Coop. "Below." She waited a moment for him to move clear before releasing it. The rope itself was quite heavy to carry, but when it dropped from a distance it became dangerous.

Sydney watched her intently, leaning back and resting her weight on her hands, quite content just to look at her. Saber was wearing a sleeveless top, which was red in color, with thick black stretch panels running down either side. Both her backpack and stickies were of the same colors, and plain black combats finished the outfit off nicely. Her long black hair was tied back in a pony tail.

Sydney wore a similar outfit, although hers were blue and grey. The blue reminded her of Saber's eyes and she groaned internally at herself. *Get a grip...I'd like to. Heh. Stop it!*

Thankfully, Coop interrupted any further thoughts. "Ready here."

Sydney waited for Saber to take in the slack. "Are you set?" When Saber tipped her head, Sydney spoke into the radio, "Climb when you're ready."

"Climbing now." Coop didn't hesitate and started to make his way upward.

"When you're on a rescue do you all stay together, or do you split up?" Sydney asked, wanting to learn more about the Mountain Rescue Service. She was interested in joining herself, but she honestly didn't know if she'd have the time, her work kept her pretty busy.

"Depends if the missing people have filed a route plan. If we know where they are we go as a team. If we don't we split up to cover more ground." Clearly seeing that Sydney wanted more, she continued, "We used to split up into groups of two—there were originally six of us."

"Let me guess, you are with Coop?"

Saber chuckled. "Actually no. When I joined, Coop was already teamed with Jeff. Once you've got a partner, you stay with them, that way you learn each other's styles, along with their strengths and weaknesses. That knowledge is vital on a rescue."

"Who are you partnered with?"

"No one at the moment."

Sydney was somewhat alarmed. "You're meant to have someone with you at all times," she said, quoting the correct safety practice for climbers.

Saber smiled at that. "I know. For the last five years I've been going with Coop and Jeff."

"Couldn't you find a replacement?"

"There's not many people around here. Besides, you've got to be highly trained. It's a lot of work for no pay, not many people are interested in that."

"Who did you go with before?"

"Charlie Bainbridge, he lives here in Shirebridge. Actually, he's your neighbor across the bridge."

"Did he leave the team?"

Saber shook her head. "Charlie? Never, he loves it too much. He works in the rescue station, he's our guy on the ground. He takes care of everything for us, from the initial callout, to arranging the chopper."

"He retired?" Sydney asked.

"No, he's only a few years older than me."

"Which is?" Sydney took her pack off and lay it beside Saber's. She retrieved her flask, taking a few swallows of her energy drink.

Saber grinned. "Inquisitive, aren't we? I'm thirty-four. You?" She shook her head at Sydney's offered flask. "No thanks."

"Thirty-two."

"Aw, you're just a baby."

Sydney scoffed. She took another drink before putting it back into her pack. "I am not...Grandma."

Blue eyes narrowed in mock indignation. "You're lucky I've got my hands full." She pulled in more slack.

"How old's Rich?"

"Twenty-eight."

"I thought he must be about that." Although Rich looked his age, he certainly didn't act it. Surely he wasn't always so juvenile? Sydney wondered what he was like while on a rescue. She knew he had to have something about him though, or he wouldn't have been allowed to join the team.

"I agree. He's immature. You should see him when he's drunk."

Sydney's hairline rose, both at Saber's effectiveness in reading her mind, and at the notion that Rich could be any more childish than he already was.

"You'll get used to it. He's a good lad, his heart's in the right place."

The corner of Sydney's mouth curled up. "He's certainly got excellent taste in women."

Saber rolled her eyes. "You've noticed that already? Is it that obvious?" She groaned at Sydney's nod. "It's gone on for years. I thought it was just a stupid crush and he'd get over it, but he hasn't. He knows I'm gay, you think he'd move on." Saber smirked. "In fact, I was hoping that he'd move on to you."

"What?" Sydney squeaked.

"You know," Saber teased, a mischievous look on her face, "the blonde hair, soulful green eyes. I thought you'd have him hook, line, and sinker."

Soulful? Sydney felt a grin emerge, and she didn't try to hide it. "Gee thanks, pass off your unwanted goods to me."

"You could distract him for me—a real friend would."

"Not this friend, pal! Ask Coop." Sydney snickered.

Saber didn't miss a step. "He's already tried. He failed miserably. He really was quite upset about it."

Sydney giggled, finding that Saber's warped sense of humor was similar to her own. "Rich definitely isn't my type."

"Oh?" Saber asked, her voice dropping an octave provocatively. "And what is your type?"

Recalling an earlier conversation in her living room, Sydney said, "You'll just have to wait and see."

Saber smirked cockily. "I think I can guess."

"Now who's confident?"

"Coop told me."

"He did?" she asked in surprise. Sydney was self aware enough to realise that she found Saber physically attractive, hell, anyone with eyes would, but she hadn't told anyone that.

"I must say, I was shocked, considering the age difference and all," Saber said seriously.

Two measly years?

"But hey, if it's true love, who am I to stand in the way? I hope you're very happy together." She sniffled dramatically.

"Whoa. Hold on, who are you talking about?"

"Coop. He said you liked his red hair." At Sydney's dismayed look, she added, "He's forty-six, you know."

Sydney fiercely shook her head. "I'm not interested in..." Saber erupted into laughter, cutting off the rest of her sentence. "Why you little..."

Saber glanced down at her long frame. "I don't think you can accuse me of that."

"Smartass."

"I had you there." Saber looked smug.

Sydney shook her head, amused. "I think I might have to tell Rich that you're in love with him."

Saber's face turned from smug to mortified in an instant. "You wouldn't?"

"Heh."

AS THE WIND carried merry laughter down the cliff face to Coop, he smiled and slowed his pace. The two women shared a natural chemistry, and he knew attraction when he saw it. He had an excellent sense when it came to such matters. It was a gift, although he rarely had the opportunity to use it.

Coop wanted to see Saber happy, and his mind ran through different scenarios to try and help things along a little—he had a feeling he'd be quite good at the matchmaking business. In fact, he'd already started, that's why he'd suggested this very excursion. After all, life was too darned short. His late wife had often told him that he was a meddler, and a born romantic. He'd always tried to look out for Saber, surely matchmaking was just an extension of that?

"YOU NEVER ANSWERED my question."

"Which one?" Saber joked. Her new friend, she was learning, had a very inquisitive nature.

Sydney grinned. "Why isn't Charlie you're climbing partner anymore?"

"He had an accident when we were out on a rescue. Charlie and I were going up The Face, on Toppling Crag." She indicated the mountain straight opposite, on the other side of the village. "We'd split up into teams, searching for a group of teenage lads who'd not only bunked off school, but decided to hike up one of the hardest mountains around here without the proper equipment."

"How can people be so stupid?" Sydney asked. "I suppose I shouldn't be surprised, I see it daily at work." She touched Saber's forearm. "Sorry, go on."

Saber looked at the hand on her arm, silently drawing strength from that simple connection. "Four were dead by the time we'd found them."

Sydney sucked in a breath, obviously not expecting that. But mountains were hostile places, especially to the inexperienced or ill-prepared.

Saber pulled in more slack before she continued. Her eyes fixed on the mountain ahead, recollecting the events. "They were about halfway up Toppling Crag. They'd taken the right footpaths, but when they'd reached the north slope, they spotted the vertical wall, which is a climb called The Face, and they dared each other to climb it."

Sydney shook her head in disbelief.

"The lads, with the little rope that they had brought—it wasn't proper climbing rope—had used it to tie themselves together," Saber said. You could tie yourselves together while hiking, in fact it was helpful as the others could assist if someone fell. Climbing was the same, as long as a person was secured to the rock. Unfortunately for everyone involved, the teenagers hadn't done that.

Sydney grimaced, as if knowing what was about to come.

"One fell, and took the others with him. Me and Charlie always took turns leading, it was Charlie's turn." Saber swallowed hard, and Sydney shifted closer. "They hadn't taken enough rope to tie all six of them together."

"Thank God for small mercies."

"The remaining two managed to squeeze onto a tiny ledge about twenty feet up." Saber tried to block out the images that came forth. "We called it in, but the rest of the team were a good way off, searching the other sides of the mountain. The boys grew more frantic with each minute we were there. We couldn't wait." She sighed. "One of them had gone into shock, he was crying and screaming for his mother."

"Poor thing," Sydney murmured.

"He was petrified. Seeing his friends like that…Well, it's a lot for anyone to see, let alone a teenager." Saber paused when a warm hand rested against her back, the contact drawing her out of her memories. Her gaze shifted to Sydney's face.

"You don't have to tell me anymore," Sydney said, her tone gentle. "Not if you don't want to."

"No, it's all right. I don't mind." The sympathetic touch remained where it was as she looked away. "As Charlie got nearer, they grew more anxious. He stopped to put in another piece of gear when one of the boys jumped and grabbed on to his back, pulling him from the rock. They both hit the ground. I couldn't do anything to stop it." Saber felt her back being rubbed softly, and she glanced at Sydney. "Charlie broke his spine, he's in a wheelchair."

Green eyes looked steadily at her. "It wasn't your fault."

Saber smiled, but it was forced. "Maybe not, but I wish I could've done something."

"You did," Sydney said. "I'm guessing you got him down off that mountain. He's alive because of you." She moved her hand, wrapping it around Saber's waist in mute comfort.

Saber nodded in quiet acceptance.

"What about the boys?"

"The boy broke his leg and shattered his elbow, but he recovered. The other lad was unhurt, physically at least."

They sat in silence for a few moments.

"Well, my respect for what you do just rose considerably. I thought my job was hard." Sydney gave her waist a supportive squeeze.

Saber smiled, and it was genuine this time.

SYDNEY WAS SITTING on the ground, leaning back against a rock, happily munching on an apple.

They had made it to the summit, and on their way back down, they'd taken another route. A less demanding route. Coop had been walking ahead of them, through a series of tall boulders, when he'd suggested that they should have lunch there. It was a lovely spot, sheltered from the wind, which even on a nice day like today, blew strongly on top of a mountain.

Coop took a sip of his tea, releasing a moan of delight. "You can come more often."

Sydney smiled at him, or tried to, her mouth was full.

"Definitely," Saber said.

"I didn't slow you down too much, then? I was worried I would." Sydney kept her tone light, but there was uncertainty behind the words.

Both black and red hair shook in unison. "No way." Saber regarded her. "You did great."

"You were brilliant," Coop added. "Especially since some of those holds were so far apart."

"Is that a nice way of saying I'm vertically challenged?"

"I meant no disrespect," he said hurriedly.

Sydney and Saber looked at each other conspiratorially, before they burst into laughter.

Coop glared at them. "Women." He shook his head in despair. "And there are two of you now!"

"You've just noticed this?" Saber asked.

"Hey!" Sydney glanced down at herself. "I'm not that flat-chested!" She tapped her chest to prove her point.

"Good Lord!" Coop spilled his tea as he quickly covered his eyes.

Saber held her side, she was laughing so hard.

Coop peeked between his fingers, and grinned at them.

By the time they'd finished dinner, they were back to discussing the team. "Let me see if I've got this right, Doug's got two kids, two dogs, and a wife." Sydney stopped at Saber's snigger.

"I'm sure Faye will be really pleased at being placed after the dogs."

Sydney looked amused, but waved the comment off. "Jeff's got a wife and kid, and Rich lives with his folks."

"Don't get him started on that," Coop said. "He's always moaning 'cause he doesn't have his own place."

"Can't he afford to move out?" Sydney asked.

"Oh, he can," Coop said, "but his life's here in the village. I'm sure you've noticed, houses are scarce around here and it's rare that they ever come up for sale."

Sydney nodded. "So I was really lucky. Wait, why didn't he try to buy mine?"

"I said he could afford a house, not a mansion."

Sydney chuckled. "One of the perks of being a doctor."

"What about you?" Saber said.

"I've worked at St. James' hospital for," she hesitated, "going on nine months, and before that I worked at The General hospital over in Wakefield, where my folks live. I miss them a lot."

"Why didn't you stay there?" Coop asked.

"The job's better here. And I've always wanted to live in the country, my parents are city folk."

Coop nodded in understanding. "My wife Mary was like that, she missed her parents something awful, but this place was her home."

Sydney picked up on his use of the past tense. "I didn't know you were married, Coop."

"I was, well I still am, in here." His eyes glistened as he placed a hand over his heart. "She passed away eight years ago."

"I'm sorry to hear that."

"She was the nicest woman you could ever hope to meet."

A ghost of a smile appeared at Saber's words. "She was." Coop glanced at Sydney. "You and her would've gotten on well."

Sydney didn't doubt it, any person who was loved and respected by these two were well worth knowing in her eyes.

"That's why I can't cook, Mary spoilt me." Coop tipped his head to Saber. "If it hadn't been for this one, I'd have starved to death by now!"

Sydney was again struck by Saber's kindness. *She has to be the most considerate person I've ever met.*

Saber shrugged humbly. "It's just as easy to cook for two as it is for one." She smirked. "I bet there were some meals that you wished I'd never made, especially when I first started out."

His lips curled. "You've certainly gotten a lot better since then."

"I'd still be waiting tables if I hadn't." Saber looked to Sydney. "You see, Coop asked Marge to give me a trial run."

Coop took over from her. "The customers were so impressed, she was hired the next day. It was perfect because Marty, the other chef, wanted to cut down his hours as his wife had a baby on the way."

"You are a brilliant cook." Sydney unconsciously returned the smile that Saber gave her.

Coop started to pack the picnic away. "Do you have any siblings, Sydney?"

"Yeah, I do. A younger sister and two older brothers."

"They doctors, too?"

"My eldest brother Thomas is, my father too, we both followed in his footsteps. My other brother started to train, but found it wasn't for him and dropped out of Uni. Boy, were my parents mad."

"They wanted him to become a doctor?" Saber asked.

"It wasn't that. Anthony didn't know what he wanted to do, he always was the rebel in the family." A sardonic look flicked across her face. "He's bumming around Europe as we speak."

Saber snickered. "Good for him. And your sister?"

"Caitlin wants to follow in my mum's shoes."

"What does she do?"

"She married a rich doctor," Sydney said wryly.

They all laughed as they shouldered their backpacks and set off walking again. Sydney found herself in between them.

Saber jostled Sydney with her hip. "I'm pleased you followed your father."

"Me, too." Of course, the one person Sydney wanted to know about most, had told her nothing about herself. She nudged her back. "Come on, your turn."

Saber's forehead creased. "There's not much to tell, you already know most of it."

"All I know is that you moved here when you were sixteen, and Marge gave you your first job."

Saber nodded.

"Do your parents still live in the village?"

Saber shook her head. "No. I moved here by myself."

Pale eyebrows rose in astonishment. *When you were sixteen?* "Oh. I misunderstood."

"It's all right." Saber paused. "I haven't seen my parents since I moved here." It was clear to Sydney that she was trying to keep her tone flat, neutral. "I don't get on with them."

Sydney noticed that Saber actually flinched with the words. She couldn't imagine not seeing her own parents for a whole year, let alone eighteen. Her mind went into overdrive, wondering what on earth could have happened to cause such a rift.

"I don't have any siblings, well at least not by blood." Saber glanced to Coop, who beamed at her.

Sydney realised that Coop had been suspiciously silent, evidently knowing about Saber's discomfort regarding her family.

"The team's a family," Coop said.

Sydney shifted her pack slightly. "I noticed that."

Saber chuckled. "You weren't saying that when you had to swim across that river!"

Sydney smiled at her, glad to see she was back in high spirits.

"It was cold," Coop said, his voice rising in protest. "Rich is always saying how fit he is, he should've gone. He's a lot younger than I am."

"You know he's all mouth. Rich thinks he's fitter than everyone on the team."

"Not everyone, you set him straight on that." Coop let out an amused grunt.

Sydney grinned at Saber. "What did you do?"

Saber gave her a look of pure innocence.

"She set a race. But not just one, she raced him climbing, running, swimming." He ticked them off his fingers. "And?"

"Cycling," Saber finished.

"That's it, cycling. After she'd thrashed him, at every single one—in front of the whole team I might add—he decided to try and get his own back by tackling her into the lake."

"Uh oh."

"She moved." Coop howled with laughter. "And he came up spluttering."

"ISN'T THIS BACKWARD?" Coop asked. "I should be walking you home."

"We pass your house first," Saber said. "I'm more than capable of walking Syd home myself."

"What makes you think you're walking me home? I could be taking you home."

Dark eyebrows shot up into Saber's hairline.

"My, my, she's forward, isn't she?" Coop said.

Sydney quickly corrected her sentence. "Walking. I could be walking you home." To her relief, she didn't turn red. She was getting used to their teasing banter.

Saber smirked at her. "Of course I'm going to walk you home."

"And again I say why are you the one doing the walking? I might want to walk you home."

Saber scoffed, as if the idea was completely absurd.

Sydney frowned at her reaction. "Am I not capable?"

"Of course you are, but..." she trailed off, clearly unable to think of a reason why.

"But?" Sydney said.

"I've always been this way, even before I met Coop and his chivalrous tendencies. It's just how I am."

"Well I'm the same."

"Maybe so, but I'm walking you home. I insist."

"Okay, you can walk me home," Sydney said, "if you can give me one good reason."

Saber looked to Coop for help, who was grinning widely at their banter. "Because...you're too short."

Sydney chuckled. "I said a good reason."

"Because you're new to the area," Coop said. Saber moved to his side, clapping him on the back in triumph.

Sydney gave in, knowing when she was defeated. "Fine." She nodded, happy in the knowledge that her newfound friends wanted to look out for her.

THEY WATCHED COOP walk up his drive, waiting for him to reach his house. Saber pointed to her left. "That one's Doug's."

Sydney followed the street until her eyes landed on a house set back from the bridge like her own. The only difference was that Doug's was the first house you came to if you went across the bridge, whereas hers was the last. If you didn't go across the bridge and you went along the road on the other side of the stream, the first building you came to was the wooden rescue station that housed the Mountain Rescue team. After that, was Jeff's house. "What's that next door?"

"That's his workshop."

They both waved to Coop, who was now at his door. He stepped inside and shouted good-bye to them. They continued in companionable silence.

Passing the next house, Saber spoke up, "That's Marge's, she can't bear to be away from her café." She tipped her head along the street to the next building, which was the café. "I can count on one hand the amount of times she's had a day off, and I've been there eighteen years. It drives Bill mad."

"Bill?"

"Her husband."

"Ah." As they walked past the café, Sydney spotted Marge bustling about behind the counter. "That's one hell of a work ethic."

Saber smiled, waving to the older woman through the glass. "Yeah, but some people are like that." She glanced at Sydney. "As a doctor, I bet you know a thing or two about long hours."

"Do I ever," Sydney said. "But I love my job, not many people can say that."

"True."

"So which is yours?" Sydney turned in a circle, looking at all of the houses in the village.

Saber raised a finger, pointing across the river. "Straight over, next to Jeff's."

Sydney followed her gaze, immediately spotting the steps leading down to the stream. Her eyes moved over the garden to the front of the house. It was small and simple, but well-cared for, and she found herself liking the place.

Although Jeff was indeed her neighbor, all of the houses in the village were a good distance apart, giving everyone a measure of privacy.

"I love the steps," Sydney said. "Did you put them in?"

"Yep. I like to just sit there, feet in the water."

"Sounds like bliss when you've been on a long hike."

Saber gave her a startled look, then smiled. "That's what made me put them in."

Sydney thought for a moment. "I think I might steal your idea." She knew the perfect place for them.

"Feel free," Saber said. "In fact, why don't you put the steps next to that big tree? Then you can sit in the shade."

Sydney was somewhat taken aback, surprised that Saber was so in tune with her. "That's exactly where I was thinking."

"This belongs to Rich's folks," Saber said, when they passed the next house.

"Is that one over there Charlie's?" Sydney pointed across the bridge.

"Yeah. The next house we pass is your other neighbor, Marty from the café."

"The other chef?"

"That's right." Saber seemed impressed. "You'll soon know everyone in the village at this rate."

"You should be a tour guide." Sydney smirked.

"Ha ha."

"No I mean it, you're really good at this. And I appreciate the fact that you're trying to help me settle in."

Saber stopped and looked at her. "I want you to be happy here."

Sydney thought Saber was going to smile or laugh, anything to make light of her statement, but she did neither. Her face showed nothing but sincerity, and it was clear she meant her words. The intensity of her clear blue eyes almost overwhelmed Sydney, and she wanted nothing more than to reach up and caress Saber's cheek. Sydney restrained herself though, she'd just moved into the village, and she knew all too well how awkward things could become if a relationship didn't work out. She'd had first-hand experience of that in her old job, and it had been one of the deciding factors in why she moved—the hospital simply hadn't been big enough for both her and her cheating ex, and the tiny community of Shirebridge was considerably smaller.

Sydney settled on linking her arm through Saber's, and they set off once more.

SABER SIPPED ON a cup of hot chocolate, stretching her long legs out in front of her.

"Are you at work tomorrow?"

Sydney looked down at Saber, from her vantage point on the couch. "Yes. Are you?"

Saber nodded, smirking toward the dining room that was still filled with boxes. "I see you haven't unpacked much."

"When have I had the time?"

Saber suddenly realised that Sydney had spent the whole weekend with her, and a shy smile formed. "I take that back."

"Mm-hmm." Green eyes twinkled. "I've had a great time though, thanks for all your help."

Saber dismissed it with a flick of her wrist. "I've enjoyed it, too." She was surprised by how much.

"How did Coop's wife, Mary was it?" When Saber agreed, she said, "How did Mary die?"

Saber sobered. "She was hit by a drunk driver. She'd been shopping for Coop's birthday."

"That's awful. What happened to the driver?"

Her face hardened. "He was sentenced to several years in jail, and ordered to pay damages. He was a rich businessman, so Coop got a good settlement—that's why he's retired. Not that it helped much. Coop was a mess for years afterward."

"You helped him through it though." It wasn't a question.

"Of course. It was hard, but he came through."

They were silent for a minute, then Sydney spoke up, "Oh, I wanted to ask you, Rich was telling me a story about this guy who you'd rescued, but Coop wouldn't let him finish. He said that it was disgusting and he shouldn't tell a lady that."

Saber sniggered. "That's Coop all right. Knowing Rich, it was about the flock of sheep."

Sydney clicked her fingers. "That's it."

"What do you know?"

"Only that you were out on a rescue, 'cause the farmer had gotten stranded on the hillside with his flock."

"Well, let's simply say that he wasn't expecting anyone, and we caught him somewhat unawares. He was very," Saber searched for a word, trying to put it delicately, "fond of his sheep."

Sydney's temple creased. "Why's that disgusting?"

"When I say fond, I mean..." Saber raised her eyebrows suggestively. Sydney took a drink, looking at her blankly. *Time for the blunt approach.* "He was shagging his sheep."

Hot chocolate went everywhere as Sydney choked on her drink in shock. "You're kidding?"

Saber shook her head, too busy laughing to answer verbally.

Sydney scrunched up her nose in distaste. "Ew! I'm not surprised Coop didn't want to rescue him!" Utter mortification crossed her face while she wiped the liquid off her chin. "He doesn't live around here, does he?"

Saber was laughing so hard, that she struggled to catch her breath. "No," she finally said. "It was a long time ago, and he moved shortly after that."

Sydney looked relieved. "I should think so, too. Ew! That is disgusting. Did you report him?"

"Why do you think he left?" Saber smirked. "He didn't live in Shirebridge though, he lived in Gransford—where you've just come from." She laughed harder. "So I'll be keeping a sharp eye on you!"

A cushion caught her directly in the face.

Chapter Four

"YOU'RE GETTING BETTER," Jeff said, when Sydney caught up to him.

Sydney smiled as they ran alongside each other, over the rocky terrain. She had been running with the team every morning for the past three weeks, and gradually, her stamina was increasing. She was a fitness fanatic herself, but even though she'd been a runner before she moved to Shirebridge, it had been over flat ground. Hill-running was a lot harder, and at first she'd found it difficult to keep up, often lagging behind.

To their credit, the team had encouraged her, and slowly but surely, her fitness level increased. The group were well spread out, but each day brought the same result. Saber came first, a good distance in front of Doug. He was followed by Rich, who despite his best efforts, had never beaten the leader. Then Jeff, and now Sydney, and finally the group was rounded off by Coop.

Sydney was really pleased with her progress so far, but she was even more thrilled by the team's response to her. Not only had they welcomed her, they were treating her like she was one of them. Over the last three weeks she'd become friends with all of them, even Rich.

"I can't wait to see Rich's face when you pass him. That'll be a sight." Jeff chortled.

Sydney looked at him in surprise. "I'm a way off yet."

"You'll get there," he said confidently.

All of the team were at the top of their own fitness levels, they had to be, but Sydney hadn't yet reached hers, which is what was allowing her to move up through the pack.

Sydney imagined Rich's face, she liked the man, but he could be awfully big-headed. Wickedly, she hoped that her fitness level didn't peak before she passed him. Ideally, she would like to run alongside Saber, but she considered that an impossibility as Saber was ridiculously fast.

Once Sydney had finished the six mile run, she made her way to the stream, where she knew Saber would be waiting for her. This was one of her favorite parts of the day, one of the few occasions that they got to be alone together.

Sydney hopped down the steps, using Saber's shoulder for support while she took off her running shoes. She let out a long sigh when she sat down and her feet joined Saber's in the cold water.

"I see you're up to Jeff."

Sydney smiled, flattered that Saber had noticed.

"You do realise, this time in a few weeks, Rich will be accusing you of being on steroids," Saber said dryly, drawing a chuckle from Sydney. "He will you know."

"I don't doubt it."

"Hey, you two," Marge shouted across the stream. She was making her way toward the café, clearly intending to open it for the day.

"Morning, Marge," Sydney called back.

Saber waved at her.

Sydney had come to realise that everyone in Shirebridge got up early, even on the weekends. The village awoke around them but neither woman paid much attention to it, focusing instead on each other.

Saber reached up and played with a piece of shaggy blonde hair, before her hand stilled on Sydney's flushed cheek. "You're warm."

"I've been running."

Saber's thumb drew idle patterns on her face. "You're getting warmer."

"That's your fault," Sydney said playfully.

"It is, huh?" Blue eyes twinkled in mischief. She leaned closer, her lips mere inches away. "Do you want me to stop?"

Sydney became serious, removing Saber's hand from her cheek and giving it a brief squeeze before letting go. "My heart says no, but my mind says yes." She let out a frustrated sigh. "It's complicated."

"Care to share it with me?" Saber asked, her tone gentle and undemanding.

"Sure." Sydney heard herself saying, surprised by how readily she agreed. Her last breakup was a painful topic for her, and one she didn't easily discuss. But she felt like she could tell Saber anything. Over the last few weeks she'd become her best friend. The best Sydney ever had in fact. She didn't want to lose that. The least she owed Saber was an explanation. Though she wasn't quite sure where to start.

Saber sat quietly, unmoving, which gave Sydney the time she needed to gather her thoughts.

"I was with Melissa for four years. I met her at work, the hospital over in Wakefield. She's a doctor too, so we both understood about working long hours. You'd think two doctors dating would be a nightmare, never having time to see each other, but we managed to make it work, and were very happy together. Or so I thought. Melissa started spending less and less time with me, and more time 'at work'." Sydney used air quotations to let Saber know that wasn't the truth. "We worked in different departments, and doctors do often have to work long hours, so it took me a while to suspect anything was going on." Sydney shook her head at herself. "I was naïve."

"No." Saber strongly put in. "You trusted your partner, which is what you're supposed to do. It's hardly your fault she wasn't worthy of that trust."

"I found them in a supply cupboard together, and they were doing anything but searching for supplies." Sydney tried to smile, but she couldn't quite manage it. "It turned out that Melissa had been seeing Wendy, a nurse who I'd foolishly considered to be a friend, behind my back for over a year. So during the day Melissa had been at it with Wendy, then at night she'd been coming home to our bed."

Saber laid a consoling hand on Sydney's back. "Melissa's a fool. She'd have to be to treat you that way." Saber rubbed her back as tears slid down Sydney's cheeks.

"I gave her everything that I had. Everything that I am, I gave to her, and still it wasn't enough. She broke my heart. I'm just not sure I can trust someone like that again, and without trust in a relationship, you have nothing." Green eyes locked on to blue. "So please don't think it's you, Sabe, 'cause it really isn't. I care about you a great deal, but I'm afraid I can't let myself go beyond that."

"I understand," Saber said. "And I care about you, too. Honestly, Syd, I'm just pleased to have you in my life, and if friends is all we can be, then I'm grateful for that. I won't push the issue again. Thank you for being honest with me." The pager at Saber's waist suddenly buzzed, and she glanced down at it in annoyance. "Sorry." She scanned the message, then gave Sydney an apologetic look. "I've gotta go. Emergency."

"Has there been an accident?" Sydney's voice rose in concern. She hastily brushed her tears away, then looked at her wristwatch. "Who goes climbing this early?"

"It might not be climbing." Saber stood. "It often happens like this, people don't realise that their family or friends haven't come home. They don't notice they're missing till morning."

"You mean they could've been out all night?"

"Possibly. I'll know more when I get to the rescue station. Charlie will have all the details."

"Do you mind if I come with you?"

"Not at all." Saber held a hand out to help her up, and smiling, Sydney took it.

SYDNEY WAS IN doctor mode. "What was the weather like up there last night?"

Charlie wheeled his way skilfully through the five other people in the room, who were all in various states of dress. He came to a stop next to Sydney, rattling a few keys on his computer keyboard. After a moment, a screen flashed up. He read from it. "They got lucky. Temperature was good, no rain, and a bit of wind but not much."

"Still, they've been out a long time," Sydney said from her perch on his desk.

"You wanna hang with me till these guys get back?" Charlie asked, as if able to tell that Sydney was worried.

"Do you mind?"

"Nah. You can keep me company."

Saber, the quickest one at everything it seemed, fastened her waterproof jacket and crossed to the shelf that held the five multicolored helmets on it. Selecting the red one, she fastened it to her backpack. She shrugged the large pack on to her shoulders, widening her stance a little to compensate for the extra weight.

Doug collected the radios that were charging on the windowsill. There was still one remaining after he'd handed one to each member, and Sydney realised it would have been used by Charlie when he used to go with them. Charlie now used the radio in the station.

The Mountain Rescue station was basic, but it did have heating, electricity, a phone, and internet access. As it was made of wood, its dark texture made the space inside seem smaller than it actually was, and the light needed to be on to see clearly — day or night.

"That's a good idea, Charlie," Doug said. "Syd, it'll allow you to see how a rescue's coordinated at this end." He zipped up his jacket. "Well, you two have fun. See you when we get back."

"Be careful, you guys." Though Sydney addressed the group, her eyes were on Saber. She wanted her to know that their previous conversation hadn't affected their friendship.

Saber gave her a warm look. "We will."

SABER SIGHED WHEN Rich repeated himself for the third time. They were currently going up Scar Peak — this mountain was used more than the others as it had the best climbs in the area.

"My legs are gonna be sore tonight. I've just done a six mile run for Christ's sake, and now this." Rich, Saber recognised, was feeling sorry for himself, and completely ignored the reality that everybody else on the team was in exactly the same position. "We don't even know where to look! I mean, what kind of idiots don't tell their folks what route they're doing? It's common friggin' sense. And I'm gonna tell them that when I find 'em."

Even Doug ignored him, they were used to his rants. The man was all talk.

Saber felt sorry for the team leader, at least the rest of them could get away from Rich's whining when they split up. She hated to admit it, but Rich did have a point, her legs would be sore by the end of the day.

I wonder if Syd will give me a foot rub. Saber silently chastised herself. She'd promised to respect Sydney's wishes, so she would do exactly that. The problem was, Saber kept replaying the incident at the hospital over in her mind. When she had first met those soulful green eyes, and when they'd touched, she'd felt something pass between them, a spark of some kind. Surely she hadn't imagined that? Had she? Not that it mattered now, Sydney wasn't willing to get into a relationship, which

Saber understood, though she found the whole situation incredibly ironic on her part—it'd been years, literally, since she'd felt any sort of romantic attraction, and now that she did, Sydney wasn't interested. A smirk crossed Saber's face, typical. Unfortunately, attraction didn't quite express her feelings for Sydney, Saber knew they ran a lot deeper than that. Way deeper. Still, she had Sydney's friendship, and she would make herself content with that. She had to.

Saber had seriously been considering asking Sydney to come along, but it wasn't her place. She knew that Sydney was keen on the idea of joining the team, and so were the rest of the group. Sydney had already been out on the mountains with them on several occasions, but they hadn't yet managed to fit in any practice runs, and Doug liked his people to be prepared. Although Saber was reluctant to put Sydney in any kind of danger, she knew Sydney was more than capable, and would make a fine addition to the team.

Saber looked at Doug. "You thinking Strong Man's Hold?"

"Either that or Little Giant."

"They that good?" she asked in surprise. "That's one of the hardest climbs around here. It's tough."

"According to the mother. She said they've been climbing since they were little."

Saber nodded mutely, the poor woman must be past herself, having both of her sons go missing.

"That's why she didn't report it until this morning. She thought they'd be all right, they know their stuff."

If that was the case, then it was likely there had been an accident. Professional climbers didn't get lost—unless it was awful weather, which it hadn't been. Saber went through various possibilities: a rock slide, a nasty fall, or equipment failure. Accidents didn't often happen regarding the latter, but when they did, the outcome was usually bad.

Doug's bushy eyebrows creased. "For their sake, let's hope they brought the wrong map and got lost."

Saber agreed, though that situation was highly improbable.

There was hardly any phone reception around Shirebridge, so mobiles were pretty useless. Even if the brothers were fine, it was unlikely they could contact anyone to let them know.

"You want us to take Little Giant?" Saber said, as they reached a fork in the trail.

"Yeah, we'll go to Strong Man's Hold." Doug went off to the left, striding over the uneven ground.

"You guys got the short straw?" Rich teased, evidently noticing which path his climbing partner was on. He halted beside Saber, grinning. "Tough call, huh? I'm glad I'm not in your shoes right now."

"You and me both." Saber walked to the right, not rising to his taunts. After several steps she stopped and turned, waiting for the others to join her.

Rich patted Jeff's shoulder consolingly as the man passed by. "Better luck next time, mate."

When Coop reached him, he simply pointed, not giving Rich the opportunity to say anything further.

Rich followed his finger, to where Doug was marching away. The smirk left his face. "Hey, Doug! Wait up!" He had to break into a jog to catch up.

Saber shook her head humorously as she watched him go.

"I'm so pleased you're my climbing partner, Coop." Jeff glanced at him. "Although I bet Doug's wanting to trade. Any takers?"

"I'd rather go up Little Giant," Coop said dryly. "In the pouring rain."

"With no shoes on," Saber added. She joined in with the following laughter, which echoed across the mountainside.

THE TRIO HADN'T yet made it to their destination. Both Jeff and Coop were ascending the steep shale incline that would lead them to Little Giant, when Saber called out from below.

"Hold up."

Saber's eyes fixed on a bit of orange material that was wedged between two large boulders. She scanned the wall behind the rocks. "Isn't there a cave around here?" Not waiting for a reply, she quickly moved toward the fabric. When she reached it, she had to tug a few times before it came free. She examined the material, then tucked it into one of her numerous pockets. Spotting a gap in the wall behind the boulders, she peered into it, waiting for her eyes to adjust to the dimmer light. She saw the source of the orange fabric, it had been torn from a jacket. The man wearing it was moving toward the entrance, having assumedly heard her voice.

"Please. We need help."

"It's all right. We'll help you," Saber said, before she pulled her head back and shouted to the others. "They're here."

"On our way," Coop called out, as he and Jeff started to descend.

Saber took off her backpack, turned herself sideways, and squeezed into the narrow gap. She dragged the pack by its shoulder strap. A few steps in, the space widened, allowing her to walk normally. It opened into a small cave. She hurried over to the men, dropping down next to them.

"I'm with Mountain Rescue, the rest of my team are on their way. Are either of you hurt?"

Both men were sat upright, their faces drawn and pale. One had his leg extended, his green trousers stained crimson. The man nearest to her, spoke up. His face was dirty, and his eyes were wide. "My brother Darren."

Saber rested a calming hand on his shoulder, knowing that simple touch was the best reassurance she could provide. She gave him a level stare. "What's your name?"

"Peter."

"Okay, Peter, my name's Saber, I need you to tell me what happened." Breaking off eye contact with him, she focused on the injured man. "Hi, Darren." She smiled at him. "I'm going to check your leg. Try and hold still for me."

"We were climbing." Peter began to fill her in on the details. "Darren was leading and he slipped. His leg caught a piece of rock that was sticking out. I managed to lower him down on the rope. There was blood everywhere." Peter looked as if he was going to be sick, but he managed to keep his stomach in check. "I wrapped his leg, but every time he moved it started bleeding again." He ran a red-stained hand through his matted hair. "It was getting dark, so I brought him in here."

Saber gently peeled back the layers of bloodied cloth that covered Darren's leg, finding a deep gash underneath. The wound had stopped its heavy bleeding, but still trickled out when she removed the pressure of the bandage. She reached for her pack, unzipping a side pocket and digging into it. Her hands came out with a fresh compress, and she pressed it tightly against the injury.

Darren let out a pained groan.

"Sorry. Whose idea was it to put the cloth outside?"

"Mine," he said, through clenched teeth.

"It was genius." Saber gave him an impressed look. "Could've gone right past you otherwise."

Darren managed a slight smile.

Saber glanced at Peter as she started to wrap the wound, binding the compress securely in place. He was nearly as pale as his brother, and he kept fidgeting nervously. "And Peter here," she said to Darren, "probably saved your life." She faced the worried Peter. "You did everything right. I would've done exactly the same."

Peter shook his head. "He's been out too long, I should've gone down last night. I was going to, but Darren didn't want me to leave."

"He was right. You never travel in the dark. And if you had left him, he could've gone into shock," Saber said. "Bringing him out of the cold was the best thing you could've done."

Coop chose that moment to squeeze into the cave. Jeff could be heard talking on the radio, updating Doug and Charlie on the situation.

Darren held a hand out to Peter, which was firmly clenched. "Thanks for saving my life, bro, I owe you one."

Peter could only nod, the enormity of the situation clearly catching him off guard.

IT WAS LATE afternoon by the time the team trudged back into the rescue station. Sydney knew from the frequent updates to Charlie, that they'd carried Darren down on the stretcher, and taken him to the hospital in the back of the Mountain Rescue Land Rover. The incident hadn't been too serious, and as they had plenty of daylight left there'd been no urgent reason to call in the helicopter. Unfortunately for the team, Charlie informed her, that meant twice as much work, because they had to descend the mountain carrying the injured man with them. Although the rescue had no complications, it'd clearly been a long day for the team, as every member looked tired.

Sydney had stayed at the rescue station all day, intent to learn all she could about the Mountain Rescue Service. She found it fascinating.

Charlie looked up from the computer screen. "How'd it go at the hospital?"

"It went well." Doug rubbed a slow hand across his beard. "The doctor said Darren's going to be fine, so that's good news."

"Who'd you see?" Sydney asked, curious to know which colleague had treated him.

"Dr. Hogarth."

Sydney nodded. Dr. Hogarth was a nice man, and good at his job. She would've said that even if he hadn't been on the interview panel that had selected her for her current position.

Charlie began to laugh as he glanced from one weary face to the next. "You guys look like shit."

Saber narrowed her eyes, smiling as she gave him the finger.

"Yeah, keep laughing if you wanna be knocked outta that chair," Rich said, in a warning tone. "I could do with rolling on home, my foot's killing me." As if to prove his point, he hobbled over to a row of seats along one wall, flopping down and hanging his head.

Charlie didn't appear to be the slightest bit offended. "I'll take you myself, buddy. You just gotta sit on my lap."

Rich copied Saber's action moments earlier, raising his middle finger.

Sydney stepped out from behind the desk and crossed to Rich, taking the seat next to him. "What's wrong with your foot?"

Rich lifted his head. "It's sore. Too much walking I think."

Sydney nodded. "Go and have a hot bath and let it soak for a while."

Rich mock saluted her. "Yes, Doctor." He quickly glanced around the room, and Sydney followed his gaze, seeing everyone was busy either getting out of their gear or sorting through equipment. Rich lowered his voice. "When's your next day off, Syd?"

She thought. "Wednesday. Why?"

"I was wondering whether you'd like to go out with me?" Rich gave an eager smile. "I know a nice restaurant, though it's a bit of a drive. I personally don't know of a place that can better Saber's cooking, but I know girls like to be wined and dined, so I'm willing to put in the effort."

Sydney didn't know quite how to respond. She supposed she should've been flattered, but not only had Rich made a date with her seem like a chore, he'd overtly praised Saber, who the whole village knew he had a crush on. Sydney easily read between the large, ill-hidden lines—'I'll date you, but I'm thinking of her!' Sadly, this wasn't the worst chat-up line she'd heard, not by a long shot. One of the perks of treating booze-filled patients, though they'd at least had the excuse of being drunk. Still, Sydney didn't want to hurt Rich's feelings, so she tried to turn him down as gently as possible.

"Rich, don't think I'm not flattered, because I am," she lied. "But I'm afraid you and I would never work out..."

Rich interrupted her. "How do you know that? That's why you date someone, to find out if they're compatible." He opened his mouth to continue, but Sydney got in before him.

"I'm gay, Rich."

Rich blinked. "Seriously?"

Sydney nodded. "Seriously."

"Oh great, another one. This isn't fair." Rich threw up his hands in despair. "Why are all of the single women in this village gay?" He looked over to Saber accusingly, who was closest to them, then back to Sydney. "How long have you been a lesbian?"

Sydney thought the question odd, but she answered anyway. "Since birth."

Her response drew a chuckle from Saber. "He's wondering if I converted you," she said.

Sydney rolled her eyes. "No one converted me." *Though Saber's certainly gorgeous enough to do so*, she thought instantly.

"At least that explains why you're not interested in me." Rich's voice perked up. "Because, obviously, if you were straight, you'd totally fancy me."

Sydney couldn't hold back her smile, his inflated ego amusing her.

Rich spoke loudly to Saber, paying no mind to everyone else in the room. "That means you're gonna get together, right?"

"What?" Saber's eyebrow shot up. "Why?"

"Because you're both lesbians," Rich said, as if that explained it.

Both Doug and Jeff whirled to face Sydney, twin smiles forming. "Is that so?" Doug asked. At Sydney's confirmation, he glanced to Coop, who didn't look at all surprised. "Did you know about this?"

"I guessed." Coop shrugged, a self-satisfied smirk on his face. "I have gaydar." He winked at Sydney when she laughed.

Saber returned her attention to Rich, her disbelief evident. "We don't automatically date on that account! That's like me saying you'd date any hetero woman just because she's straight."

"I would if they were hot!"

"How very big of you." Saber's tone dripped sarcasm.

"And I wouldn't even hesitate if it were either of you." Rich shook his head critically. "Are you both blind?"

"SIT YOURSELF DOWN and put your feet up," Sydney said, feeling a bit cheeky for bossing Saber around in her own home. She was doing it for the right reasons though, as she'd seen how tired Saber was on the walk over from the Mountain Rescue station. Sydney had to consciously slow her pace, whereas normally she had to take twice as many steps just to keep up with the taller woman's stride. Seeing Saber's fatigued state, Sydney had taken it upon herself to see that she got settled. "I'll get you a drink and something to eat. What do you fancy?"

Saber followed Sydney into the living room. She surprised Sydney by taking a seat on the sofa. "I'm all right, thanks."

Sydney remained upright, hovering over her. "Did you manage to eat something when you were out?"

"I had a couple of trail bars in my pack."

"That's not enough, I'll fix you a sandwich."

"You don't have to do that. I'll just go and get a quick shower, then I'll be back." Saber moved to stand.

Sydney clasped her shoulder, keeping her in position. "The shower can wait. You don't smell that bad!" She smiled teasingly.

A weary chuckle. "Even if that's true, which I doubt, Marge will kill me if I scare away all the customers." Saber stood up, her body brushing against Sydney's as she did so.

Sydney's jaw dropped. "Please tell me you're not thinking of going to work?"

"Not right now, no."

Sydney let out a relieved breath. She'd thought Saber was being serious for a moment, which was ridiculous, considering how tired she was.

"But in a few hours I will be, hence why I need the shower."

"You are kidding, right?" Sydney's voice rose in disbelief.

"No." Saber looked bewildered. "I've got a late shift. I'm doing some extra hours."

"For when?"

"From eight until midnight."

"Midnight?" Sydney repeated.

"Yeah. It's a pub too, remember?"

"Sabe, you're exhausted now, you can't possibly go to work like this."

A frown. "Yes I can. It wouldn't be the first time, and I'm sure it won't be the last."

Sydney shook her head, annoyed by Saber's stubbornness. "I see you've inherited Marge's work ethic."

"I can't let her down now, there's only a few hours to go."

"Sabe." Sydney softened her tone, trying another tack. "You can't honestly believe you're going to last till midnight? You're dead on your feet. Marge will understand."

"I don't want to go," Saber said. "But I don't want to let Marge down either. It's good enough that she allows me to go running out at a moments notice when there's an emergency."

"So you're saying Marge gives you time off for these incidents?" Sydney couldn't believe that Saber would even consider working in her current condition, she clearly didn't take very good care of herself.

"She does, yes."

"Well, this is part of one of those incidents. You need time to recover," Sydney said rationally.

"I suppose." Saber paused for a second. "But only on two conditions."

"Name them," Sydney said confidently, hoping she hadn't just dove off into an empty pool.

"One, Marty has to be able to cover my shift."

Sydney nodded. She'd expected as much, Saber wouldn't leave Marge to fend for herself. "And the second?"

"You stay here and we watch a movie together?"

Sydney smiled. "I'm sure I can manage that. But first, let me go and make that sandwich."

"I'VE BEEN WANTING to ask you, since our conversation earlier got interrupted, when did you and Melissa split up?"

Sydney thought for a moment. "Over a year ago."

Saber was hungrily devouring her sandwich. After swallowing a mouthful, she said, "I bet it was awkward for a while, you two working at the same hospital?"

"It certainly wasn't pleasant. That was one of the reasons why I took this job—though what I told you and Coop was true, I've always wanted to live in the country."

Saber nodded. "I understand why you didn't tell us that part earlier, we had just met after all."

"I did try to stick it out, thought that since we were in different departments perhaps it wouldn't be so bad." Sydney took a sip of her coffee before she shrugged. "I was wrong."

Saber gave her a sympathetic look. "I'm sorry."

Sydney waved it off. "It's not all bad. I love my new job, the people. I finally live in the country, and my new home is the best house I've ever owned, or at least it will be after it's decorated." Sydney smiled at Saber's chuckle. "And my neighbors are some of the nicest people I've ever met."

"Sounds pretty good." Saber seemed impressed by Sydney's positive take on things.

"And I haven't even got to the best part yet."

"Oh?" Saber raised an inquisitive eyebrow.

"I've got some great new friends, and one in particular that I'm especially fond of." Sydney locked gazes with Saber and smiled, letting her know who she meant.

"Rich will be pleased," Saber joked, causing Sydney to burst into laughter. Though Saber had made light of the comment, she still met Sydney's sparkling green eyes, dipping her head in acknowledgement and returning the warm smile. They stayed that way for quite some time, just looking at each other.

It was Sydney who broke the silence. "So anyway, I figure all in all, maybe things worked out for the best. Melissa simply wasn't who I thought she was." Sydney reflected on that for a long moment. "Most people go through some kind of heartbreak at one point or another. I'm sure I'm not the only one. What about you?"

Saber swallowed rather hastily and pushed her now empty dinner plate to one side. She brushed her hands together, as if to rid them of breadcrumbs. "I've had my heart broken," Saber finally said, her voice flat, quiet. "But not in the way you're meaning, not by a partner."

Sydney's interest was piqued. Though she felt she was coming to know Saber, she had to admit she knew little about her past, Saber was surprisingly tight-lipped about anything before Shirebridge. She recalled that Saber actually flinched when her parents had been mentioned, so she made the logical guess. "Your parents?"

For a second, Saber looked surprised, but then her face cleared. "You're observant."

"Comes with the job." Sydney held up a hand to stop Saber from continuing. "But I can tell this is an uncomfortable subject for you, so you don't have to tell me. Trust takes a while to build, believe me, I understand."

"That's not it." Saber strongly shook her head. "I do trust you. Completely. It's just I don't...I can't, talk about it. I realise that's not very fair, given that you've just opened up to me about Melissa." She ran a frustrated hand through dark hair. "But I...If I'm honest with myself, I've never dealt with what happened, and the only way I've coped is to shut it out. Now I know that's not healthy, but it's worked for me so far. That said, though I can't give you the details, I can give you an overview."

Sydney slid across the sofa and lightly gripped Saber's bicep, offering both silent support and comfort.

"Let's just say my parents didn't agree with my lifestyle."

"They had a problem with the fact you're gay? Is that why you left home when you were sixteen?"

"They didn't give me much of a choice." Saber's eyes started to glisten. "Do your family know?"

Sydney nodded. "Yes. My friends and colleagues too. I'm very open about it."

"I am too, though I'll admit that after my parent's rejection it took me a while to confide in anyone else."

"Was it Coop?" Sydney asked. She wasn't surprised when Saber nodded, she'd seen how close the two of them were.

"He helped me a lot. It sounds dramatic, but Coop and Marge helped restore my faith in people. I'd have been completely lost without them. Still would for that matter."

Sydney gave Saber's arm a rub. She'd always appreciated how lucky she was to have such a supportive family, but now even more so. She tried to imagine what it would've been like if they hadn't accepted her. She stopped a few seconds in, the thoughts too painful for her to continue. "Thank you for telling me that. And please know that I'm here for you, Sabe, if you ever do want to talk about what happened. You can talk to me."

Saber held her gaze. "Thanks, Syd. I mean that."

"As do I."

Saber smiled, patted her knee, then stood and crossed to the DVD stand, which was next to the TV. She indicated her large collection of films. "Right. What movie do you want to watch?"

Chapter Five

SABER'S EYES POPPED open at the unusual sound. She was surprised to see that not only had she fallen asleep on the sofa, but she was being held hostage by a small blonde woman, who was sprawled across her possessively. She found the source of the noise—Sydney's pager was vibrating.

The vibrations bounced off the table's wooden surface, making it louder than normal. She glared at the pager, which chose that exact moment to stop buzzing. "That's better."

Saber peered down at Sydney, her dishevelled hair making her look even cuter than usual. "Syd?" Saber croaked, then after clearing her throat, she tried again. "Syd?"

Sydney opened her eyes slightly, blinking a few times to clear her vision from sleep. "Sabe?" she asked in surprise. "Not that I'm not pleased to see you, but what are you doing in my bed?"

Saber chuckled, deep in her throat. "First off, we're not in a bed. Second, we're not even in your house, and third, we're on my couch. We must've drifted off watching the movie last night."

"Oh." Sydney yawned. "Crap. I'm gonna be late for work." She sat up quickly, and would've fallen off the sofa if it hadn't been for Saber's quick reflexes. Smiling gratefully, Sydney got to her feet.

"Your pager's been going off," Saber said, as she stood and stretched out her long frame. She then handed Sydney her pager, smiling softly at her. "Why don't you call in the café after work for something to eat? My treat. To say thanks for taking care of me last night."

"You don't have to do that."

"I know, but I want to."

"Okay. Sounds great."

SYDNEY ACTUALLY LEFT work on schedule for a change, and as Saber suggested, she drove to the café. As soon as Sydney perched herself on one of the chairs in front of the counter, Saber appeared from the kitchen, placing a steaming plate of food in front of her.

"You said you liked the gammon."

Sydney looked at the meal, then at Saber. "You're an angel."

Saber grinned. "You've got the blonde hair." She retrieved the utensils and condiments, placing them in front of Sydney. "Do you want apple juice?"

"Orange please." Sydney sprinkled some salt onto her chips. A drink was placed next to her plate. "Thanks."

Saber nodded. "How was your day?"

"Hectic." Sydney smiled. "Everyone thought I must've had an accident, I'm never late."

"Yeah, sorry about that."

"It was hardly your fault. I should have set the alarm clock on my phone." Sydney bit a chip in half.

"Coop's been teasing me about it all day."

"Why? Were you late to work, too?"

"Apparently the guys were wondering why we both didn't show up for our run this morning."

Sydney put a hand over her mouth. "I'd completely forgotten about that."

"Coop tells me it looks 'suspicious.' And apparently Rich has been telling everyone that we're having, and I quote, 'hot lesbian sex.'"

Sydney surprised them both by saying, "I've heard worse rumours."

A shy, but flattered smile crossed Saber's face, making her even more endearing to Sydney. "I tried telling Rich the truth, that I was exhausted and you fell asleep on the couch, but that only made him worse."

Sydney waved a dismissive hand. "Don't worry about it. Let them think what they want."

"You're not upset?" From her expression, Saber clearly assumed she would be.

"Not at all." Sydney was startled to find she actually meant the words. Normally, people gossiping behind her back annoyed her, but this time it didn't. The speculation pleased her. Since she'd woken up that morning in Saber's arms, something had shifted inside Sydney. She wasn't quite sure yet what it was, but she found she was no longer as averse to the idea of a relationship with Saber. She still wasn't ready to take things to the next level, but the door to her heart, which previously had been locked and bolted, now stood open—Saber had somehow, without her knowledge, slipped inside and opened it.

SYDNEY'S DESSERT WAS a chocolate fudge cake, topped with ice cream and even more chocolate. It made her feel guilty for missing her run that morning, but she enjoyed every bite. As she finished, Coop came into the café.

He came straight over. "Do you mind?" He indicated the seat next to Sydney.

"Be my guest." She wiped some remaining chocolate from her mouth.

"We missed you and Saber on the run this morning." Coop's brown eyes twinkled mischievously.

Jump straight in, why don't you? Sydney smirked at the man. "We slept in. Sabe was tired after last night's rescue."

His face creased in happiness. "I'm glad you were there to take care of her," he said seriously, no hidden meaning behind the words. "She needs someone to look out for her, she's too hard on herself."

"I've noticed that."

"I try to, but we both know it's not the same." Coop squeezed her forearm lightly. "I'm really pleased that you've come into her life. I mean that."

Sydney swallowed around a lump in her throat, recognising the statement for what it was — acceptance from the closest person to Saber. The man was giving her his blessing, in his old-fashioned way. She placed a hand on top of his, giving him direct eye contact. "We're not a couple, Coop."

Coop nodded confidently. "Not yet."

Sydney shook her head in despair, but she couldn't stop a smile from emerging. "Have you eaten?"

He shook his head. "I think I fancy one of those fudge things that you've just had. They look like a whole meal in themselves."

"They are pretty big." Sydney looked around, suddenly realising that the café was full. She didn't recognise the group of men in the corner. "Who are they? By the window?"

Coop subtly glanced behind. "No idea. Look like outdoor types though, probably staying at the caravan site."

Sydney raised her eyebrows questioningly.

"You know the road that goes through the mountains that cuts off before you reach this village?"

"Yes."

"If you go along there for about ten miles or so, there's a caravan site. Campers stay there, too. It's where any climbers, or walkers and the like stay if they plan on touring the area," Coop said. "It's set well back from the road, that'll be why you've never noticed it."

Sydney gave the men a wary look. They were growing rowdy from the beer they were drinking. "So they come here for a meal?"

"Or a drink. It's the nearest pub to the site." As if sensing her discomfort, he added, "Don't usually have any trouble though."

Usually?

Rich chose that moment to enter the café. Crossing to them, he leaned up against the counter, next to Sydney. "Hey, Syd. Coop."

They greeted him.

The strangers laughed loudly, and Rich glared at them, visibly annoyed. "I didn't know there was a zoo around here." When Coop and Sydney chuckled, he grinned, clearly pleased he'd amused them.

Marge came forward, from behind the counter. "What can I get you? Anything else, Sydney?"

"Another orange juice would be great." Sydney noticed Marge was seemingly unbothered by the noisy men, and suspected she was more than used to such behaviour.

Coop indicated Sydney's empty bowl. "One of those please, Marge."

"A beer for me," Rich said.

Marge scribbled on her pad. "Be right with you."

IT WAS GETTING late and the café had almost cleared out. All that remained were themselves, and the four strangers in the corner. Sydney had a bad feeling about the men, she'd had it all night, despite Coop's attempts at reassurance.

She'd enjoyed the evening with both Coop and Rich, but was disheartened that she hadn't seen much of Saber. That said, the café had been really busy, and she knew Saber had to work.

"Oh, I forgot." Rich looked keenly at Sydney. "We're ahead of schedule on the job we're currently doing, and Doug says we can start on your place at the end of the week, if that's all right by you?"

Sydney nodded enthusiastically. She was excited at the prospect that work was soon going to start on her house. The living room wallpaper was slowly driving her insane.

"So I can tell Doug that you're okay with it?"

"Absolutely. Although I'll be leaving the house at eight to go to work, so I'll come and drop the keys in before I go."

"What time do you get back?"

"Depends on what shift I'm doing. Thursday and Friday this week, I'm on the shortest shift rotation, so if I finish on time, it should be six-ish."

"What's the longest?" Coop asked.

"There's no limit," Sydney said. "It's not unusual for me to pull back-to-back shifts."

Coop let out a low whistle. "I hope they pay you enough. You pull some long hours."

Rich took a swig of beer. "Of course they pay her enough—look at her house, and her car. Hell, if I'd known how much they paid, I'd have become a doctor."

Sydney smiled. Rich really was all talk. Once you learned that and didn't take him seriously, he became more amusing than annoying. "That's one of the reasons why I do get paid a lot. I work long hours, and even when I'm not there I could be on call."

"What? You mean you've just gotta drop everything and go to work? No matter the time?"

"Yes. Sometimes."

"Screw that. I've changed my mind, I'm happy doing my own job thanks."

Coop and Sydney shared a humorous look. A loud bang startled them and they whirled around.

One of the strangers slammed his bottle down again on the table, roaring with laughter. They were visibly drunk.

Rich opened his mouth, as if intending to set the group straight.

Sydney had treated hundreds of people in hospital that'd come off worse in situations just like this. She didn't intend to become one of them. Laying a hand on Rich's forearm, she gripped it to get his attention. "So, Rich, how long have you worked for Doug?"

Rich looked down at his arm and smiled. "Since I was twenty-one."

"Tell her what you do, Rich," Coop said, apparently realising what Sydney was trying to do — keep them from a bar fight.

"I'm a handyman," Rich said, full of self-importance. "Jeff's the carpenter, so he specialises in woodwork, you know, making banisters, chairs, that sort of thing. So say Jeff's made a banister, I'm the one who goes in and fits it. I'll do the painting, wallpapering. If you want any carpets laid or any walls knocked out," he pointed to his chest, "that'd be me. I'm basically the guy who does all the hard work."

"Is that right?" Sydney asked, trying not to laugh at Coop's expression, which was a mixture of amusement and annoyance. "You sound like a good man to have around."

Rich became smug. "Oh, I am."

Sydney bit her lip to keep a straight face at his self-assuredness. There was a fine line between confidence and arrogance, and Rich had just crossed it.

"Don't let Doug or Jeff hear you talking like that," Coop said, in a cautionary tone.

Rich nodded to him.

Sydney watched as Marge, who was busy cleaning the tables, moved over to the strangers. "Time to leave, fellas. We're closing," Sydney heard Marge say.

"Aw, can't we have one more?" the guy who'd been slamming his bottle said. He stood up, using his tall muscular frame to try and intimidate the much smaller woman.

Saber immediately appeared, stepping between Marge and the man without a moment's hesitation. She was slightly taller than he was, and she looked unflinchingly at him. "You heard the lady. Place is closing."

A wolf whistle came from another man at the table. "Where did you come from, darlin'? You wanna come and sit on my lap?" The four strangers laughed.

"Not right now, thanks, I've got something I'd rather do." Saber smiled darkly at him.

"Yeah?" he asked. "What's that?"

"Poke out my eyes," Saber said flatly. From beside Sydney, Rich sniggered.

"Ooo, we've got a live one here," Bottle-slammer said, his face inches from hers.

"'Fraid so, cemetery's that way." Saber jerked her head forward, stopping just before she struck him, a clear warning to back off.

He flinched and took a step back in shock. The men laughed again.

Saber smirked when color stained his cheeks. She raised a defiant eyebrow, as if challenging him to do something—he did. Bottle-slammer roughly grabbed her arm, and her smirk widened, it became predatory.

"Get your hands off her."

Saber's head turned at the angry voice, looking surprised to find Sydney standing right alongside her. Rich stood next to Sydney, while Coop led Marge behind the counter out of harm's way.

"Another one!" A smaller man stood up, trying to get a better view of Sydney.

"Don't even think about it," Saber growled.

"Hey!" Bottle-slammer shouted, tightening his grip on Saber's arm. "I'm in charge here." He nodded to his friend. "Go for it, Lewis. She's more your height anyway." He chuckled.

Lewis started out from behind the table, and Rich moved to intercept him.

Sydney gave Rich bonus points for that. Then she was being pulled backward, and she struggled for an instant before she realised it was only Coop. "What are you...? She needs help." Sydney raised her voice in protest. "Let go of me."

Coop didn't release her. "Saber needs space. She won't want you getting caught in the crossfire."

"If Rich is helping, I am too."

"Feisty little thing, aren't you?" Marge said, pulling Sydney behind the counter.

"Please." Coop scoffed. "She doesn't need Rich either, but he's just gotta be involved, you know what he's like."

Sydney tried appealing to his chivalrous side. "Coop, how can you let a woman fight while you're hiding behind a bar?"

"I can't fight like she can."

"Who can?" Marge said.

As if seeing the worry on Sydney's face, Coop patted her arm. "Come on, Syd, I wouldn't be standing here if I thought she was in any danger."

"It's true, Sydney, he'd just be in her way."

Coop nodded sheepishly at Marge's statement.

"She'll be mad as hell with Rich. He's only doing it to try and impress her." Marge shook her head.

"Just watch," Coop said, still not releasing his hold on Sydney's arm. Three sets of eyes watched the tableau in front of them unfold.

Lewis threw the first punch, nailing Rich in the jaw.

Saber seemed to take that as her cue and caught Bottle-slammer with a powerful hook. The man stumbled backward, and a lazy kick to his behind sent him sprawling over the table and into the chairs. He landed with a grunt.

Saber glanced at Rich, who was holding his own, for now.

The other two men lunged at her. She dodged their wild, drunken swings with apparent ease, felling one with a four punch combination: jab, hook, jab, uppercut.

The remaining man used that time to pick up a chair, swinging it savagely at her head.

"Sabe!" Sydney yelled in warning.

Saber ducked at the last possible second. She turned and lashed out with a long leg, causing the man's head to snap back with the force. Both he, and the chair, dropped to the floor.

Rushing over to Rich's side, Saber grabbed Lewis's arm as he was about to punch Rich in the gut. This allowed Rich's punch to connect and the drunk fell.

Bottle-slammer got to his feet, pulling out a pen-knife from his pocket.

Sydney couldn't keep quiet any longer. The man had now made things even more dangerous. She knew Saber could take him, she'd just proved that, but there was no way Sydney was going to risk it. One lucky swipe with that blade could cause Saber serious harm.

"You take one more step," Sydney spoke strongly, surprising herself with the steadiness of her voice, "and we phone the police. Then I'll personally get on to that camping site you're staying at, and I'll have you thrown out and banned for life." She took a gamble that Coop was right, hoping that they were indeed campers.

Bottle-slammer hesitated. "You can't do that."

"Watch me," Sydney said. "They're good friends of mine," she lied. "Do you really think they'll want people like you around here? Causing trouble for everyone?"

He glowered at Saber for a long moment. "Don't do that. I'll get my buddies and we'll go." He folded his pen-knife and put it away. Helping one of his friends to his feet, they staggered toward the door. Lewis and the last man followed.

Saber closed the door behind them, locking it securely. They waited for the men to drive off before letting out a collective sigh.

Proud blue eyes found green. "That'a girl."

Sydney's face lit up in a beautiful smile.

Coop patted Sydney on the back. "Remind me not to play poker with you."

"That was quick thinking." Marge gave her an approving nod.

Rich sat down on a chair, touching his swelling cheek cautiously. "I had him, you know," he said to Saber, clearly referring to the fight.

Saber sat next to him. "I know." She patted his knee pacifyingly.

Sydney squatted beside Rich, her professional side surfacing. "Let me see."

"Those punks are lucky you scared 'em off when you did. I was just getting warmed up." Rich flinched. "Ow!"

"Sorry," Sydney said, as she probed a sore spot. "You need to put some..." She smiled at Marge when a bag of frozen peas was suddenly thrust into her hand, wrapped inside a towel. "Thanks." She turned back to Rich, placing it carefully on his cheek. "Hold it there."

Rich winced at the cold, but did as instructed.

Sydney shifted her position and began to examine Saber's bruising hands. "Have you got another one, Marge?"

Marge nodded and headed back toward the kitchen.

Saber smiled at Sydney. "You were amazing."

"You should've been standing where I was." Sydney shook her head in astonishment. "Where did you learn to fight like that?" It really was a shame that she'd been so frightened, she hadn't had a chance to fully appreciate Saber's skill.

"I used to do a lot of martial arts."

"Used to? Looks like you haven't lost your touch."

"I manage. I'm not as good as I used to be though."

"Why'd you give it up? Make a fist for me."

Saber did so. Her left hand was the worse of the two and she couldn't shut it all the way. "That's as far as I can close it."

"All right, stop there." Sydney took hold of her hand, checking each joint carefully. When she was satisfied that nothing was broken, she took the frozen package from Marge and placed it on top. "Are you left handed?"

"No."

"That's unusual." Sydney's brow creased. "You fought more with your left."

Saber remained silent.

Sydney knew Saber was holding something back, she could sense it. That knowledge hurt, but she had to trust that Saber would tell her when she was ready. She stood up. "Well, you're both fine. The ice will keep the swelling down to a minimum."

"Coop?" Saber caught his gaze. "We should really make sure those guys get back all right. We don't want them causing an accident."

"I'll ring Patsy now." Coop stopped tidying up the café and moved to the phone. "What car are they driving?"

"Red Frontera," Saber and Sydney said in unison, causing Rich to roll his eyes.

Marge chuckled. "You and your cars." She regarded Saber. "Yours was just like that one, except it was blue."

"Marge." Saber sighed, as if knowing what was coming.

"I still don't understand why you got rid of that car. It was your pride and joy." Marge walked over to Sydney, who was setting a table upright.

Saber got up to help.

"Don't you dare." Sydney gave her a stern look. "Not with those hands."

"They're bruised, not broken," Saber said.

"You listen to her, y'hear? She's the doctor." Marge pointed at Saber, then glanced to Sydney. "If she gives you any trouble, you come and see me, I'll soon sort her out."

Sydney chuckled. At both Marge's words, and at Saber's reaction — she waved a hand in front of her eyes, as if to check that she was still visible.

"Where was I?" Marge slid a chair under the table. "Oh yes," she spoke solely to Sydney, "It took her years to save up for that car, and she spent more hours than I care to say, tuning this, changing that. And then suddenly, one day, it was gone." Marge clicked her fingers in demonstration. "Just like that." She gazed sadly at Saber. "It was your pride and joy," she repeated.

"It was only a car," Saber murmured, somewhat pensively.

Sydney cast her a troubled look, knowing Saber well enough to realise that wasn't her honest opinion. She mentally filed the question away for later, adding it to the numerous others already there. The woman was more complex than a jigsaw puzzle — a puzzle with no picture on it.

Coop put down the phone and leaned on the counter. "Patsy's going to keep an eye out for them, and if they're not back soon she'll call the cops. They won't be coming here again."

Sydney righted another chair. "You asked her to ban them?"

"Didn't have to. She told me they've been causing problems all week, this was the final straw."

"Good." Rich stood up. "I'll see you guys tomorrow." He tried to give the frozen peas back to Marge.

"You keep it," Marge hastily said. "I can hardly serve them to customers now."

"Cheers. Night." Rich paused when he reached the door, glancing behind to both Saber and Sydney. "Remember to set your alarm clock." He winked, giggled, then left the cafe.

Marge's brow lifted. "What was that about?"

"Nothing," Saber said. "Just Rich being Rich."

Marge seemed to accept that explanation, apparently knowing how he could be. Coop set the last chair upright, and she looked pleased that her beloved café was back in order.

"We all set here, Marge?" Coop asked. "I'll walk you home."

Marge smiled, clearly appreciating the courtesy. She retrieved her keys so she could lock up for the night. Once outside, they said their good-byes, Coop and Marge going off to the right, while Saber and Sydney went left, each heading home.

Sydney broke the silence. "I'd ask how your day was, but from what I've seen it was pretty crummy."

Saber chuckled. "Mm, I've had better days. Though it was worth it, I got to see you put those idiots in their place."

"I'm not normally like that," Sydney said introspectively. "I'm not sure what came over me. I was scared, I guess."

"I wouldn't have let them hurt you."

Touched, Sydney linked an arm through Saber's. "I wasn't scared for me." She looked up into alluring blue eyes. "I was scared for you."

Saber swallowed, then a soft smile formed. "There was no need. Everything worked out. We're both fine, our friends are okay, and Rich too." Her humor had the desired effect.

Sydney giggled. "His face is going to be swollen tomorrow."

"He'll be showing off his battle wounds. We'll never hear the end of it." Saber shook her head. "He could've saved himself a whole lotta hurt if he'd stayed out of it."

"He was trying to impress you."

"I know." She sighed. "I respect him for trying to help. I do. I only wish he was doing it for the right reasons. I'm never going to feel like that about him, no matter what he does."

"Maybe you should show him the definition of gay in the dictionary?"

Saber chuckled. "And get it tattooed on my arm."

"That's too discreet. It'd have to be your forehead, so he can see it every time he looks at you."

"Good point. You know, in the movies, there's always that guy trying to have sex with a lesbian, or a couple, trying to convince them to have a threesome. I always thought that was so clichéd, so unreal, yet Rich is exactly that guy."

"He is." Sydney laughed. She drew to a stop, they'd reached her house. Raising herself up on her tiptoes, she kissed Saber's cheek good night, then continued up her driveway. After waving good-bye, Sydney closed the front door, noticing Saber's absence immediately. She felt oddly alone.

Chapter Six

THURSDAY ARRIVED AT last, and Doug and his team were due to start work on Sydney's house. With Saber's help, Sydney had cleared out the living room the night before, so work could start straight away.

Sydney wanted all of the rooms to be decorated, but the living room was priority as she spent the most time there, and the wallpaper was hideous. She could have decorated herself, but she wanted the wall between the dining room and the kitchen knocked out. That way, the main rooms downstairs would all be open, and form a large L-shape. The only rooms that wouldn't be open would be the hall and the cloakroom under the stairs.

There were five big double bedrooms upstairs, plus the main bathroom, en-suites, and the landing, but she hadn't yet decided what to do with them.

Although it was her house, she was very aware that it was treasured by the people in the village, in particular, Saber and Doug. She'd mentioned this to Doug, who promised her they could keep the character of the place intact and still modernise it.

She'd asked for Saber's opinion more than any other, and was pleased to find that Saber had a lot of the same ideas that she did regarding the house's redesign.

Sydney had finished her run, showered, and was having breakfast when she heard a knock on her front door. She smiled when she answered it. Saber stood there, holding a large parcel in her hands.

"Have you got a new job?" she teased.

"Gotta make extra cash somehow." Saber gestured down the road with her head, indicating the postman who was now driving away. "I was on my way over anyway, thought I'd save Scott a trip."

"Well come on in, I'm just finishing breakfast." After closing the door, she followed Saber down the hall and back into the kitchen.

Saber put the cardboard box on the table, next to the breakfast items already there. Instead of reaching for the box, Sydney took hold of Saber's hands, examining the fading bruises.

"They're healing nicely."

"Yeah, they're a lot better now." Saber made a tight fist with each hand to prove her point.

"I bet they're still sore though?"

"A bit."

Sydney shook her head, an amused smile playing on her lips. "Don't play butch with me, I'm a doctor, I know exactly how you feel."

A dark, delicate eyebrow rose. "Is that so?"

Sydney gave a confident nod, her smile growing.

"Then I'm in so much trouble." Her comment made them both laugh, and she sat down as Sydney began to open the box.

Sydney noted that it'd been redirected from the hospital's address, which was strange. She saw why as soon as she looked inside — it was some of the things she'd left behind at Melissa's house, and since she hadn't given her ex her new address, nor would she, Melissa had sent them to the hospital where Sydney worked. She'd clearly asked around to learn of Sydney's new post, for Sydney hadn't told her that either. Fortunately, the hospital's policy of not giving out personal information extended to the staff members as well as the patients.

"Is something wrong?" Saber asked.

Sydney rifled through the box, withdrawing CD's, a bottle of perfume, some items of jewellery, and photographs of herself and Melissa. "It's the stuff I left at Melissa's. Why didn't she just throw it out? All of these were presents from her, that's why I left them." Sydney dumped everything she'd unloaded back into the box. "They're going straight in the bin."

Saber picked up one of the photographs. Next to Sydney, striking a pose, was a beautiful redhead. "She's very pretty."

Sydney's retort was immediate. "Only on the outside." It wasn't the words so much as her tone that conveyed there was no love left between them, especially not on her part. All that remained was anger. Sydney closed the box, sighed, then rubbed her temple. "I've put her behind me, but I could've done without the reminder."

Saber stood and enfolded Sydney in her arms. Sydney returned the embrace, but after a few moments Saber withdrew.

Sydney smiled up at her. "Thanks, I needed that."

Saber merely nodded. She moved on to another topic. "Don't bother taking the keys to Doug's, I'll let him in."

Sydney hastily glanced at her watch, then back to Saber in appreciation. "That'd be great. I'd best get going or I'll be late." She snatched up the box, intending to throw it in the outside bin, and was halfway to the door when she whirled around. "What did you want to see me about?"

"Huh?" Saber's confusion was written on her face.

"You said you were on your way over, that's why you took the parcel."

"It's my day off. Doug mentioned there was a lot of work, so I told him I was free to help out."

Sydney was again struck by how generous Saber was, especially with her friends. "That was nice of you."

A modest shrug. "I like DIY. Besides, I'll have fun with the guys."

Sydney suspected they would indeed have fun, and wished she herself had the day off so she could stay too. She pointed at Saber. "As soon as your hands start to hurt, I want you to stop."

A small smile appeared. "Yes, Dr. Greenwood."

SYDNEY PICKED UP her private office phone on the third ring. "Dr. Greenwood speaking."

"I've got a call on line two for you — a doctor over at The General hospital."

"Which doctor?"

"She wouldn't say. I asked three times, she just said you were expecting her call."

Sydney frowned. She wasn't expecting any call. That said, she still kept in touch with a lot of people from her old job, so assumed it was one of them calling. "It's fine, Sara, put them through."

She actually heard Sara's sigh of relief through the phone, whoever it was had clearly rattled her. Sydney waited for the line to connect.

"This is Dr. Greenwood, who am I speaking to?"

"Sydney it's me, Melissa." No wonder she hadn't given her name, she'd known Sydney wouldn't have taken her call.

"Is this about a patient? A medical case?"

"No, I..."

"Then I have nothing to say to you. Now I'm very busy, so if you don't mind..."

"I won't take long. I just wanted to check that the parcel I sent arrived? I sent it a while ago now."

"I received it this morning actually."

"Sure took its time. Still, at least you got it."

"I did, thank you." Sydney was polite, if nothing else. Coop would be proud.

"You're welcome. So how are you, Sydney? How's the new job?"

"The job's great, people too. And yourself?" Sydney grimaced as soon as the words left her mouth. She truly wasn't interested, and had asked solely out of habit.

"I've split with Wendy."

Sydney didn't know what to say to that, so she stayed quiet.

"I see that she was a mistake now. I shouldn't have cheated on you." When Sydney didn't speak, Melissa continued, "I want us to give it another go. We were good together."

"Were. Past tense. You ruined it." Sydney bit off each word in anger. She couldn't believe Melissa's nerve.

"It was one indiscretion. You need to get past it, Sydney."

"How dare you say..." Sydney was cut off.

"And it's not fair of you to put the blame all on me. There must've been something lacking on your part, or else I wouldn't have gone elsewhere."

The words stung. Melissa always had known how to manipulate people, her in particular, playing on her insecurities and doubts. While together, Sydney had gotten used to it, but she realised she shouldn't have put up with it, and certainly wouldn't do so now. She threw the comment back in her face. "If I'm so lacking, Melissa, why do you want me back?" Her retort stunned Melissa into silence. "You want me back because I was the best thing that ever happened to you and you know it. No one else will put up with your crap. And you have the audacity to come crawling back without so much as an apology, asking for another chance." Sydney barked a laugh. "There's no way in hell I'd get back with you."

"You've met someone else, haven't you?" Melissa asked, annoyance plain in her voice.

"That's none of your business." Sudden realisation struck. "Is that why you sent my stuff back? To try and weasel your way back into my life?"

"Of course not."

Sydney knew she was right on the mark. She'd heard enough of Melissa's lies to know when she was speaking the truth, and she wasn't now. "The whole box went straight in the bin. Every last bit of it."

Melissa exhaled noisily in irritation. "I don't know why I bothered."

"I don't either," Sydney said. "And frankly, I wish you hadn't. I'm so over you, Melissa, and I don't want to hear from you ever again." She hung up the phone.

I MUST BE going mad. I'm imagining her now. Sydney shook her head as she wandered around the town on her lunch break. Normally, she'd have eaten in the hospital cafeteria, but she wanted some air to try and clear her head. She was still angry from Melissa's earlier phone call.

Twice now, she'd thought she had seen Saber across the street, but they'd been fleeting glimpses as the woman disappeared into a hardware shop. *Lots of women have long dark hair. Just because I want it to be her, doesn't mean it is.* She found herself crossing the road though, heading for the shop. Sydney was about to go inside when the woman came out again—it was indeed Saber. They almost collided with each other.

"Sorry." Saber didn't seem to register her, she was too busy balancing a collection of timber in her arms.

"Fancy meeting you here," Sydney said, feeling happier already. Saber's presence always had that effect on her.

Saber grinned, and she looked at Sydney in surprise. "Why hello there, little lady," she drawled.

Sydney gestured to the load Saber was carrying. "Do you want a hand with those?"

"No, I've got them, thanks. You could come and open the car boot for me though."

"Sure." Sydney walked alongside her, toward the busy car park. Although the town wasn't exactly heaving, she longed for the quiet of Shirebridge. "What's the wood for?"

"You can't ask that question."

That only made her curiosity grow more. "I just did."

"It's a surprise."

"Uh oh. What are you and the guys up to?"

"They've got nothing to do with it. They're too busy with the house. It's a surprise from me."

"I don't know whether that's better or worse," Sydney teased.

Saber chuckled, stopping beside Doug's car. "The keys are in my pocket." She indicated her ripped, paint-spattered jeans.

Sydney reached into her front pocket. She pulled out the keys and pressed the unlock button. The car responded and she opened the boot.

Saber dumped the timber inside, then sat down on the bumper. "You'll like it. I promise."

"I know. I trust you." Sydney sat down too, realising the truth of her words. She did trust Saber. Completely.

Saber smiled, nudging Sydney with her shoulder. "Everything all right? You look a little down."

Sydney didn't bother to deny it, Saber could read her well. "Melissa rang."

"Oh? And what did she have to say for herself?" Saber's disdain was clear in her tone.

"She wants me back. She's split with Wendy."

Saber noticeably swallowed. "What are you gonna do?"

"Nothing. I don't and could never trust her again. I couldn't make it work even if I wanted to, which I don't."

Saber released a breath, her expression one of relief.

"I told Melissa that. In no uncertain terms."

"Good for you."

"You know she actually had the balls to blame me for what she did."

"She did what?" Saber shook her head in disbelief, then held up a hand to forestall Sydney's response. "Hold up. When are you due back at work?"

Sydney glanced at her watch. "Half hour."

"Have you eaten?"

"Not yet."

"How about we have lunch together, and you can tell me all about it?"

Sydney smiled. "I'd like that."

SYDNEY PULLED INTO her driveway. It was Friday night, and she was pleased it was her weekend off. She was also looking forward to her surprise. Saber hadn't finished it yesterday, and wouldn't show her until it was completed—despite Sydney's attempts to persuade her.

She'd just locked her car in the garage when movement caught her eye. She spotted Saber walking along the path that led to the back garden.

Sydney chuckled when Saber got closer, she was covered in mud. "What on earth happened to you?"

"You ready for your surprise?" Saber asked excitedly, holding out a dirty hand.

Sydney took it instantly and was led up the path. They were soon crossing the lawn, and as they neared the stream, Sydney spotted her surprise under the large tree. "I can't believe you did this," she said quietly.

She walked down the new steps that led to the waters edge—over the last two days, Saber had dug out the mud at different levels for the steps to fit into. The wood she'd bought held back the dirt, and pieces of grey stone made up the steps themselves. She knew Saber's own steps were covered with gravel, but the flat slabs of stone would be much more comfortable for her to sit on. Plus, they looked a lot nicer.

Saber appeared panicked when Sydney turned tearful eyes to her. "Don't you like it? I can put it back."

Sydney shook her head strongly. "I love it."

"Then what's the matter?"

"This is the nicest thing anyone's ever done for me," Sydney whispered. "Thank you. I don't know what else to say."

Saber gave one of her modest shrugs. "You don't have to say anything."

The difference between Saber and her ex had never been so startlingly apparent to Sydney, and with regret, she realised how unfair she'd been to Saber, not allowing her to get too close because of her ex's mistakes. She could see now that Saber would never do the things Melissa had, it just wasn't in her. They were complete opposites—where Melissa was abrasive and cruel, Saber was kind and considerate. Perhaps it had to do with the short timeframe between events, but Melissa's insulting phone call yesterday had woken Sydney up. Not only to the fact that her ex was a real bitch, but to the fact that she was ready to move on, to love again. With a sudden revelation, Sydney realised that she already had—she was completely in love with Saber, and had been for some time, she just hadn't had the courage to face her feelings.

Sydney reached up and cupped Saber's cheek. Her thumb moved back and forth, caressing. She held Saber's gaze, then moved in and wrapped her arms around her, squeezing tightly.

"Your suit," Saber said, though her protest was mild.

"It'll wash."

Saber apparently didn't need any further encouragement, for she returned the embrace. She sniggered at Sydney's outfit when they withdrew — it was smudged with mud. "The guys will have a field day over this."

AS PREDICTED, RICH started in as soon as they entered the living room, via the back patio doors. "My my, someone got a warm welcome."

Saber gave Sydney an amused, I-told-you-so look.

Doug immediately joined in. "Don't tell me, you fell over?"

Rich hooted with laughter. "Good one. That's almost as good as Saber's excuse this morning." He changed his voice in imitation. "I just happened to be waiting for you."

"I was!" Saber said. At Sydney's questioning glance, she added, "Since I was here before them this morning, they all think I spent the night."

"Having hot lesbian sex!" Rich slapped his hands together.

Saber covered her eyes. "Will you please stop saying that? You're obsessed!"

"I don't know why you're bothering to deny it, we all know what's going on," Rich said. "That you two are an item."

"Oh." Jeff put down his work tools and turned to them, as if he found the conversation much more interesting. "I have an important question for you."

"We both have." Doug also set his tools aside. "Jeff and I have been wondering about this for a while now."

"I hope you're not after pointers," Saber said dryly, causing both men to snigger. She received a slap to the abdomen from Sydney, who found the whole situation hilarious.

"Who made the first move?" Jeff asked.

"No one. We're not together." Saber tried again to tell them.

"Why'd you wanna know that?" Sydney said.

"You're not helping," Saber mumbled to her.

Jeff wiped his mucky hands on his dark green overalls. "We've got a bet going."

Saber looked surprised. "Who's we?"

"Just me and Jeff." Doug indicated Saber. "I bet you made the first move."

"And I bet Syd."

"You both lose. Neither of us did, because we're not together!" Saber said, in an exasperated tone.

Rich waved her comment off. "You're wasting your breath."

"Clearly," Saber muttered. "And if you ask me, you've all got way too much time on your hands."

"Speaking of time, have you finished those steps yet?" Doug picked up a scraper and handed it to Saber when she nodded. "There's plenty of wallpaper to remove. You wanna work your magic and save us a lot of effort?"

"Sure." Saber moved to the far corner, squatting down to peel a piece back.

"I'll just get changed into some scruffs, then I'll come and give you a hand."

"Okay, Syd." Doug smiled and nodded his appreciation.

Sydney went upstairs and quickly got changed. She didn't think she'd been gone long, but when she returned Saber had removed half the wallpaper on one wall—a wall that'd previously been untouched.

"How did you...?" Sydney broke off with a shake of her head, she must've been mistaken.

Her jaw dropped as she watched Saber pull off an entire strip of wallpaper, it all came off in a single piece and fluttered to the floor. Or it would've done if she hadn't been in the way. It draped over her head.

"Oi!" Sydney cried, her voice slightly muffled by the paper.

Rich and Doug laughed at the other end of the room. Jeff, who'd been in the kitchen, stepped in to see what the fuss was about. The men were completing the finishing touches to the wide archway that was now in place instead of the wall.

Sydney removed the wallpaper from her head, her eyes narrowing accusingly at Saber. "You did that on purpose!"

Saber looked innocent. "My aim's not that good."

Sydney tried to take some wallpaper down, a small square broke off in her hands. She watched while Saber casually yanked off another whole strip. "You've got the easy bit," she said, as hers tore again.

Saber rolled her eyes. "Fine, swap places." She proceeded to drag Sydney's strip off in one clean motion.

Sydney glared evilly. "I loosened it for you."

Saber smirked. "Of course you did."

Sydney tried tugging on the paper like Saber had done, and she growled in frustration when it ripped in her hand. "How are you doing that?"

"There's a knack to it."

Rich sniggered. "Yeah, and you don't have it."

"You can say that again," she muttered.

"Don't worry about it, Syd, none of us have it," Doug said. "Only Saber can do it. Believe me, I've tried."

"Here, I'll show you." Saber stepped behind her. Reaching around Sydney's front, she took hold of her arms and guided them to the wall. "Peel that piece back. Make sure you've got a good hold on it." Saber waited until she'd finished her task, then she moved Sydney's arms in a quick, but smooth movement.

The whole strip came off. "I did it!"

Saber dropped her hands to Sydney's waist, giving her a congratulatory pat before stepping aside.

Doug and Jeff began to clap, applauding her. "A new apprentice is born," Doug joked.

SYDNEY FELT LIKE she'd been questioned on every single part of her life, and the questions just kept on coming. She was rambling along the steep path that led up to Scar Peak. It was Saturday, and as the team were all off, Doug had organised a practice rescue using people from the village. His two children had volunteered as always: his son Michael had just turned eighteen, and his daughter Lauren was sixteen years old. Doug had gotten engaged at a young age to his high-school sweetheart, Faye. They were still happily married to this day.

Both of Doug's kids were really nice, and they were very inquisitive, like Sydney herself was. She, however, stopped to take a breath, whereas these two didn't seem to need to.

"When did you first know you were gay?" Lauren asked bluntly.

Sydney nearly swallowed her own tongue at the new turn to the conversation. It was completely unexpected and it threw her for a loop. "Wow, that's direct."

"Oh, sorry, don't you like to talk about it?" Lauren asked yet another question.

"No, it's not that. I didn't know..."

Michael interrupted, "You didn't know that we knew?"

Sydney had barely nodded in response, when they both spoke again.

"Dad told us," Lauren said.

"Everyone knows," Michael added.

"Yeah. So when did you know? How old?" Lauren was apparently determined to get an answer.

Sydney was sure that her brains were leaking out of her ears. "Hold up." She stopped in her tracks, using her authoritative voice. They both regarded her expectantly. "Everyone knows?"

"Well not everyone." Lauren overemphasized the last word.

"But everyone in the village knows," Michael said.

Sydney looked from one to the other. "You're pulling my leg, right?"

They shook their heads. "It's hard to keep secrets around here. It's a small place." Lauren pushed a piece of mousy brown hair behind an ear. "How old?"

"About thirteen," Sydney said. She was skeptical. "I do find it hard to believe people are that interested in my sexuality."

"You can't blame them. This is juicy stuff," Michael said. "We don't often get new gossip out here."

Sydney could see his point. In such a small community, she supposed everybody knew everyone else's business. Not that it at all bothered her, but she found the contrast between her old home and the new startling—in a good way. Her old neighbors could barely be bothered to remember her name, whereas the new wanted to know every detail about her. Sydney could happily adapt to that, but knew it would take time. She realised that's what made Shirebridge the nice community it was, because people cared for each other. She wanted to be a part of that.

Lauren misunderstood her meaning. "Don't worry, everyone's open-minded around here. Even Uncle Coop's all right with it, and he's as old-fashioned as they get!"

"I heard that," Coop cried out from behind. He shook his head at Jeff, who was walking alongside him. "Kids today have no respect," he said it loudly so they would hear.

"Sorry, Uncle Coop," Lauren called back. She moved closer to Sydney. "He's not really our uncle, but we've known him since we were born, so we've always called him that."

Sydney nodded in response, she thought it was sweet.

Michael smiled at her. "Dad says you're going to join the team?"

"I hope so."

"We are too, when we're a bit older," Lauren said. "That's why we go on these practice runs, to learn as much as we can. And it's fun to be carried around like a princess while everyone else does the hard work."

Sydney laughed. "I'll remember that when my back's breaking from hauling your butt down the mountain."

"She weighs a ton, too," Michael teased. "I want to join now, but dad won't let me. He says I'm too young."

"Here we go." Lauren sighed dramatically. "And I do not weigh a ton!"

"Saber joined when she was about my age."

"She was twenty," Lauren said. "And I bet Saber was way better than you are."

"It's only two years," he muttered.

Lauren ignored him and switched her attention to Sydney. "Saber was the youngest person to ever be allowed on the team, you know. The first woman, too—at least in these parts."

Sydney hadn't known that. "It doesn't surprise me, she's an exceptional climber." She couldn't stop herself from adding, "And an exceptional woman."

"Who are we talking about?" Saber asked, suddenly appearing beside them.

"You actually," Sydney said, trying not to blush.

"Is that so?" Blue eyes twinkled. "Exceptional, huh?" She grinned at Sydney. "Careful, I'll get a big head."

"Like Rich," Lauren said.

Saber placed an objective hand on her hip. "That's a bit harsh."

Lauren glanced over her shoulder. "Rich is right at the back, chatting with my dad. He can't hear me."

"I meant to me!" Saber winked at Lauren, who giggled like the schoolgirl she was.

Sydney humorously noted that both siblings shared similar tastes, for both were fawning over Saber, staring at her with big, puppy dog eyes. She now understood why Lauren had been so persistent regarding the age she'd known about her sexuality—Lauren was questioning her own. If Lauren was indeed gay, Sydney wanted to be there when Rich found out. She imagined he would say something along the lines of 'Not another one' or even, 'Is there something in the water around here?' Whatever his reaction, Sydney expected it to be comical.

She idly wondered if everyone in the village was in love with Saber. Sydney herself was, so she could hardly judge. Saber, it seemed, was one of those incredibly annoying women who were born with everything. Other women were naturally envious of her, that is, if they weren't already infatuated themselves. Sydney hadn't yet met a person who'd been immune to Saber's charms, nor did she think she was likely to.

The track narrowed up ahead, and Saber slowed her pace. "You two know where we're headed?"

"Of course." Lauren sounded insulted she'd asked.

"Good. Then why don't you lead the way?"

"All right," Michael eagerly said, seemingly happy to be given this little bit of responsibility.

Saber pointed at them. "Just until you reach the climb."

Both nodded in acceptance before striding away, their newfound enthusiasm putting a spring in each step.

ONCE LAUREN AND Michael were out of hearing distance, Saber said, "Thought you could do with an intervention."

Sydney gave her a grateful smile. "I swear, Sabe, sometimes you can read my mind."

She chuckled. "Ah, you found me out."

Sydney bumped her with her hip as they walked. "I'm serious."

"I just pay attention."

"To me?"

"To everyone." Saber saw disappointment cross Sydney's face and it confused her. She was getting mixed signals. Sydney told her she didn't want a romantic relationship, so Saber backed off, but lately Sydney had become more physically affectionate, which Saber felt contradicted her words. Had Sydney had a change of heart?

Saber watched her carefully when she said, "Though you more than most."

Sydney's smile was radiance itself, and Saber found herself returning it. She had her answer.

"I BET YOU could do with a hot bath?" Saber whispered in her ear.

Sydney let out a little whimper. "That would be heavenly." She unzipped her rain-soaked jacket, which Saber took and hung on a peg in the rescue station. Sydney wasn't wearing the matching red and black outfits that the others wore as they still had to be ordered. But apart from that, she felt like she was one of the team, and she thought the practice rescue had gone really well. Of course, the fact she was a doctor had helped considerably, and her experience of climbing was the icing on the cake. "I still can't believe how much equipment you carry in these packs." She hefted the rucksack she'd been carrying and moved it over to the others, leaving it in the corner with them.

"It's a lot more than regular climbers take. I'll take you on a few hikes with the pack, let you get used to the extra weight," Saber said.

"Good idea."

Coop smiled. "You've done the rest of us a favor though. Some of the weight's spread out over six packs now, instead of five." That was true, but each pack contained the necessities to survive—in case of separation.

"Glad I could help."

"I bet your shoulders disagree with you," Saber said dryly.

"You did great today." Coop patted Sydney on the back. "I completely forgot that it was your first time, it was like you'd been with us for years."

"One of the team," Saber said, pride written clearly on her face.

Sydney beamed.

Doug sat down behind the desk and beckoned Sydney over. His kids had gone home, saying it was no fun unpacking and checking the equipment. "Normally, I'd send you on loads of courses to help train you up, but I think I can safely cross you off the first aid training." Doug chuckled. "I've never seen anyone take to it as quickly as you. It takes a lot to impress me, my wife will tell you that, but, Sydney, I'm impressed." He held a hand out to her.

Sydney grinned as she shook it, her own hand swallowed by his much larger one.

"I'll run you through the post-rescue equipment checks, and then you can go and get some rest." Doug stood and led her around the desk.

Jeff patted her arm when she passed him. "Well done."

"Cheers, Jeff." Sydney felt like she was on top of the world, even with her aching muscles. Although Saber's opinion was the most important to her, Doug would determine whether or not she would be allowed to join the team. It seemed she had passed both of their expectations with flying colors, and she couldn't help but be pleased with herself.

On the way back down the mountain, Doug had told her that she'd been lucky to practice a rescue in bad weather, because that made the situation much harder. Mountain ranges were used to heavy rain, and the team often found themselves caught out in it. The weather was actually the cause behind a lot of the accidents. Sydney's cold body didn't feel particularly lucky, but her mind understood the man's logic.

She was surprised when Doug pressed a bottle of wine into her hands. "What's this for?"

"You've been here a month today. It's to mark the occasion."

Sydney was moved by his kind token. She stretched up and kissed him on the cheek. "Thank you."

Doug grinned. "Hell, if I'd known I was gonna get that kinda response I would've brought two!"

"Now don't go getting jealous, Saber," Rich teased, giving her arm a playful punch. Saber shoved him in response, nearly causing him to trip over his own feet. "Ooh, hit a nail, did I?"

"It's nerve, idiot. And that's not the only thing that'll be hit if you don't cut it out."

"As if you could catch me!"

Saber made a lunge for him, and Rich darted out of the rescue station with a girlish squeal. "You'd better run!" Saber called after him.

Distracted by their teasing banter, Sydney now turned back to Doug. She held up the wine. "Do you want to open it now?"

"That's probably not a good idea. My stomach's kinda empty."

Saber rolled her eyes. "Nicely played, Doug."

Sydney raised a questioning brow, the play going completely by her.

"He wants dinner," Saber said. "But he's too polite to ask outright." She turned her gaze to him. "Anything but a breakfast."

"You decide." Doug shrugged. "Whatever you want to make."

Rich's head popped through the door. "Did I hear someone mention food?"

"We'll stay here and run the post-rescue checks," Doug said, "while you go and get dinner ready."

Saber shook her head good-naturedly. "Why do I suddenly feel like a housewife?"

Chapter Seven

"MORNING, SYD," RICH shouted across the gravelled driveway.

Sydney turned from unlocking the garage door. "Hi, Rich. Doug. Jeff. You guys are here early." She looked at the extra addition. "Hi, Coop, didn't expect you today."

"Thought I'd give them a hand."

"We've got a lot to do," Doug said, opening the double doors at the back of his van. "The early bird catches the worm and all that."

"Saber inside?" Rich's suggestive smirk was not at all subtle.

Sydney nodded. "Door's open, go on in."

"We haven't even had time for breakfast," Rich said.

Sydney shook her head, she was positive the team would starve to death if Saber didn't feed them. "Help yourself to stuff in the fridge."

Rich darted forward at the offer. "Bye, Syd."

Jeff unloaded a holdall from the van, then gestured to Sydney's outfit. She was wearing a smart navy trouser suit, with a white blouse underneath. "You look nice."

Sydney smiled at him. "Thanks, Jeff."

Doug picked up the other bag. "Have a good day at work."

"You, too. See you tonight." Sydney stepped into the garage and got into her 4x4.

Passing the gate that marked the entrance into the village, she increased her speed. As she crested the hill, she instantly spotted a dark set of skid marks. They looked fresh.

Sydney slowed, her eyes following the marks off the road. At the bottom of the bank lay an overturned car, steam billowing out of its engine. She immediately slapped on the hazard lights and stopped her car.

Sydney removed her mobile phone from its hands-free holder on the dashboard, before jumping out of the vehicle. Quickly moving to the boot, she opened it and retrieved a first aid kit.

Sydney glanced at her phone, praying that there'd be a signal—she was in luck. She briefly considered phoning for an ambulance, but realised they were too far away, and it would take forever to get here. Selecting her house phone, she hoped someone would pick up. It rang. "Come on, come on."

After the fourth ring, it was answered, "Hello?"

"Sabe, there's been an accident. I need you and the guys to come and help." Sydney wanted to be on the move, but she consciously kept herself in one spot. She couldn't afford to lose the signal.

"Are you all right?" Saber asked, concern evident in her voice.

"I'm fine, but the car's letting off a lot of steam, I'm worried about a fire."

"Can't you get out?" She sounded anxious now.

"It's not my car, I wasn't involved." Sydney took a breath, she wasn't explaining this very well. "A car's rolled down the bank, just passed the village gate."

"We're on our way. We'll be with you ASAP."

Sydney could tell that Saber was already moving through the house, the cordless phone allowing her to do so. "Bring the gear and the spinal boards."

"Will do. Don't take any chances."

Sydney hung up, pocketing the mobile. She started to make her way down the slope. When she neared, she could hear a woman calling for help.

"I'm coming. I'm on my way down. I'm a doctor, everything's going to be all right."

"Oh, thank God! Please hurry!"

Sydney stumbled, fighting to keep her balance while she hurried down the steep bank. She made an effort to slow her pace, knowing she would be of no use to them with a broken neck. "How many are in the car?" she called out.

"My husband and my little girl." The woman started to cry.

"What's your name?"

"Helen," she sobbed, then suddenly grew frantic. "I think the car's on fire!"

Sydney saw plenty of steam, but no flames. "There's no fire, Helen. It's just steam." She finally reached the car and dropped to her knees. Peering into the shattered window on the driver's side, she spotted Helen in the passenger seat, suspended upside down by her seatbelt. "Helen, my name's Sydney. Are you hurt?" She reached into the car, feeling the driver's neck for a pulse.

"My arm, I think it's broken."

Sydney couldn't feel the man's pulse: she had to act quickly. She lay flat and crawled into the car, trying to ignore the glass shards cutting into her stomach. "What's his name?"

"Colin. Is he okay?"

"He's not breathing." Sydney struggled to unfasten the seatbelt. "I need to get him out of the car." Looking through the gap between the seats, her eyes took in the little girl—she was hanging limply, blood dripping down her face and turning her pale hair pink.

Sydney could only help one at a time though, and she jabbed again at the belt's release. It came free. She wriggled backward, crying out as the glass dug deeper into her skin.

Pulling Colin out of the car, she dragged him until he was laid flat, then started CPR.

"Help him!"

"Helen, I need you to talk to your daughter, try and wake her up." Sydney gave her something to do to try and distract her.

Helen twisted in her seat. "Madeline? Madeline, sweetie, it's Mom, can you hear me? She's bleeding!"

"Come on, Colin." Sydney compressed his chest.

"I can smell petrol!" Helen shouted in dread.

Sydney's hands didn't falter, but her head whipped toward the car in alarm. This was bad. "Helen, can you get out of the car?"

"I think so." She pressed the button to release the belt. Nothing happened. "My seatbelt's stuck!"

"Is there anything in the glove box to cut it with? A penknife?" Sydney looked up to the road, desperate to see the team. If she left Colin, he would die, but she needed to get the others out of the car if petrol was leaking. She could feel the heat coming off the engine and worried about a spark igniting the petrol.

Helen was scrabbling in the compartment. "There's nothing here."

Sydney had a penknife in her own car, why hadn't she remembered to bring it? She cursed silently. "It'll be all right, Helen. My team are on their way," she said it to reassure herself as much as Helen.

"The nearest hospital's an hour away!"

"No, they're not paramedics, they're Mountain Rescue. They don't live far."

"Mountain Rescue?" Helen swore. "My little girl's bleeding! She needs a doctor not Mountain Rescue!"

"Calm down, Helen. I can assure you they're fully trained. And I promise I'll see to your daughter as soon as they get here."

"Where are they?" Helen cried desperately.

Sydney peered down at her own wound as she administered CPR. Her shirt was ripped, and she was bleeding all over herself. She really needed to put a compress on the nasty gash in her stomach, but she didn't have any free hands. She suspected some glass had wedged its way in. It hurt a lot when she moved.

Sydney nearly wept with relief when she heard the sound of a vehicle approaching, and seconds later the Mountain Rescue team roared into view. The car stopped alongside Sydney's own and the team clambered out, grabbing backpacks and medical supplies before rushing to help.

Saber headed straight for Sydney, and practically sprinted down the hill. Her face was a mask of concern. "Syd, are you all right?" She knelt next to her, pulled a dressing from her pack, and pressed it securely against Sydney's stomach.

"Argh." Sydney couldn't manage to stifle her cry.

"All right. Easy," Saber said. She looked troubled by the amount of blood that covered Sydney's blouse. She called Coop over.

Coop stopped as the rest of the team rushed by. "I'll take over," he said.

Saber carefully moved Sydney back, allowing Coop to continue the CPR.

"There's petrol leaking," Sydney shouted to the team. "Need to get them out. Mother in front, child in back, both on passenger side."

"We've got it," Doug yelled. He rounded the rear of the overturned car. "Get yourselves clear."

Sydney made a move to stand, intending to help. But before she knew what was happening, Saber whisked her up, off her feet and into her arms. Sydney found herself being gently cradled, and suddenly felt like she was in a Harlequin romance novel.

Walking away from the overturned car, Saber moved slowly, clearly trying not to jostle Sydney's injury.

"I need to treat the little girl."

"Doug will get them clear, he'll bring them to you."

"Sabe," Sydney said in protest, taken aback by the strength of the woman that held her. "I'm not that hurt, I can walk you know." All of her worries melted away — even the pain lessened. She felt perfectly safe in Saber's arms.

"Humor me," Saber said tensely. She carried Sydney a safe distance away before setting her down. She placed a hand over Sydney's own, which was holding the bandage in place. "Keep pressure on it."

"Yes, Doctor."

A smile flicked on to Saber's face, but it was gone just as quickly. "Are you sure you're okay?"

Frightened blue eyes hurt Sydney more than her wound did, and she laid a hand on Saber's cheek, needing to convince her. "I'm fine. I will need a few stitches though."

"Looks painful." Saber winced in sympathy. She gave Sydney's shoulder a reassuring squeeze. "I've gotta help Coop, but you stay here. I mean it, Syd."

At Sydney's nod of acceptance, Saber ran back over to Coop.

Saber swiftly unhooked a spinal board from her backpack and unfolded it, just as Coop finished another cycle of CPR. He checked Colin's pulse, then gave the watching Sydney a thumbs up — they'd got him back.

Colin was transferred onto the spinal board and carried out of harm's way, placed next to Sydney. Insisting she could keep an eye on Colin's vital signs, both Coop and Saber left her to it, rushing back into the fray to help the others.

They passed Rich and Jeff on route, who were supporting Helen between them. Worriedly, there was still no sign of Doug or the little girl.

SABER PUT ON a surge of speed, and soon rounded the upturned car. She saw Doug, flat on his back, fighting to cut through the girl's restraints.

The entire team heard the petrol ignite — from the front of the car, a loud crack pierced the air.

Saber crawled into the passenger seat, knowing time was running out. They had only seconds to act.

"Get out of here," Doug said.

Saber ignored him and squeezed between the two front seats. She snapped her own penknife open and began to saw at the seatbelt. Smoke gushed through the front air vents, and she felt heat at her back. She sawed harder, and Doug also increased his pace.

"Out," Coop shouted, stationed just by Saber's feet. The fast-moving flames were progressing too quickly. "You've gotta get out now!"

Saber heard her name being yelled in panic—it was Sydney's voice.

The material snapped, causing the girl to drop. Doug caught her in his huge arms, and began to shuffle backward. His progress was too slow, so Coop simply grabbed his ankles and pulled, hauling them both out.

Saber was already up by this point, so she, with Coop's assistance, yanked Doug onto his feet, the little girl still in his arms.

As the flames spread toward the petrol tank, the three of them sprinted away, hoping for a few more seconds.

They didn't get many. The blast was deafening, and it knocked them clean off their feet.

"I'M GETTING TOO old for this," Coop mumbled from his position on the ground.

Saber lifted herself off the ground quickly, intending to stop Sydney from dashing over and making her stomach wound worse. "We're all right," she shouted.

"Ouch. Better get your hearing checked, Sabe."

Warm hands were suddenly on her, and Saber glanced at Sydney in shock. *How on earth?* She looked at the distance Sydney had covered. "I thought I was fast!"

"Nothing motivates me quicker than seeing my friends almost blown up." Sydney pressed Saber's hand to her chest. "I wouldn't recommend it though."

Saber could feel the thunderous heartbeat. She pulled Sydney to her, holding her close. "I'm all right."

From the ground, Coop loudly cleared his throat. "I am too, in case you're wondering."

Sydney chuckled, giving him a hand up. "Glad to hear it, Coop."

"Where'd your compress go?" Saber shook her head critically when Sydney shrugged.

"It wasn't exactly high on my list of priorities!" Sydney said.

Saber continued to shake her head. "Doctors really do make the worst patients."

Sydney scoffed. She set to work checking on Doug and the little girl in his arms.

Coop coughed a couple of times due to the smoky air. He tossed Sydney a playful look. "Come on, Saber, I'll help you find another compress."

Saber smiled, draping a long arm over his broad shoulders. "This time, I'll tie it to her."

Sydney glared at them, but her eyes glimmered in amusement.

"Knowing her," Coop winked at Sydney, "she'll probably still manage to lose it."

"SHE'S PERFECTLY FINE though, right? No lasting damage?" Saber asked again. God, she sounded like Rich, repeating herself over and over. She was probably driving Sydney and the doctor, who Sydney had informed her was Dr. Stein, mad. The whole ordeal had shaken her, though. She'd never had someone she loved so much in danger before.

Saber wondered how she was going to cope with Sydney on rescue missions. Of course, the team had been in lots of perilous and potentially life-threatening situations over the years, and they'd been injured, sometimes badly—Charlie being a prime example. But although she cared for them deeply, especially Coop, it just wasn't the same intense love that she felt for Sydney. It was the first time she'd felt this way, and she was somewhat overwhelmed by the depth of her feelings. What would she have done if Sydney had been seriously hurt, or worse? Saber couldn't bear to think about her life without Sydney in it, and when she tried, she almost gasped at the raw pain that came forth. Her jaw clamped shut.

Sydney, who was sat upright on the bed, must've noticed, for she laid a hand on Saber's stomach. She frowned when Saber's eyes fixed on her face. "Sabe? Are you all right?"

Saber was startled that Sydney could read her so well. "I'm not the one in the hospital bed." She smiled tightly, then turned to Dr. Stein. "So?"

"We've removed all of the glass and stitched her up. In a few weeks she'll be as good as new. It was pretty deep, and although there's no internal damage, I would recommend time off to allow it to heal properly." He smiled at his colleague. "I've already taken care of your sick note, and given it to the boss myself."

"Thanks, John, that was kind of you."

"I've given you two weeks, if you need any longer just let me know." Dr. Stein passed her a white paper bag. "Here are your meds, you know the drill. In case you've forgotten the directions are on the packet." He grinned.

Sydney chuckled. "I'm sure I'll manage." She carefully shuffled to the edge of the bed. "I'm glad those people are going to be all right."

"They're lucky you happened by when you did."

Saber took hold of her forearm, helping Sydney to her feet. "Okay?" As Sydney nodded, Saber guided her forward. "We'll take it nice and slow."

Dr. Stein pulled back the curtain, allowing them to leave unhindered. "See you in two weeks, Sydney."

"Thanks, John."

"Thank you," Saber added, tipping her head to the doctor. He seemed to be a nice man, and she found herself liking him. She was pleased Sydney had him for a colleague.

He spoke to Saber, "You make sure she takes it easy now."

"I will." Saber nodded to him. "Nothing but bed rest for her."

"There's no way I'm spending the whole two weeks in bed!" Sydney said, her tone serious.

Dr. Stein laughed quietly. "Good luck with that."

"NOW ARE YOU sure you've got everything you need?"

Sydney smiled as Saber affectionately tucked her into bed. "Everything but one."

Saber studied the bedside cabinet. It had Sydney's medication, a drink, a bottle of juice in case she needed anymore, some snacks, magazines, books, and the TV remote on it. What had she missed? Her brow creased in puzzlement. "It's nearly dinner time, I can make you some lunch?"

Sydney shook her head.

"Do you want me to put a DVD in for you to watch?"

Sydney held out a hand, which was immediately taken. "I just need you." She paused for a moment. "Will you stay here with me?"

"Of course." Sydney patted the bed, so Saber lifted the duvet and climbed in. "Why don't you try and get some sleep?"

Sydney nestled into Saber, closing her eyes without protest.

With a smile, Saber said, "I'll be here when you wake up."

"ARE YOU POSITIVE they're both asleep?" Rich whispered to Coop, who was creeping back downstairs.

Coop nodded. He pushed Rich toward the living room. That was the sweetest thing he'd ever seen, not that he would ever admit it to anyone.

The guys were hungry and had told Coop to go up and see what was going on. He'd been selected as he was the closest to Saber, and the others felt that if he walked in on anything 'hot' as Rich so delicately put it, he would get less of a beating than the rest of them. They all knew that Saber wouldn't touch a hair on any of their heads, but Coop agreed, simply because he was the only proper gentleman in the group.

So he'd snuck upstairs, peeking through the door into the master bedroom. Both women were sound asleep, curled up in each other's arms. The intimacy of the moment reminded him strongly of Mary, and he'd simply looked at them, pleased to see that his friends had found happiness with each other.

"What shall we do about lunch? I'm starved," Rich said when they entered the living room.

Doug rubbed his bearded chin. "We could always get it ourselves for a change."

"Or we could make a racket? Wake them up?" Rich moved to the table, raising his hand to bang on the wooden surface.

"Don't you dare!" Coop said sternly. He received a surprised look, but Rich didn't lower his hand. "Sydney needs her rest," he added, pleased when the younger man stepped away, nodding. That was Rich's main problem, he never thought things through.

"Can anyone here cook?" Jeff asked.

"Never needed to." Rich shrugged. "Mum does all my cooking, well her or Saber."

Coop smiled up at the ceiling. "Saber's too good to us." He heard everyone murmur their agreement, even Rich.

Doug clicked his fingers. "We could go to the café?"

"Yeah, why don't we bring something back for the girls?" Jeff said.

"Good idea." Doug herded them out into the hall, closing the front door as they left.

BLUE EYES OPENED slowly, blinking in shock when they landed on the clock—3:00 p.m. Saber hadn't intended on falling asleep herself. She'd only closed her eyes for an instant, but she was so comfortable, surrounded by Sydney's warmth. *I must've dozed off.* She smiled. *For a few hours.*

"What's that grin for?" Sydney mumbled quietly, as if not fully awake.

"How can you tell?" Saber asked. Sydney couldn't see her face.

"Can feel it." Sydney was still on her back, and she moved her head out from under the hollow of Saber's neck to look at her. "Hmm?"

"I couldn't believe I've been asleep so long. I bet the guys are munching on the furniture down there."

Sydney's lips curled upward.

Saber frowned. "I'm surprised they didn't wake me up." She went still. "Can you hear anything?"

Sydney listened for a few seconds. "Nope."

"Maybe they've all passed out from hunger."

Sydney giggled, then swatted Saber's arm. "No jokes. Laughing pulls on my stitches."

"Sorry."

Despite her words, Sydney joined in. "Maybe Coop cooked something? Maybe he's killed them?"

"No, we'd have heard the screams of pain as they choked down his food."

Sydney laughed, though she soon stopped with a wince.

"Sorry," Saber repeated. She clutched Sydney's hand, watching in concern until the hurt left her face. "What time can you take your next lot of pills?"

Sydney glanced at the clock on her bedside cabinet. "Not yet."

Saber ran tender fingers through Sydney's short hair. "Is there anything I can do?"

Sydney managed a small smile. "You're already doing it."

"I wish I could do more." Saber locked her gaze with Sydney's. "Anything you want, just ask it. Anything at all."

"That's quite a proposition." Sydney didn't smile, apparently able to tell that Saber was being serious. "All right. I want to ask you something, and I want you to promise that you'll be completely honest with me. Don't tell me what you think I want to hear. Only the truth."

"I promise," Saber said.

"Do you still have a crush on me?"

"No. I never had a crush on you."

"But I thought..." Sydney looked completely thrown. "At the stream, when you tried to kiss me..." Saber's finger covered her lips, silencing her.

"My feelings for you have always run deeper than that, even at the beginning. I've never loved anyone more than I love you."

Sydney's voice broke. "Past tense?"

"I did try to stop after you told me you only wanted friendship," Saber sighed. "But, Syd, you're the most lovable person I've ever met. It'd be easier for me to stop breathing than it would be to stop loving you."

A tear rolled down Sydney's cheek, and Saber gently brushed it away.

"I hope those are good tears?" Saber could barely control her stampeding emotions, and she swallowed hard.

As if hearing the uncertainty in Saber's voice, Sydney didn't keep her waiting. "They're definitely good tears. I love you too, Sabe. Completely. It frightens me how much. But I promise I won't run away this time, I love you too much." Sydney took a breath. "You asked me what I wanted? Well more than anything, Sabe, I want to be in a relationship with you."

Saber felt happiness bubbling up inside her. "I want that too."

Sydney's smile was breathtakingly beautiful.

Saber was completely taken with Sydney's expression, and she mentally tucked the image away, storing it into a cherished place in her heart.

Sydney started to close the distance between them. "And one more thing?"

Saber raised a teasing eyebrow. "I'm not enough?"

Sydney's smile grew. "More than enough."

"Go on, ask away. I can see you're going to be high maintenance."

Sydney laughed. "Kiss me."

"YOU KNOW, THE first time we touched at the hospital, I felt something pass between us."

Sydney was surprised by her words. "I did, too. Still do for that matter, every time you touch me. We definitely have a connection."

"A connection," Saber repeated. "I like that."

Their lips met. They explored slowly, each content to take her time. Saber wound a hand behind Sydney's neck, drawing her closer still. Sydney cupped Saber's cheek, gently cradling her face as their tongues caressed each other. Their kisses consumed them, the intensity steadily rising until it was near breaking point. Sydney whimpered, which seemed to snap Saber out of it.

"God, I'm so sorry. Did I hurt you?" Saber drew back, looking at her with fretful eyes.

"No," Sydney said, panting slightly. "You didn't hurt me, I'm more than okay." She pulled Saber to her, her tongue fighting Saber's for dominance.

"I think," Saber said in between kisses, "we should..." She let out a groan as hands found her naked skin. "Stop, we should stop."

Sydney tucked a strand of dark hair behind her ear. "What's wrong?"

"You're stomach."

Sydney's tone was droll. "I'm hurt, not dead."

"I don't want to hurt you further." Saber moved away ever-so-slightly.

Sydney's gaze softened. "You won't," she said with certainty. "I trust you."

"I think we should wait till your better. I'm not going to risk hurting you."

"Sweetheart." Sydney again cupped her cheek. "I'm touched, I really am, but I assure you, you won't hurt me."

Before Saber could respond, Sydney heard the front door open downstairs, and in came the team, all chattering amongst themselves. They still had work to do on the living room.

Sydney released a frustrated groan. "Their timing sucks."

Saber chuckled, brushing blonde hair off Sydney's forehead. "I should really fix us something to eat anyway. You need to keep your strength up."

Sydney couldn't argue with that. And as a doctor, she knew the truth of her words.

Saber got out of bed, then leaned back over and gave Sydney a kiss. "I'll be back soon, love."

Sydney smiled at the affectionate term. "I'll be waiting."

Saber was true to her word, and returned in under two minutes. Doug followed. They both carried a bag and a bottle of juice.

"That was quick."

"Yeah, the guys brought us back some dinner from the café."

"That was thoughtful." Sydney nodded gratefully when Doug handed her a bag. He placed the juice on the bedside cabinet.

"No worries." Doug scratched his beard. "Are we all right to continue working, or do you want us to call it a day? I realise you won't be able to get much rest with us making a racket."

Sydney was mightily tempted to accept, so she and Saber could finish what they'd started. But now that she'd managed to get her hormones in check, she had to admit that it probably hadn't been such a good idea. At least not yet, her stomach was extremely tender, and would probably restrict her participation—she wanted their first time together to be special.

"No, I'm good." Though she declined his offer, Sydney appreciated the consideration. "And the sooner it gets done the better, so feel free to crack on with it."

"Will do. Well, I'll leave you girls to it." Doug paused at the foot of the bed. "Oh, and Saber?" When she looked at him, he grinned. "You've got lipstick on your neck."

SYDNEY'S ALARM CLOCK woke them. She'd forgotten to unset it. She slapped groggily at the device, fumbling with the buttons for a moment before it finally stopped beeping at her. Rolling over, she found Saber peering back at her.

"Morning." Saber gave her a soft kiss.

"Mmm. That's a good way to start the day." Sydney rubbed noses with her. "Waking up and finding a beautiful woman in my bed."

"Finding?" Saber's lips quirked. "If I recall correctly, I believe I was invited into this bed."

Sydney grinned. "So you were." She returned the kiss. "My mistake." Although they'd shared the same bed, they hadn't yet been intimate.

"I'll forgive you," Saber whispered, placing light kisses along Sydney's throat as she continued, "But...just...this...once." She grew serious. "How are you feeling?"

Sydney considered her response, internally assessing her body. "About the same."

Saber gave her a careful hug. Since she'd stayed over, she'd borrowed one of Sydney's longest night shirts, but it was barely legal on her much taller frame.

Sydney ran her hand up a long, bare leg. "I think you should wear this every day."

A low chuckle answered her. "You clear it with Marge and I'll do it."

"Who on earth would protest?" Sydney asked.

"I can think of a few."

"Name one?"

"The law." Saber was still chuckling. "It's a pretty important one."

"There's a law about restricting natural beauty?" Sydney teased, enjoying the faint blush that crept over Saber's skin. She nibbled an earlobe.

"No, but there is a law about indecent exposure." Saber gave her a cheeky look. "Unless you want to join a nudist colony?"

"Now there's an idea!"

Saber played with blonde locks affectionately. "I love your morning hair. Makes you look like a cherub."

Sydney ran her fingers through it, trying to neaten it. "I bet a cherub wouldn't do this." She reached around and pinched Saber's bum.

"Hey!" Saber said, chuckling in surprise.

"Nice muscle tone."

A smile. "And speaking of muscle, I suppose I'd best get ready for my run."

Sydney pouted. "Must you go?"

Saber's smile turned flirtatious. "Not if you can convince me to stay."

Green eyes sparkled. "I'm sure I can come up with something."

Chapter Eight

"HOW DO YOU FEEL?" Saber asked as she entered Sydney's bedroom.

"Like I'm ready to get out of bed," Sydney grumbled. She slammed shut the book she was reading.

Saber sighed. "We've had this conversation before."

"I've been in bed for the past three days, Sabe, that's more than fair. I am..."

"A doctor, I know," Saber finished teasingly. "But actually it's only been two and a half days."

"It'll be three days in another hour," Sydney muttered unhappily. She was so bored she'd been reduced to counting hours. Saber had been downstairs helping the guys with the decorating for most of the day, while she'd been stuck up in her room, alone and fed up.

Saber sat down on the bed next to her and ruffled her blonde hair. "You've been a star patient."

Sydney smiled. She could never stay mad with Saber around. "I'm going to remember this, you know. Wait till you get sick, then you'll see."

"I don't get sick."

Sydney rolled her eyes. "Sabe, everyone gets sick."

"Not me."

The response infuriated Sydney even more. "I'm just letting you know, paybacks are a bitch," she said in a warning tone. Saber winked at her. She tried to scowl, but couldn't quite manage it.

"Thank you for humoring me." Saber rubbed the back of Sydney's hand.

"You're welcome." Sydney pushed the bed covers away. "But don't think I'm spending one more second in this bed, I'm going to come down for lunch."

"You can't do that." Saber put the blankets back over her.

"Sabe!" Sydney said testily.

"Just hear me out." Saber's lips twitched when Sydney blew out a frustrated breath. "I'm not supposed to tell you this, but they've nearly finished decorating the room, they want it to be a surprise."

Her resolve weakened slightly. "How long's it going to take?"

"I said I'd keep you up here till tea time today."

Sydney's expression lifted. "Does that mean you'll stay and keep me company?"

"Absolutely." Saber grinned. "And I've brought you a present." She left the bedroom for an instant and came back holding a box. "It's my Playstation 3. I wish I'd remembered it earlier. You can spend days on this thing. You won't want to leave, I guarantee it." She started to connect it up, tossing some games on the bed. "Pick one."

"I'm not very good at computer games." Sydney selected a case to look at.

"You will be." Saber gestured emphatically at the game Sydney was holding. "That's a great one."

Sydney smiled at the childlike wonder on Saber's face. These sort of games had never been her thing, but she was willing to try it for Saber's sake. "This one it is."

Saber finished what she was doing and took the box from her, putting the disc into the machine. She then closed the curtains.

Sydney smirked. "Did you have another game in mind?"

Saber chuckled. "It's for atmosphere, you'll see." She sat next to Sydney as the game screen loaded up. "I'll start afresh, that way you can get to know the story."

It has a story?

TWO HOURS LATER, Sydney was screaming at the screen, "Kill it! Kill it!" She hid behind Saber's shoulder as Saber wrestled with the control.

A gunshot was heard. "Got it," Saber said enthusiastically.

Sydney peeked out once she was sure that the monster was dead. She let out a scared laugh. "Jesus Christ!"

Saber giggled.

Sydney didn't know what she'd been expecting, but this wasn't it. This was fabulous. The graphics were stunning, and the game did indeed have a story. It was superb.

Saber's head tilted to one side. "You hear that?"

Sydney heard a scraping sound. "Someone's coming. Get your gun up!" She glanced briefly to Saber, and grinned at her eager face. She was clearly enjoying herself, they both were.

As Saber moved the character forward, through a deserted laboratory with dead bodies and blood spattered walls, the lights went out.

Sydney squealed in alarm. The scraping came again, nearer this time. "Get your torch out." They heard ragged breathing closing in on them from the left. Sydney had speakers dotted around her room, and the surround sound made it even creepier.

The character pulled out her torch, lighting up a snarling creature in front of her, which was dragging a crow bar along the floor. It lunged.

"Holy shit!" Saber cried out.

Sydney screamed in fright.

Saber pressed a few buttons, bringing the shotgun up. She fired, blasting the thing in half. The lights came on. They quickly scanned the scene, but no one else was there.

Saber looked at Sydney. "How are you doing? All right?"

Sydney relaxed her death grip on Saber's thigh. She smiled. "Fine. This is by far the best game I've ever played."

Saber held out the control to her. "You gonna give it a go yet?"

"Hell no, not on this game. If I was holding that, I'd run out the room screaming."

Saber chuckled. She put the control down. "I'll put something else on if you want to try that?"

"Later. I wanna kick some more monster butt." Sydney sniggered. "God, I never thought I'd hear myself say that." She shifted slightly. "Unless you've had enough?"

"No way, I was just being polite. Like I said, I can play this for days."

"We'll have to get supplies in beforehand." Sydney grinned. "You're really good."

Saber acknowledged the compliment with a shy look. "Practice. You're forgetting I've played this before, so I knew what was coming. Well, up until this level, I've never reached this far until now."

Sydney picked up the other games, looking at them with a newfound interest. "You've got a few."

"I've got more at home." Saber pointed to the screen. "This one's my favorite though."

They turned their attention back to it when a low groaning sound emerged from the speakers. Saber picked up the control, as Sydney's arm wound its way around her waist.

"GOOD GRIEF!" COOP said, as Sydney let out another scream. "What in heavens name is going on up there?" He looked to the others for an answer: Rich smirked, Jeff chortled, and Doug raised his bushy eyebrows, an impressed expression crossing his face. Coop pointed to each man individually. "You three get your minds out of the gutter."

"Oh God," Saber shouted.

Coop's skin turned the color of his hair.

Doug started to laugh, and he glanced at Jeff. "Maybe we should have asked for pointers?"

Jeff nodded mutely.

"Don't they know we can hear them?" Coop asked, mortified.

Rich patted his back condescendingly. "I don't think they're giving us a lot of thought right now."

DOUG WAS BUSY cleaning the last of the paint from his brushes when Jeff walked into the kitchen, carrying a duffel bag.

"When's the new carpet coming?"

"Next week, I think Syd mentioned Tuesday." Doug dropped the brushes into the open bag. "We all cleared away in there?"

"Yeah, I'll just take this stuff to the van."

Doug crossed into the living room, examining it and giving a satisfied nod. The cream walls went really well with Sydney's brown sofa and furniture. "What do you think, Coop?"

"It's nice," he said. "I think Sydney will like it."

Rich came in carrying the coffee table. He placed it where it had originally been. "All done."

"Great. Coop, you wanna go up and tell Saber she can bring Syd down?"

"No. I'm not going up there." Coop shook his head. "I'm not going to risk disturbing...anything."

Rich made a show of listening. "They've quietened down now, you'll be fine to go up."

"Well if you're so sure, why don't you go up? I went last time."

"Fair's fair, we are a team after all. Rich, it's your turn." Doug grinned, shoving the man forward.

"You're kidding?" Rich objected loudly. "You haven't done it yet either." He looked as if he was about to protest further when Jeff came into the room. Rich quickly passed the buck on to him. "Jeff, you're up."

"What for?"

"It's your turn to get the girls down here," Doug said.

Jeff chuckled. "You guys too chicken?"

"I don't see you rushing to do it," Rich muttered.

"I'll do it. I don't mind." Jeff went into the hall. "Saber? Syd?" he shouted. "You can come down now."

There was silence for a long moment, then Doug laughed. "Damn, why didn't we think of that?"

"Be right there." Saber's voice came back.

Jeff looked smug when he walked back in. "The three of you couldn't come up with that?"

SABER SMILED WHEN she spotted Coop waiting at the bottom of the stairs, offering his hand to Sydney when she reached him. Saber was on one side, so he took the other.

Sydney nodded to him. "Thanks, Coop, you're such a gentleman." She blinked as she entered the newly completed living room, seemingly impressed with the transformation. "Wow. You guys, this is great. Thank you so much."

"Do you like it?" Jeff asked.

"I love it. It looks wonderful."

"You've done a good job," Saber said, as she guided Sydney to the sofa.

Rich clapped Saber on the back when she passed him. "Way to go,

Saber," he whispered, winking at her.

Saber looked blankly at him, having no idea what he was referring to. His smirk and thumbs up only added to her confusion.

Coop covered his eyes, as if embarrassed.

A thought suddenly occurred to her. "You told him about the lipstick, didn't you?"

Doug held his hands up in a defensive gesture. "I didn't say anything. I didn't have to."

"What lipstick?" Rich pounced on the opening. "Doug, have you been holding out on us?"

"See? I haven't told anyone. I thought you'd wanna do it yourselves."

"Told us what?" Rich asked impatiently.

Saber glanced to Sydney, who nodded and took hold of her hand. "We're a couple."

"We know!" Rich said. "Though it's about time you admitted it."

"We've just got together," Sydney said.

"Uh-huh." Rich rolled his eyes. "No one's buying that."

"It's true!"

Rich gestured toward the ceiling. "We heard you having sex!"

Coop covered his face once more.

Saber's eyebrows disappeared into her hairline. "I don't see how, I've only kissed her."

"All that moaning was from a kiss?" Doug said. "My God, we do need tips!"

"What moaning?" Sydney looked confused.

"Well, crying out, shouting, that kind of thing. It wasn't very clear. We assumed..." Doug smiled suggestively.

Realisation dawned on Saber. "We were playing computer games! You guys have filthy minds!"

Coop, Jeff, and Doug all turned red in embarrassment. Only Rich remained unaffected by Saber's scolding, instead, he looked disappointed. "Wait. You've only kissed? After all this time?"

"We've just got together," Sydney repeated impatiently. "Not that it's any of your business."

"Truly?"

"Yes," Saber drew the 's' out in exasperation. "That's what we keep telling you."

Doug began to laugh. "You've just ruined your own reputation, Saber. After those moans, Rich thought you were a real stud. Casanova reincarnated."

Saber now understood his earlier wink. "Perhaps I should've kept my mouth shut?"

As everyone laughed, Rich said, "So what's this about lipstick?"

"Remember the other day when you brought food back from the café? Doug noticed I had lipstick on my neck. That's how he knew. So I don't want anyone to feel like they were the last to know, because we intended to tell you all together." Saber looked specifically at Coop, who nodded in understanding.

Coop perched on the sofa's arm and laid a hand on Saber's shoulder, giving first her, then Sydney, a warm smile. "I'm glad you've finally been able to see what I've seen all along—that you two are perfect for each other."

Both women returned his smile, and Sydney squeezed Saber's hand, which was still entwined with her own.

Rich, never one to allow himself to be overlooked, egotistically added, "I told you guys you'd get together. You should've just listened to me, I'm always right."

"I CAN'T BELIEVE that would happen," Sydney spoke up as the credits rolled.

"What? That the ship sank?" Saber joked. "It's *Titanic*, what did you think would happen?"

Sydney swatted the arm that was around her shoulders. "I meant, I can't believe that someone like Rose would get together with someone like Jack, it's just not realistic. Kate Winslet is way too cute for him."

Saber chuckled. "I agree. You know, I think I've changed my mind about sitting on the sofa. It's much nicer than I remember, although I think a lot of it has to do with the company."

Charmed, Sydney snuggled back into position against Saber's chest, smiling when she felt her hair being played with. "Coop will have a fit when I tell him that. He's been trying for years, and I'm the one to convert you."

"I hope you're talking about the chair," Saber teased. "'Cause I've always been attracted to women."

Sydney sniggered. "I kinda gathered that, honey. You've got this butch macho thing down to a fine art."

"You can talk! You wouldn't even let me walk you home without an argument."

"But you did end up walking me home, so you're more butch than me."

Saber seemed to concede the point. "I am very protective. Does that bother you?"

Sydney instantly shook her head. "Not at all. I like the fact that you want to take care of me. It's incredibly sweet." She cleared her throat, becoming self-conscious. "Besides, that would be hypocritical of me, considering I talked you out of your shift after that rescue." Sydney peeked up at her. "Were you mad at me for that?"

Saber grew serious. "No. I'm sorry if you thought I was." She sighed. "It's just that I'm not used to people looking out for me, except for the team. I've never had anyone. You were right though, I'm pleased you convinced me to take the night off."

Sensing the change in her mood, Sydney took hold of her hand. "You'll soon get used to it. I'll take good care of you," she said, raising Saber's hand and kissing it.

A touched smile. "I don't doubt it."

A thought suddenly struck Sydney. "You've never had anyone? So is this your first relationship?"

"No, but it's my first serious one. It took me a long time to accept who I was, my parent's negative reaction bound me for a lot of years. I didn't dare to be myself."

Sydney softly stroked her stomach, giving her comfort. She didn't ask any questions, though she badly wanted to, she had to trust that Saber would tell her when ready.

A short while passed, then Saber took a deep breath, as if collecting herself. "But as you can see..." Playful fingers tracked up Sydney's thigh. "I got over that."

Sydney stretched up and kissed her. "I'm very glad you did."

Chapter Nine

"DO YOU MIND if I take your car?" Saber asked, as she peered into the fridge. "We need some more supplies. The guys are bound to want feeding at lunch."

Though the living room was finished, work was due to start on the hall. Sydney had hoped that her bedroom would be decorated next, but since she'd been holed up in there for the last few days, she'd had no choice but to revise her plan. Knowing that Sydney wanted the whole house decorated, Doug had suggested they do all of downstairs first. Seeing the logic in that, Sydney had agreed with him.

"It's all yours. Want some company?" Sydney asked hopefully. She really wanted to get out of the house for some fresh air, she hated being cooped up. Although on the plus side, she got to spend a lot of time alone with Saber, which was never a bad thing.

"You don't want to push yourself too hard." Saber rummaged through the cupboards, clearly trying to determine what was required from the shop.

"I'll wait in the car. I just want a change of scenery."

"If you're sure?" Saber turned, and Sydney nodded steadily at her. "It'll certainly make the journey more fun."

Sydney gave her a warm look. "How did you get about before?"

"I had my own car until a couple of years ago, now I go with Coop. You don't mind if he comes along this morning, do you?"

"No, of course not."

"We always go together. I don't want him to feel pushed out." Saber closed the cupboard door. "I'd go in his car, but he drives like an old man." She chuckled.

"Why'd you get rid of yours?" Sydney watched her closely for a reaction, not wanting to pry if Saber didn't want to talk about it. "Sounds like you spent a great deal of time on it."

"Yeah, I did. I had a lot of fun with that car." Saber leaned against the kitchen worktop. "You know I said I didn't...don't, get on with my parents?"

Sydney tipped her head.

"Well one day, out of the blue, my Aunt calls me—on my mother's side. God only knows how she found me, I sure as hell didn't tell any of them where I was."

Sydney was shocked by the amount of venom in her voice and instinctively crossed to her side, resting a hand on Saber's crossed arms.

"Anyway, my Aunt tells me my mother's sick and they need money to go private."

"What was wrong with her?"

Saber laughed humorlessly. "She wouldn't tell me, she said it wasn't my business because I wasn't part of the family anymore."

Sydney frowned. "Then why was she asking you for money?"

"They couldn't afford the operation, so they tracked me down."

"A private op?" Sydney asked, confused. "It can't have been life-threatening or the NHS would've taken care of it."

"That's what I figured," Saber said quietly. "My Aunt told me that it was the least I could do, since I'd ruined their lives and all."

Sydney gasped. "She said that?"

"Of course she did. They all hate me for being gay, you know that."

"I didn't realise they were that awful."

"What? You thought I wouldn't speak to my family for nearly twenty years over a little tiff?" Saber said angrily.

Sydney looked upset but she didn't back away.

"I'm sorry," Saber added gently. "Truly." She sighed. "This is why I don't talk about it. I'm sorry."

"It's all right. No, I didn't think it was a little tiff but..." Sydney grew annoyed at Saber's Aunt for hurting her. "How can people be so horrible?"

"You must see that frequently in your line of work?"

"Mm. It still upsets me though, especially if it involves you."

"I sold the only item that was worth anything—my car. I sent them the money."

"And?" Sydney needed the answer, even though she knew it wasn't going to be pleasant.

Saber's blue eyes were sad. "I never heard from them again."

"Sweetheart," Sydney whispered.

"I don't know why I did it." Saber swallowed. "I guess I thought it might build some bridges, even after all this time." She produced a self-deprecating look. "Stupid, huh?"

"Not at all. They're still your parents, it's understandable that you care about them." Sydney touched Saber's cheek, caressing the soft skin there. "So you gave up your pride and joy," she quoted Marge's phrase.

Saber shrugged ever so slightly.

"This just confirms what I've always thought about you."

"That I'm a sap?" Saber asked mockingly.

Sydney's brow knit. "No. That you're the kindest, most thoughtful person I know. You amaze me, you really do." She gave Saber a kiss. "I don't understand why you haven't told Marge or anyone else about this though."

"Coop would've given me the money, I didn't want that. The others..." Saber ran a frustrated hand through her hair. "I was so angry with myself for being taken in like that, I didn't want them to think any less of me."

Sydney shook her head. "They wouldn't have."

"Maybe not, but I didn't want any questions. I'm not very good at talking about it, as I'm sure you've noticed."

"You're doing fine," Sydney said. "Thank you for trusting me with this. I mean that."

A hint of a smile appeared on Saber's lips.

"Come here." Sydney hugged her.

"I WANT IT done by the time we get back," Sydney yelled out the car window.

"You want the whole hall done in two hours?" Rich snorted. "Yeah right." He took the bag that Jeff handed him. They were unloading the van.

"That's the price of my dinner," Saber said seriously.

The men looked at her in horror. "You're kidding!" Rich said.

Saber's face creased into a grin. "Yes. Do any of you guys want anything while we're there?"

"What are you going to cook for lunch?" Rich asked.

"Whatever you want from the looks of it," Saber said wryly.

Rich walked to the car, pulling out his wallet and handing her a twenty pound note. "Get them steaks that I like. And some beer, we've got none left at home. Oh and chocolate, you know which kind."

Saber raised a dark eyebrow. "Anything else?" she said sarcastically, causing Sydney to snigger. She sighed as Rich kept them waiting for a moment while he seemed to think about it.

"How come he gets a specific request for lunch?" Doug suddenly appeared at the window beside him.

Saber groaned, dropping her head against the steering wheel with a thump. "Why did I ask?"

Sydney opened the glove box, searching.

"I hope you're looking for a gun," Saber muttered.

When she pulled out a pen and paper, Doug said, "Well done, Syd, it always pays to be prepared."

Sydney wrote down the items. "Anything else, Rich?"

"Some flowers for my mum," he added quietly.

Sydney gave him a surprised look. "That's sweet, Rich." He became self-conscious, so she refocused on the pad, scribbling it down.

Saber lifted her head and waved Jeff over.

"Some red wine. Half a dozen of them crusty rolls, the Missus loves those." Doug listed. "A six pint of milk, too."

"What do you want for lunch?" Saber leaned back in the seat, rolling her eyes. "God, I am a housewife."

"With none of the perks." Doug winked playfully.

Saber scrunched her nose up. "I wouldn't want any of your perks, mate. No offence."

Sydney chuckled beside her.

"Ouch!" Rich clasped the leader's broad shoulder.

Doug laughed good-naturedly. "None taken."

"Jeff, anything you want?" Saber asked, as if knowing he wouldn't just barge in like the others. After Coop, Jeff was the most considerate of the men.

"I'll have the same as Rich for lunch."

"You sure? I'll be doing something different for Doug anyway. I could get you one of those fish that you like so much?" At his hesitation, she said, "I really don't mind."

Sydney spoke up when Jeff nodded his approval, "It's been ages since I had fish, I think I'll join you."

"Saber does it just right," Jeff said.

"From her cooking so far, I don't doubt it."

Saber smiled at the compliments. "Doug?" As he seemed to ponder the question, scratching his beard, she said, "The place will be closed at this rate." Saber shook her head. "It's all right, Jeff, I'll get the money when I come back."

"Okay." Jeff removed his hand from his pocket. "Thanks, Saber."

"Right, I know what I want."

Saber apparently knew what he was going to say. "Let me guess, lamb chops with mint sauce?"

Doug closed his mouth and grinned at her.

Sydney wrote it down. "What do you want, honey?"

"I'll have a steak." Saber waved to them as she drove off. Leaving the drive, she continued straight ahead to Coop's house. "Remind me to never ask that question again." She honked the horn when they came to a halt.

Coop came out almost instantly, tapping his watch jokingly. "You're late, Saber." He got into the back seat. "Morning, Syd."

"Coop." Sydney handed him the pad of paper. "That's why we're late."

He examined it. "This is a shopping list for the entire village!"

"Practically." Saber pulled the car away from the curb, driving forward once more. "By the time we get all of this lot, they may indeed have finished the hall."

Coop passed the list back to Sydney. "Glad to see you're feeling better."

"It's all the TLC Sabe's been giving me. Works wonders. Although I'm starting to feel a little spoiled."

"Nonsense," Coop said. "I'm pleased she's looking after you properly. She's never even had a pet. I was wondering how she'd cope looking after a person."

Saber scoffed. "I managed just fine, thanks." She glanced across to Sydney, doubt appearing on her face. "Didn't I?"

Sydney touched her arm in assurance. "You couldn't have been better, sweetheart. I think it's the only time I actually enjoyed being laid up."

Saber gave her a happy look before using the rear-view mirror to stick her tongue out at Coop.

Coop smiled. "Did you have any pets, Syd?"

"Yes. 'Cause there were four of us we've had most things over the years."

"Like what?" Saber asked.

"Dogs and cats, rabbits and hamsters, fish, birds, lizards and snakes, a tarantula." Sydney reeled them off from memory, knowing how lucky she'd been. Both her and her siblings hadn't wanted for anything. Her parents had seen to that. She wouldn't consider herself to be spoiled, but she'd certainly led a privileged life.

"A tarantula?" Coop's tone conveyed he thought it an odd choice.

"I didn't say it was mine," Sydney said in defence.

"I bet it was your brother's, the one who went backpacking? What was his name again?"

"Anthony. Yes it was actually. Oh, and we had a chinchilla, too."

"My goodness," Coop's voice rose a notch, "your house must've been like a zoo!"

Sydney giggled. "We didn't have them all at once."

"Which was your favorite?" Saber asked.

"My dog, Merlin. He was a Labrador. I had him when I was a teenager, he was the last pet I had. I was too upset after he died to get another."

"Doug's got a couple of those," Coop said. "Nice dogs. One's so pale it's almost white, the other's brown. Guess what he calls them?" Coop halted briefly. "Salt and Pepper." He laughed. "You should see Saber with them, she's like a big kid."

Saber smiled, not denying it. "I love dogs."

"And speaking of Doug, he told me that Faye's finally agreed to sell her cookies at the café."

Saber's amusement was clear. "She's given in, has she?"

Coop sounded unrepentant. "Only after some insistent pestering on mine and Marge's part." He eagerly rubbed his hands together. "Wait till you try them, Syd, they're to die for. Doug should be the size of a whale, what with both Faye and Saber feeding him." His voice became reflective. "You know, that's two things I've been right about lately, Faye's cookies and…What was the other again? Remind me, Saber?"

"Yeah yeah, me and Syd." Saber grinned at him through the rear-view mirror.

"You seemed to know even before we did," Sydney said. "How could you tell?"

"It was your eyes, the way you looked," Coop snorted, "or rather, gazed at each other."

Green eyes met blue, and they smiled.

Coop burst into laughter. "That's it!"

SYDNEY TURNED IN the passenger seat, wanting to see Coop's expression. "I've finally gotten her to sit on the sofa."

His rusty eyebrows shot up. "How did you manage that?"

"We were curled up watching a movie one night, and since then she sits on it."

"Only when you're around," Saber said.

"Ah. I didn't know that."

"You've got an unfair advantage, Syd, you can offer her an incentive — you. No wonder you won."

"Technically I didn't win, as she," Sydney gave Saber's arm a poke, "still sits on the floor when I'm not there." She raised an inquisitive eyebrow. "I thought you said it was comfortable?"

"It is." Saber lowered her voice secretively. "But I miss you when you're gone. I don't notice it so much on the floor."

"Aw, Saber, you big softy," Coop teased, smirking when Saber glared at him through the rear-view mirror.

"You are so sweet." Sydney's smile was tender as she reached out and gave Saber's thigh a squeeze.

"My reputation's in ruins," Saber muttered.

Coop sniggered. "Wait till the guys hear about this."

"Don't you dare!" Saber said. "I'll never hear the end of it."

Sydney giggled. She'd missed the banter between these two. It's not like Coop hadn't been around, but from upstairs she hadn't seen a lot of it. She remembered what Saber had said in the kitchen that morning — about not wanting him to feel pushed out. She decided to address the issue. "Coop, you do know that you can come round at any time? You don't need an invitation."

"You girls deserve your privacy."

Sydney appreciated that, but she didn't want him to be left out either, especially as Saber was so close to the man. "Just because Sabe and I are now an item, that doesn't mean things have to change between you and her. I respect that you two do a lot together, and I don't want that to change on account of me."

"It will change, Syd, because now they'll be three of us." Saber smiled. "The three musketeers."

"In Sydney's case, I think it should be mouseketeer."

"I'm not that small," Sydney said.

"If you're sure I won't be in the way?" Coop asked.

"You're family to Sabe, that means you are to me too. And family can't be in the way."

Coop sounded touched. "All right, but only on the understanding that you'll tell me if you want some space. I won't take offence."

Saber chuckled. "We'll tell you to get out, don't you worry about that."

"Okay then, it's settled."

A happy smile crossed Saber's face. She took hold of Sydney's hand and brought it to her lips. "You are the most wonderful person I've ever met."

The comment caught Sydney unawares, and her breathing hitched, her eyes filling with tears. She was rendered speechless, so she simply squeezed the hand that held her own.

As Saber's gaze returned to the road, Coop pointedly cleared his throat. "Most wonderful woman I've ever met," she said.

Sydney laughed as she regained her composure.

Coop nodded his head in acceptance. "That's better."

SYDNEY OPENED THE car door when she noticed the overloaded shopping trolley heading her way. "Did you leave anything in the shop?"

"Barely." Coop pushed the cart toward the back of the Range Rover.

Saber stopped beside the passenger door. She dug into a carrier bag and pulled out three bars of chocolate, handing them to Sydney.

"These all for me?"

"I figured we could do with something on the trip back, by the time I cook everything we'll be starving." Saber also removed three bottles of pop, and rested them on the dashboard.

"Thanks, I'm parched." Sydney opened one and took a sip. "How much did it all come to?"

Saber fumbled in the bag, then passed her the receipt. "I've gotta take off what the guys owe."

"I'll give you the rest after that."

"No you won't."

"Sabe, I know you like your independence, but there's no way I'm letting you pay for all that."

"You're too stubborn." Saber lay a finger against her lips to forestall the protest that was about to emerge. "We'll go halves on everything, how does that sound?"

Sydney gave her finger a lick. "Sounds reasonable."

Saber laughed.

"But just so you know, you're the stubborn one."

"So according to you, I'm butch, sweet, and stubborn. Geez, what a combination, however do you put up with me?" Saber leaned toward her.

"Luckily for you, I'm the patient one," Sydney whispered. "Besides, I can think of a few reasons why I put up with you." She gave her a kiss. "That being one of them."

A clatter came from the boot.

"I think Coop's dropped the shopping." Sydney giggled.

They both looked to Coop, who was turning crimson.

"I think you're right," Saber said. "I'd better go and give him a hand."

Coop shook his head at Saber as he lifted the bags from the trolley and transferred them into the boot.

"What?" Saber asked innocently.

"You did that on purpose." He shook his head again. "It's a good thing that bag didn't have Doug's wine in it, that's all I can say."

Once they'd finished loading the car, they set off.

Saber tossed a chocolate bar to Coop. He was hit in the chest. "What in the...Oh thanks, Saber." Sydney passed him the pop. "Thank you. Phew, it was busy in there."

"Everyone comes shopping on a Friday to stock up for the weekend. In a few hours half the shelves will be empty." Saber glanced to Sydney. "That's why we come on a morning."

"You only go once a week?" Sydney was contentedly munching on her chocolate. She unwrapped Saber's and handed it to her.

Saber smiled gratefully, then took a bite. "In summer. Once every two in winter, roads get blocked by the snow."

"What happens if the roads don't clear?"

"Don't worry," Coop's voice came from the backseat. "We've got our own snow plough. It attaches to the front of our Land Rover. We need it to get to stranded motorists."

"And the odd sheep farmer," Saber joked.

"Ew." Sydney wrinkled her nose.

Coop sounded aghast. "Don't tell me you told her?"

"It wasn't her fault," Sydney said. "I was curious as to what had happened, I asked her to tell me. Frankly, I wish I hadn't."

Saber chuckled, and Coop scolded her, "It's not funny, young lady."

"Coop here, bless him, kept trying to block my view."

"Which let me tell you, is extremely difficult when she can see over the top of my head."

Sydney hastily swallowed her drink, imagining the scene. These two were a riot, and never ceased to make her laugh.

"I thought you were going to be sick," Saber said.

"I very nearly was."

Sydney was still laughing. "How did you manage to keep a straight face?"

"It was a long trip back to the car. From what I can recall, we didn't say very much."

"I've never eaten lamb since," Coop said.

"JEFF, YOU WERE RIGHT." Sydney rested her cutlery on the now empty plate. "That fish was delicious."

"It was."

"Spot on as always, Saber." Rich patted his full stomach.

"Thank you for a wonderful meal," Coop said, as well mannered as ever.

"Yeah, the lamb chops were perfect."

Coop's entire face scrunched up in disgust, and Sydney had to restrain herself from sniggering.

Saber received the praise with a modest nod. She got up, as if intending to clear the plates away.

"We've got it," Doug said. He and the other men got to their feet.

"We'll wash up." Coop nudged Saber in Sydney's direction. "Go and take that girl of yours into the living room. She should be resting."

"Cheers, guys." Saber followed Sydney out of the kitchen. They both crossed to the couch and settled onto it. She lay a gentle hand on Sydney's stomach. "How's this doing?"

Sydney was pleasantly surprised by the lack of objection from her wound. "It's fine."

"Good."

"Why don't you bring the Playstation down? We could have a rally with the guys? It'll give their food a chance to digest."

Saber grinned. "I've got you hooked, huh?"

"You had me hooked the first time I saw you." Blue eyes sparkled at her words. "Oh you mean the game?" Sydney batted innocent eyelashes. "Yeah, I love it."

"NO FAIR!" RICH shouted as Sydney overtook him on the racing circuit. "You're a damn pro!"

"I've only been playing on it since yesterday."

Saber gave her a high five when Sydney completed the track. "Nice one, sweetheart." She marked another notch on the paper. "That's four to the girls, one to the boys."

"Can't we change our team name?" Coop said. "It's hurting my manhood being called a girl."

Sydney giggled. "There are two girls and one guy, we outnumber you, so no."

Coop, Sydney, and Saber, were on one team. Jeff, Doug, and Rich, the other. Sydney passed the control to Coop while Rich handed his to Jeff.

Doug was the expert on the other team. To give both teams an equal chance, the experts raced against each other. Saber and Doug had raced twice now, and it was one each.

Coop was surprisingly apt at it—considering he spent half the time admiring the graphics instead of keeping an eye on the track. "Did you see that? Looks like the Colosseum." He took his finger off the accelerator button, slowing down to get a better look.

"Coop!" Sydney shouted. "He's catching up."

Saber hurriedly slammed her finger onto the button. "It's a race, Coop, not a scenic tour!"

"It's only a game, you know." Coop laughed as Jeff whizzed past.

"Too slow, old man," Rich teased.

Coop's eyes narrowed. "Right, now you've asked for it." He floored the accelerator, catching up to Jeff after a few reckless corners. He slammed his car into Jeff's, sending them both careening off the road.

Jeff's red Subaru Impreza spun out, while Coop's blue Mitsubishi Evo managed to find its grip and reach the edge of the track. It picked up speed as its tires gripped the tarmac.

"That's cheating!" Rich yelled.

"Eat my dirt," Coop said.

Saber clasped his shoulder when he passed the finish line. "Way to go, Coop." She gave an additional point to her team, marking it down on the sheet.

Coop gave them a bow, looking rather pleased with himself.

"How on earth did you do that slide?" Sydney looked at the control eagerly when Coop pointed out which buttons to press. "That was so cool."

"Yeah, why don't you drive like that in real life?" Saber joked.

"I wish I could."

"Me, too," Sydney added. "Although I don't think I'd want the repair bill afterward." She gestured to the screen. "Look at that dent."

Saber waved it off. "The prize money will take care of it."

Jeff crossed the line a few seconds later, then handed the control to Doug. "That was some nice driving, Coop. Completely illegal, but nice nonetheless."

"Come on, Doug, you've gotta win this one," Rich said.

"What's the score?" he asked.

"Five to one," Saber said cockily.

Doug frowned. "It is not."

Saber held up the pad of paper, showing the large numbers in black and white. The five was under the girls' column.

Doug flexed his hands in show, then pointed at Saber. "I'm going to wipe that smirk off your face."

"Don't make promises you can't keep."

The green lights came on and both sets of car tires squealed.

"I wonder how much more exciting it would've been if we'd made a bet," Sydney said.

Saber immediately pressed the pause button, giving Doug a questioning look. "Care to put your money where your mouth is? Not just you, the whole team." She glanced to the others.

"Sure, but not money though. How about if I win, you and Syd have to kiss." Doug grinned.

"I'm game," Jeff said instantly.

Saber laughed. "You're obsessed. And that's enough incentive to make me lose on purpose." She winked, and Sydney gave her an enchanted smile.

"Hang on, if this is a team thing, what do you want me to do?"

Coop asked, looking worried.

"Nothing. You can enjoy it like the rest of us," Doug said forthrightly.

Coop shook his head. "I'll do no such thing. It's private."

Sydney got into the spirit of it. "If Sabe wins, you've gotta wash Coop's car and mine, once a week, for the next month."

Coop's headshake turned into a nod. "I'm in."

"Me, too." Rich's enthusiasm was clear. "Wait, wait, let's got one thing clear, you've gotta kiss properly — on the lips, tongues and all."

Coop became flustered. "Dear Lord, what kind of people am I hanging out with?"

Sydney chuckled. She touched Saber's arm. "Is that okay with you?"

Saber pouted. "You and Coop get your cars washed, what exactly am I getting out of all this? I'd rather lose and get kissed thanks."

Sydney thought. "I'll give you two kisses if you win."

"Well I'm throwing the race," Doug said.

"In private," Sydney added.

"You've got yourself a deal." Saber reached over and shook Doug's hand. "I win either way." She smirked.

"Exactly," Jeff said. "So you might as well be kind and let us enjoy it, too."

Sydney sniggered. "Nice try. I want my car washed."

"You do realise, Doug," Jeff said. "If you lose this race, we'll never forgive you."

"Yeah, you better win."

"I'll never forgive myself." Doug looked amused. "No pressure."

"Ready?" Saber clasped the control. Doug nodded, so she pressed the pause button and the game roared to life, blue car alongside red as they raced for the first corner.

They were neck and neck up until the last lap, when Saber pulled out in front. She crossed the finish line a few inches ahead.

"Damn it." Doug dropped the control unhappily.

"Good try, mate, you almost had her." Jeff gave his back a consoling pat.

"You obviously underestimated how much I wanted that kiss." Saber's smile was smug. "Or should I say kisses?"

Sydney ran a hand over Saber's cheek, closing the distance. She stopped just before her mouth met Saber's. "You'll get your reward later."

Saber licked her lips, trying her best not to close the gap herself.

"Oh my God!" Rich whispered.

Sydney noticed they were being avidly watched, and burst out laughing as she withdrew. "Sorry guys, you lost."

"Aw, Doug!" Rich said. "That would've been the hottest thing I've ever seen. You owe me, man."

Saber grinned wickedly at them.
"You owe me big!"

Chapter Ten

SABER HAD FINISHED her morning run, showered, and was now sticking a load of clothes in the wash. She'd stopped at her house on the way back from her run, intending to change and pick up some spare clothes at the same time. It'd been Sydney's suggestion, to save her from flitting back and forth between houses. Saber had happily agreed, and after loading the washing machine, she went upstairs and began to pack her night clothes, some fresh running gear, and other essentials into a rucksack.

It made sense to stay at Sydney's, not only because of her injury, which was healing nicely, but because once Sydney returned to work, she sometimes had to rush out at a moments notice, so it was easier if she had everything to hand. Saber preferred Sydney's house anyway, even in its unfinished state.

The weather forecast had informed her it was going to be a scorcher of a day, and feeling warm already, Saber changed out of her T-shirt and into a plain black vest top, which matched her black jeans. She then tied her hair back, letting the air get to her tanned neck. She hoped it wasn't going to get too hot, for she was helping the guys again with Sydney's house, and manual labour wasn't at all fun in sweltering heat.

Slinging the rucksack on to her back, she went downstairs, locked up her house, and made her way to Sydney's. Letting herself in the front door, she headed up to the bedroom so she could put her spare clothes away, in the drawer that Sydney had thoughtfully emptied for her. She didn't get that far.

Sydney came down the stairs, and as she passed Saber, she slipped.

"Syd!" Saber grabbed her, catching her before she could fall. "Are you all right?" Once Sydney found her feet, Saber studied her worriedly.

"You can't wear that!" Sydney said, her voice flustered.

Saber looked down at herself, her face creasing. "Why not?"

"Because I'll never be able to concentrate! Look what's just happened!"

Saber raised a slender eyebrow, a flattered smile playing on her features. "You're saying this was my fault?"

"Absolutely. Jesus Christ, Sabe, have you looked in a mirror?" Sydney's gaze ran over Saber's figure. Twice. She swallowed.

"Judging from your expression I don't think I need to."

Sydney swallowed again. "You have to get changed. Please?" she said. "I'll lend you a T-shirt...A baggy one."

"It's too hot. I'm sweating already. See for yourself, feel me."

"Don't tempt me." Sydney fanned her face. "You have to take off that top."

"Why?" Saber was having fun teasing her.

"'Cause if you don't I'm going to ravish you on the stairs."

"And that's a reason to take it off?" Saber dropped her voice an octave. "I think that's a reason to keep it on."

"I'm serious." Sydney's hands, the first to rebel, started to caress Saber's stomach.

"So am I," Saber whispered huskily. She kissed Sydney passionately, their tongues duelling for a few moments. Then she abruptly wrenched herself back. "What time is it?"

"Huh?"

Saber took hold of Sydney's wrist, examining her watch. She groaned, but it wasn't in the way she wanted.

"What?" Sydney asked.

"The guys will be here soon."

Sydney let out an aggravated sigh. She tugged on Saber's belt loops, leading her up the stairs and into the bedroom. "Well at least you'll have time to take off that top."

Saber's face twitched mischievously. "Okay, if that's what you want." She pulled it over her head, leaving herself half-naked except for a matching black bra.

Sydney stared. "Sabe," she whispered. "You really are the most beautiful woman I've ever seen."

"That's not possible, because I'm looking at her."

Sydney smiled. She reached out to Saber, her fingers stopping just before they met bare skin. Saber inhaled sharply, anticipating her touch. Green eyes twinkled. "I meant you should change your top, you know."

"Oh? Sorry, miscommunication."

"Is that so? Here I was thinking you were teasing me."

"Me?"

"Yes, you. And enjoying it, too." Sydney's fingers traced a two-inch scar that ran along Saber's collarbone, on her right side. "A surgical scar," she said, as if in comment to herself. Sydney looked curious, but didn't ask any questions, clearly trusting that Saber would tell her when ready.

"I don't see you rushing to find me another top to wear."

Sydney gave her an impish grin. "Busted."

Saber took hold of Sydney's T-shirt, slowly removing it. Since Sydney was still in her bed clothes, she wasn't wearing anything underneath. At the sight of her, Saber couldn't restrain herself any longer. She pulled Sydney to her, kissing her strongly.

Sydney unhooked Saber's bra and let it fall, releasing a soft moan when their naked flesh met. Hands cupped Sydney's buttocks and lifted her off her feet. She wrapped her legs around Saber's waist, her tongue never leaving Saber's mouth.

Saber carried Sydney to the bed, setting her down in the middle.

Sydney lay back, pulling Saber on top.

"Wait," Sydney suddenly said. "What about the guys?"

Saber reached for the phone by the side of the bed, quickly dialling Coop's number from memory. On the third ring, he picked up. "Hi, Coop." She tried to make her voice level.

"Saber? What's up? I was just on my way over."

"I need you to do me a favor."

"Sure. Are you all right? You sound...different."

"Uh, no, I'm fine."

"Is it Sydney? Is she okay?"

Saber was pushed onto her back as Sydney reversed their positions, climbing on top of her and straddling her hips. "Syd's fine."

Sydney smiled at that. She ran her tongue up Saber's taut stomach, causing Saber's breathing to catch.

"Yes...it's about that actually. Could you give us a couple of hours?"

"Sure thing." She was grateful when Coop didn't question her reasons.

Saber let out a gasp, Sydney's mouth had found her breast.

"Saber?" He started to chuckle, sounding embarrassed. "Would you like me to pass the message along to the rest of them?"

"I'd appreciate that."

"We both would," Sydney added loudly.

Coop laughed upon hearing her. "I'll take care of it. How does lunchtime sound?"

"Even better. Thanks, Coop." Saber hung up the phone, a low moan escaping her as Sydney slid a thigh between her legs.

Sydney smiled. "Nice thinking."

SYDNEY HAD NEVER been so aroused and the fire in her loins grew tenfold when their lips met once more.

Tongues battled, and hands explored. When Sydney pressed herself intimately against Saber and began to slowly rock back and forth, Saber inhaled sharply.

"Syd." Another gasp. "God. You've gotta stop, I'm going to..."

Sydney cupped her cheek with a hand, holding her lust-filled gaze. "I want you to." She gave Saber a sensual kiss, then made her hips move faster. "Just let go."

Saber's release was immediate, and Sydney kissed her through it, watching her face as it transformed in pleasure. Sydney often thought about Saber's beauty, but seeing her like this literally took her breath away. She knew instinctively that she would never tire of seeing her this way, and before Saber had even recovered, Sydney was making her way downward, greedily, hungrily seeking more. She locked on to Saber's hot center with her mouth, sucking at her clit.

Saber released a guttural moan, and her hands buried themselves in Sydney's hair, pressing her closer still. Sydney's hand snaked up and squeezed her breast, playing with the firm nipple. Saber's hand joined Sydney's, their fingers entwining together.

Soon Saber's hips began to gyrate, and as she thrust herself up to meet Sydney's mouth, her strong leg muscles lifted both her and Sydney off the bed. Sydney ceased at her attempt to devour Saber, smiling at the whimper of protest that came from Saber's throat. Instead, Sydney pushed her tongue inside, lapping at Saber's slick wetness.

Saber gasped and arched her back, her hand tightening around Sydney's. Sensing Saber's need for closeness, Sydney withdrew and laid a kiss on her inner thigh.

"I'm right here," she said, watching Saber closely. "Do you want me to come up there?"

Saber was panting heavily, but she managed a smile. "Don't you dare."

Sydney giggled, not resisting as Saber pushed her head back down. Sydney's tongue ran over the velvety folds, and Saber began to writhe against her, clearly desperate to peak. Between gasps, Saber called Sydney's name, over and over, until the wave of euphoria passed, and she collapsed back on the bed, looking completely spent.

Sydney crawled up her long body, laying kisses as she went. She sprawled over Saber, and tenderly brushed some hair off her face.

Blue eyes, still a bit dazed, locked on to Sydney's. "Have I told you lately that I love you?"

"I love you too." Sydney kissed her devotedly. She moaned into Saber's mouth when a hand cupped her breast, and Sydney was surprised by Saber's quick recovery. She supposed she shouldn't have been, Saber was exceptionally fit.

The touch pushed Sydney past the edge of reason, and she ground herself against Saber's well-muscled thigh. "Please, Sabe," she whispered, desperate for release.

Saber was blessedly merciful. Since Sydney's body was half strewn across her, her legs were already apart. Saber raised one leg higher, as if to give her better access, then delved inside, her fingers slipping into Sydney's warmth.

Sydney gave a startled cry, delighted yet eager for more at the same time.

Saber set a steady rhythm, her thrusts slow but powerful. Sydney felt her desire build, and Saber heightened it further by plunging her tongue into Sydney's mouth.

The kiss drove Sydney wild, and gasping with need, she rolled further onto Saber, forcing her fingers deeper inside. Her hips rolled in tandem with Saber's impaling thrusts, and she groaned in increasing pleasure. When Sydney's movements grew frantic, Saber, with her other hand, pushed on Sydney's rump, driving herself deeper still.

"Oh yes, Sabe. Yes!" Sydney's panting grew louder, completely unrestrained, and as she climaxed her whole body shook.

She sagged against Saber, whose arms instantly wrapped around her. Sydney took longer to recover, but once she'd caught her breath, she said, "God, Sabe, that was incredible." She blew out an impressed breath. "Though that word doesn't even begin to describe it."

Saber released a satisfied chuckle. "You can say that again. Wow." She softly kissed Sydney's brow. "You're all right, though? Your stomach?"

Sydney had forgotten all about her injury. She peered down at the bandage, then lightly probed at the spot. "It's fine." She smoothed lines of concern from Saber's face. "Don't worry." Moments passed, then a mischievous smile emerged. "Besides, what do doctors always say?"

Saber shrugged. "Take your medicine?"

"No," Sydney giggled, swatting her arm.

"What then?"

Sydney's smile became seductive. "That exercise is good for you."

Saber chuckled, low in her throat. "Better follow the doctor's orders." She drew the duvet over them both.

Chapter Eleven

"SYDNEY," MARGE GREETED when she entered the café. She beckoned Sydney over with a towel. "How was your first day back?"

Sydney couldn't believe that she was already back at work. The time off had flown by, the sick note running out much sooner than she would've liked. Not that she wasn't fit to return to work, because she certainly was, but she'd enjoyed spending so much time with Saber, and now her work would cut into that time. Before Saber, her work had been everything, but not anymore. Saber was everything to her now.

At that realisation, a wide, happy smile crossed Sydney's face. "It was fine. Glad to be home though."

As if reading her mind, Marge tipped her head. "She's out back. Go on through."

Sydney eagerly rounded the counter and went into the kitchen. Her eyes found what they were searching for—Saber was standing by the grill, frying sausages.

Saber looked up, producing a smile that was reserved for Sydney alone.

Sydney returned it. "Hey."

"How was your day? Did your stomach give you any grief?"

"Not a twinge."

Saber seemed pleased. "Good. You want some sausages?" She expertly turned them over in the frying pan.

Sydney leaned against the wall, quite content to watch Saber work. The smell was tempting her taste buds. "That'd be great."

"How'd you want 'em? In a bread bun? With chips? Potatoes?" Saber placed a few more sausages into the pan, making it spit furiously at her. "Yeah, yeah, temper, temper," she muttered to the object.

Sydney chuckled, Saber often talked to the kitchen appliances when she cooked, it was a habit of hers that she found endearing. She imagined that's how Saber kept herself entertained during the long shifts—there was no one else around to talk to, except for Marge, but she was mostly out front with the customers. "In a bread bun's fine."

"I can easily do something to go with it? I'm doing chips and beans with mine." Saber glanced at her. "Do you mind if I eat with you?"

"Tch. You kidding? I was going to insist. If you're doing chips I'll have some. And some beans too." Sydney shook her head. "It's a good thing I exercise."

"That's the nice thing about keeping fit, you can eat all you want and not feel guilty. We've got a fresh load of Faye's cookies in." Saber's glance told Sydney she knew of her weakness for them. "I thought we could have some for dessert."

"Ooh," Sydney murmured. "I'm doomed."

"You're perfect as you are."

Sydney snorted. "You won't be saying that when I'm the size of that whale Coop mentioned."

"Yes I will," Saber said confidently.

Sydney gave her an affectionate look. "The same goes for you too, honey."

"You'd never let yourself get that fat anyway. You couldn't cope with being in bed for a few days, so I can't see you living like that."

"I was a good patient!" Sydney went silent for a second. "You do have a point though."

"I happen to think you're in fabulous shape." Saber's face twitched. "Especially for your age."

"For my age? I'm younger than you!"

"That's exactly what I mean, your body hasn't had as much training as mine has, I've got two years on you." Sydney could tell Saber was teasing. Neither of them were conceited over their high fitness levels.

"You sound like Rich."

Saber scowled. "That was uncalled for."

"You're right, it was. I'm sorry, love."

Saber smiled. "You're forgiven. But only because you used emotional blackmail by calling me love."

"You noticed that, huh?"

Saber poured some cooking oil into the pan, peering at her from under long lashes. "Mm-hmm."

Sydney let out a short chuckle. "Damn. I thought I was being subtle."

"Nice try."

"It still worked though," Sydney said cockily.

"Yeah, I'm a sucker for a pretty face." Saber laughed. "I remember thinking that when I first met you, that's why I convinced Rich to get seen to."

"I wanted to thank you for that. Knowing Rich as I do now, I know he'd never have stayed if you hadn't done so yourself."

"The best decision I've ever made," Saber said with certainty.

Sydney smiled brightly. "For both of us."

Saber turned the new sausages over, causing them to hiss at her. "So did you save any lives today?" She sounded proud.

"You make it sound so dramatic."

"That's because it is. You're just too mod...Son of a..." Saber pulled her hand back sharply, glaring at the frying pan.

Sydney was by her side in an instant, guiding her quickly to the sink. Turning on the cold water, she directed Saber's hand under the flow.

"It's fine." Saber gave the sausages an evil look. "It just spat at me."

After a few moments, Sydney removed her hand from the spray.

"Let me see."

"The sausages will burn," Saber said, though her objection was mild.

"Let them," Sydney said. "I'm not in love with the sausages." Except for a red mark on the top of Saber's hand, it was no worse for wear. She glanced up to find Saber staring at her with such a look of amused tenderness, that she simply couldn't stop herself from stretching up and kissing her. "Mm, I've been waiting all day for that."

"I've got you beat." Saber lightly took hold of her chin. "I've been waiting for you all my life."

Sydney sucked in a breath, the remark earning Saber another kiss, longer and more passionate. Saber really did say the most beautiful things to her.

With a smile, Saber gave Sydney's hip a pat, then moved back to the oven.

Marge came bustling in. "Saber, haven't you taken your break yet?"

"I'm about to. I'm going to sit with Syd."

"Good." Marge nodded to Sydney. "I can see you're a good influence. She hardly ever takes her breaks, no matter how many times I tell her. She is so obstinate."

"She can be." Sydney grinned cheekily as Saber's jaw dropped.

"I bet you keep her in check, don't you?"

"I try. She's quite the handful," Sydney teased.

Marge patted her arm sympathetically. "I know, dear, she can be quite trying at times."

Saber scoffed in outrage.

Marge dismissed Saber with a wave of her hand. "She's lucky you're so tolerant. Don't you give up now, y'hear? I've noticed a world of difference in her since you moved into the village."

"Is that so?"

"She never stops smiling for one. You two are good for each other." Marge switched her gaze to Saber. "Haven't you finished cooking yet? Poor Sydney's starving to death while you stand there yakking." She shuffled out of the kitchen, leaving Saber gaping comically in her wake.

Sydney was delighted by what Marge had told her. "You never stop smiling?"

Saber scrubbed her cheek self-consciously. "My reputation's in shreds."

"Yes it is."

"Oh well, my reputation had a good run. You wanna go and grab a seat? This is nearly ready."

"Okay, I'll get the drinks." Sydney dug into the fridge, pulling out a can of coke and a juice carton.

"Don't let Marge see you."

"My, my." Marge stepped back into the kitchen. "It seems Saber's rubbing off on you, too." She sighed at the chef.

"How is this my fault? I'm over here in case you hadn't noticed."

"I'm only trying to save you some work." Sydney closed the fridge door.

"You even sound like her." Marge smiled, taking the drinks from her hands. "That's a nice sentiment, dear, but if I came in halfway through an operation and started to stitch your patient closed, would you let me?"

Sydney blinked at the visual image. "Well, no."

"Precisely. Now, go and put your feet up, I'm sure you've had a long day." Marge ushered her to one of the tables, then rested the drinks on the surface.

Sydney hadn't thought of it like that, and she could see Marge's point of view. "Sorry, Marge."

"Hush now, no need to apologise for being considerate."

"I'll let you wait on me hand and foot from now on."

Marge chortled. "I'd appreciate it. Now if you could only get your other half to do the same." She shook her head as Saber stopped to collect the condiments for the food. "I swear, that girl never stops." Marge hurried over and picked up the items before Saber could. "Will you go and sit down!"

"Yes, ma'am."

Sydney didn't have the heart to tell Marge that the same was true about herself, the older woman was always on the go. Saber put the plates on the table and sat opposite her.

"Finally, she sits," Marge said, her tone one of exasperation. "Anything else I can get you?"

"A couple of those chocolate chip cookies," Sydney said.

"Coming right up." Marge left the two of them alone. Though she called back to Saber, "And I don't want you returning to that kitchen a minute before your break's over, y'hear me?"

Sydney giggled, finding their relationship adorable. She took a bite of her sausages, savouring the taste. "Sabe?"

"Hmm?"

"Is there anything you can't cook?"

"Ice cream. It always melts."

Sydney nearly choked on a chip.

"I'VE A GREAT IDEA," Sydney said. She was leaning back against Saber, and had to turn her head to observe her. "Are you sure I'm not squashing you?"

They were lying in a hot bath, relaxing. "I'm fine. Trust me," Saber said. "What's your idea?"

"Why don't we get a bigger tub?" Sydney used the term 'we' unconsciously and they both smiled. "I'm getting the bathroom redone anyway, there's plenty of room for a larger bath. We could get one with a whirlpool."

"A spa bath?"

"Yes, one of those. I bet they feel wonderful."

"Why don't you just go the whole way and buy a hot tub for the back garden?" Saber joked sarcastically.

Green eyes grew wide. "Now that's a great idea!"

"I was kidding!"

"Well I'm not." Sydney slid her fingers up Saber's thigh. "I bet we could have some fun in a hot tub."

"Not outside we couldn't."

Sydney smiled. Saber was somewhat shy about sex, at least where she could be seen in public. "It's a private garden," Sydney said, as if Saber didn't already know that piece of information. "In a secluded village, miles from anywhere."

Saber sniggered, shaking her head.

"I'm sure I could convince you." Sydney shifted in her arms, kissing her lovingly.

"I'm sure you could."

"Where do you think it should go?" Sydney asked excitedly.

"You're serious, aren't you?" At Sydney's nod, Saber tilted her head, looking thoughtful. "You don't want to set it too far back from the house, you'll freeze your ass off going back and forth."

Sydney giggled. "I'm sure that would ruin the romance. I've seen some with structures around them, even a roof." She tickled Saber's stomach. "It'd give you some more privacy, little miss modest."

Saber chuckled, squirming as the tickling increased.

"I'll ask Doug about it." Sydney ceased her torture. "I bet he knows someone. He knows everybody." She glanced around the room. "This place is going to be great when it's finished."

Saber grew serious. "Hot tubs aren't cheap. What with the renovations, are you sure you can afford all this? I don't want you overstretching yourself." She seemed uncomfortable, as if knowing it wasn't her place to say how Sydney should spend her money.

"I earn a lot and I'm good with my finances," Sydney said simply.

"I'm not trying to tell you what to do."

"I know you're not, honey, you're just looking out for me. And I appreciate that." Sydney gave her a gentle kiss.

Saber visibly relaxed, clearly pleased Sydney wasn't offended. "Imagine Coop's reaction to a hot tub, he was astonished by your reclining sofa."

Sydney laughed. "You're right. He'll die when he sees it."

"I don't know if it's such a good idea after all, he'll never be away."

"We'll give him a key to the gate, and then he can let himself in."

Saber's hand moved slowly up Sydney's stomach and cupped her breast. "Mind, if you do that, you'll never convince me to make love outside."

"It's retracted," Sydney said swiftly.
Saber smiled. "Of course, we're inside now."
"Hmm, so we are."

"SYD, SWEETHEART, WE'RE going to have to get up." Saber ran a hand through Sydney's blonde hair.

Sydney, settled against Saber's chest, released a sigh. "I think we should leave the rest of the house like it is, the décor's not that bad."

Saber chuckled. "You hate the décor."

"True, but I can learn to live with it if it means I get to stay in bed with you."

"Now who's the sweet-talker?" Saber's smile could be heard in her voice. "So I take it that means you're not going to get up?"

"Nope." Sydney snuggled further into her human pillow. "I don't see you getting up any time soon either."

"I am kind of pinned down. Not that I'm complaining mind you."

A few minutes passed, then Sydney relented. "All right, I'll let you go." She tried to move, but found herself held firmly in position. She giggled. "It seems I'm stuck."

"I can be bought." Saber smirked. "For a kiss."

"Only one?"

The one turned into a dozen, and Saber rolled them over so she was on top.

Using her fore-finger, Saber drew a line from Sydney's lips down to the top of her shorts. She pushed Sydney's T-shirt up, until her flat, well-toned stomach was revealed. Swallowing audibly, Saber slid slowly down her body, and Sydney felt her breathing catch.

Sydney trembled when warm air reached her uncovered skin. She looked down to see blue eyes sparkling back at her. Saber's tongue darted out, taking its time licking around her navel. Sydney's eyes closed in pleasure.

Saber's mouth locked around Sydney's bellybutton and she blew hard, making a loud raspberry sound.

Sydney bolted upright, giggling like a banshee. "Sabe!" she chastised, or at least tried to, it was difficult to tell someone off when she was laughing so hard. Grabbing a pillow, she flung it at Saber, who was looking pretty pleased with herself.

Saber took the hit, then dove for another pillow. She came up swinging.

Sydney leapt off the bed, squealing loudly as she was chased around the room. "I can't believe you did that!" She found another pillow, and they fought for a few moments.

"It got you out of bed, didn't it?" Saber surrendered, and tossed the pillow on top of the duvet cover.

"Why you little..."

"We've had this conversation. I'm not the one who can't reach the top shelf."

Sydney threw herself at Saber.

Saber deftly sprang onto and over the bed, racing for the en-suite bathroom. She got the door closed before Sydney reached it, and the click of the locking mechanism was heard. "Heh," Saber said.

"Just you wait." A plan came into Sydney's head. She dropped her voice to a low purr. "You know, if you let me in, we could share a shower together."

Silence.

Sydney pumped her fist in the air, knowing Saber was considering opening the door. She raised her pillow in readiness.

The door lock didn't click.

"A nice long shower, just you and me. I could wash you, you could wash me. What do you think?" Sydney asked seductively.

"I think..." Saber cleared her throat. "You're good. You almost had me there." A short chuckle. "Almost. But I'm not getting a shower, you forgot that I haven't been for my run yet."

"Damn it!" Sydney narrowed her eyes. "Almost, huh? I'll have to work on that."

More chuckling from behind the door. "You do that."

Sydney burst into laughter. She started to put the bed back into some semblance of order.

"MM, I KNEW there was a reason I was dating you," Sydney teased, taking another bite of crispy bacon.

Saber chuckled. "Ah, I see, you're just after my cooked breakfasts."

"It's a good motive."

Slicing her egg, Saber looked up good-humoredly. "I hope it's not the only reason?"

Green eyes latched on to blue. "That and the fact that I love you."

A dazzling smile lit up Saber's face, making her even more striking than usual. "And I love you."

Sydney got out of her chair and moved to Saber, sitting down on her lap. She draped an arm around Saber's neck, feeling long limbs encircle her waist. Sydney picked up a slice of toast from the plate and held it up to Saber's mouth, offering it to her.

Looking amused, Saber took a bite. Then Sydney ate some herself. When the toast was finished, she raised a piece of bacon.

Saber snickered. "I can see this getting awful messy."

"Just wait till we get to the beans."

Breakfast took them longer than expected, and they were just finishing up as the team arrived. Sydney let them in, and they went straight through to the kitchen to dump their work tools.

"Jesus, Saber." Rich gestured to her. "You're a messy eater. You've got bean juice all over your top!"

"Blame her!" Saber said, pointing to a laughing Sydney.

Before Rich could inevitably ask what they'd been up to, Doug pulled out some booklets from his duffel bag and handed them to Sydney. "I brought you some brochures for those hot tubs. The numbers are on the back."

Rich came excitedly forward, looking at the pictures with Sydney as she leafed through them. "Are you guys thinking of getting one?" He whistled as Sydney nodded. "They sure are something."

"Ooo, look at this." Sydney showed Saber a large hot tub that had, for all intents and purposes, a gazebo built around it. It offered the hot tub some privacy.

Saber chuckled as Sydney winked at her. "I have to admit it does look nice."

"You could fit the whole team in one of those," Doug said, his hint none too subtle.

Saber shook her head, her doubt clear. "No way?"

"Yes way." He turned the pages over a couple of times, as if searching for a particular photo. "See?"

Saber's eyes widened. "There are twelve people in there."

"We can easily fit six in then," Doug said, causing Sydney to chuckle.

"It's like a communal bath." Coop's tone was disapproving.

"Coop." Saber sniggered. "It's not like you're naked, you wear a bathing suit."

"That's no fun," Rich mumbled. Coop swiped his shoulder. "Yow!"

"It's outside. Why would anyone want to take a bath outside?" Coop asked. "Surely you'll catch a cold?"

"It's very relaxing," Rich said knowingly.

Jeff's brow lifted. "How did you ever get to use a hot tub?"

"In a gym."

"You were in a gym?" Coop teased. "Get out."

"Very funny." Rich crossed his arms over his chest, not looking the least bit amused.

Sydney tried not to smile at Rich's reaction, the man was more than eager to make fun of other people, but he couldn't take a joke himself.

"I've never been in a hot tub," Doug said.

"You're all welcome to use it," Sydney said without hesitation. She peered at the pictures while Saber continued to leaf through them. "As soon as I decide which to get. I didn't think they'd be so many."

Coop's voice rose as he pointed to the prices. "All that for a glorified bathtub?"

Both women shared a humorous glance.

Doug nodded. "They're not cheap."

"When I get my own place," Rich said, "I'm gonna get one of these."

Sydney had to stop herself from rolling her eyes.

Rich looked keen. "Can I have the brochure after you're done with it?"

"Sure," Sydney said.

He leaned over and snatched the brochure out of Saber's hands.

"I wasn't finished!"

"You are now." Waving the brochure in torment, Rich fled from the room. Saber bolted up from her chair and raced after him.

Doug shook his head in amusement. "Kids."

RICH WAS CAREFULLY painting around the edge of a doorframe. "I wonder how long it'll be before they move in together." He received surprised looks at the question. "What? You know what women are like," he said, as though he'd had loads of experience in that area. "Hell, they practically live with each other now."

"They do spend a lot of time together," Jeff said.

"It seems daft to pay for two mortgages," Rich continued. "I know Syd's got money to burn, but even so." His face lit up. "Hey! I wonder if Saber will sell her house to me. Then I can finally have my own place. That would be so cool."

"You'd have to do your own cooking." Doug smirked. "Your own washing, too."

Rich's face scrunched up at that realisation. "Surely it can't be that hard? And the café's only across the street."

"You wouldn't be able to afford to eat out all the time, Rich, you'd be paying a mortgage, or at least rent. Not to mention electricity, water rates, the list goes on," Doug said sensibly.

"Then I'll just have to learn." Rich nodded to himself, only slightly deterred. "I'm sure Saber will help me. I'll have to ask her about it when I next see her."

"You'll do no such thing." Coop stopped painting his section. "Those two girls can make up their own minds about who they do or don't live with, they don't need you sticking your nose in."

"They can't possibly need two houses."

"Maybe not, but it's their decision. Saber would ask you first if she were moving out, she knows you want your own space. But they need to come to that conclusion in their own time, when they're ready."

Rich sighed unhappily. "I hope they don't take too long."

"You could always use this time to start learning," Doug said. "Then when the time does come, you'll already be prepared."

Rich pointed at him, his eyes wide. "Genius."

Chapter Twelve

SABER WAS BUSY sorting through some old boxes. Sydney had mentioned that the hospital was having a jumble sale this weekend, trying to raise funds for a new MRI scanner. Donations of clothes, books, knick-knacks, and other oddments would be gratefully received, so Saber was doing her part.

Sydney was working late to help cover for a colleague, who was away on holiday. Since Saber didn't expect her back for a few hours, she'd thought she might as well do something productive, rather than sit and count the minutes till Sydney returned. Humorously, Saber shook her head at herself, wondering how she'd managed to be alone all those years.

Saber glanced to the small pile that was to be donated. There wasn't much. She'd been genuinely surprised by how little she had, not just to donate but in general. It seemed all her money had been spent on clothes and accessories for outdoor pursuits. That and computer games. She spied a few items that she no longer wore, and added them to the pile.

Eyeing the last remaining box, she hoped it was full of old clothes, so she'd at least have something substantial to donate. She tore through the box's tape, not remembering why she'd sealed it until she tipped it on to its side.

Just like the contents of the box, her memories came tumbling forth, long-repressed feelings, buried for so many years now overwhelmed her completely.

SYDNEY WAS SURPRISED to see lights on at Saber's house. The lights themselves weren't unusual, given that it was after 9:00 p.m., but Sydney thought they'd be on at her house, not Saber's. She pulled onto the smaller driveway and parked her car.

At the front door, she wondered whether to knock, but something told her not to, so she slipped quietly inside. After a quick check of the ground floor, Sydney headed upstairs, to Saber's bedroom.

The room was a mess, boxes and clothes were strewn everywhere, over the bed and on the floor. Except for one orderly pile, off to one side. Amidst all this, sat cross-legged on the floor, was Saber. She had her head in her hands, and was staring down at a green jumper in her lap.

"Sabe?" When she got no response, Sydney knelt directly in front of her. She lightly gripped Saber's arm, expecting the contact would draw her out of her trance-like state. It didn't. She got no recognition whatsoever.

"Hey." Sydney's tone was soft, but the worry could be heard. She gently lifted Saber's head, raising her face with a hand beneath her chin. That still didn't bring Saber out of it. Her fixed, faraway stare didn't change. She looked through Sydney, not at her.

Sydney cupped her face in both hands. Her fingers stroked Saber's face, caressing. "Sabe, look at me."

Saber blinked, and awareness seemed to dawn. "Syd?"

"Yes it's me, love. Are you all right?"

Saber rubbed her eyes, then shook her head as if to clear it. "I thought you were working late?"

"It's after nine."

"It is?" Saber glanced to the clock in disbelief. Surprise crossed her features when she saw the display. "I must've lost track of time."

"What were you doing?" Sydney gestured to the mess around them.

Saber paused for a second, frowning in thought. "I was sorting donations for the hospital."

"When I came in, you were staring at that jumper." She indicated the item, which was still in Saber's lap. "You were completely out of it."

Saber gave a sad nod. "Brought back some bad memories. I was wearing this the day I left home. I don't know why I kept it, it's the last connection I have to that life I guess." She peeked up at Sydney. "I wasn't allowed to take anything with me, but I was wearing this."

Sydney gave her an encouraging smile, but didn't press with any questions. She wanted it to be Saber's decision.

Saber nervously chewed on her lower lip. "I'm ready to talk if you're willing to listen?"

"I'm here," Sydney said.

Saber held out her hand, as if needing the contact. Sydney took it instantly, cradling it between her own. "I'm not sure where to start."

Sydney rubbed the top of her tense hand. "Relax, it's only me."

Saber took a deep breath, then said, "I was never close with my parents. We had a lot of differences and hardly ever saw eye to eye, but they were never abusive toward me. Climbing and martial arts were two of the few things that we did agree on, well, me and my dad anyway. My mum wanted me to stop being so tomboyish. She said I'd scare off any boys who were interested in me, because my muscles would be bigger than theirs. That didn't bother me in the slightest, as I'm sure you can understand."

Sydney nodded in wordless agreement.

"My dad got me into both sports, he is..." Saber stopped, looking reflective. "I don't know what he does now, I don't know anything about them anymore." She paused for a long moment. "He was...a martial arts instructor. That's why I know so many types, he taught me. I'm not a patch on him though, he was incredible."

Upon hearing that information, Sydney's stomach rolled. She

didn't know how, but she suddenly knew that Saber's scar was directly connected to him. She prayed that she was mistaken, but knew in her heart she wasn't.

"Climbing meant everything to me, I was always out and about, mostly by myself but sometimes with my dad." Saber's gaze turned wistful. "Those were the best times."

Sydney gave her hand a sensitive squeeze.

"I didn't dare tell them I was gay, it took me years to gather up the courage. When I was sixteen, I decided enough was enough and I had to tell them."

Kelly walked into her parent's living room, a sense of quiet foreboding settling firmly over her shoulders. She tried to shake the feeling as she strode to the television and switched it off.

"Hey!"

"Kelly!" Charlotte yelled.

"I won't be a second, Mum," Kelly said.

"I was watching that, the fight's about to start." Her father, Robert, patted the seat next to him. "Come and join us, I bet you twenty quid Anderson's gonna kick his ass."

"No way. Reilly will win easily." Kelly sat next to her dad, not realising that this was the last time she would be treated as part of the family, the last time she would be looked at without disdain, disgust, or hate. She would've appreciated the moment if she'd known, she would have cherished every second of it.

Robert snorted, holding out his huge hand, which Kelly firmly shook. "You're about to lose twenty quid."

If truth were known, she was about to lose a lot more than that. Her life, everything she knew and loved, was about to be lost, gone forever.

"Hurry up and tell us then," Charlotte said. "You know how your father hates to miss anything."

Kelly took a deep breath. "Okay, now I don't want you to be mad. This is something that I've thought a lot about, and I don't want you thinking that it's a phase or a fad or whatever. I'm serious about this."

"Oh my God! I hope this isn't about College?"

"You are going to College and that's the end of it," Robert said angrily. "I thought you wanted to teach climbing?"

"I do, that's not..."

"They don't just accept any riff-raff, you'll need to be qualified," Charlotte said.

"I am going to become qualified."

"Yes you are," he all but shouted.

"You should be grateful you've got an advantage, a lot of kids don't know what they want to do at your age."

"Let's have no more of this nonsense."

"That's not what I was going to say." Kelly managed to get a word in.

"No? Well that's a relief, what was it then? Be quick before your father puts the TV back on."

Kelly really didn't want to tell them now. If they'd reacted that way over College, God only knew how they would handle her sexuality. They would have to find out eventually though, so she decided to get it over with. "I'm gay," she said.

The cup Robert was about to drink from shattered in his hands. He looked at her with cold, dark eyes. "I don't find that funny."

"Apologise to your father at once."

"I'm not joking," Kelly said quietly. This wasn't going well.

"You're sure?" His voice held no emotion.

"Yes."

Robert grabbed Kelly around the neck, hauling her roughly out of the chair.

"Dad!" Kelly gasped in a breath before he cut off her air in his strong grip.

"Don't you ever call me that again. I'm not your father. To think I've had you under my roof all these years. You and your perverted thoughts."

Kelly kicked and struggled against him, but he held her fast. Robert dragged her out of the room. Kelly panicked, realising he was taking her to the garage. The room had been converted into a gym. They often sparred there together.

He threw her down roughly, onto the mat. "Get up."

"Please," Kelly said, wheezing as she tried to pull in oxygen. "I'm sorry if I've disappointed..." She coughed. "I didn't mean to."

Charlotte appeared in the doorway. Kelly glanced at her mother desperately — she was impassive. "You've brought this on yourself."

As Kelly got to her feet, Robert didn't hesitate, he threw himself at her. She could tell he was furious, but also knew that as an expert it wouldn't detract from his efforts, he would only channel it.

Kelly barely escaped his first strike, lurching backward at the last second, avoiding his punch. He shot an elbow directly into her face. Her head snapped back, blood erupting from her nose and mouth. She didn't have time to recover, he followed with a kick to her abdomen. She crumpled, falling to the floor, hard.

"I thought I'd taught you better than that," Robert said. "Let me down there as well." He paced aggressively. "I'll give you to the count of five to get to your feet. One."

Kelly couldn't breathe, he had winded her. Her head swam.

"Two."

"I really wanted grandchildren," Charlotte cried. "You're my only child. If I'd known you were going to turn out like this...I would've chosen anything but this."

"Three."

"You can't have picked it up from me, I don't have defective genes."

"Four." Robert looked at his wife. "Are you saying that I do?" he growled.

"No of course not. No child of ours could possibly turn out like this."

"She isn't our child anymore." Robert turned back to the mat, looking surprised to find Kelly standing. "Did you hear that? As from tonight you're not our daughter. We never want to see you again."

"What will the family say? The neighbors? Oh, Robert, this is too awful."

"See how upset you've made her? What kind of kid would do that to her own mother?"

Kelly's throat was thick with terror, but she managed to throw the statement back at him. "What kind of father beats up his daughter?"

"I'm giving you the chance to fight back, girl, it's not my fault you're not up to the job."

"You trained me." As soon as the words left her lips, something in him changed, she saw the shift, his eyes took on a dangerous glint. Dread flowed through her.

He lunged.

Kelly blocked a few blows, but he was much more advanced than she was. Robert kicked out her legs, flipping her over so that she was face down on the mat.

"You're right handed, aren't you?" He took hold of that arm and wrenched it behind her back.

Kelly cried out.

Robert straightened her arm as he stood, placing his foot on her shoulder blade. "You've taken everything from us. All these years lost, and all because of your godforsaken perversion. Now it's my turn to take from you." He slammed his foot down as he pulled up with his powerful arms.

Kelly felt, and heard, her shoulder dislocate. She yelled in agony. She would have begged him to stop, but she was in too much pain to formulate any words.

"Now I can't take everything I've taught you back, but I can make damn sure that you're never able to use those skills again." Robert stamped his foot once more, giving her arm another forceful tug for good measure.

Kelly screamed.

"Pitiful," Robert said, letting her arm drop to the mat. He knelt down next to her. "Within a few weeks we'll forget you ever existed, we'll move on. But you can't. No matter how hard you try you won't be able to climb again, or throw a decent punch, and you'll always know that I did that to you, that I won." He got to his feet. "I hope it was worth it, I really do. And if you ever come back...I'll do a lot worse." He moved to the wall and pressed a button.

The garage door started to slide upward.

"Leave your stuff, we'll dispose of that. I want you gone."

Her mother had been silent throughout the beating, but now she spoke up, "We both do."

"I still don't know how I got to my feet."

"Sabe," Sydney said her name so quietly, it was almost inaudible. She wondered how she could hate people that she'd never met, but she did. A new level of anger emerged within, and her heart broke as the final piece of the puzzle slid home. Tears flowed freely down Sydney's face, but she could see that Saber was trying to fight hers. She cupped her cheek.

Blue eyes met green.

"Let them fall," Sydney said. She knew Saber had never dealt with it, never grieved. Never told anyone, until now. She was both deeply touched and humbled that Saber felt able to talk to her about it.

As if a dam opened, the tears fell, cascading down Saber's cheeks unchecked and unhindered.

Sydney embraced her, holding her close. "Let it out, sweetheart, let it all out." Saber's frame shook with sobs, and Sydney tightened her hold, crying with her. She rocked her gently. "I'm here, Sabe, I'm right here. I'll always be here."

SYDNEY RESTED AGAINST the bed's headboard. Saber lay between her legs, leaning back into her. "I can still remember it as though it was yesterday, every little detail. I used to have nightmares, but they faded with time."

Sydney kissed dark hair. "Sweetheart, that's awful. I don't know how I'd have coped with that now, let alone at sixteen." The knowledge that Saber had sold her car for them, after all they'd put her through, only distressed Sydney further. She honestly didn't know if she could've been that forgiving. She was in complete awe of the woman.

Her hands stroked Saber's stomach. "How did you get to the hospital?" she whispered into her ear.

"I went," Saber cleared her throat, her voice unsteady from crying. "I went to the neighbors, told them my folks were out. They took me. They gave me a funny look when they saw the car in the driveway. I made up some excuse about it being broken, said my parents were out in a rental car, they probably knew I wasn't telling the truth."

"Didn't they ask you how you did it?"

"Yeah, I said I'd been practicing a new spinning kick and I'd fallen awkwardly. My face would've told a different story though. I never was any good at lying.

"Luckily, I had my bank card on me, I'd forgotten to take it out of my pocket. There wasn't much in my account, but it was enough to take me far away. I came here. I didn't even mean to, I stopped at Gransford and asked around for any work, and they told me that the caravan place was hiring. I hitched a ride." Saber gave her a meek look. "I know that wasn't very smart, being a young girl and all, but I wasn't thinking very clearly."

"That's understandable, love."

"Anyway, I spotted Shirebridge on route. The guy dropped me off, and I walked the rest of the way. Marge and I clicked instantly, she gave me a job."

"Where did you sleep?"

"Marge knew I'd run away from home. She gave me a room at her place, she really went out on a limb for me."

Sydney's respect for the café's owner grew tenfold.

"Wasn't much use to start with, what with my arm, but she never gave up on me. I owe her everything."

"I'm surprised they don't have any kids themselves."

"I asked Bill about that once, since they were so good with me. He told me that although they'd never wanted kids, Marge thought of herself as my surrogate mother, and he was grateful that I'd come into their lives."

"She really does treat you like her own."

"Scoldings included."

Sydney smiled softly. "Those, too."

"Shortly after that, I met the Mountain Rescue team and knew that's what I wanted to do. I didn't tell them how serious my injury was, I just said it was dislocated. I didn't want them to bar me from getting on the team."

"You had a purpose again."

Saber looked up at her, as if surprised by how well Sydney understood her. "Exactly."

"How serious was the injury?"

"The first yank dislocated my shoulder. The second damaged the tendons. One was torn, hanging on by a thread, so the surgeons had to go in and stitch it back together."

Sydney's jaw clenched in rage, recognising how much force would be needed to cause such an injury. Though her blood boiled, she didn't let it come through in her voice, her anger wasn't for Saber. "I'm amazed you can climb."

"Doctors told me I'd never climb again."

"I'd have agreed with them."

"I spent a lot of time doing intensive physio. The one time being stubborn really paid off." Though the joke fell flat, Sydney placed a kiss in her hair. "That's why I gave up martial arts, punching jars it too much."

Clarity hit Sydney as she recalled the brawl in the café. "And that's why you hit more with your left."

Saber nodded. "You're the only person who's noticed. After two years I started climbing again, nothing major, just getting used to it. I learned to climb more or less one-handed at first, which was difficult."

"I bet."

"Gradually, I was able to use both arms properly. But for the more difficult maneuvers, or anything that's gonna put a strain on it, I use the left."

"There must be some occasions when you have to use it though?" Sydney asked logically.

"Of course. It's been getting better over the years, it would ache afterward but nothing serious."

Sydney was struck by a sudden memory. "So that's why you were holding your arm when I first met you?"

"Yep, takes the pressure off slightly."

And that's why she flinched when Rich hit her in the car, Sydney thought quietly, knowing old injuries could still cause discomfort. "But I still don't know how you're so fast, surely you should be slower?"

"I knew I needed to be able to keep up with Mountain Rescue or I had no chance of being accepted. I spent another two years practicing with one hand, every spare hour I had, I practiced, getting my speed up to a decent level. And as my other arm got stronger, I kept getting quicker. I was so angry, I used that to push myself. My father had already taken away martial arts, I wasn't going to let him take climbing as well. I wouldn't let him win."

Sydney laid her hand on Saber's collarbone, over her scar, wishing that the light touch could take away all that had happened. "He hasn't."

Saber was quiet for a long moment, then her hand rose and rested on Sydney's. "I know." She looked as if a weight had been lifted from her shoulders. Sydney imagined that was exactly how she must feel, not just from the knowledge that she'd triumphed, but from the release of her emotions—Saber's darkest secret, now come to light, could hurt her no more.

"I'd become good friends with Coop by this point, and he was teaching me all about the Service. Then when I was twenty, one of the guys left the team. I filled the position and bought his house."

"Lauren told me you were the youngest person to ever be allowed on the team."

"I had an early start," Saber said modestly.

Sydney shook her head in disbelief. "You go through all that and you dismiss it, you should be really proud of what you've achieved. I know I am."

Saber regarded her. "You are?"

"Yes. I'm very proud of you."

Saber smiled for the first time since recounting her story. "That means the world to me, coming from you."

"You're welcome, sweetheart."

THEY'D DECIDED TO spend the night at Saber's house. After Saber had finished recounting her story, the emotional drain had exhausted her, so Sydney gently pushed her down onto the bed, covered her with the duvet, and climbed in beside her. Their bodies melded together as they always did, and they settled down for the night.

Half an hour passed, and Sydney was still awake, though her eyes were shut. She sensed that she was being watched, and when she opened them she found Saber studying her intently.

Sydney raised herself up on an elbow. "Can't sleep?"

"I was just thinking how blessed I am to have you. There were times after I left home when I wondered why I kept going. I had no one. I didn't think I could survive like that, and to be honest, most days I didn't want to." Sydney brushed Saber's face with the back of her knuckles. "But now, I look at you, and realise that every minute, every single second, was worth it. And I would gladly go through it all again if I knew you were at the end of it."

"I wouldn't let you," Sydney whispered.

"I just wish I'd known that then. It would've made things a lot easier."

"I wish you had, too."

Saber stroked blonde tresses for a while, staring at Sydney with quiet wonder on her face. "You're so beautiful. I've went from having nothing, to having everything." She gave Sydney a loving kiss. "I can't believe how lucky I am."

"Well believe it, 'cause you're stuck with me."

"Is that right?"

"Mm-hmm. You forget, I know where you live."

Saber sniggered. "So you do. I guess it's a good thing I like having you around then."

A grin surfaced. "Oh you do, do you?"

"Yep. And I plan on keeping you around for a long time."

Sydney dropped her voice back to a whisper. "How long's that?"

Saber's expression was heartfelt. "As long as you want."

Sydney went quiet for a few moments, the emotion between them palpable. "How does forever sound?"

Blue eyes shone with tears, but this time they were tears of happiness. "Perfect."

Chapter Thirteen

Six Months Later

"I WANT A REMATCH," Rich said, when he drew to a stop alongside Sydney. He was greedily pulling in air, trying to catch his breath.

"You'll get one tomorrow. We do go running every day." Doug glanced to Sydney. "I'd better watch my back, you'll be overtaking me next."

Sydney was chuffed with herself, she'd finally managed to pass Rich, although it'd been a close thing.

"You must be on steroids. Performance enhancing drugs."

Both women shared a look, it was an old joke between them. "It was a close call, Rich, I might've just gotten lucky," Sydney said.

"Yeah." He nodded, still panting. "We'll have to see if you can keep up the pace."

Saber winked at Sydney, then gave her an impressed smile.

Sydney was breathing hard, but she managed a return grin.

"Have you been giving her extra lessons or something?" Rich's tone was accusing.

"Nope, she beat you fair and square," Saber said bluntly, causing Rich to frown.

Jeff jogged up to them. "Nice run, Syd."

Rich scowled further.

Coop came in last like always, and he was holding his side as if he had a stitch. He was laughing raucously. "I could hear you protesting all the way from the back, Rich." Coop draped a sweaty arm over Sydney's smaller shoulders. "Well done, lass."

"Thanks, Coop." Sydney lowered her voice so that only he could hear. "Can I drop in after work? I need to talk to you in private."

Coop nodded. "Is everything all right?"

Sydney gave him a reassuring look. "Everything's fine, I just want to get your opinion on something."

"Sure. I'll put the kettle on."

"IS THAT ALL?" Coop looked relieved.

"What do you mean is that all?" Sydney's voice rose. "This is huge! I don't want to frighten her off!"

"I'm not sure I see the problem, Saber lives with you now."

"Yes, but this would make it official. You don't think it's too soon?"

"Do you? You and Saber are the only ones that count in this."

"No." Sydney smiled. "I've wanted to ask her for ages, but I'm not really impartial to the situation." That's why she had come to Coop, he was always so sensible, and she trusted his judgement.

Coop gazed steadily at her. "You love her, don't you?"

Sydney didn't hesitate. "Yes. More than I've loved anyone in my entire life."

"And I know she feels the same about you." Coop nodded. "I think it's a good idea."

"I'm worried about moving too fast." Sydney took a sip of her tea. "I don't want to pressure her."

"How long have you been together?"

"Nearly seven months, though I've known her for eight."

"I suppose that is pretty quick," Coop said. "But do you think you'll feel any different in say, a year's time?"

"No. I'm positive about that."

"Well then, I don't see why there's a reason to wait."

"That's what I thought," Sydney said. She came to her decision. "I'm going to ask her. I'll do it tonight." She finished her tea, then got to her feet.

"Please let me know how it goes." Coop walked her to the front door.

"I will." Sydney embraced him. "Thanks, Coop, you're a good friend."

"It's my pleasure, Syd. And don't worry, I'm in no doubt as to what her answer will be—she'll say yes. You're the best thing that's ever happened to her." He waved good-bye. "I'd wish you luck, but you're not going to need it."

Sydney held up crossed fingers as she walked to her car.

SABER SNIFFED THE air appreciatively as she hung her coat on one of the hallway pegs. She kicked off her shoes, leaving them beside the doormat.

"It's just me," she called out, letting Sydney know she was back.

"In the kitchen."

Saber went straight there, though she hovered in the doorway at seeing Sydney cooking. "Is it safe to come in?"

"Tch." Sydney narrowed her eyes. "I burn the bread once, and I'm tainted for life."

"Burn?" Saber chuckled. "It was on fire."

"It was your fault for distracting me! You and your kisses."

"I may have played a small part." Saber held up a forefinger and thumb, not even an inch apart.

Sydney was busy at the stove, stirring some sauce. Hands encircled her waist, and Saber began to kiss her neck. Sydney turned in her arms, bringing them face to face. Like magnets, their lips met, drawn together by an unseen force. The first kiss was soft, one of greeting, but it soon deepened, lips parting for tongues to slip inside.

When Sydney moaned, she drew back. "Careful, or the sauce will burn too."

Saber twisted the dial on the hob, knocking the heat down. "I'm sure I can make it quick."

"I'm not sure that's something every girl wants to hear."

A chuckle. "You didn't let me finish." She backed Sydney up into a cupboard, then pinned her against it. "You've put so much effort into this dinner, the least I can do is take care of dessert."

"Sabe, dessert comes after a meal." Despite her words, Sydney pressed their hips together.

"Yes, but this is just an appetizer. A taste of what's to come." She ran her tongue teasingly over Sydney's lips.

"Mm, I like the sound of that." Sydney's nipples stiffened against her blouse, and her back arched as Saber fondled them.

"I thought you might." Saber unbuttoned Sydney's trousers, her hand darting inside and cupping Sydney possessively.

Sydney inhaled sharply. She tried to capture Saber's mouth, but Saber kept on torturing her, teasing her lips with her tongue.

Saber timed it exactly, so her fingers delved into Sydney just as she relented and soundly kissed her.

Sydney moaned, long and deep, sounding delighted by the dual entry. She gasped as Saber moved in her, stroking her higher and higher. With a cry, Sydney's legs buckled, but Saber had no difficulty keeping her upright. Sydney's orgasm suddenly hit, and she trembled fiercely in Saber's hold. Saber didn't give her a chance to come down, her thumb beginning to rub Sydney's clit, hard and fast.

"Sabe, I can't...it's too much," Sydney's eyes rolled back in her head, as though she was going to pass out from such intense pleasure. Her body nevertheless responded, hips surging forward for more. Sydney clung to Saber desperately, writhing against her as another climax built.

Sydney was panting strongly, and she cried out when Saber flexed her fingers inside her. Saber began to thrust into her again, while continuing to massage her clit.

"Oh, Sabe. Oh!"

Saber increased her pace, which sent Sydney hurtling over the edge once more, and she collapsed in Saber's arms.

Propping Sydney up, Saber tenderly held her until she recovered.

"And you wonder why I burn things," Sydney mumbled into her neck.

"Maybe I do play a bigger part than I gave myself credit for."

"Uh-huh. You're so damn irresistible."

"Wait till you see what's for dessert."

Sydney chuckled. "Good thing I made dinner after all, we're clearly gonna need the energy."

SABER DUG EAGERLY into her salmon. "Syd, this is really good."

Sydney was flattered. Since Saber was such a good cook, her opinion meant a lot to her. She dipped a potato in hollandaise sauce, then took a bite.

Saber gestured to the immaculate, candlelit table. "A girl might think this is in aid of something."

Sydney laughed. "You got me." She put down her cutlery. "I've been thinking about us a lot lately, we've been dating for nearly seven months."

"The best seven months of my life."

Sydney smiled, touched. "Mine too." She paused, trying to think of the best way to phrase her next words. After a moment, she just came out with it. "I want you to move in with me."

Saber's gaze was laced with affection. "Really?"

Sydney nodded. "Really."

Saber leaned over and thoroughly kissed her.

"Is that a yes?" Sydney asked breathlessly.

Saber laughed. "It's a yes. I would love to move in with you."

"THANKS FOR COMING over on such short notice, Coop," Saber said as she opened the front door. "We've got some great news."

"There was nothing worth watching on TV anyway." He smirked knowingly. "Did you say yes?"

Saber looked surprised and raised a questioning eyebrow to Sydney.

Sydney shrugged. "I may have mentioned it to him. She said yes." Sydney smiled at Coop happily.

"What did I tell you? That is good news." His eyes twinkled. "That's another thing I've been right about. I really am rather good at this."

Saber keenly patted his shoulder. "Will you give me a hand with some of my stuff?"

"Now?" Coop asked, in evident disbelief.

"Mmm. Just some clothes and things."

"Sure. Why wait till morning when you can see properly?" he teased good-naturedly.

"I'll go get my rucksack." Saber took the stairs two at a time. "Can I use yours too, Syd?"

"Yes. You know where it is."

Coop laughed. "I think she's excited."

Sydney grinned. "We both are."

"Mind, I'll give you a word of advice. Don't tell Rich until you've decided what to do with Saber's place, he'll hound you otherwise. You'd probably find him camped out on your doorstep."

Sydney felt her eyes grow wide. "He wouldn't?" At Coop's look, she said, "Of course he would." She chuckled as Saber came bounding down the stairs. "Why don't we move the wardrobe from the spare room into ours? Then you've got somewhere to put all your clothes?"

"Sounds like a plan. We can move it when we get back."

"Isn't it funny how things work out?" Coop said. "Saber's wanted to live here since she first arrived, and now she's finally going to."

"Is that true?" Sydney asked her.

"It's always been a dream of mine. That, and to have someone to love and share it with." Saber smiled. "Although frankly, given the choice, I'd happily live in a tent with you."

Sydney was moved by the words. Saber said the most beautiful things to her — even when she least expected them.

Saber pointed at Coop, as if to forestall his comment. "If my reputation's already ruined, I might as well go down in flames."

Coop pulled her toward the door. "Come on, Romeo."

Saber threw a rucksack at him.

"SYD?" COOP SHOUTED.

"I'm in the bedroom." Sydney had been designated the task of packing Saber's clothes. She was currently packing her underwear into the rucksack.

Coop came in. "Goodness, I...I'm sorry," he said, practically tripping over himself to try and leave the room.

Sydney giggled at his reaction. Coop was blushing profusely, his face matching his hair color. "It's all right, Coop, they're just clothes."

"They're most certainly not just clothes, young lady."

Sydney shut the drawer containing the offensive items. "There, all gone."

Coop peeked around, turning fully now that nothing inappropriate was visible. His eyes narrowed suspiciously at Sydney.

"What?"

"You know exactly what. Those pretty green eyes don't work on me."

"How was I to know you had a phobia of underwear?" Sydney joked. "Though, if you don't mind me saying, that is a bit unusual."

"I don't have a phobia of underwear." Looking flustered, Coop rubbed his chin.

"No? Then I can continue packing?" Sydney went to open the drawer.

"No you certainly cannot," he said quickly.

Sydney relented, grinning at him. "Did you want me?"

"Yes. Saber sent me up to get the rest of her computer games, she said you'd know where they are?"

"They're in that corner." Sydney indicated a wooden DVD stand. "I would take the whole thing, Coop, we'll need a place to put them all anyway."

"Right you are." Coop lifted the stand with apparent ease, careful that nothing fell out. "How many of these things has she got?"

"A lot."

"I have to admit, it is fun. Some of those games are so realistic."

"Tell me about it. You know that snowboarding one? Every time my character comes off their board, I wince. I'm positive they'd be dead in real life if they took a tumble like that."

Coop nodded. "That part's not realistic then." His nose wrinkled. "Thank heavens."

"I'd never finish the race if it was."

"You do like to crash a lot, don't you?"

"Hey! I'm still learning the controls."

"I hate to break it to you, Syd, but if you haven't learned them by now, you never will." He moved toward the door, stopping when Sydney retaliated.

"You're the one who had that close encounter with a tree." Sydney sniggered.

Coop winced. "Ouch, I remember that."

"So does the tree," Sydney said dryly.

"Getting cocky, are we? Just you wait, we'll have a rematch when we get back, then we'll see who wins."

"You're on." Sydney yanked open the drawer, grabbing a bra and dangling it in front of him.

"Sydney!" Coop cried, unable to block his view since his hands were full.

Saber chose that precise moment to enter the bedroom. "I was going to ask what was taking you so long, but now I can see that you're distracting yourself with my unmentionables."

"We weren't...We...She..." Coop said, causing Sydney to break into laughter.

A single dark eyebrow rose. "Well, whatever turns you on."

Coop pushed past Saber and left the room, muttering under his breath.

Saber chuckled as Sydney collapsed onto the bed in hysterics. "Have you been teasing Coop again?"

Sydney was too busy laughing to answer.

"I'll take that as a yes." Saber took the bra from Sydney and held it up. "You are too cruel." She shook her head. "How come I never thought of that?"

SABER WAS HANGING her clothes up in the wardrobe. Coop had left long ago and she was nearly finished unpacking the items they'd brought over.

Sydney picked out another top from the bag. "This one's nice." She put it on a hangar and passed it to Saber.

Saber hung the tight-fitting burgundy vest top up. It left very little to the imagination. "Gee, I have no idea why you like that one."

Sydney stuck her tongue out. "I like the color."

Saber snorted. "What do you think I should do with my house?"

"That's up to you, honey."

"It's up to both of us. If I'm going to be living here, I need to pay my way."

Sydney pulled a face. "Sabe, I don't want you to think of it like that, paying me rent. I'm not your landlord, I'm your partner, and I want this to be your home too."

"That's not what I meant. I'll pay half the mortgage and the rest of the bills."

"You don't need to do that."

"I want to. That way, this is my home. I don't want you spending most of your money on a house that is for both of us."

Sydney didn't argue, as if knowing Saber wasn't going to budge on this. "I know you're fiercely independent, Sabe, and I respect you for that. But I don't want you stretching your much smaller paycheck too thin."

"I can manage. Trust me."

Sydney gave a nod. "Okay."

Saber looked pleased. "So, what do you think?"

"Sell it or rent it you mean?"

"Rich would keep renting it all year round, so we wouldn't have to worry about it sitting empty."

"Do you still have a mortgage on it?" Sydney passed her the last top.

Saber took it and put it away. "Yes."

"That means you'd be paying two mortgages. That hardly seems fair."

"Rich's rent will easily cover that mortgage, and the rest I can use to top up my payment for this one. I'll have to check the figures but I probably won't be paying much more than I am now."

"Then I'll have twice as much because I'll only be paying half of this mortgage." Sydney's pale hair shook. "Not gonna happen. What's the alternative?"

"Sell it and pay a chunk off this one."

"That's definitely not fair. It's your money."

Saber rubbed her temple in irritation. "It's our money."

Sydney scoffed. "Now it is. A moment ago, you didn't want me paying the mortgage alone because it was my money. I don't see the difference."

Neither did Saber. She sat down on the bed. "And you say I'm stubborn." Sydney perched next to her. "What do you think we should do?"

"I think you should sell your house and buy yourself a car."

Sydney rested a hand on Saber's thigh. "I was heartbroken by what happened to your other vehicle, and though I can't change that, perhaps this might go a ways to help."

Saber's face lit up. "That'd be a hell of a car! I could get one like yours." She shook her head. "That's not very practical though."

"We're not making much progress, are we?"

Saber snickered. "I thought you were good at this?"

"I am, usually. I would like for you to have your own car. I'm at work all day and you should be able to go out when you need to, you shouldn't have to wait for me or rely on anyone else. If you sell your house, you can buy one outright. Whatever's left, do what you," Saber gave her a look, "we want with it."

"I'd want to pay off this mortgage."

Sydney frowned. "We're back here again."

"Hang on, I've got it. How much is this place worth? And how much is your mortgage for?"

Sydney told her. "More when the renovations are finished."

"The mortgage is a quite a bit less, where's the rest of it?"

"I paid it off using the money from my last house."

"Ah-ha! If you did that, why can't I?"

Sydney opened her mouth to respond, but clearly had no argument. "You've got me." Saber looked smugly at her. "Don't think you've won yet, I'll only allow you to put the same amount in, not a penny more—fifty/fifty remember?"

"Don't worry, I won't have a penny more."

"But what about your car?" Sydney's voice rose in protest.

"If it's between that or paying my way, I'll pay my way thanks," Saber said, absolutely serious.

Sydney scrunched her face up. A moment later, it cleared. "Then I'll get you a car. What about for your birthday? I could buy..."

Saber interrupted. "Absolutely not."

"Sabe."

"I mean it, Syd, I won't accept it."

Sydney sighed, her annoyance visible. "I'm only trying to take care of you."

Saber's stern look softened. "And I'm grateful for that, truly, but I don't want you thinking I'm with you for your money."

"Is that what this is about? I know you too well to ever think that of you."

"Well this way you'll never doubt that. It's nothing personal, I'm the same with everyone else, just ask Coop."

"I'm not everyone else, Sabe, I'm your partner!" Sydney said angrily. "Is this how it's going to be? Every time I want to buy you a present I have to check with you? Ask permission? That's not how I operate. That's not going to work."

"That's how I am."

"Do you think I'm with you for your money?" Saber wasn't given a chance to respond. "After all, I allowed you to pay for those steps down by the stream."

"Don't be ridiculous, that was a present."

"Mine would be too."

"There's a big difference between some pieces of timber and a car, Syd," Saber said, hearing the defensiveness in her own voice.

Sydney visibly bristled. "Not to me there isn't. It's the thought behind it that counts."

"You would say that, you're rich."

Sydney placed her hands on her hips. "What's that supposed to mean?"

"Money's not important to you."

"You're right, it's not. I'd rather make someone happy than worry about how much it costs."

"That's because you can."

"I've worked hard to get where I am today, Sabe, I earn every penny I make."

"I'm not disputing that."

"Then allow me to spend it on what and who I want. You're the most important person in my life, I want to share it with you." Sydney's tone gentled. "Please let me."

"You're making me sound awful," Saber muttered.

"I'll put it another way. When we go running or climbing or whatever, you always come out ahead, do you put in more effort than I do?"

Saber shook her head. "Of course not."

"And at work, do I put in more effort than you do?"

"Your job's much more important than mine."

"That's not what I asked. I've seen you at work, Sabe, you never stop," Sydney said. "It doesn't matter to me that you come out ahead in regards to the physical stuff, and it shouldn't matter to you that I earn more money. The same amount of effort goes in."

The corner of Saber's mouth curled up. "Good analogy. Sneaky though."

"Did it work?" Sydney asked hopefully.

"I don't know, what's the question?"

"I think we should get a joint account, all our money goes in one pot. Then it's not your money or my money, it's just ours. Everything can be put in both our names. It'll make things a lot simpler."

Saber hesitated. This was ridiculous, she'd supported herself for her entire life, and hadn't been dependent on anyone. And she never thought that she could be. Yet here was Sydney, asking her to change all that, and she was seriously considering it. She knew from Sydney's outburst it obviously meant a lot to her, and Saber understood that it wasn't only about the money. Sydney wanted them to depend and rely on each other for everything, not just financial matters.

"It would be fair too," Sydney added. "Please?"

Green eyes tugged at her, and Saber was shocked to realise that she'd become dependent on Sydney a long time ago. She really couldn't do without her. "Will that make you happy?"

"Very. Is that a yes?"

Saber over exaggerated a sigh. She nodded, laughing when Sydney leapt onto her knee and kissed her gratefully. "Next time, remind me to just agree, I hate fighting with you."

"Me, too." Sydney locked gazes with her. "Thank you."

Saber smiled softly. She kissed Sydney, and it was filled with promises of their future. "So when do you want to go car shopping?" She gave in completely, folding like a paper tissue.

Sydney grinned. "We can start looking this weekend if you like? Then when the house sells, we can go and get it straight away."

"Shouldn't take long, Rich will be in ASAP. So we're settled? We're going to sell it?"

"Yes. Then whatever money is left over from your car, we'll use to pay a chunk off this mortgage like you suggested. That'll reduce the payments quite a bit, which will give us more money each month."

"Seems sensible to me."

"I bet I can guess which color car you want?" Sydney teased.

Saber smirked, looking around at the recently finished bedroom. "I believe you picked out the color for these walls."

"I must've imagined someone pushing me over to the blue section then."

Saber chuckled. "It's my favorite color. You have to admit it looks good."

"It does," Sydney said. "Not much left to decorate now."

"Just the back room. That reminds me, the hot tub company rang today, they'll be here a week Monday to fit it. I'm gonna ask Marty to change shifts with me."

"I can't wait to try it out." Sydney gave her a suggestive look.

"I'd better get used to exposing myself now then." Saber started to remove her top.

"DO YOU THINK I should take the bed?" Saber asked the next morning, while walking Sydney to her car.

"Bring anything you want. The back bedroom still needs furnishing, so it's a good idea."

"I thought I'd bring my electronic stuff over. I figured I could put the little telly in the kitchen, and then I can watch TV when I cook." Saber smirked. "I don't suppose Marge would let me have one at work."

Sydney grinned. "Probably not."

"The stuff we can't use—like the sofa—I'll leave in the house for Rich, he's not going to be able to afford much to start...mmpfh."

Sydney kissed her soundly.

"What was that for?" Saber asked dazedly when Sydney withdrew.

"Just for being you. You're so thoughtful." Sydney ran a finger down Saber's nose. "Make sure you get one of the guys to help you, I don't want you carrying all that stuff yourself."

Saber ruffled blonde hair. "Coop's gonna help, I asked him last night."

"Good old Coop," Sydney said affectionately. "What would we do without him?"

"Mm, he's a good mate." Movement caught Saber's eye, and she smiled as she looked up. "Speaking of..."

Coop walked up the driveway, and gestured overhead to the cloudless blue sky. "Nice day for it."

"Thanks for helping out today, Coop," Sydney said.

"No bother. It keeps me out of trouble." He smiled. "And we're in luck, Doug and the team are out all day, which means Rich won't be pestering us as to what we're doing."

"I'd best be off," Sydney said, giving Saber a soft kiss on her lips.

Coop glanced discreetly away, clearly trying to give them their privacy.

"Bye, sweetheart." Saber closed the car door behind Sydney.

The window slid down as Sydney drove off. "You two be good," she called.

Coop waved good-bye. "Would we be anything but?"

"She knows you too well." Saber pushed him playfully.

"Me?" he said indignantly. "I think not."

"PHEW!" COOP ARCHED his back, as if trying to stretch out his spine. "I think I've given myself a hernia."

Saber put the TV on the kitchen worktop and grinned at the sweating man. She glanced at the clock, they'd been working nonstop for hours. "We can take a break if you want?"

"No, I'm good."

"There's that bed to put back together upstairs, why don't you do that?"

Coop looked relieved for the easier task. "I can do that. I'll put those drawers and other units back up as well."

"Great. There's not much left, a few knickknacks. I'll go get them."

"What about that bookcase?"

"It's solid. We're better off doing that last." Saber chuckled. "Then we can collapse afterward."

"I'll stick it in my car. Drive it over."

"I think we'll have to."

SYDNEY OPENED THE front door, immediately struck by how quiet the house was. She stepped out of her shoes and walked into the living room. She stopped abruptly, an easy smile crossing her face. Saber lay face down on the floor, fast asleep, and Coop was stretched back in the recliner, also out for the count.

Sydney tiptoed out of the room, going upstairs to change out of her work clothes. She noticed a few extra things in their bedroom and she checked the other rooms too, pleasantly surprised by how well Saber's furniture fit in with her own. It again confirmed their similar tastes.

"What do you think?" Saber whispered directly into her ear.

Sydney jumped. "Jesus, Sabe!"

Saber put a calming hand on her back. "Sorry." Her lips twitched with amusement.

Sydney scowled at her. "You don't look very sorry."

Saber clearly tried to keep a straight face, but she failed miserably. "I am."

"Uh-huh."

Saber grinned. She indicated the room. "It matches well, don't you think?"

Did this woman read minds? "Yeah it does."

Saber covered her mouth as she yawned, then rubbed at her eyes as if to clear them of sleep. "If there's anything you want moving, I can..."

"It's perfect," Sydney said. "I love that entertainment unit in the living room, you can keep all your games in it."

"Exactly." Saber led her from the spare room, back into their bedroom. "We put the bookcase in here."

Sydney peered at the contents. "Shouldn't that be DVD case?"

Saber gave her a sheepish look. "There's a book."

Sydney couldn't see one. "Where?"

Saber bent down and pointed toward the far corner of a shelf. "There."

Sydney giggled. "Oh, excuse me, there is indeed a book. I'm not sure that constitutes it being a bookcase though."

Saber rolled her eyes. "I hope you like it there, 'cause it can't possibly be moved—me and Coop almost busted a gut getting it here."

"It's fine where it is," Sydney said. "Did you manage to get everything sorted?"

"Yep, all done."

"So you're all moved in?" Sydney clasped her hands behind Saber's neck, drawing her close.

"Yes, we're officially living together."

"I think that deserves a celebration." Sydney kissed her sweetly, and her breasts brushed against Saber's.

"Me too, but Coop's downstairs."

"He's asleep. He would never come up uninvited anyway." Sydney could see that Saber wasn't comfortable with it, so she relented. "Okay, delayed gratification and all that."

Saber bent her head, giving Sydney an intense, passionate kiss. "Something to keep you going till later."

Sydney's body was now completely on fire. She shook her head, trying to clear her thoughts. "That wasn't nice."

"It wasn't?" Saber's expression turned impish. "I thought you said I was a good kisser?"

"Not the kiss," Sydney said, exasperated. "That was…" She had to shake her head again. "You are such a tease."

Saber flashed her a grin.

WHEN RICH ENTERED the café, Sydney immediately tried to catch his eye. He didn't seem to notice her, for he walked straight to the counter, and called through to the kitchen. "I'm here, Saber."

"I'll be with you in a minute." Saber's voice came back. "Syd's in the corner."

Rich looked Sydney's way, then crossed to the table where she was seated, sitting opposite her. "Hi, Syd. What's this about?"

Sydney nodded in greeting, since her mouth was full of spaghetti. They'd asked Rich to meet them here, but hadn't given a reason why. As she swallowed her food, she said, "I'll tell you as soon as Sabe gets here."

"Okay." Rich sat back in the seat. "Hell, we had an exciting day today, we had to go rushing over to the hospital."

Sydney grew concerned. "Why? What happened?"

"The woman we were working for went into labour." He turned green. "It wasn't a very pretty sight, let me tell…Well, I guess you'd already know that."

"I didn't see you."

"We asked where you were, they said you were on your lunch — we didn't stay long."

"No one told me," Sydney muttered. She knew messages often weren't passed on, people were too busy for that. In this case, it had likely been a good thing. If someone had told her that one of her friends had been in hospital, she'd have been frantic wondering if it was Saber.

"Anyway it worked out well, we've got the rest of the week off."

Saber came out of the kitchen, carrying a plate full of food. She placed it down in front of a customer, nodding at his thanks. Sydney shuffled over to make room for her, and as she sat down, Rich looked to them both expectantly.

"We've moved in together," Sydney happily said.

"Hey that's great, guys, congratulations."

Sydney smiled at his enthusiasm, pleased that Rich had finally gotten over his crush on Saber.

"I'm going to put my house up for sale, and I know you're looking for a place, so..." Saber trailed off.

Recognition dawned on Rich's face. "Are you saying I can buy your house?"

"Sure am."

"Wow, that is so awesome! When can I move in?"

Sydney knew he'd ask that. "It's a good thing you're off for the next few days."

His eyes grew wide. "Really? I can move in now?"

"Don't see why not, I'm already out. The finances will come through when they're ready."

Rich slapped a hand excitedly on the table. "I'll have to go shopping!"

"You might wanna check what you need first."

Rich looked confused. "I've only got the stuff in my room, my TV, bed, that's about it. The rest belongs to my folks."

"What Sabe means is, she's left you a lot of her stuff, we don't need all of it and I'm sure you'll put it to good use."

"No way?"

Saber shrugged. "We can't use two sofas."

"I..." Rich shook his head, grinning from ear to ear. "I don't know what to say."

"That's a first," Saber joked.

"Thank you. Really, I mean it, thanks very much." Rich stood up, opening his arms to the chef.

Saber stepped into them, patting him on the back. "You take good care of the place."

"I will." Rich pulled away, then beckoned Sydney forward. "You, too."

Sydney hugged him, chuckling when she noticed the curious glances from other patrons.

Rich drew back, still grinning like a Cheshire cat. "I'm gonna go pack!" He turned and ran out the café, whooping with delight.

Chapter Fourteen

WAYNE'S ALARM SOUNDED. He smacked it off in annoyance and soon fell back to sleep. When he woke of his own accord, he cursed loudly as he spotted the time—5:00 a.m. His friend Philip would be arriving any minute now, and he was a stickler for punctuality.

Wayne leapt out of bed, glad he'd packed his climbing gear the night before. He quickly used the bathroom and got himself dressed.

A quick glance at his appearance belied the fact that he was thirty-one years old—he looked older. Yawning widely, he ran a comb through his short, dark curly hair.

He heard a car pulling up outside.

Wayne ran into the kitchen, skidding to a halt in front of the refrigerator, wishing that he'd also packed his lunch last night. Removing a glass bottle of coke, he started to search frantically for his sports bottle, intending to transfer the liquid over.

A knock on the door.

"Shit!" Wayne grabbed a few bars of chocolate and pushed them forcefully into a side pocket of his backpack. Opening a cupboard, he retrieved a few of packets of crisps and added them to his collection.

His stomach rumbled. He secured the glass bottle on to his pack, which would allow him easy access to it.

Another knock.

Grabbing his walking boots, he hopped to the door while putting them on. Unlocking it, he tried to appear as though he hadn't been rushing about. "All right, mate."

"Ready to go?" Philip smiled, seemingly in a good mood. Wayne didn't think he'd ever seen Philip in a bad mood, his smile was nearly always present.

"I've gotta grab my bag." Wayne ushered him inside, stopping to tie his shoelaces. He returned to the kitchen, grabbing a bread bun. He didn't have time to put anything in it, so he would have to eat it dry.

"Don't tell me that's your breakfast?"

"No way, man, I'm starving that's all," Wayne lied. "Want one?"

Philip shook his completely hairless head. The man wasn't old, in fact he was the same age as Wayne, but the onset of baldness happened early in his family, and he was no exception. "Good, because this is going to be one of the hardest climbs we've ever done, you'll need your energy."

"I know." Wayne took another bun, meaning to eat them on the drive. "Okay, I'm all set. Did you tell your Missus what time we'll be back?"

"I did. I gave us an extra couple of hours leeway, in case it's more difficult than we think."

"We won't need it."

"Best to be on the safe side," Philip said. "I don't want her worrying if we're late back."

"You mean you don't want her bitchin' at you." Wayne put on his jacket, then picked up his backpack.

"That too."

SYDNEY WAS IN a fully fledged bad mood. It was early Thursday morning, she was on call, and she'd been reluctantly pulled out of bed at 5:45 a.m. She realised that she should be grateful that she'd only gotten up a quarter of an hour earlier than usual, but she was annoyed that she was missing her run. She didn't want her fitness level to drop, especially since she'd finally managed to pass Rich.

She'd left the house at 6:00 a.m., giving her sleepy partner a kiss before leaving.

Sydney looked at the digital clock on her dashboard. It was 6:30 a.m., she was halfway to the hospital.

A smile formed as she remembered coming out of the bathroom that morning, only to find that Saber was no longer in their bed. She found her downstairs, preparing Sydney some breakfast. Saber really didn't need to do that, but she had, never once complaining about the day's early start.

Sydney's thoughts were interrupted as a VW Passat came toward her. She hardly ever encountered people on this route, let alone this early in the day.

She pulled her 4x4 off the road, flashing the other car to continue past her.

As it neared, she saw two men in the car. The driver, a man with no hair, signalled his thanks when he passed. The passenger gave her a thumbs up.

Sydney nodded to them. As she was higher up than they were, she noticed the rucksacks in the backseat. She now knew why they were here so early, they were going climbing. It was nice to see people taking notice of the weather forecast for a change. It was due to get foggy later, and they'd clearly set off early to avoid it.

"Finally, some people with sense."

If Sydney had known what was going to happen later that day, she would have blocked the road with her car and physically forced them to turn back.

WAYNE TURNED AROUND in his seat, trying to get another glimpse of the blonde woman they'd just encountered. He whistled. "Man, did you see her? She was smokin' hot."

"Yeah, she was kinda cute."

"Kinda? Come on, man, Sheila's not here now."

Philip laughed. "Okay, she was gorgeous."

"Damn right. Nice car, too." Wayne watched until the large black 4x4 dipped out of sight.

"Her husband's probably loaded."

Wayne sighed in acknowledgement. "Girls like that are never single."

"WHERE'S SYD?" DOUG asked, as Saber joined them for their morning ritual.

"Is she okay?" Jeff sounded worried. "She's not sick, is she?"

"No." Saber smiled to back up her words. "Hospital called her in early." The team met at the same spot every day, at the start of the track that led up to Toppling Crag. They were now only waiting for Rich to arrive, and then they could begin their run.

"Poor thing." Coop looked sympathetic. "She's going to have a long day."

Saber nodded. "Yeah, but she's off tomorrow and Saturday this week so that's something."

"I could never get used to that," Coop said. "When I used to work, I liked my weekends off."

"Sometimes she gets them, depends on the rotation. She always gets two days off together though."

"Julia would go mad if I didn't spend most of the weekend with her," Jeff said.

Doug tipped his head. "Faye would, too."

"It's fine for us because I work different days a week too. Though granted, not as many. I swap my days off to match with hers," Saber said. "I'm really lucky that Marty's so flexible. Marge too for that matter."

Coop pointed at Saber's — soon to be Rich's — door as it opened. "Here he is."

Rich jogged over. "Hey guys, isn't it fantastic about my new place?"

"Sure is." Doug smiled at him. "I bet your mum's going to miss you."

"I told her I'd only be across the street."

Jeff held out his hand. "Welcome, neighbor."

Rich grinned, shaking it. "I promise I'll keep the noise down."

"I'll hold you to that."

Rich turned to Saber. "Everything's great, thanks again for that."

Saber knew he was referring to the items that she'd left for him. "No problem."

"Do you need a hand with your stuff?" Doug asked.

"No thanks, there's not much and my dad's gonna help. He can't wait to get me out. He wants to turn my room into a gym."

"Clive does?" Jeff's shock was clear in his voice.

"I know, right? My dad's never worked out a day in his life." Rich shook his head. "Mum reacted the same way, she thinks he might be starting a midlife crisis. She says as soon as he starts dying his hair, she's sending him to therapy." He laughed along with the rest of them.

"Well if it is that, you're best off out of it," Coop said.

"Has Clive even got any gym equipment?" Jeff asked.

"Nope, not a thing."

"It's going to be a pretty empty gym then," Saber said, her tone droll.

Doug clasped a hand on to Rich's shoulder. "Tell him he can come running with us. It'll be a lot cheaper than buying all that equipment, and just as effective."

"I already suggested that. He's worried I'll show him up," Rich smiled, and it was filled with self-satisfaction, "which of course I would."

Coop mumbled into Saber's ear, "No wonder he doesn't want to come."

"HERE, HAVE MY banana." Philip tossed the item to Wayne.

They were sitting underneath Jagged Flint — the first of the two climbs that were soon going to challenge them in every possible way.

"I can't believe you didn't bring a proper lunch," Philip said in disbelief.

"I'll be fine." Wayne peeled back the skin. "I've had enough sugar to keep me going." Despite his words, he could already feel his energy waning, and they hadn't even done any proper climbing yet. Though they had been walking for hours, and had also done some scrambling on the way up.

Philip glanced at his watch. "We're slower than I thought we'd be, I'm pleased I gave us the extra two hours. Sheila's not expecting us back till three o'clock."

"What time is it now?"

"Just after ten."

Wayne felt a bit better knowing that — they'd been hiking for a little over three hours. "We must be nearly there then, the guidebook said it'd take six hours round trip."

Philip checked the map before looking up at the vertical wall. "There's this one to climb, then we follow the trail round to Black Mount." He traced the route with his finger, showing Wayne. "That'll take us to the top." He examined his watch again. "It's gonna be close."

Wayne was confident. "It's quicker coming down anyway."

CHARLIE LOOKED OUT of the rescue station's window. "Those clouds are moving in fast."

Saber joined him, seeing that the weather was deteriorating quickly. "Anyone filed a route plan for today?"

"No, but you know as well as I do, that doesn't necessarily mean that no-one's up there."

Saber murmured in agreement. "What's the forecast?"

"Heavy rain and high winds. It's gonna get cold up there. Oh and your personal favorite, thick fog."

"Peachy."

"Look on the bright side, the helicopter rescue team gets a day off."

"We have to go out in the fog," Saber muttered.

"Yes, but your instruments don't stop working. The fog interferes with the helicopter's equipment."

"Excuses, excuses," Saber joked.

Charlie chuckled. "Mind you, it's probably a good thing, 'cause if it crashed you'd have to go and rescue them, too."

"I take it all back," Saber said quickly. "Every word."

"It's days like these when I really appreciate being stuck at this station." Charlie grinned at her.

"Thanks, pal, rub it in, why don't you?"

Charlie did exactly that. "I'll be nice and dry, sheltered. Oh, and I've got my little heater here." He rolled over to the desk and patted the item caringly. "And of course the fact that I'll be able to see more than two feet in front of me, I find that a plus on any day."

"Laugh it up while you can, we might not even get a call out today." He gave her a pointed look. Saber groaned. "I've just jinxed myself, haven't I?"

"You and the rest of the team."

"Damn it! Don't you dare answer that phone, Charlie. If it rings, tell them we've all gone on a team building exercise."

"I thought you said not to answer it?" Charlie teased, clearly not taking her seriously.

"Smartass."

WAYNE WAS TWO-THIRDS of the way up the first climb. Philip was waiting at the top for him, and he suspected his friend would be growing more impatient by the second—Philip wanted to keep their schedule.

Wayne wasn't particularly bothered, it's not like Sheila would have a go at him. As long as they made it to the top, he would be happy.

His energy levels were depleting quicker than he'd hoped, and the climb itself was providing him with a tough challenge. And this climb was supposed to be easier than the next.

Wayne stopped his ascent, resting for a moment.

Even Philip had struggled in some places, and he was the better climber. Not that Wayne would ever admit it.

"Tight rope," Wayne shouted. He was gasping for a drink. Feeling the rope go taught, he let go of the rock and sat in place in his harness.

Low dark clouds covered a lot of the view.

Reaching around to his small pack, he unfastened the coke bottle. His hands shook from the exertion but he managed to open the top, swallowing a few gulps.

"Weather's coming in, pick up the pace," Philip called from above.

Wayne cursed, hastily trying to tie the glass bottle back on to his pack. It slipped. He watched it fall a good way before it landed on a small outcrop, shattering into numerous shards.

"Fuck!"

It was a hard climb, and Wayne really didn't want to go down and have to do it again. More than that though, he didn't think he would physically be able to. Philip wouldn't be happy to give him the extra time either. He looked down at the glass. They hadn't seen a single other person up here, so in the scale of things, what could it hurt to leave it there?

Wayne grabbed hold of the rock and continued his ascent.

PHILIP STARTED TO laugh as Wayne pulled himself to the top. "You look like I feel."

"I'm sweating like a pig, man."

"I am, too." Philip indicated his sweater. "You should put a jumper or your jacket on, you don't want to cool down too fast."

"Are you sure we can spare the time?" Wayne asked sarcastically, pulling out a coat from his pack.

"It's noon, we can still make it back for three. Like you said, it's quicker going down. There was a village nearby, I can call Sheila from there, I'm sure they'll have a payphone."

Wayne was hopeful. "Is Black Mount that short?"

"I don't think we should do the next part, we're not going to have the time."

"No way, man! I haven't slogged my guts out all day to turn back now, we're on the final friggin' stretch."

"Look how long it's taken us to do that last part, we're going to be hours behind."

"I'm sure you've got OCD or some such shit. What's a few hours here or there?"

Philip opened his mouth to retaliate.

"Come on, man, you can't tell me you won't be disappointed to turn back now, not when we're so close."

"I would be. But even if you forget about the time, there's the fact that we might not be able to climb it. That one nearly did me in."

Wayne could tell Philip wasn't happy, but if there was one thing he was good at, it was manipulation. "I tell you what, why don't we go to Black Mount, you said it wasn't far?"

"Round there." Philip pointed along the trail that they were currently sitting on. It disappeared out of sight round the mountain.

"We'll just go and take a look at it, see what we think and decide from there," Wayne said, although he had no intention of leaving without at least trying to climb it.

Philip apparently saw no harm in allowing this small excursion, for he nodded his consent.

SURPRISE WAS ETCHED all over Philip's features. How had Wayne managed to get that far up?

When they'd first arrived, Wayne had insisted they attempt the climb, sweetening the deal by saying that he himself would lead.

Philip had agreed, purely because one look at the climb itself told him that Wayne wouldn't get very far. Black Mount was a lot higher than Jagged Flint, and it would have to be climbed using the multi-pitch technique.

Wayne now sat on a ledge halfway up, signalling for Philip to come and join him.

Philip had little choice in the matter, knowing Wayne wouldn't come down now. He sighed, highly aggrieved.

PHILIP FELT THE wind buffeting him as he climbed. This side of the mountain was a lot more exposed. His spirits had risen though. He was starting to believe they could do it.

It had been drizzling for the last hour and the holds were getting slippy.

Philip had wanted to turn back, but Wayne pointed out that if they got to the top, there was an alternative route down — an easier, quicker route. That had clenched it for Philip, knowing that Sheila's worrying would be cut down somewhat. He was also hoping that his phone might get a signal at the peak.

"You gave us too little credit, man, we can do this." Wayne grinned down at him.

Philip climbed the last few feet to his friend's position, then sat on the ledge and tried to catch his breath.

The heavens opened and the wind picked up.

PHILIP ROLLED BACK the sleeve on his raincoat, checking his watch for the umpteenth time — 2:00 p.m. They'd been sitting on the ledge for ages, waiting for the downpour to cease.

Neither of them wanted to risk climbing with the high winds, so they'd simply huddled together. The ledge was a decent size, and with their backpacks to the wall, they were able to stretch their legs out fully.

Philip's hands were going numb, despite the gloves that he wore. Undoing the clasp on his helmet, he took out a hat from his pack. He put it on, not wanting essential body heat to escape through his head. Placing the helmet back on top, he found that he couldn't refasten it with his cold fingers. It didn't matter, they weren't going anywhere yet.

Another half hour passed.

"I think we should go down," Wayne said, his teeth chattering.

Philip glared at him, annoyed beyond words.

Wayne sighed heavily. "Doesn't look like it's going to shift anytime soon."

Philip was watching the dark grey clouds. "It's too late now."

"What do you mean?" Wayne's voice rose in alarm. He tipped his head back, following Philip's finger as he pointed upward, indicating the reason behind his statement.

A thick blanket of fog was headed their way, and it settled over them with an icy grip.

Philip stretched his arm out in front of him—he lost sight of it before it'd even reached its full extension.

Both men shared a look of despair. They now had no choice but to stay where they were. Any attempt to move would likely end in disaster.

In an obvious attempt to try and make himself comfortable, Wayne unclipped from the rock.

CHARLIE BURST INTO laughter as the phone rang, and he pointed at Saber tauntingly. "You jinxed it."

Saber buried her face in her hands. After a moment, she decided to look on the bright side. If this was a genuine rescue call, it at least meant she would get to see Sydney earlier than usual. Despite the situation, she found herself smiling.

Charlie picked up the phone. "Mountain Rescue Service."

"DR. GREENWOOD?"

Sydney looked up from her paperwork. "Yes?"

"There's a call for you." Sara, the young secretary, looked flushed. She'd clearly been searching high and low for Sydney.

"Who is it?"

"Mountain Rescue. They asked for you specifically."

Although they could have contacted Sydney on her mobile, she'd asked them not to, since hospital policy banned their use inside. Sydney frowned, assuming there must've been an accident. She hastily followed

Sara to the nearest desk and picked up the phone.

"Line three."

She pressed the button. "Hello?"

"Syd, it's me."

A pleasant warmth filled her chest at the sound of her partner's voice. "Hi, Sabe. What's up?"

"We've been called out, can you get away?"

"My boss will sort out cover. He knows I'm Mountain Rescue. It'll take me the best part of an hour to get back to you though."

"Doug and the guys are out, too. They've gone shopping to Gransford, so it'll take them the same time to get back."

"Okay, I'll set off as soon as I can." Sydney wanted to know more about the situation, but time was of the essence and she couldn't walk and talk on a landline.

"Drive safe, it's nasty weather out there."

Sydney smiled. "Will do, honey."

"DOUG?"

"Charlie?"

"Yeah, it's me. We've got a call out."

"Hang on just a sec." Doug lowered his mobile, and hastily walked down the shopping aisle to catch up to the others. "Pack it up, guys. We've gotta go, it's Charlie."

"Aw, in this weather?" Rich said.

"Go and take your things to the checkout." Doug pushed him forward, then returned his attention to the phone. "Charlie, give me the details."

Doug was relieved that Charlie had managed to get through to him — mobiles didn't have a very good signal around Shirebridge, but they worked all right in town.

"Received a phone call from a Mrs Sheila Morton not ten minutes ago," Charlie said. "Her husband and his friend are both climbers, and they set off at five this morning to travel to The Water Tower. With the car journey, they planned to reach the mountain at seven."

"Does she know which climbing route they were going to take?"

"No, and apparently they were planning on doing two climbs today."

Doug shook his head. He really didn't want to split up his team in bad weather, but he might not have much of a choice. "What time were they supposed to be back?"

"Three."

"It's just past that. We'll give them some extra time."

"That's why Sheila's so worried, her husband Philip already added two hours leeway."

Doug thought for a minute. "So they expected to be around six hours, give or take. Look up which routes take that amount of time, should narrow it down some."

"If it was only the one climb they'd intended to do, it would've left only a couple of choices. But as they're doing two...They could've backtracked or anything, Doug. It's going to be much more of a guesstimate than actual fact. And that's if they've calculated correctly, which assuming they haven't had an accident, they obviously haven't done."

"Okay. Well they've been out for eight hours now, so work between the two timeframes, in case they have simply miscalculated. Focus on the routes that are relatively close together, that add up to between six and eight hours. It's likely to be the weather that's slowed them though."

"Will do," Charlie said. "I'll have them for you when you get back."

"Have you told Sydney yet? If you can't reach her I'll pop in and get her on the way past."

"She's already on her way."

"Coop and Saber?"

"Saber's gone to get Coop now." Charlie chuckled. "He's over at the café stuffing his face full of your wife's cookies."

"Sounds about right. See you soon." Doug disconnected the phone and followed the other men out to the car.

Jeff was trying to console Rich. "At least you got most of it. We can come back for the rest later."

"It's not that. I'm trying to remember where I put my gear."

Doug groaned. "You can't be serious?"

"Hey I'm between two homes right now, I think I took it to my new place. God knows where I put it though."

Doug handed him his mobile. "Get your mum to hunt it out, we're going to be pushed for time as it is."

Jeff raised a curious eyebrow. "Is the weather expected to get worse?"

"Yes, unless the forecast's changed from this morning. The heavy rain's going to make it dark earlier, too."

"Great," Jeff said flatly.

SABER WAS PACKING food into two lunchboxes when Sydney came into the kitchen.

"Hello, beautiful." Sydney stood on her tiptoes and kissed her.

Saber smiled. Sydney noticed that she was already dressed in her climbing gear, and had her black waterproof trousers on over the top.

"I'll go and get changed. Be back in a tick." Sydney left the room. Her clothes were laid out on the bed, waiting for her. Checking her rucksack, she found her harness, stickies, and everything else she needed alongside Saber's. When they got to the rescue station everything would be transferred into the packs there. "You are too good to me," she spoke her thoughts aloud.

"Never. Nothing's too good for you."

Sydney jumped. As she'd been about to step into her trousers, she stumbled and fell onto the bed. She scowled at Saber, who was chuckling in the doorway. "Sabe! Must you sneak up on me like that?"

"You need to get your ears checked. I ran up those stairs."

"Sneakily ran," Sydney murmured.

Saber placed the two lunchboxes inside the rucksack. "I'd put another top on over that if I were..." She broke off as Sydney held up a jumper. "Okay, I'll just shut up now."

"Heh." Sydney put the jumper on. She caught her hat as Saber threw it to her and slipped it onto her head. "Where's yours?"

"Downstairs with my coat." Saber picked up the pack and carried it out of the room.

"I could've carried that, you know, you didn't need to come upstairs to get it."

"I didn't." Saber descended the stairs, then turned around to face Sydney. "I wanted to watch you get dressed."

Sydney giggled. "Here I was thinking you were being chivalrous."

"Nah. I just wanted to get an eyeful."

Since Sydney had stopped on the bottom step, she was higher than usual. "And did you?"

"Two in fact." Saber leaned forward and kissed her. Then she reached up and pulled the hat down, over Sydney's eyes.

"Oi!"

"Aw, so cute."

Sydney pushed her hat up. "You are in so much trouble."

"Oh yeah?"

"Yeah."

"What are you gonna do about it?" Saber turned away and started for the kitchen.

Sydney darted past her, holding her arms out to stop Saber. She whispered into her ear, hearing Saber's breathing catch at the words.

Saber's eyes filled with desire. "You'd do that?"

Sydney took her hand and led her to the fridge. Opening the door, she retrieved an aerosol can of whipped cream. "I plan to do that."

Saber swallowed, hard.

The phone rang.

"That'll be the guys." Sydney returned the item to the fridge and shut the door. "Best get moving." She gave the still stunned Saber a kiss. "Hold that thought."

"Now who's the tease?"

Sydney smiled, pleased with herself. "Paybacks are a bitch, huh?"

"IT'S A GOOD thing it's still summer," Coop said. "Or we'd already be losing light."

Sydney watched the dark clouds. The helmet she wore kept both her hat and head dry, but it did nothing to protect her face. Freezing rain pelted her relentlessly, and she was relieved to get into the Land Rover.

Rich, as always, voiced his opinions. "Shit that weather is bad. I'm not looking forward to being out on the mountain in this. Get blown off the damn cliff."

Sydney actually agreed with him for a change. She wasn't exactly thrilled at the prospect herself. At least Doug was going to drive to the foot of the mountain, which would save them some time.

Jeff glanced out the car window. "Looks foggy up there."

"Mm, it is. Seems to have settled at the summit for now. Let's hope it doesn't come any lower." Doug started the engine. "The last thing we need is to be swamped by fog."

"Amen to that," Coop said.

Sydney's hand was surrounded by warmth as Saber took hold of it, the gentle squeeze reassuring her more than words ever could.

"RIGHT, LET'S SET up base camp here," Doug said.

"Do you want all three tents put up?" Rich asked.

Saber shrugged off her pack, letting it slide to the ground. "Just the one for now, we'll store everything we don't need in there. If we find them quickly we can still make it down safely, if not we'll have to camp the night. We can assess the situation later."

Sydney wiped a hand across her dripping brow. It wasn't the rain that soaked her, it was sweat. The rain had relented an hour into the trek. After a further thirty minutes they'd reached this small plateau. She took a moment to catch her breath: Doug had pushed them hard, but she knew that he'd had too. The fog could shift any minute, and they'd be no good to anyone if they had to hold their position.

As Saber, Doug, and Rich set up one of the four man dome tents, Sydney looked around. Doug had picked a good spot. The small space was sheltered mostly by the large peak behind it. The wind was blowing from the north, and as they were on the south side they were relatively protected from the strong gusts. There was also plenty of space for the other tents if needed.

"Tough hike." Jeff stepped up beside her.

"I'm pleased you said that." Sydney smiled at him. "Glad to know I'm not the only one who thought so."

"It doesn't help that Saber and Doug haven't even broken a sweat."

"Sickening, isn't it?" Sydney chuckled, admiring her partner's stamina.

"They can't be human," Coop said in all seriousness as he joined them. He dropped his pack to the ground and sat on it. "We should really test their DNA."

The tent was soon assembled and they all went inside, immensely pleased to be out of the cold air.

Saber pulled Sydney down onto her lap, wrapping long arms around her. "Better?"

Sydney could feel her body heat, even through the layers. "Much."

"You wanna try that, Jeff?" Doug teased. "Looks real cosy."

"Sure does. Not with you though, mate." He laughed as Doug pretended to be offended.

"Ew. Don't get me wrong," Rich added hastily to Saber, "two women are hot, but I can't get my head around two blokes." He shivered. "Gross."

Both women rolled their eyes.

"Right," Doug said, his tone growing serious. "We'll rest here for five minutes then we'll split up, usual teams. Rich, you and I will take the east side. Coop, you and Jeff the west. Saber and Syd, the north."

They all nodded.

Rich's earlier phrase 'be blown off the damn cliff' sprung unwillingly to Sydney's mind.

"As soon as the fog starts to descend, I want you to come back to base. No heroics. Understand?"

Murmurs of agreement came forth.

"Same goes for darkness. We've got a tough night ahead, but I'm more than confident that each and every one of you will be up to the challenge." Doug looked at them individually, his calm level stare assuring all of the team.

They started to unload their packs, taking only what was necessary for the climbs ahead.

Chapter Fifteen

DOUG WAS BELAYING Rich from a top rope, while keeping a close eye on the weather. He hoped that someone would call in over the radio, telling him they'd found the missing climbers.

He was uneasy about the fog. He'd led countless rescue missions, and it was the only weather condition that truly bothered him — you could easily step off a cliff edge if you couldn't see it.

Looking down, Doug saw that Rich was closing fast, and he had to give the man credit, he was on the ball tonight.

Something caught his eye a few holds up from where Rich was, it stood out against the rock. He strained to see it.

"I'M JUST PLEASED the rain's stopped." Saber stepped into her climbing harness. She brought it up around her waist, tightening it accordingly before tying on to the rope.

Sydney had already attached to the other end, and was busy securing herself to the rock. "Let's hope it holds off. Now if only the wind would do the same."

The wind howled, and Saber grinned. "I think it heard you."

"It didn't listen though, did it?"

"It must be male."

Sydney sniggered. *I am so happy.* She realised the absurdity of the thought instantly, even though she knew it to be true. Here she was, stood on a mountain at dusk, dripping wet, freezing cold, aching and exhausted, and yet she was content. She smiled across at the reason why. "Sabe?"

Blue eyes looked up from tying stickies.

"I love you."

Saber seemed to forget what she was doing, for the laces fell from her fingers. She returned Sydney's soft smile. "I love you, too."

RICH WAS GETTING closer, climbing nimbly.

Doug finally recognised what was on the rock. "Rich, don't put your hand on there." He pointed straight down. Unfortunately, the wind buffeted around them at the wrong moment, obscuring his words. Rich glanced up at him questionably, but didn't halt his climb. "Don't put your hand there." He tried again.

Rich tapped his ear and shook his head. He kept climbing.

Doug, although tied on, braced himself, pulling the rope taut.

Rich reached up toward the rock. He gripped it firmly. "Urgh!" His face scrunched up as he pulled his hand away, losing his balance and peeling off the cliff.

"WAYNE," PHILIP SPOKE loudly. "Don't you dare fall asleep on me."

"I'm not, man, I'm just resting my eyes," he mumbled.

"Well don't."

Wayne shook his head, as if trying to rouse himself. "I'm so fucking cold."

Although they were huddled close together on the ledge, inside a survival bag, their combined temperatures did little to protect them from the assault by the constant wind.

They both sat cross-legged on an insulation mat, which was keeping the cold from seeping up the rock and into them. Neither man was in any doubt that both the mat and the bag were what had kept them alive and conscious this long. They couldn't do so forever though.

Wayne shivered uncontrollably, and was clearly growing drowsy — Philip knew they were both symptoms of hypothermia.

Philip warmed his hands under his armpits, flexing his fingers to keep them from stiffening up. If the time came, he needed to be able to climb.

"What time is it?"

Philip glanced at his watch, careful not to let too much heat escape from the bag. "Quarter to seven."

"Jesus, we've been here for..." Wayne frowned in concentration. "Hours." He looked surprised that he couldn't calculate correctly. "Where the hell's our rescue?" His anger seemed to bring him further out of his sleepy state.

"The weather will be holding them up."

"Does that mean we've gotta spend all night out here?"

"Maybe. It'll be getting dark soon, if they haven't found us by then..." Philip couldn't bring himself to finish, he didn't want to think about being stuck here overnight.

"Man, we are so screwed."

"This fog can't stay here forever. As soon as it shifts, we'll move. Rescue or not," Philip said. At least then they would be trying, he hated just sitting here like this, slowly freezing to death.

Wayne nodded. "Sheila will have told them, won't she?" Doubt crept into his voice.

"Yes. But it'll take some time to mount a rescue, especially since the weather's so bad."

"Really?" Wayne asked sarcastically. "I hadn't noticed."

"They might not set off till morning." Philip shrugged, he didn't know how these things worked. "Depends on the team, I guess."

"Let's hope they're not a bunch of pussies."

RICH HADN'T FALLEN a foot, Doug had expected his reaction. The man could be such a drama queen.

"Doug!" he shouted. "Why didn't you tell me there was bird shit there?"

"I tried." Doug grinned.

"Next time, try harder." Rich wiped his hand against the rock. "Sick."

COOP PICKED UP his radio. He and Jeff had been given the nearest part of the mountain to explore, and they'd just finished their sweep. "Nothing to report. Area search completed, there's no one here."

Doug's voice replied, "Roger that. Return to base."

"On route now."

"I expect a hot drink waiting for me when I get back." Doug's hint was none too subtle.

Jeff chuckled from beside Coop. "If you're lucky," he said into the radio.

Coop was watching the light fade from the sky. "We're running out of time."

"The others might have more success than we did." Jeff dug his gloves out of a side pocket, putting them back on now he'd finished the climb. "Temperature's falling fast."

"We'd better get back and set up the rest of the tents, looks like we're spending the night."

SABER FINISHED PUTTING in a cam, seating it securely into the rock. She gave it a firm tug to test it before she continued upward.

The workout was warming her up nicely.

Saber stretched up to grab a hold high above her, gripping it firmly. She placed her other hand there also, and used her stickies to walk up the rock as there was nothing to use in the way of footholds. Squatting there, she assessed the options available to her.

Above on the left was an outcropping of rock, to the right, a few finger tip holds. Time was of the essence so she went for the easier of the two. She reached up with her left, clamping it on to the outcrop.

Pain erupted from her hand. Saber gasped, recoiling quickly. She lost her balance, her feet slipping out from under her. Her remaining hand still had a good purchase and she managed to keep on the rock. There was nowhere for her feet though, so she had to hang there for a moment, suspended by one arm.

Saber lifted her hand to assess it. A piece of glass protruded from the center of her palm, about an inch wide. Her fingers were covered in numerous cuts, and she could already feel blood trickling down her wrist. "Son of a goddamn bitch!"

"Sabe?" Sydney called anxiously from below.

"Give me a minute," Saber said instantly, not wanting Sydney to worry. She looked around for a way to climb down to her last piece of gear. There was none that she could do one-handed, not with her weaker arm anyway.

There wasn't much distance between her and the equipment, only six feet. That meant she would drop twelve. "Syd, I'm peeling off."

Saber watched as Sydney steadied herself against the cliff for the jolt, so she wouldn't lose her stance. "Okay, I've got you."

Saber let go. She was jerked to a halt a few seconds later, and used her good hand to try and stop herself from slamming too hard against the rock. Despite her best efforts, her knee crashed into the wall and she winced, knowing that she'd soon have a flourishing bruise there.

Sydney lowered her quickly but smoothly. When Saber was safely down, Sydney detached herself and crossed to her side.

Saber was struggling to undo the rope attached to her harness with one hand. "Could you?"

Sydney untied it and pulled it free. She took gentle hold of the motionless hand by Saber's side. "Have you sprained your wrist?" Raising the limb, she looked dismayed to find it covered with blood.

"No. Some genius left smashed glass up there." Her tone turned wry. "And this genius grabbed it."

Sydney turned the hand palm up, green eyes flashing with anger at the sight. "Just when I think people can't get any more stupid, they do. It's as if they want to prove me wrong. Fucking imbeciles."

Saber's eyebrows shot up at her harsh language, Sydney hardly ever swore. She gave her shoulder a brief squeeze.

Sydney became sheepish. "I'm supposed to be comforting you here. Sit down, love."

Saber sat, legs crossing neatly underneath her.

Sydney retrieved her pack, pulling out the medical supplies that she needed. Sitting in front of Saber, she examined every cut carefully with a magnifying glass. "There's only one piece of glass. It's deep, it'll need stitches."

"Okay."

"I can stitch it at camp, but I need to take the glass out now, if you stumble on the way back you could do even more damage to it. I'll give you some analgesic to numb your hand."

Saber shook her head. "I need to be able to feel it, I might have to use it."

"I knew you were going to say that." Sydney's pause was brief. "I'll give you a strong painkiller instead. It'll take away the pain, but it won't numb anything."

"Will it impair me in any way?"

"It might make you a bit light-headed."

"Then I don't want any, I need to have a clear head."

"Sabe..."

"No," Saber said.

Sydney sighed as she took out a pair of tweezers. "You're so stubborn. Paracetamol will have to do then. But I'd really prefer to give you something stronger." At Saber's headshake, Sydney sighed again. "I need you to keep perfectly still." She brought one of her knees up. "Rest on there."

Saber moved her hand without comment.

"When the glass comes out they'll be a lot of blood, but that's normal," Sydney said, giving Saber a direct look. "Are you ready?"

Saber nodded.

Sydney used her other hand to keep Saber's fingers flat. The tweezers seized the glass between their tips and slowly started to withdraw, dragging the glass reluctantly behind.

Blue eyes sealed shut at the flare of pain in her hand. She could feel the shard tearing through her flesh.

"Sabe?"

The tearing stopped.

"Breathe normally for me, Sabe," Sydney said, her tone perfectly calm.

Saber's eyes snapped open. *I am breathing normally.*

Sydney smiled at Saber's bewildered look. "You're holding your breath."

Saber sucked in a lungful of air, surprised to find that she was short of breath. She looked at Sydney in admiration, she hadn't even realised herself. "You're good," she said, still greedily pulling in oxygen.

"Deep breaths, Sabe, nice and slow." Sydney took a few long breaths herself, clearly intending that Saber copy her. Though her attention was fixed on Saber's face, her hands didn't falter, they remained completely still.

Saber followed her lead. "Sorry," she said a few moments later.

Sydney waited patiently, giving her an affectionate glance that translated to don't-be-stupid.

"I'm all right now."

Sydney arched a pale eyebrow. "Yes, Doctor."

Saber managed a tight smile, in spite of the throbbing in her palm. "That look is copyrighted, you know."

"Well if you're taking on my role of doctor, the least I can do is steal one of your trademark expressions."

"I don't do it that often."

Sydney grinned, shaking her head. She then got down to business, returning her focus to the tweezers. At Saber's nod, she proceeded.

The rest of the glass came out cleanly and blood came gushing out of the wound.

Sydney dropped the instrument, grabbing a compress to stem the flow. "Hold this." Saber took it from her. Sydney uncapped a bottle of water. "I need to wash the dirt out. I'll clean it thoroughly when we reach camp." She pulled out a cloth.

Saber was annoyed to see that her injured hand was shaking. Sydney wrapped gentle fingers around her wrist, keeping it in place. Saber swallowed, flinching as the water struck and the cuts made themselves known with a vengeance. She would've pulled her hand away if Sydney hadn't been holding it.

Sydney delicately removed some of the muck with the cloth before again dousing the hand with water. "Almost done."

Saber sat as rigid as a stone, the only thing moving were the muscles in her jaw. Clenching and unclenching.

Sydney handed her a fresh compress. "Put that one on now. Hold it tight." She washed the blood off her own hands and dried them on another cloth.

Saber had come to the conclusion in the last few minutes that she was a complete wuss. She was utterly relieved that Sydney was going to wait until they reached camp to do the stitches, and that relief made her angry at herself — she never used to be so soft.

Sydney rested a tender hand on Saber's cheek. "You did great, sweetheart."

Saber smiled whole-heartedly. Her insecurities melted away, drifting into nothingness.

"Before I wrap it, move your fingers for me."

"This reminds me of a certain bar fight." Saber winced when she moved them. "Hurt then, too."

"It was you then, too. I think I should start charging you for my services — retire early." Sydney started to wrap a bandage around Saber's hand. "I can see you're one of those people who finds trouble wherever they go."

Saber snorted. "Well excuse me for having bad luck. You're the one who found that exploding car. I hardly think some drunks and a bit of glass compare to that."

Sydney made a face. "It wasn't an exploding car, don't be so dramatic. It was on fire."

"Fine, have it your way. It was a burning, exploding car." She saw Sydney give her a humorous glance. "Did it or did it not explode?"

"Yes, but..."

"Then it was an exploding car."

"If I recall correctly, you were the one who was nearly blown up, not me," Sydney said.

"Uh-huh, and where were you?" Saber looked questioningly at her. "Well?"

"I was treating the patient."

"Really? I thought Jeff was treating the patient by then. You were too busy bleeding into a pool of your own blood."

Sydney scoffed. "It was hardly that bad."

"And you say I'm the troublemaker?"
Sydney grinned. "We're as bad as each other."
"What a pair."

"WE'LL HAVE TO do something about that glass," Sydney said. "We can't leave it up there."

Saber was watching the weather with a wary eye. "I agree."

"I'll need something to put it in." Sydney started to rummage through her pack. "Do you think you can manage to belay me?"

Saber nodded confidently. "You've done such a good job on my hand I could probably climb."

Sydney looked at her sternly. "Flattery won't work, Sabe."

"The other climb we've gotta check is just round there." Saber gestured up the mountain.

"We don't even know that they're there. Now unless you want me to pull you up the rock, you're not going." Sydney held up a thick sock. "Think that'd do?"

"That'll work."

"I'll retrieve your gear while I'm there. Then once I've secured the glass, I'll go up and check the last route."

Saber glared, getting to her feet. "You most certainly will not."

Sydney frowned. "Sabe, you said yourself, it's only round there."

"It's thick with fog. Basic rule number one—never climb alone."

"I wouldn't be climbing, I'd be walking," Sydney said. She stood up too, tucking the sock into her jacket pocket.

"Not gonna happen. Not unless I come with you."

"Basic rule number two—never climb when injured." Sydney threw the comment right back at her.

Saber scowled, recognising that both points were perfectly valid. "Give me your hand." Sydney offered it, and Saber wrapped her injured hand around Sydney's, squeezing it firmly, determined to make her point. She winced infinitesimally.

"I saw that," Sydney said, her tone once again gentle.

Saber couldn't help but smile. "It hurts yes, but I can grip well enough."

"That you can, but the answer's still no."

"You haven't stitched it yet, so it's not like I'm in danger of reopening the wound."

"You'd still be aggravating it, which would make it worse." Sydney wasn't backing down. "I am the doctor, you know."

"So you keep telling me." Saber sighed. "Fine, I'll stay put, but you're not to go off by yourself."

Sydney tipped her head, as if knowing Saber was right on that issue. "Okay. I'll just get the glass."

"We shouldn't really go up there anyway. Doug would kill us, that fog's really thick."

"You're right, basic rule number three—never climb when you can't see," Sydney joked.

Saber laughed. "I think that should be number one."

"PHILIP, LOOK." WAYNE pointed upward. "I can see through the fog."

Philip followed his friend's gaze. "Hey you're right." Shuffling forward, he peered over the ledge. "It's moving downward."

He considered Wayne's condition. The man was shaking like a leaf and in no fit state to climb. Philip would have to go himself. He got out of the survival bag and waited for Wayne to do the same before cramming it into his pack.

The little warmth they had mustered evaporated as the wind hit them. "Bloody hell. I swear if we get out of this I'm moving to somewhere hot and sunny."

Slightly cheered by his jest, Philip clapped Wayne on the chest, surprised when his hand struck something solid. He gripped the item, recognising its odd shape instantly.

"What are you doing, man?"

Philip smiled. "You know you couldn't find the whistle in your pack?"

"Yeah?"

"Well I know why. 'Cause it's in the pocket of your jumper."

"No way, man, I never put anything in there."

Philip undid Wayne's jacket hurriedly, reaching inside. He withdrew the whistle, a triumphant look on his face.

"What was it doing in there?" Wayne asked dumbly.

"Hell if I know." Philip put it to his lips and blew. A sharp trill burst forth, echoing off the fog around them.

SYDNEY LIFTED SABER'S pack, helpfully hooking it over her taller shoulders. Sydney had cleared away the glass, and it was tucked safely inside one of the jumpers in the main compartment of her backpack.

"Thanks," Saber said with a grateful smile. She clipped her gear back on to her belt. "Looks like we made it just in time, fog's beginning to move down."

They both started down the mountain, walking quickly to try and keep ahead of the approaching fog.

"That next climb we were going to do, it's not the same north slope that Charlie had his accident on, is it?" Sydney angled her feet to get a better grip on the incline they were descending.

"No, that was over on Toppling Crag."

"That's right." Sydney felt relieved. She knew it would bring up bad memories for Saber. "Have you ever been back there since?"

"Yeah, but not on a rescue. Though that's bound to happen sooner or later. Can't say I'm looking forward to it." Her expression only backed up her statement. "I've been lucky I haven't had to do it yet."

"You've never had a direct call out to there?"

"Nope, just the area, so like now the team was split up to search. Doug always made sure that he and Rich went up there."

Not for the first time, Sydney appreciated what a good leader Doug was.

Saber suddenly stopped. "Hold up. Stay still." She tilted her head, listening intently.

Sydney didn't move, her ears straining to hear whatever had caught Saber's attention. They waited for a minute. Silence.

"My mistake." Saber stepped forward.

"Wait." Sydney placed a restraining hand on Saber's abdomen. She heard it. "A whistle."

They turned and ran back up the incline.

"I'm leading," Sydney told her, in a tone that brokered no argument.

Saber submitted with a nod. "You rig it. I'll radio the others."

"Will do." Sydney knew they shouldn't be going up there, not with the fog. But now that they were positive the men were there, neither Saber nor herself could leave them. If they did, in this weather, the men would likely be dead by dawn. The fog was distorting the whistle, making it echo oddly. "Sounds high up."

"Yeah, it's definitely coming from the north. Poor buggers." Sydney recognised that Saber was referring to the wind. They would be getting the full brunt of it round there. "We've found them," Saber spoke into the radio. "They're on Black Mount. We need assistance."

Coop's voice came through. "Jeff and I are on our way, we're at base so we'll be with you within the hour."

"What's their condition?" Doug asked.

"Don't know yet, we haven't reached them. We can hear their whistle."

"We'll make our way to you," Doug said. "Keep us informed."

"Be advised, the fog is coming down, it may block your path."

Sydney, who was readying herself for the climb, finished changing from her walking boots into her stickies. They'd both left their harnesses on, as speed had been of the essence when they were planning on outrunning the descending fog.

"Only proceed if you can reach them safely."

"We're going up Jagged Flint now, we'll reassess from the top." Saber lifted her foot when Sydney tapped it. Crouching, Sydney helped to put on her stickies.

"Roger that." Doug ended his transmission.

"I could hear his teeth grating from here."

Sydney smiled. She started to set up the belay for Saber. "The weather's making it trickier than usual."

"We need to both reach the top before the fog hits," Saber said matter of factly.

Sydney glanced at the oncoming haze. It was going to be close. She felt Saber's hand cup her face, and she looked into reassuring blue eyes, finding all the strength she needed there.

PHILIP COULDN'T MAKE up his mind. "Maybe we should wait?"

"What for?"

"The fog might shift lower, in which case we can rappel off. It'll be quicker than climbing up the rest of the way."

Wayne looked downward, to the fog settled below. "It's been there for the last few minutes, it might stay there for hours." Glancing up, the route was clear above them. "Or worse it might come back up, we've gotta move while we can," he mumbled, his words beginning to slur.

"But..."

"This might be our only chance. We've gotta take it." Wayne pursed his blue lips.

Philip realised that his friend didn't have time to waste. "I might be able to get a signal on my phone up there. If they know exactly where we are, they might come and get us." He knew it was doubtful, but he was trying to give Wayne some hope. Even false hope was better than none at all. "I'll be able to reach the top on this rope. I'll rig a pulley so I can help you up."

Wayne held out a hand and Philip clasped it. "Let's mount this bitch."

Two major mistakes were made: Philip, in his haste, forgot to refasten his helmet, and Wayne, exhausted and hypothermic, didn't secure himself back on to the rock.

WITH EVIDENT DISBELIEF, Sydney shook her head as Saber dropped down next to her. "You're quicker than me even when you're one-handed."

"You were leading, of course I was quicker." Saber didn't smile, she was too busy trying to ignore the piercing pain in her hand. It hurt more than she'd expected.

They cleared the edge and started to walk along the trail to the next climb. They didn't make it very far before the fog reached them.

Saber stepped in first, running her hand along the wall to keep contact with the rock. She felt her way carefully, it was thick and she couldn't see much. Sydney kept a good distance behind her. Although a rope connected them, if either were to fall, the other would need enough time to react.

The wind picked up when they neared the north slope.

Saber got down on all fours, feeling the linking rope lower as Sydney did the same behind her. She was thankful that her injured hand was the one tracing the wall and not the one supporting her weight. A few feet farther, the rock started to curve inwards. Following it round, she emerged on the north side. She took a moment to steady herself, the wind threatening to batter her against the cliff face.

"I quit," she shouted so that Sydney could hear. Muffled laughter answered her.

Saber crawled forward, relieved when the density of the fog lessened. After numerous seconds she crossed into clear air. She waited for Sydney to join her.

"Oh my God," Sydney said, pure horror coating her voice.

"What?" Saber whirled in alarm. "What's wrong?" She followed Sydney's gaze up Black Mount.

They had found the climbers, but both men were mere moments away from death.

Chapter Sixteen

PHILIP WAS RELATIVELY pleased with himself as he looked back to Wayne. He had climbed quite a distance. It hadn't been straightforward though: it had been too difficult for him to climb directly upward, and over the course of the climb he'd gradually moved more and more to the right. It didn't matter, as long as he could reach the top.

The equipment he was placing would be lost, it would have to stay in the rock for another climber to claim. Wayne would usually follow behind and collect the pieces when he passed them, but there would be no possibility of that in his current condition. They each had more gear on them anyway, so they'd be able to get down the mountain safely.

Philip was surprised at how quickly the rock was drying out, and he knew he had the strong wind to thank for that.

He still slipped though.

"Bloody hell!" Philip yelled angrily as he fell, he couldn't afford to make mistakes, having neither the time nor the energy to repeat things. He would have to climb the last sixteen feet again. At eight feet, he fell past the last nut he had placed, and waited for the same distance again, fully expecting to be tugged to a halt. He wasn't. He kept falling, his speed increasing with each passing moment.

Philip briefly wondered if Wayne had finally lost consciousness to the cold, and the rope — his only lifeline — was sliding through Wayne's belay unnoticed. He fell past the ledge from where he had started, and although he was a good distance away, he was able to see it clearly.

"Wayne!" Philip shouted, terrified. There was no one on the ledge. Only Wayne's pack remained.

Philip heard the man yelling, the sound coming from high above. He spotted him. Wayne was being roughly hauled up the mountain by the rope. He still had hold of it.

Philip's logical mind registered that, and a brief glimmer of hope appeared. As long as Wayne held the rope he would stop. They both would. They would be in a bloody awkward predicament, but they would stop nonetheless.

His hope was snuffed out like a candle when the equipment he had placed — due to the excess strain — started to pop out of the rock. One went, then the next, causing a zipper-like effect to occur. Each piece held for a second, jerking him strongly and slowing his speed some. He prayed that he would stop before the last piece went.

Philip reached frantically for the rock, but he was too far off. He understood that at this speed, his arms would likely be ripped from their sockets, but he had to try. He didn't want to die.

Another jolt and his arms flailed wildly, knocking the helmet from his head.

Wayne was still yelling, and Philip knew that he had to be getting extreme rope burn. He begged him to hold on.

The trail below hurtled toward him frighteningly fast.

To add insult to injury, Philip realised that if he could see the trail, the fog had once again shifted its position. If they'd waited, he would be rappelling down right now — perfectly safe. His mistake would cost him dearly, and he would pay with his life.

Only two nuts stood between him and a lethal impact with the ground.

Philip was pulled forcefully to a halt. The savageness of the motion caused him to careen back toward the solid wall. He couldn't get his hands up quickly enough, and his head collided with the rock. Everything went black.

BOTH WOMEN INSTANTLY weighed up the situation.

Saber got the rope off her pack. It was a lot longer than the one they'd been using, and they would need it here. She passed it to Sydney, who started to quickly set up the belay.

Neither discussed who would go. Time was in very short supply, and even Saber would struggle to save either man.

"Keep well clear of the higher, I'll go for the lower of the two."

Sydney read her unspoken words clearly, Saber couldn't save both of them, and the unconscious man hanging limply from his harness was the safer bet. Sydney fixed herself to the rock in two places, one on each side. She could feel in her gut that this wasn't going to go well, and knew that she would need a firm unshakeable stance.

The two women shared a parting glance, every possible emotion passing between them.

Saber took off up the rock, moving fast despite her injured hand.

Sydney watched, finally comprehending what Coop had meant when the three of them had gone on their first climb together. He'd told her that she hadn't seen anything yet regarding Saber's climbing abilities, and she now understood his statement. The woman was phenomenal — even if she wasn't biased she would have said so. Hand over hand Saber moved, hardly stopping to place her gear. Sydney could tell the equipment was carefully placed though, she saw Saber testing each piece before moving on. Sydney wished she were in any other situation than this, so she could appreciate Saber's technique fully.

"We're Mountain Rescue," Saber called out to the conscious man high above her. "Stay where you are and we will come to you. Do not move."

Sydney could hear Saber clearly, and she only now noticed that the harsh wind had dropped. The cliff face was deathly silent. It sent a shiver crawling down her spine.

"Help us!" he cried.

"Stay calm," Saber said, not breaking her momentum. "What's your name?"

"Wayne."

"Wayne, can you put in any more gear? You need to secure yourself."

"There's nothing, I've already looked."

"Keep looking. And your friend?"

"Philip. Is he okay?"

"I'm nearly there, just hold on." Saber climbed higher. "Philip? Can you hear me?"

There was no response.

"Oh man, he's dead, isn't he?" Wayne cried.

"He's unconscious," Saber said.

Sydney recognised the comment for what it was: an attempt to keep Wayne from panicking further. Nothing more. Saber had no way of knowing whether Philip was simply unconscious, the man could indeed be dead. He hadn't so much as twitched, and Sydney could see that Saber wasn't yet close enough to tell if he was breathing.

One of the nuts popped out. The two men dropped.

Wayne let out a startled shriek of alarm. "Hurry! There's only one left, it's not gonna hold!"

Saber didn't increase her speed, and it was obvious to Sydney that she was already going as fast as she could. Swiftly, Saber put in some more equipment. "Wayne, I need you to look around for a hold, anything."

"I told you there's nothing."

From the ground, Sydney strained to see farther up the cliff face, but it was no use, Wayne was higher up still, and she was too far away to offer anything of value.

Saber tipped her head back, clearly giving his position a quick once over. "There's an outcrop below you, you need to make a grab for it."

Wayne glanced down. "I see it."

"Focus on it, keep your attention there. If you fall let go of the rope and grab on to the rock. Do you understand?"

"What about Philip?"

"I'll take care of him. You need to do this, Wayne."

"Okay." Wayne went quiet, as if following Saber's instructions.

Saber was nearing Philip, but time was quickly running out. Another piece of gear went in.

The last remaining nut flew out of the rock.

THERE WAS ONLY one thing that Saber could do to save Philip, and she physically readied herself, she wouldn't get another chance. She clasped the hold as tight as she could with her injured hand.

Philip plummeted toward her.

Saber latched on to his harness, getting a secure grip. His dead weight yanked harshly on her shoulder, and she cried out as she felt her arms being pulled in opposite directions. A sharp bolt of pain shot up into her neck, causing her hold on the wall to loosen.

Saber knew she was going to fall, but she wasn't the slightest bit worried about that — she trusted Sydney completely. She was anxious, however, about her grip on Philip, her shoulder couldn't take another jolt. She wrapped her legs around him, crossing them together at the ankles.

Saber's hand gave way. She was wrenched from the rock.

SYDNEY GASPED AS she realised what Saber was about to do. She was gripped with fear while she watched the scenario unfold in front of her. Her heart almost beat out of her chest when she heard Saber cry out, and it was all she could do to keep herself from climbing up after her.

It was a testament to Saber's strength that she was able to catch Philip at all, let alone hang on to the cliff face for as long as she did.

Sydney was ready for their fall, knowing that she would have to get them down quickly, as Saber couldn't hold him for any prolonged period.

She was concerned about Saber's shoulder. A pull like that could seriously damage a healthy shoulder, let alone an injured one. Saber's cry of pain had told Sydney all she needed to know. Saber hadn't made a sound over the incident with the glass, and the wound required stitches, it was deep. So for her to actually cry out, she must be in agony.

The rope snapped taut as their combined weight landed on it, and Sydney was pleased that she'd had the sense to brace a knee against the wall. She would have been slammed against it otherwise, the extra weight pulling her off balance.

Sydney let the rope slide through the belay rapidly, while still maintaining a controlled descent. She slowed it when they neared the ground, before stopping it completely.

With her legs, Saber laid the still unconscious Philip flat on the trail. Her legs were now pinned underneath him, and since Saber couldn't use her hands to help herself — one arm supported the other in obvious pain — she was having difficulty extracting them. Seeing this, Sydney surprised them both by pulling on the rope and lifting Saber to her feet, the adrenaline coursing through her blood making her stronger than usual.

Saber gave her a grateful look. Then she peered up at Wayne, clearly pleased to see he'd survived—Wayne had managed to grab hold of the outcrop, and his feet had found purchase also.

Sydney was astonished that neither man had fallen to their death. They'd been extremely fortunate. She turned her attention to Philip.

"Wayne, try and fix yourself to the rock," Saber shouted.

"Already have."

"Great. Just sit tight, we'll come and get you."

"How's Philip?" Wayne called.

Sydney was busy concentrating, so she didn't answer. She felt Saber's questioning gaze on her, but Saber didn't disturb her.

"The doctor's with him now," Saber said to Wayne. She sat down suddenly, as if her knees had buckled beneath her.

The fog had moved farther down, leaving their pathway clear. It would likely hinder their way back to camp, but Coop and Jeff would hopefully be with them by then. The night sky was approaching quickly—they weren't out of the woods yet.

Sydney finally looked up. "He has a serious concussion. He'll have to be closely monitored."

"He's bleeding a lot," Saber said hoarsely.

"Head wounds always do." Sydney started to bind Philip's scalp. More than capable of doing two things at once, she assessed Saber's tense form—she was clutching her arm like she had done when they'd first met. Her jaw was clenched, her skin pale, and Sydney hadn't missed the pain in her voice. Her bandaged hand was now red instead of white, the blood evidently still flowing freely from the damaged limb. "You look awful, Sabe."

"I've certainly had better days. But at least I don't look as bad as Philip there." Saber swallowed, looking decidedly queasy. Intense pain was often accompanied by a feeling of sickness, so Sydney let her rest quietly for several minutes, not asking anything further.

In that time, Sydney finished treating Philip. He was now covered with a heat-retaining blanket, and his neck was in a brace to restrict movement. She moved and sat in front of Saber. "Is the pain bad?"

As if it hurt too much to play butch, Saber nodded. "Very."

Green eyes winced in sympathy. She laid a gentle hand on Saber's thigh. "I need to examine you, sweetheart."

"That's not a good idea. Unless you're fond of being thrown up on?"

"Granted it's not my favorite pass time, but I'm sure I can cope." Sydney tried levity to lighten the mood.

Saber gave her a distressed smile. "We need to get Wayne down first."

"Nice try. He's secured to the rock. Besides, I need to know you can belay me before I can go up and get him, and I can't do that until I've checked you over."

Saber's forehead, already creased in agony, scrunched up further at the logic behind Sydney's statement. "Touché." She carefully eased her supporting hand free and wiggled bloody fingers at her. "I can belay you with this one."

Sydney gave her a look that told her exactly what she thought of that idea. "It could be dislocated, the pain will lessen instantly if I put it back in."

"It's not dislocated."

"How do you know?" Sydney asked incredulously.

"Because I've experienced that before, remember?"

Sydney could hardly forget. She brushed Saber's face with her knuckles, the gesture earning her a sad smile. "I need to take your coat off." She helped Saber slide her good arm out first, then she gingerly slipped the jacket over her other. She put it down and indicated Saber's shoulder. "May I?"

Saber tipped her head.

Sydney cautiously probed around the area. "You're right, it's not dislocated." She took hold of Saber's arm at the elbow. "I need to check your range of motion, love. I'll be as gentle as I can."

"Okay," Saber said tightly, her teeth clenched together.

Sydney slowly raised the arm, toward herself. She lifted it quite a way before Saber inhaled sharply. "All right," she said soothingly, lowering her arm. "What did it feel like? Is the pain constant? Or shooting?"

"Made the glass feel like a mere scratch in comparison."

Sydney grimaced. "That bad?"

"Mmm, it's constantly there but it's worse when I move it, stabs from my shoulder into my arm."

"I need to lift it outwards, to the side." Sydney hesitated briefly, hating to be causing pain to the woman she loved. It needed to be done though, so she could treat Saber properly. This time, she only managed to raise the arm slightly, alarmed when Saber let out a whimper. Sydney had seen enough, she guided the arm back, Saber automatically clutching it.

She noticed that Saber had paled even further, and was now as white as the chalk in her bag. Her hands shot forward, one clamping on Saber's waist, the other behind her neck, intending to steady her should she pass out.

"Stay with me, Sabe." Sydney raised her voice, trying to keep her attention. In the last hour and a half Saber had been on the receiving end of two accidents, the latest of which was obviously causing her considerable pain. Sydney knew both mishaps, combined with the likely fact that the adrenaline surge was wearing off, had made her light-headed. The pain induced when Sydney lifted her arm had clearly been the final straw.

Saber began to slump forward.

Sydney recognised that Saber wasn't going to win this battle, and she shifted closer, holding Saber to her. "I'm here, Sabe, I've got you," she said softly, her thumb running lightly over the back of her neck.

As if on cue, Saber sagged against her.

SABER WAS ROUSED by gentle words of comfort being whispered in her ear. Although she was confused as to what had happened, she couldn't think of a nicer way to wake. Her head was being cradled tenderly on Sydney's shoulder, and she could feel a warm hand caressing her back. As her eyes fluttered open, the hand on her neck moved to her cheek. She blinked a few times, her vision slowly clearing. When it did, she found herself looking into attentive green eyes.

Sydney smiled at her. "You're all right, sweetheart."

Saber's brow creased, her aches and pains starting to seep back into her consciousness. "Ow," she murmured. "What happened?"

"You passed out."

"What?" Saber immediately tried to sit up, embarrassed.

Sydney had apparently expected the response, for she quickly tightened her hold. "Just stay where you are. Give your body time to adjust."

Saber didn't even try to argue. It took too much energy, and she rarely won when Sydney had set her mind on something.

Sydney patted her cheek playfully. "Good girl."

Saber gave her a small smile, but she couldn't manage any more.

"I don't suppose you'd allow me and the guys to carry you back to camp?"

Saber scoffed.

"I knew you wouldn't go for it, but I had to try." Sydney sighed. "It would save you a lot of grief."

"True, but you'd be replacing it with another—Rich will never shut up about it."

"Does that really matter?"

"It does to me."

"I know." Sydney shook her head. "I can't pretend I understand it though."

"That's because you're not butch."

"And you are?"

"I used to be." Saber paused. "Not so much since you've been around."

"I don't like seeing you hurt, Sabe, especially when I can do something about it." Sydney turned pleading. "At least let me give you some morphine? It'll make the hike down comfortable."

"Okay."

"Coop and Jeff will be here any minute, so you don't...What?"

"Okay." Saber lifted her head off Sydney's shoulder, settling back onto crossed legs. "Give me some of that." The others would be able to help Sydney if the drug did impair her in any way. She knew Sydney was more than capable, but she would be damned if she was going to leave her partner in a potentially perilous situation alone, she would rather be in pain than endure that.

Sydney looked pleased by Saber's compromise. She searched through her medical supplies, pulling out a fresh bandage and compress, a hypodermic needle, a small vial, and a sling. Unwrapping the syringe, she filled it with the contents of the vial, measuring out the correct dosage. She tapped the needle before rolling Saber's sleeve up, then she pressed it into her flesh, administering the drug.

The relief on Saber's face was instantaneous, and she released a happy breath as she looked at her angel of mercy. "Have I told you lately that I love you?"

Sydney chuckled.

"GOOD LORD," COOP said, when his gaze landed on Saber.

"You should've seen her earlier," Sydney murmured.

Both women were standing talking to Wayne, trying to keep the man calm by assuring him that the rest of the team would be here shortly to get him down. Even with the morphine, Saber was in no condition to belay.

Saber's coat was only zipped halfway, and Coop gestured to the sling underneath. He then pointed to her other hand, which was bandaged. He glanced worriedly at her. "Are you all right?"

"I'm fine. Syd has dosed me up with painkillers." Saber was impressed by how much better she actually felt. Her arm was held in position by a sling, but the rest of her body was able to move freely, even her bruised knee was no longer painful to walk on.

Coop looked to Sydney for confirmation.

"Is it broken?" Jeff asked.

"No." Sydney regarded her questioningly, as if to see whether Saber minded her embellishing further. Saber nodded her consent, so she continued, "She's damaged some tendons in her shoulder quite badly." Sydney indicated the prone man behind them. "While she was saving Philip's life," she added proudly.

"Yep, sounds like you," Coop said.

"Good work, Saber."

Saber was modest as always. "Anyone else would've done the same."

"It'll heal all right, though?" Coop still looked concerned. "Given time?"

"I'll have to run some more tests at the hospital, but with time and hard work it should, although it will be the weaker of the two." Sydney rested a consoling hand on Saber's back.

Saber wasn't looking forward to another load of physiotherapy.

She'd had enough of that last time.

"Nothing she can't handle." Sydney's eyes met Saber's, searching them. "I'll be there to help you, every step of the way," Sydney said.

The worry over the physio vanished completely. Last time, Saber had been alone, with no one to help her but herself. She had succeeded then and she would again. When Sydney was beside her, she truly felt like she could do anything. Saber gave her a loving smile, seeing it instantly reflected.

"Us, too," Coop added.

"Yeah, anything you need," Jeff said.

Saber was touched by their offer. This round of physio was certainly going to be different from the last, she was now surrounded by people she loved, who loved her back unconditionally. "Thanks, guys."

"I'll go up and fetch..."

"Wayne," Sydney said.

Jeff nodded. "Best get a move on, it'll be dark soon."

WAYNE WAS SUBNORMALLY cold to the touch and he was shivering uncontrollably. Sydney knew he had hypothermia. He was also looking at her strangely.

"Do you drive a black 4x4?" Wayne's voice shook.

Sydney was taken aback by his question, but she nodded.

"I thought it was you." A tired smile appeared.

"I'm sorry, do I know you?" Sydney gave Jeff a grateful glance as he passed her the man's backpack. "Do you have any spare clothes in here, Wayne?" It was always advisable to take a change of clothes along, for exactly this purpose, but she knew not everyone followed the guidelines.

"No."

Jeff knelt, pulling his own rucksack over. "You can use mine, he looks about my size."

"Perfect." Sydney unclipped Wayne's helmet. "Are you hurt anywhere?"

"I can't tell. I'm freezing cold."

Sydney noticed his torn gloves and removed them, seeing the harsh rope burns underneath. Since he wasn't losing any blood, his body temperature was her first concern. "I'll treat your hands when we get back to camp. How did you manage to hang on?" She wasn't only referring to his hands, he was shaking constantly.

"I was too scared not to. The outcrop was a good hold and there was a crack alongside it, so I was able to fit a cam in quickly."

"You did really well," Sydney said.

"No I didn't. It was my fault." Wayne stared sadly at his friend, who was being monitored by Coop. "Is Philip going to die?"

"He's got a concussion. I'll have to keep an eye on him."

"You didn't answer my question."

"Head wounds are tricky things. I'd feel a lot better if he regained consciousness. We need to get you into these dry clothes. We'll do it in stages, starting with your top half." Sydney undid his jacket for him and Jeff slid it off.

Wayne's other layers followed. "I'm glad the wind's dropped," he muttered, while Jeff put a dry T-shirt over his head.

"I bet," Jeff said, helping the man into a jumper. A zip up fleece came next. "What did you mean it was your fault?"

"I didn't clip on to the rock. Philip fell and I was pulled off the ledge. If he dies it's all my fault. I'll have killed my best mate." Wayne started to cry. "I'm so sorry, Philip."

"The hypothermia would've interfered with your judgement. It was an accident," Sydney said knowingly. "You kept hold of the rope, Wayne. You could've tried to save yourself and let him fall, but you didn't. You did your best." She touched his arm. "That's all anyone can do."

Wayne kept crying, not stopping until all of his clothes had been changed.

"He shouldn't be exerted further," Sydney said quietly to Jeff, as she wrapped a heat-retaining blanket around Wayne.

"I'll get a stretcher. We'll have to carry them one at a time until the others arrive."

Sydney realised her team mate was right — only three of them here could carry a stretcher, even with only one person at each end there wasn't enough. Without Doug and Rich, the team was incomplete. She poured a warm cup of sweet tea from her flask, handing it to Wayne. "Drink this." She gave him a chocolate bar. "And eat this, too."

Wayne sipped the drink. "Thank you."

"Everything's going to be all right," Sydney said, hoping she sounded more confident than she felt. Daylight was running out quickly, and since the others hadn't yet arrived it would be slow going to get them down. "Now, how did you know I drove a black 4x4?"

"We passed you this morning."

Sydney thought for a second. "That was you? Well I can see there's nothing wrong with your memory."

"Take more than hypothermia to make me forget someone like you."

Oh boy. Sydney gave him a polite smile — a look she'd perfected over the years due to being hit on at work.

Jeff returned at just the right moment, board in hand.

"Wayne, we're going to put you on the stretcher and carry you down to our camp. Don't worry, you'll be perfectly safe."

SYDNEY AND COOP carried Philip round to Jagged Flint. She

hadn't wanted to leave Saber, but she had to monitor Philip, and someone needed to stay with Wayne.

Since Saber was injured, another team member would've normally stayed with her, but as they had little time, there was no alternative. Sydney wasn't happy about it, but because all Saber had to do was sit and wait, she allowed it.

Jeff was a few steps ahead. He was going to rig the equipment to lower the stretchers down. Everyone had their own task, and it was vital that they did it.

Sydney was relieved the fog had moved farther down the mountain, it rested on the slope where she and Saber had first heard the whistle. Although they would soon reach it, at least they could descend this climb safely.

"SABER?" WAYNE CALLED out from the stretcher.

She leaned over him. "Yes, Wayne?" Although he looked far from warm, Saber knew Wayne had to be pleased to be out of his cold, wet clothes. The insulated blanket kept further cold from getting to him, and also kept his body heat contained. His limbs were strapped securely to the board, and his head and ears were covered by a thick hat.

"That's unusual, is it a nickname?"

"Surname."

"I thought maybe you were a fan of *Star Wars*?" At her odd look, Wayne said, "You know... lightsaber?"

Saber let out a short laugh. "That's a new one. Usually people think I'm named after the cat—Sabre-toothed tiger. Spelling's wrong for that though."

"But you're not?"

"No."

"Okay...Listen, I wanted to ask you something, while we're alone."

"Shoot." The wind picked up again, and the temperature dropped further. She hoped Wayne appreciated the blanket as a shiver ran through her.

"Do you know Sydney well?"

"Very."

"Great. Is she seeing anybody?"

"Yes," Saber said directly. "Me."

Wayne's eyes widened in surprise. "You're a dyke?"

"I'm gay, yes. As is Sydney."

"That's a waste."

Saber tried not to be offended. "Not to me. And I can assure you I appreciate Sydney just as much as any guy would. More actually."

"Well credit to you. At least you managed to bag yourself a doctor. I bet that went some way toward appeasing your folks."

"Excuse me?"

"Don't get sensitive. It's just I can't imagine any parent wants to hear that their child's gay. But I bet one look at Sydney won them over. She's gorgeous."

"She is," Saber said, purposefully ignoring the rest of his sentence.

"You'd better mark your territory before someone else snaps her up."

"She's not a tree!"

"You know what I mean. Is she a GP? Or does she work at a hospital?"

"Hospital."

Wayne's nose scrunched up. "You'll have stiff competition then, there are hundreds of people in those places, and she can take her pick from any of them."

"Sydney loves me."

"My ex said the same thing, emphasis on the ex. Didn't stop her from leaving."

"That's your relationship, not mine."

"Women aren't that different, they all want the same thing."

"Oh, and what's that?"

"They want to be taken care of. And in Sydney's case it's even more important. She looks after sick people all day, so she's not gonna want to do that after hours now, is she? She'll want someone attractive, which you certainly are, but you also need to be able to stimulate her mentally as well as physically, she's a doctor, so she's obviously clever. What do you do?"

"I'm a chef at a café." She hadn't even gone to College.

"Is the pay good?"

"Not particularly."

"I see a problem already."

Saber scoffed. "Why? Because I'm not rich? Sydney's not like that."

"You'd better hope not, because how can she be on equal footing with someone who gets everything from her and gives nothing in return?"

"A relationship isn't based on money." Saber was growing impatient, annoyed at both Wayne and herself as doubts began to form. Saber had months of physiotherapy ahead to fix her shoulder, if it could be fixed at all. She knew that she would need help, like one of Sydney's patients. What if she became a burden to her? It wasn't exactly going to be fun, who would want to stick around for that? *Sydney promised she'd be there every step of the way and she will be,* her rational mind told her. On any other day she would have listened, she had never questioned Sydney or their relationship, but she had been through a lot today, and she ignored both her logic and her heart.

As Wayne had pointed out, she should be taking care of Sydney, not the other way around. She wasn't weak, and she certainly didn't want Sydney to think that of her. Saber intended to prove to Sydney that she was capable, that she wasn't a liability.

After all, she could easily be replaced. Sydney could find a woman who was more capable than she was, a woman who had a good education, a fancy well-paid job, and two arms that worked, everything that she herself didn't have. Most importantly though, a woman who didn't pass out like a girl! Jesus that had been embarrassing.

Saber started to feel sick again, though this time it wasn't down to pain, not in the physical sense anyway. Wayne was right, Sydney could have anyone. Why would she settle for her?

Wayne was still rambling. "I bet you anything she's used to dating doctors like herself."

Saber grimaced. Wayne was spot on the mark about that, was he right about the rest of it too? She was hardly an expert on relationships.

The uncertainty multiplied, and started to chip away at Saber's tired, overworked defences.

NOT WANTING TO talk to Wayne anymore, but knowing she had to stay with him, Saber spoke into the radio, "Doug? How far out are you?"

"Ten, fifteen minutes. We're going as fast as the weather permits. Damn fog." Doug could be heard panting slightly. "How's everyone holding up?"

"Fine. We've got two casualties, one's concussed and unconscious, the other's got hypothermia."

As everyone on the team could hear the conversation through their own radios, Saber wasn't surprised when Sydney's voice came through. "We need to get them to camp ASAP."

"Roger that," Doug said. "Coop, Jeff, good work for setting the rest of the camp up, that wouldn't have been much fun in the dark."

"No problem." Coop's voice added to the mix, easily accepting the compliment.

"Where are you now?" Doug asked.

"We're about to descend Jagged Flint," Coop said.

"Right, we'll meet you on the trail down."

"We might not have reached that far. We'll need you or Rich to help carry the stretchers."

Doug sounded puzzled. "I thought there was only two injured?"

"Saber's hurt, too," Coop continued.

"It's no big deal, I just hurt my arm," Saber spoke up, trying to make light of it. She didn't need to be mothered. She was a grown woman for Christ's sake.

"Sydney?"

Doug went over Saber's head, infuriating her. She was beginning to wish that she hadn't started this conversation. "I said I'm fine," she ground out through a clenched jaw.

Sydney still answered him. "Sabe's strained some tendons in her shoulder, I've had to put her arm in a sling. Some glass got into her other hand, it needs stitches."

Saber rolled her eyes as Sydney gave him the full account, but she knew the welfare of the team was both Sydney's and Doug's first concern. She also didn't fail to notice that Wayne tensed up at the part about the glass.

"Is she all right to walk?" Doug asked. "Do we have to stretcher her down?"

Saber's teeth grated together, knowing fine well that Sydney's preference was to carry her down.

"No, she can walk." Sydney respected Saber's wishes, even though Saber knew she didn't agree with them herself.

Saber realised that Sydney could have insisted. Doug would've backed the doctor's decision without question. She was relieved Sydney hadn't pushed. Despite Saber's bad mood, a small smile formed, she had the best partner in the world.

A dreadful thought snuck in. But for how long?

IT WASN'T IN Saber's nature to feel sorry for herself, but at the moment a rather large self-pity party was going on inside her head. She kept imagining what her life would be like without Sydney, how empty and alone she'd be. She had excellent friends, not to mention Coop, but it just wasn't the same. Sydney made her happy.

How had she managed all those years before? She thought she'd been happy then. Now she knew that she'd only been content in her routine.

Fortunately, Coop and Jeff soon arrived, and they picked up Wayne after strapping both his and Saber's pack to the stretcher.

Saber would have insisted on carrying the backpack herself, but as she could only put it over one shoulder it threw her off balance, and she was already slightly unstable from the drug.

Saber walked slowly at first, but picked up her pace when she heard them closing the distance. She really couldn't bear to hear another word out of Wayne's mouth. She also suspected that he was the idiot who had left the broken glass behind.

SYDNEY'S FULL ATTENTION seemed to be on Philip, the man had regained consciousness. She was asking him questions and filling him in on what had happened.

Saber was relieved for the distraction. Sydney could read her like an open book and she didn't want to talk about it.

Jeff and Coop set the stretcher down alongside Philip, and the two injured friends started to converse with each other.

Saber caught Jeff's eye and signalled him over. She held up the end of the rope. "Tie me on, would you?" She hated asking him to do that, it was so degrading. She probably could've managed herself, but with only one hand it would take a while, and she wanted to get down before Sydney noticed her.

"Sure." Jeff tied her on to the rope.

"Thanks. I'll go first." Saber walked toward the edge.

Jeff quickly connected himself. "Shouldn't someone go with you?"

"Nope, you're lowering me down the cliff, I've just gotta sit there."

"Syd will want to..."

Saber cut him off. "She's busy with Philip." He looked unsure, and she grew impatient. "I'm only sitting in my harness, Jeff, you're doing all the work," she said testily.

"How are you going to keep yourself from banging into the rock?"

Saber waved her bandaged hand at him. "This one still works." She tried another tack. "They're both needed for the stretchers anyway, it's not like we've got time to waste."

Jeff nodded in agreement. "Okay, if you're sure?"

"Positive." Saber leaned out over the edge and started to descend. After a few steps she pushed off, allowing Jeff to let the rope out quicker. She continued like that, rappelling to the bottom. Once down, she fumbled with the rope, annoyed when it resisted. Finally managing to detach herself, she stepped away from the wall and kept going until she was well clear.

Sitting down, Saber rested her head in her hand, closing her tired eyes. She needed some time to get her emotions under control.

SYDNEY FINISHED PREPARING Philip's stretcher for the cliff descent. She was tied on to another rope to help guide it down. She searched for her partner. "Where's Sabe?"

Coop glanced up, a frown crossing his face. "She came with us."

Her gaze landed on Jeff, who was busy coiling rope. *Don't tell me she..?* Sydney hurriedly moved toward him. "Where is she?"

Jeff tipped his head. "Down there."

Sydney felt her voice rise, along with her temper. "You let her go alone?"

"I told her she should wait. She assured me she was fine."

Sydney clenched her hands. "Of course she did."

"Shouldn't I have let her go?" Jeff's face creased with worry. "She was kind of insistent."

Her damn macho pride. Sydney looked at the apologetic Jeff, it was hardly his fault Saber was so awkward. "I gave her a strong dose of painkillers, she needs supervision." She crossed to the cliff edge, easily spotting Saber below. The only reason Sydney had left her alone with Wayne, was because there was nothing physical involved.

"Sorry, Syd, won't happen again."

"No harm done, she's just sat waiting for us." Sydney strode back over to Coop.

"Are you going to give her what for?" he asked, clearly reading her stern expression.

Sydney was furious, she had never been so mad at Saber. "Damn right."

"She never did know when to quit, always pushing herself too hard. Give her some from me too."

Chapter Seventeen

SYDNEY GAVE SABER an intense glare as Saber helped detach the stretcher from the rope. Sydney didn't get a chance to protest about Saber's condition, for Saber quickly lifted the stretcher one-handed, gripping the middle hold in the board.

"Let's move him over there," Saber said. They carried Philip out of the way and set him down on the ground, so the next stretcher could descend.

Sydney lightly touched his arm. "You all right, Philip?"

"Yeah, that was kinda fun."

Sydney smiled at him. "I'm just going to talk to my colleague for a minute. If you start to feel ill or need me for anything, shout out and I'll be right here, okay?"

"Take your time. I'm not going anywhere."

Sydney patted his arm, then left. She took hold of Saber's elbow and led her away, giving them a little privacy. "What the hell was that?"

"What? Giving you a hand with the board? I thought you'd appreciate some help."

"Don't get smart, going off by yourself down the cliff that's what."

"Jeff did all the work."

"That's not the point and you know it. And since you brought it up, you shouldn't be lifting anything with that hand."

"It doesn't hurt."

"You could still be damaging it!" Sydney took a furious breath. "I could've made you go on the stretcher, I wanted too, but no I respected your feelings on the matter, and this is how you repay me? By going off gung-ho? Thanks a lot."

Saber's voice rose in objection. "I can look after myself."

"When did I state otherwise?" Sydney asked. "What if something had happened?"

"It didn't."

"But it could have. I'm not having you put yourself at risk because of your pig-headed pride. I warn you, Sabe, one more stunt like that and I'll change my mind about the stretcher."

"You wouldn't?"

"I would. I won't take a chance with anyone's safety, let alone yours."

Saber started to pace back and forth. "I'm not one of your patients, I can take care of myself and I can take care of you, too."

Sydney's brow knit over the odd statement. "I know that. You're very good at it."

Saber whirled sharply. Too sharply. She swayed on her feet, and squeezed her eyes shut for a second. Sydney gripped her waist sturdily, but Saber pulled away, rubbing an impatient hand across her eyes. "I'm all right."

Sydney was hurt by the rejection, and she gazed at Saber with the pain written on her face. "I don't understand. Before the team came you were fine with me looking after you, what's changed since then?"

Saber was still blinking rapidly, and it was apparent her vision hadn't yet cleared. Sydney stayed where she was, despite wanting to go to her.

"Did you mean that? You feel I take good care of you?"

Sydney didn't hesitate. "Yes." She saw Saber's face flash with the same level of relief that it had when she'd delivered the morphine earlier. Sydney frowned strongly, this plainly ran deeper than her pride, but she had no inkling as to what it was.

"Are you happy?" Saber asked quietly.

"Not at the moment no."

"No." Saber's voice cracked and a single tear rolled down her cheek.

"Sabe," Sydney whispered softly. She took a step toward her and again Saber backed off. "See? How can I possibly be happy? My partner's upset, I have no idea why, and she won't let me comfort her. Please, Sabe, tell me what's wrong?"

"Are you happy with me? I need to know."

"I've never been happier." Sydney gave her a smile to back it up. She didn't know where this sudden insecurity came from, but she was going to stop it here and now.

"You're not just saying it?"

"I love you."

"Exactly, don't spare my feelings if it's not true."

"I wouldn't lie to you. I am very happy. Trust me." Sydney kept her eyes locked on Saber's. To her dismay, more tears fell.

"So you're not going to leave me?"

"Oh, Sabe." Sydney moved forward again, relieved when Saber stayed put. She gently wiped her tears away. "Never. I want to spend the rest of my life with you."

"I can get another job if it'd make you happier. I'd have to train up another chef first, but..." Saber stopped as fingers were laid on her lips.

"Where's all this coming from, sweetheart? How long have you been thinking like this? I'm upset you didn't feel able to talk to me about it."

"I can talk to you. I do. Wayne said something that struck a nerve with me I guess." Saber looked beyond confused, and it was clear to Sydney that her mind was in turmoil.

"What did he say?"

Saber rubbed her forehead, as if trying to ease the tension there.

"Doesn't matter. Maybe I'm being oversensitive."

"I doubt that." Sydney made a silent promise to have a word with Wayne. "Why would I want you to change your job? I thought you loved being a chef?"

"I do."

"You're brilliant at it. The only reason I'd want you to change jobs is if you weren't happy with it." Sydney caressed her cheek, which was still damp from her tears. "All right?"

Saber wrapped her hand around Sydney's back, seeking security.

Sydney willingly obliged, enfolding her into a hug. Wayne had really done a number on Saber's confidence, and she wondered what on earth he'd said to her. She knew one thing for certain — she was going to find out.

SYDNEY STRODE PURPOSEFULLY toward the tent. She had finished treating Philip, and Doug and Rich were watching over him. She was happy with Philip's progress, and she'd already stitched and re-bound his head wound. To be fair, the injured had been split up amongst the team, each pair having their own patient to watch over. Doug and Rich had Philip, Coop and Jeff had Wayne, and Sydney had Saber. As the doctor Sydney had to treat all three, and she trusted the team to come and get her if any of their conditions changed.

Saber had been distant and withdrawn for the whole journey back to base camp, and Sydney was worried. She'd wanted Coop to stay with her, but Saber declined, stating she wanted to be alone.

Sydney wanted answers. She stopped outside the tent and took a calming breath, she wouldn't get them if she stormed in and demanded them — as much as she wanted to.

She entered the tent. Off to one side, passing time by playing cards, were Coop and Jeff.

A smile appeared on Wayne's face as Sydney approached. He was sat upright with a blanket wrapped around him. His shivering had ceased.

Sydney touched his forehead, feeling some warmth returning. She sat down in front of him, indicating the bag she was carrying. "Put your hands out please, I need to see to those burns."

Wayne complied with her request.

Sydney examined both hands, before she numbed the area and started to clean them. "Wayne." She kept her voice casual, light. "What were you and Sabe talking about?"

"When?" he asked dumbly.

"Up on the trail, when you were both alone."

"We were talking about you actually."

"Me?"

"Not in a bad way," Wayne hastily added. "I just asked if you were single, you're very attractive." He smiled charmingly. "Saber said you and she were an item, and I simply gave her some advice on what she'd have to do to keep you."

"To keep me?" Sydney's voice rose an octave in disbelief.

"Yes. A woman like yourself will have loads of suitors, and since you work at a place that has hundreds of people coming and going, you can take your pick."

"I've already picked. I chose Sabe."

Wayne looked annoyed at the interruption. "Do you want to hear what I said or not?"

Sydney kept her temper in check. She finished wrapping one hand, and started on the other. "Let's hear it."

"No doubt you're used to dating doctors, or professionals at least, so Saber needs a good job with a lot of money. I said, and I quote, how could you possibly be on equal footing with someone who gets everything from you and gives nothing in return. You can't respect someone if they're not on level ground."

Sydney's jaw hurt she was clenching it that hard. So that was the reason Saber had brought up jobs. And she was already sensitive about money. Sydney glanced up at Wayne in annoyance. *Brainless ass.* Saber had little experience of relationships, and this buffoon had come along and shaken everything that she thought she knew.

"What else? Oh, and she needs to take care of you, you don't want some wuss who needs to be pampered all the time—you do that at work." Wayne wrinkled his nose. "Frankly, I don't know how you do it."

That's why she's being extra butch. And now with her arm needing so much work... Sydney winced internally. *She thinks she's a burden.* She wondered if Wayne knew how much harm he'd caused, worse still, he probably wouldn't care.

Sydney continued working on his hand in tense silence. She wanted to slap him for his ignorance. She waited until she'd finished treating him to speak, rocking back on her heels.

"First off, Wayne, you know nothing about our relationship, nor any other, from what I can gather."

"Now wait a second..."

"No you wait!" Sydney erupted angrily. "How dare you scare my partner with your arrogant, unfounded opinions."

"Hey!" Wayne's tone was indignant. "It may be different for you dykes, but it's..."

"Now hold on a minute." Coop threw down his playing cards and got to his feet.

"It's fine, Coop." Sydney held up a hand to stop his advance.

"You will apologise right this instant," Coop said hotly.

"For what?" Wayne raised a defiant eyebrow. "That's what she is."

"What the hell's going on?" Saber entered, no longer wearing her helmet, jacket, or shoes. Presumably, she'd heard the raised voices and come straight over. Saber looked to Wayne expectantly, as if somehow knowing that he was the cause. "Well?"

"We had a difference of opinion," Wayne said.

Saber's eyes narrowed. "I bet you get a lot of that." She turned to Sydney. "Are you done here?"

"Yes, I'm finished." Sydney peered down at Saber's sock-covered feet. "Where are your shoes?"

"I was getting ready for bed."

"I would've helped you."

"I know, but..."

"You didn't want to be a burden," Sydney finished. "I know what Wayne said to you, and let me tell you right now that every last word is bullshit. I promise you that."

Wayne mumbled something incoherent, no doubt insulting. He was ignored.

Saber's expression turned sheepish. "Yeah, I know."

"You do?"

"I realised in our tent, I just needed some time to think."

Sydney opened the tent flap and stepped outside, zipping it closed after Saber exited. She glanced at Doug's well-lit tent, surprised that he hadn't come over to see what the commotion was about. It was then that Sydney noticed the distance between the three tents. They were much farther apart than usual. Doug obviously hadn't heard. She knew instantly that this was Coop's doing, he was giving them their privacy. She smiled, he was such a gentleman.

The night air was cold, and Sydney immediately wrapped an arm around Saber's jacket-less form to give her some warmth.

Blue eyes shone with affection. "You really do like taking care of me, don't you?"

Sydney smiled up at her. "I really do."

"That's good, 'cause I really like it too."

"Does that mean you're going to drop the butch act? At least with me?"

"I won't give you any more grief," Saber said with a nod. "Now come and help me get the sleeping bag out, it's stuck in your pack."

Sydney bit her lip in amusement.

"My hand needs stitching too."

A grin formed.

"And you might wanna take a look at my knee," Saber teased.

Sydney chuckled. "Looks like I'm in for a busy night."

"I DON'T KNOW how those two are even friends. Philip's such a nice guy, and Wayne..." Sydney shook her head. "He's a complete moron."

"Mm." Saber was laid on her back, with Sydney's arm and leg draped snugly over her. "Whoever came up with the idea for a dual sleeping bag should be given an award."

"Gets my vote."

"I'm sorry I ever doubted us," Saber said quietly. "I can't believe I ever listened to that jerk. I'm sorry."

Sydney stroked her dark hair, saying nothing.

"As soon as I had time to seriously think about it, I knew he was wrong. I was wrong."

"He hit a nerve." Sydney sighed. "And after all you've been through today, I can see why you reacted like that, you weren't thinking clearly."

"I still hurt you though, didn't I?"

"You did," Sydney said. "I thought you trusted me enough to know that I would never leave you."

"I do trust you. Completely. You've never given me reason to doubt you. To doubt us."

"But you did."

Sad green eyes were ripping at Saber's heart. "I know. I'm sorry."

"You do know that I wouldn't change a thing about you? I love you exactly the way you are. Every single part of you." Sydney paused, as if to ensure that her words sank in. "Your job, the money, all of the things that Wayne said, none of it matters to me, I need you to believe that."

"I do. Wait, you wouldn't even change my stubborn will?"

Sydney smiled. "No, not even that."

"It won't happen again," Saber said. "I give you my word." Their eyes held for a long moment. "Please forgive me?"

Sydney gave her a gentle kiss. "Already done."

"I'd rather rip out my other arm than hurt you again."

Sydney tucked a loose strand of hair behind Saber's ear. "I think that's a bit extreme, but I appreciate the sentiment."

"Let me make it up to you." Her bandaged hand slipped under Sydney's nightclothes.

"No way, Sabe. No," Sydney swallowed, "way."

"Please?" The nipple beneath her fingers stiffened, responding to her touch.

"I've just stitched your hand; I'm not going to let you..." Sydney broke off at Saber's mischievous look. "What?"

"I don't need my hands." Saber grinned enticingly.

"I know that, smartass, but I..." Sydney left the sentence unfinished, seemingly losing her train of thought as Saber began to kiss her neck. After a moment, she said, "I'm surprised you want to, we are only in a tent after all."

Saber smirked. "You must be a bad influence. Anyway I'm just building up for the spa. You know me, one..." she kissed down Sydney's throat, "step...at...a...time." She returned to Sydney's face, awaiting her response.

"On one condition." Sydney held Saber in place beneath her. "You stay exactly where you are. You don't move."

Saber hesitated. Sydney took her breath away with a mind blowing kiss. She blinked a few times, dazed.

"Deal?"

Saber would've agreed to anything after that. "Not one muscle."

"SABER." COOP JOGGED over as soon as she and Sydney exited the tent. "How do you feel this morning?"

"Syd's given me some more painkillers, so I'm fine at the moment."

Coop lightly touched her strapped forearm. "We'll soon get you checked out at the hospital."

"You're meant to be making me feel better, not worse."

Sydney placed a hand on her hip in protest. "Hey I work there!"

"And that's the only redeeming feature about the place."

Sydney smirked at her. "Good recovery."

Saber winked. "I thought so."

Sydney hefted her pack, which contained her medical supplies. "I'm gonna check on Philip and Wayne, then I'll be back to help with the tent, okay, Coop?"

"Take your time, I can manage."

"I could..." Saber broke off as twin glares were directed her way. "Sit here quietly and wait," she said, planting herself down on a nearby boulder.

Coop's surprise was clear. "My goodness, did she just follow the doctor's orders?"

"Looks like." Sydney laid an appreciative kiss in Saber's hair. "I just want what's best for you. And you know I'm right."

Saber gave her a droll glance. "You're telling me that you're right."

"My vote automatically trumps yours," Sydney teased.

"Let me guess, 'cause you're the doctor?"

Sydney grinned. "Now you're getting it." She turned thoughtful. "That doesn't bother you, does it? Pointing out that I'm a doctor and you're not? I didn't mean anything by it, I'll stop if it..."

Saber firmly shook her head. "I hadn't thought twice about it. Besides, it just reminds me that I'm the modest one."

"Tch. One of the after-effects of growing up in a big family, highlighting your achievements, always fighting for attention."

"You'll never need to fight for my attention." Saber slowly tickled Sydney's abdomen. "You might have to fight off my attention though."

Sydney giggled. "Never." She tilted Saber's head up and kissed her. Then she headed for Doug's tent to check on Philip.

Ten minutes later she emerged, pleased. Philip would still need to be carried down since he needed to be kept immobile until the x-rays had been completed, but as long as there were no unexpected complications he would recover fully.

Wayne was talking to someone as Sydney approached the tent he was in, and she was surprised when she heard Saber's voice. She couldn't help but hear what they were saying.

"Look, I'm not in the mood for your excuses, Wayne. I'm just asking for you to think through your actions. The glass you left caused an accident, and it could've been a whole lot worse than it was."

"I don't need a lecture," Wayne muttered.

Seeing red at that information, Sydney barged into the tent. "Well apparently you do if you were stupid enough to leave broken glass on a handhold of a well-used climb. Didn't it occur to you what might happen?"

"I'm not stupid," Wayne said.

"So it did occur to you but you just did nothing about it?" Sydney shook her head in disapproval. "I don't know what's worse."

"Look, what do you want me to do about it?" he asked. "I can't rewind time. I'm sorry, okay. Satisfied?"

Sydney was anything but. Her words had probably gone in one ear and straight out the other. She crouched down and began to examine him. After a few moments of tense silence, she said, "Your temperature's back up, you should be all right to walk down. If it gets too much for you, tell someone and we'll carry you the rest of the way."

"I'm sure I can manage," Wayne said cockily.

"That's up to you." Sydney got to her feet, and ushered Saber ahead of her. They both left the tent. She noticed that Saber was trying to hold back a grin, but was failing miserably. "What?"

"You can be so butch when you want to be. It's cute."

Sydney snorted. "Can you be cute while acting butch?"

"You just were."

Sydney was oddly pleased. "Hm."

Saber linked their arms together as they walked. "Riding in on your white horse."

Sydney sniggered. "I don't know about that. Though if you're into that kind of thing I can probably get Doug to carry me on his back. Will he do?"

Saber laughed. "I'd pay to see that."

They drew to a halt alongside Coop, who was packing their tent away into a bag. Sydney went to help him, smiling when Saber automatically sat herself down on the boulder.

"Coop, I wanted to thank you," Sydney started.

"There's no need, it didn't take long."

"No, not for the tent. For last night." At his confused look, she said, "Standing up to Wayne. You didn't have to do that."

"I most certainly did! Now I know you could've handled it, Syd, but let this old man have his way." Coop's brown eyes twinkled. "I'm only watching out for my family."

Sydney smiled at him. "Thank you. That means a lot." She kissed his cheek, making him blush. "And you're not old."

"Hey, Saber," Rich suddenly shouted, pointing at them. "He's making moves on your girl."

"And right in front of me too," Saber teased. "Have you no shame?"

Sydney giggled. "It was my fault. I kissed him."

"A confession!" Rich said excitedly. He looked to Saber expectantly. "You know what you have to do."

Saber stared blankly at him.

"You must take her over your knee and spank her."

Doug magically appeared at the remaining tent's entrance. "That's the only way," he added, grinning when Saber shook her head at him. "I wasn't going to miss this."

Saber held up her bandaged hand. "How unfortunate," she said sarcastically, causing Sydney's giggle to advance into full-throated laughter.

"I'll do it." Rich and Doug stepped forward simultaneously.

Coop tutted in reproach. "Perverts."

"I wasn't getting kissed a moment ago," Rich said.

Coop turned a deeper shade of red, and Sydney patted his back condolingly.

"They're at it again!" Rich cried.

Sydney snatched her hand away, playing along. "It was an innocent gesture."

Saber gave her an amused look. "If it was so innocent, why did you deem it necessary to say so?"

"Umm..." Sydney nudged Coop. "Help," she squeaked.

"Because she didn't want you to overlook the obvious?"

Saber narrowed her eyes. "Are you saying I'm stupid?"

Coop smiled as he nodded. "Yes."

Saber chuckled. "Walked right into that."

"Never mind him, spank your woman already," Rich said impatiently. "Or kiss her or something."

Doug shrugged. "We're not picky."

"Perverts rarely are," Coop muttered.

"Touché." Doug grinned for a moment, then he sobered, becoming all business again. He looked to Sydney for her medical opinion. "How are the patients? Are they all right to travel after we've finished packing the tents?"

"Yes. Philip still needs to be stretchered, but Wayne can walk. Though he still needs supervision. As does Sabe."

"Okay. Rich, you and I will take Philip for the first stretch," Doug said. "Coop and Jeff, you'll take Wayne. Then we'll switch."

No one protested, they'd been split into their usual teams.

"And I'll take Sabe." Sydney wrapped an arm around her.

Saber smiled, whispering in her ear, "You can't right now, sweetheart, we're in public."

Sydney's libido roused, not that it'd been sleeping, it never did when Saber was around—she was insatiable around her. "You are so bad."

"I didn't suggest it!"

SYDNEY STOPPED, TAKING in the view across the valley. She hadn't been able to appreciate it on the way up, the weather had seen to that. Now, the sky was a clear blue and she could see for miles.

"It's strange not being in front." Saber drew to a halt beside her. "Not that I mind, it certainly has its compensations." She smiled mischievously.

"What's that look for?"

"Just admiring your bum," Saber said bluntly.

"You weren't?"

"You were admiring your view, I was admiring mine." Saber patted the part in question. "Mine wins hands down."

A small smile crept across Sydney's face. "There's no way I'm going to be able to walk in front of you now. Especially if you don't stop looking at me like that."

"You have the cutest little wiggle."

"Sabe, I do not wiggle!"

"You do. Watch, I'll show you." Saber paraded away in a straight line, hips swaying provocatively from side to side.

Sydney clapped a hand over her mouth, mortified. "I don't walk like that. Please God, tell me I don't walk like that."

"I may have exaggerated it a little." Saber grinned, crossing back to her side.

"I'm so glad we're at the back of the group," Sydney said self-consciously.

"It is extremely sexy." Saber tilted Sydney's head up. "Trust me."

"You have to say that, you've got a vested interest."

"Yeah, but I wouldn't lie to you. You want the truth?"

Sydney nodded.

Saber leaned closer. "The truth is, ever since we've set off from camp, I've been seriously reconsidering your offer."

"Offer?"

"To take me here and now," Saber said. "You know how shy I am." When pale eyebrows rose, she added, "At least regarding sex, well, when other people are around."

"You do like your privacy."

"Exactly. That's how hot your walk is."

Sydney looked impressed. "Really?"

Saber kissed her, long and sweet. "Yes."

"Heh."

"Are you convinced?"

Green eyes sparkled as Sydney smiled. "Definitely."

"That's a shame."

"Why's that?"

"I had another way of proving it to you."

"What was it?"

Saber lowered her voice. "I was gonna put your hand down my pants and show you how sexy it was to me personally."

Sydney swallowed. Hard.

Saber winked at her. She moved away, continuing on her walk down.

Sydney stood for a moment, stunned. Then she chased after her. "Did I say definitely? I meant not in the slightest."

Chapter Eighteen

SABER HAD BEEN sent for a scan to find out the full extent of the damage. Half an hour later they were still sat waiting for the results, and she was tapping her feet nervously.

Sydney couldn't blame her, she was apprehensive herself. She placed a calming hand on Saber's thigh.

Saber stopped moving. "What if...?"

"Hey, you mustn't think like that." Sydney knew that it was easier said than done. "Sabe, look at me." She twisted in the uncomfortable chair and turned Saber's head toward her, until scared blue eyes met her own. "Everything's going to be all right."

"But..."

"But nothing, Sabe, we need to wait and see what the test says, don't jump to conclusions, honey."

"I need to climb. I won't let my dad win. I can't."

Sydney's hand shifted from Saber's chin to her cheek, completely oblivious to everyone else in the waiting room. "He won't."

"What if it is bad news?"

"You've been told that you couldn't climb before, did you let it stop you?"

Saber shook her head.

"Well then, why would this be any different?" Sydney let that sink in. "I know how stubborn you are." She tweaked her nose.

Saber's lips twitched ever so slightly. "And this time, I've got my own personal doctor at my beck and call."

"That you do." Sydney held her gaze. "We'll get through this. Together."

Saber nodded. "Okay, we can do this."

"That's my girl."

"Yes I am." Saber returned her smile. "All yours."

THE SCANS CAME back as Sydney thought, the tendons had been pulled badly, but no permanent damage—bar the weakness there, would be left.

Saber was given pain meds, and had made her first appointment with the physiotherapist before leaving the hospital. Sydney also spoke to her boss, managing to get some last minute time off to take care of her injured partner.

"You know, you can drive faster than a snail," Saber said to Doug flatly.

Rich laughed. "He's driving like Coop." His laughter increased when an insulted grunt came from the back of the car.

"I'm only being careful," Doug said.

"Leave him alone. I think he's driving perfectly." Sydney appreciated Doug's consideration. "You don't want your shoulder jarred."

"Painkillers are wonderful things. I can't feel it."

Rich immediately turned in the front seat, his hand slowly creeping toward Saber's sling. Sydney slapped it strongly away. "Don't."

"Ow! Jesus! What did you do that for?"

"I don't want you touching her arm," Sydney said in a stern tone.

"I was only gonna pinch it, see if she could feel that."

Sydney shook her head in disbelief. Rich was so immature. She could feel Coop and Saber chuckling silently on either side of her.

"Ouch." Rich rubbed his sore hand. "Talk about overkill."

"Protective is the word," Coop said. "And there's nothing wrong with that."

"Tell that to my hand."

"Thanks," Saber whispered to her. "I would've done it myself but..."

Sydney nodded, knowing full well that Saber's other hand was also hurt.

"Hey, I've just had a thought."

"That's a first," Rich muttered.

Saber ignored him. "I'm not going to be able to cook for a while, at least not until my hand heals. I know my arm will take longer, but I'm sure I can flip a burger one-handed."

Rich's face was aghast. "What are we going to eat?" His voice rose, sullen mood seemingly forgotten.

"Marty will still cook."

"His isn't the same," Rich said. "And he'll only cook for us in the café."

"God forbid." Saber shook her dark hair.

Sydney shook her head also. Rich was acting as if he'd just been informed the world was ending.

"This is going to be awful." Rich looked expectantly to Sydney. "When will she be able to cook?"

"A few weeks."

"A few weeks! We're never gonna survive that long." Rich gave Saber an annoyed glance. "This is all your fault."

Saber scoffed. "I hardly did it on purpose."

"You should've watched where you were going."

"It could've happened to anyone, Rich," Doug spoke up from the driver's seat.

"And not content with just one, you have to go and bust up your other, too. Great, well done."

"That's uncalled for," Coop said.

"What did you want me to do? Let him die?" Saber leaned forward in her seat, her irritation clear.

Sydney wanted to slap Rich again, hard across the face this time. She knew everyone was tired and emotions were running high, but he was acting like a petulant child. Saber had been the only person on the team injured, while saving someone's life she might add, yet she was having to defend her actions to a man who was pissed off because he wasn't going to get his dinner. Unbelievable.

Rich frowned. "No, but you could've found another way."

"When? There wasn't time for me to do anything." Saber didn't resist as Sydney pulled her gently back into the seat.

"You could've done something different."

"Maybe, but I'm lucky to have been able to save him at all."

"Now we've all got to suffer," Rich muttered.

"You weren't even there!" Sydney exploded. "I have no idea how you think you can sit there and judge! You didn't see it, she was amazing, and not you or anyone else on the team, me included, could've even managed to reach half of the distance needed, let alone save him. She did everything right, and you should be praising her, not whining because you can't get your bacon buttie! Do you know how that makes you sound? You need to grow the hell up!"

Rich sat mutely, his eyes as wide as saucers. After a long moment, he cleared his throat. "Saber, I'm sorry. I got carried away. Syd's right, you did really well. I am sorry."

Saber, never one to hold a grudge, nodded once.

Rich faced forward, and Doug switched on the car radio to block out the silence.

Sydney felt a squeeze on her arm and shoulder. Jeff and Coop were quietly congratulating her.

Saber was looking at her with a mixture of worry and delight. "Are you all right?"

Sydney sighed heavily. "Yesterday's stress is catching up with me I think."

"I'm not surprised." Saber planted a kiss on her forehead. "You must be exhausted, sweetheart."

"No more than you."

"Yes more than me, you were called in early for work yesterday, remember? You need a good night's sleep."

Was that only yesterday? It seemed like forever ago. "You've got a better memory than me." Sydney yawned suddenly. "So I was, you got up with me though."

"True, but I wasn't at work all day like you, I had the day off."

"But you were dragged off a cliff face and I wasn't." Sydney smiled. "I win." She bumped their thighs together. "That's way worse than an exploding car."

Saber chuckled. "A burning, exploding car."

Sydney rolled her eyes. "Whatever. It's still worse, so I win again. That means you attract more trouble than me." She grinned. "Heh."

"We'll see."

"Come on, how am I ever going to top that?"

"Quite easily, since it's you we're talking about."

"Tch."

"What can I say? I believe in you." Saber smirked.

"Aw. Hey wait a minute, you're not saying that in a good, sweet way, you're saying you believe that I'll get into endless amounts of trouble."

"Yep."

"That's not sweet at all."

"Nope."

"I'm not the one who was dragged off a cliff!"

"You would've been if I had let you go."

"Let me?"

"Mm-hmm. You'd be the one with the busted arm."

Sydney started to protest.

"You're welcome." Saber patted her cheek condescendingly.

Green eyes narrowed, but in spite of her best efforts, she giggled. They shared a smile, then Saber shifted, sliding down the seat and leaning against Sydney, who laid her head on top of hers. Within a few moments, Saber was fast asleep. Sydney felt herself starting to drift off, and knowing that the guys would wake them when they reached home, she surrendered to it, allowing sleep to take her.

"I HAVE A QUESTION," Saber said from her position on the bed.

Sydney was kneeling at her feet, removing Saber's trousers. She looked up. They had both decided to get a shower before going to sleep. Although it was mid-afternoon, they were worn out, and knew that once they were in bed they'd be reluctant to leave it.

"Either I'm overtired or I'm stupid."

"The first." Sydney smiled at her. "What's the question?"

"How, if I'm meant to keep this one," Saber held up her bandaged hand, "dry, and this one," she indicated her sling, "immobile, how am I going to be able to bathe myself?"

"You really haven't had anyone to take care of you before, have you?" Sydney rose up on her knees and kissed her tenderly. "I'll do it, love."

"That's another reason I'm glad you're here, imagine Coop doing it, I'd never be clean."

Sydney laughed. "You're right. He couldn't stand to look at your bra. I'm sure Doug and Rich would offer though."

"I'd be filthy if that was the case, I wouldn't let either of those two come near me."

"It's a good thing I am here then."

"I have another question," Saber said. Sydney regarded her humorously. "What am I supposed to wear? I can't get anything over my head. Should I just walk around in my bra all day?"

"Now there's an idea, but I've got a better one."

"No bra?"

"You really are a mind reader." Sydney giggled. "I know the answer but I'm not sure I want to give it to you, I rather like the idea of you walking around half naked."

"What about when I go back to work? Rich will certainly get an eyeful then."

"It'll probably set off his crush again," Sydney said. "Okay, I'll tell you." She moved to Saber's cupboard, pulling out a top that zipped up the front. "Slip it on one arm at a time. Plus," the zipper came down, "easy access for me."

"Always thinking ahead."

Sydney smirked.

"All right, smartass, how do I get this jumper off? There's no zip."

"Ah, that one's a bit more tricky. If it's baggy enough I can get it off without having to cut it."

"It's not fitted, it is quite loose," Saber said.

"Let's do it now." Sydney removed the sling. "Keep it perfectly still," she added unnecessarily.

They managed to remove both the jumper and the T-shirt without too much coercing. The bra and panties followed. Saber shivered as she sat on the bed, completely naked. "Are you going to join me in this strip show?"

Sydney thoughtfully wrapped a night gown around her. She grabbed the plastic bag that she'd brought upstairs, putting it over Saber's bandaged hand and securing it in place with an elastic band.

Saber frowned at her covered hand. "I feel ridiculous." Her hair bobble was removed, allowing dark locks to spill over her shoulders.

"Well you shouldn't." Sydney removed her own clothes. Once nude, she led Saber into the shower, making sure her partner didn't slip. "Aren't you glad we got the double size?"

"I've been glad about that for a long time now." Saber's soft lips met Sydney's. They were both too tired to go any further, but they still enjoyed a few pleasurable moments reaffirming their love and devotion to one another.

Later, they crawled into bed, their bodies melding together in a perfect embrace.

SABER SANK FARTHER into the bubbling water. "This is going to work wonders on my shoulder."

Sydney eyed the large hot tub. "It's certainly a gentler form of exercise, we can have our very own hydrotherapy sessions in here."

"Sounds like a plan." Saber smiled impishly as she tipped her head toward her bandaged hand, which was resting out of the warm water, on the tub's edge. "My hand's feeling left out though."

"Is that so?"

Saber pouted, as if knowing Sydney couldn't resist that look.

Sydney chuckled, leaning over and giving the hand a kiss. "How's that?"

"It's fine now." Saber smirked. "But my lips are jealous."

"Can't have that." Draping her arms around Saber's neck, she kissed her slowly.

Saber's hand found its way into short hair. "I love you."

Sydney's eyes twinkled. "I love you, too." Their lips met again. She moaned into Saber's mouth.

Saber pulled back. "Did you hear something?"

It was Sydney's turn to smirk. "That was me."

Saber gave her a dry look. "I know that. It wasn't you, something else."

"I didn't hear anything." Sydney distracted her with another kiss.

Saber pressed her body into Sydney's, letting out a groan of desire as she did so. Both women sported bikinis, although they didn't expect to be wearing them for very long.

This time it was Sydney who moved away. "I heard something, too."

Saber's smile was smug. "That was me."

Sydney returned the look that been given to her moments earlier.

In unison, they turned toward the garden gate. "Oh my God!" Saber said as they spotted the rest of the team standing there, all clad in bathing shorts.

"Funny, that's just what Rich was saying." Doug wore a wide grin. Jeff's expression was the same, and Rich's jaw hung open.

Sydney burst into a fit of giggles.

Coop, who was being held captive by Rich, managed to work the hand off his mouth. "I tried to tell you."

Rich jostled him. "You did tell them, Coop, you and your stupid mumbling. It was starting to get good."

"I thought it was already pretty good," Jeff said. "Phew!" He flapped a hand in front of his face, in a clear attempt to cool it.

Looking embarrassed, Saber buried her face in Sydney's chest. "Didn't you lock the gate?"

"I didn't see the need to." Sydney observed the men accusingly. "You're not supposed to be here till noon."

Doug tapped his watch. "It is noon."

"Ah." Sydney gave Saber an apologetic look. "I guess we lost track of time." *Great, now I'll never get her to make love out here.* She glared at them. "Thanks a lot, guys."

"I think we should be thanking you." Doug snorted with laughter.

Surprisingly, Saber chuckled. "Next time, sweetheart, lock the gate."

Sydney peered down at her in hope. "Next time?"

Saber stood up, giving her lips a quick kiss as she passed them. "Yep, you convinced me."

Sydney smiled brightly.

"Are you just gonna stand there or are you coming in?" Saber rested a hand on her hip.

Only Coop came forward, climbing into the spa eagerly. "Wow," he said excitedly. A few seconds passed. "I now see why these things are so expensive."

"Well? Are you guys coming or what?"

Sydney realised what had captivated the men so fully, rooting them to the spot. Saber stood high out of the water, dripping wet, clad in nothing but a skimpy black bikini. She took a moment to appreciate her partner's beauty, Saber really was perfect. Turning to the team, Sydney said, "Down boys, she's all mine." She tugged at Saber's wrist. "Honey, sit down, you're distracting them."

Saber's brow creased with confusion, but she lowered herself back into the water.

"She has no idea how gorgeous she is," Sydney said to Coop.

A nod of red hair. "Not a clue."

Saber winked at Sydney, taking a seat between them. "What do you think of the spa, Coop?"

"Worth every penny." He let his head rest against the side and closed his eyes. "Feels good on these old bones."

The rest of the guys clambered in, settling down into seats of their own.

"This is nice," Jeff said.

"Be great after a rescue." Doug smiled, his hint perfectly clear.

Saber laughed when she caught Sydney's eye. "Told you. We'll never get rid of them now."

"That's fine, as long as they abide by one simple rule."

"What's that?" Coop asked.

"If that gate's locked, clear off." Sydney grinned.

Rich sniggered. "We could get you a 'do not disturb' sign."

Saber nodded. "That would work, too."

Epilogue

SYDNEY CARRIED THE shopping out of the car and into the house. Saber hadn't gone with her as she'd said she was tired. Sydney didn't call out her usual welcome, not wanting to disturb her if she were asleep.

Sydney opened the fridge, finding an envelope waiting inside with her name etched on it. She recognised Saber's writing.

"Uh oh. What's she up to now?" She chuckled to herself.

Opening it, she read the brief message — *Come to the rescue station. Love Sabe.*

Sydney smiled, at both the love part, and the fact that Saber had signed off using the shortened name that only she used for her.

Sydney hurriedly put the shopping away, wondering if they were needed for a rescue. Perhaps Saber hadn't been able to get hold of her on her mobile? The signal rarely was any good around these parts. Saber had evidently left the note there, knowing that was the first place she would go to.

Sydney picked up the phone, calling the station's number. On the second ring, it was picked up.

"Mountain Rescue Service."

"Hey, Charlie, it's Syd. Have we been called out?"

"No, nothing like that. Just get over here."

"So I don't need to get changed or bring my kit?"

"No, only yourself."

Sydney was confused. "Is something wrong?"

"Everything's fine."

"Then I don't understand."

"Saber, speak to your woman, she's being awkward."

Sydney frowned, hearing the phone being passed over.

"Syd?" Saber's voice came through.

"I'm not being awkward, I merely want to know what's going on."

"Get your cute little butt over here and you'll find out," Saber said. Laughing came from the background. "See you soon." She hung up.

Sydney gave the phone a questioning glance as she put it down. She left the house and headed directly for the rescue station. When she arrived, the door opened to reveal the entire team inside, all looking at her.

"Hi," Sydney greeted somewhat apprehensively. She faced Saber. "I thought you were tired?"

Saber tugged at her ear, a sheepish expression on her face. "Err, yeah. Sorry about that, but I didn't want to blow the surprise."

Sydney's face lit up. "Surprise? What surprise?"

"Happy birthday!" Coop yelled.

Sydney's brow knit. "It's not my birthday for ages. You know that."

"He's joking," Saber said. "That's not why we're here."

"Oh?"

Doug came forward. "Now we know that you've been a member of the team for some time now, but these came through today, and we wanted to do it properly. Formally."

Jeff opened a large box on the desk, pulling out two items and handing them to her.

Sydney recognised them to be Mountain Rescue clothes. "Oh, wow!" She inspected them enthusiastically; she would finally look the part. "These are great. Thanks, you guys."

"We're really pleased that you're with us," Jeff said.

"I second that." Coop gave Sydney's arm an affectionate pat.

"If they don't fit, blame Saber," Doug joked.

"Let me take those from you." Rich stepped closer, so he was alongside Sydney.

Sydney handed the clothes to him. "Thanks, Rich."

"Close your eyes and hold out your hands," Saber said playfully.

Sydney smiled amusedly, but didn't protest.

"Wider."

She moved her hands farther apart, feeling something light being placed on top.

"Open your eyes."

Sydney found a white helmet resting in her hands. This wasn't an ordinary helmet though, it had been personalised for her. On the back was a large red cross, indicating her as the medic on the team. A smaller cross was on the front. "Thank you. All of you. I love it, I really do."

A chorus of voices replied, all saying the same thing, "Welcome to the team."

The End

Other Yellow Rose Titles You Might Enjoy:

Amazonia
by Sky Croft

What happens when you finally find the woman of your dreams, but your twin sister despises her?

Amazonian twin sisters Shale and Kale are as different as night from day, but they have an unbreakable bond—a bond that is tested to its limit when their tribe is brutally slaughtered by an unknown assailant.

Seeking revenge, redemption, and a new place to call home, the twin warriors travel to another tribe, where they find an ally in Blake, an Amazon princess. Shale and Blake form an instant connection, much to Kale's obvious unease.

As Shale strives to make friends and fit into their new tribe, a matter made all the more difficult by jealous rivals, power struggles, and her forthright twin, she must also let down her guard to Blake and surrender her heart, a most unnatural task for a warrior.

When the deadly assailant suddenly reappears, not only is the blossoming love between Shale and Blake threatened, but the lives of the entire tribe. Will these warring Amazons find common ground and ultimately unite? Or will the entire Amazon nation fall?

ISBN 978-1-61929-066-2

It'sElementary
by Jennifer Jackson

Tolerance and acceptance are growing in society, but don't tell that to a parent of a school-aged child. Teachers are supposed to be straight, wholesome, and good examples for the children they teach. This is why one vague rumor about a slightly effeminate teacher at Baxter Elementary resulted in a mob of angry parents demanding his removal. Victoria was a first hand witness to the carnage, which is why she vowed to never let her personal life mingle with her professional life. It was a good plan. That is until a most-certainly-not-her-type, absolutely adorable, first-year teacher got under her skin. And, when a confused and desperate parent targets her protégé, Victoria must decide which is more important: her career or love?

ISBN 978-1-61929-084-6

OTHER YELLOW ROSE PUBLICATIONS

Brenda Adcock	Soiled Dove	978-1-935053-35-4
Brenda Adcock	The Sea Hawk	978-1-935053-10-1
Brenda Adcock	The Other Mrs. Champion	978-1-935053-46-0
Janet Albert	Twenty-four Days	978-1-935053-16-3
Janet Albert	A Table for Two	978-1-935053-27-9
Janet Albert	Casa Parisi	978-1-61929-015-0
Georgia Beers	Thy Neighbor's Wife	1-932300-15-5
Georgia Beers	Turning the Page	978-1-932300-71-0
Carrie Brennan	Curve	978-1-932300-41-3
Carrie Carr	Destiny's Bridge	1-932300-11-2
Carrie Carr	Faith's Crossing	1-932300-12-0
Carrie Carr	Hope's Path	1-932300-40-6
Carrie Carr	Love's Journey	978-1-932300-65-9
Carrie Carr	Strength of the Heart	978-1-932300-81-9
Carrie Carr	The Way Things Should Be	978-1-932300-39-0
Carrie Carr	To Hold Forever	978-1-932300-21-5
Carrie Carr	Trust Our Tomorrows	978-1-61929-011-2
Carrie Carr	Piperton	978-1-935053-20-0
Carrie Carr	Something to Be Thankful For	1-932300-04-X
Carrie Carr	Diving Into the Turn	978-1-932300-54-3
Carrie Carr	Heart's Resolve	978-1-61929-051-8
Sky Croft	Amazonia	978-1-61929-066-2
Sky Croft	Mountain Rescue: The Ascent	978-1-61929-098-3
Cronin and Foster	Blue Collar Lesbian Erotica	978-1-935053-01-9
Cronin and Foster	Women in Uniform	978-1-935053-31-6
Pat Cronin	Souls' Rescue	978-1-935053-30-9
Verda Foster	The Gift	978-1-61929-029-7
Anna Furtado	The Heart's Desire	1-932300-32-5
Anna Furtado	The Heart's Strength	978-1-932300-93-2
Anna Furtado	The Heart's Longing	978-1-935053-26-2
Melissa Good	Eye of the Storm	1-932300-13-9
Melissa Good	Hurricane Watch	978-1-935053-00-2
Melissa Good	Red Sky At Morning	978-1-932300-80-2
Melissa Good	Storm Surge: Book One	978-1-935053-28-6
Melissa Good	Storm Surge: Book Two	978-1-935053-39-2
Melissa Good	Stormy Waters	978-1-61929-082-2
Melissa Good	Thicker Than Water	1-932300-24-4
Melissa Good	Terrors of the High Seas	1-932300-45-7
Melissa Good	Tropical Storm	978-1-932300-60-4
Melissa Good	Tropical Convergence	978-1-935053-18-7
Regina A. Hanel	Love Another Day	978-1-935053-44-6
Maya Indigal	Until Soon	978-1-932300-31-4
Jennifer Jackson	It's Elementary	978-1-61929-084-6
Lori L. Lake	Different Dress	1-932300-08-2
Lori L. Lake	Ricochet In Time	1-932300-17-1
Lori L. Lake	Like Lovers Do	978-1-935053-66-8
K. E. Lane	And, Playing the Role of Herself	978-1-932300-72-7
Helen Macpherson	Love's Redemption	978-1-935053-04-0
J. Y Morgan	Learning To Trust	978-1-932300-59-8
J. Y. Morgan	Download	978-1-932300-88-8

Author	Title	ISBN
A. K. Naten	Turning Tides	978-1-932300-47-5
Lynne Norris	One Promise	978-1-932300-92-5
Paula Offutt	Butch Girls Can Fix Anything	978-1-932300-74-1
Surtees and Dunne	True Colours	978-1-932300-529
Surtees and Dunne	Many Roads to Travel	978-1-932300-55-0
Vicki Stevenson	Family Affairs	978-1-932300-97-0
Vicki Stevenson	Family Values	978-1-932300-89-5
Vicki Stevenson	Family Ties	978-1-935053-03-3
Vicki Stevenson	Certain Personal Matters	978-1-935053-06-4
Cate Swannell	A Long Time Coming	978-1-61929-062-4
Cate Swannell	Heart's Passage	978-1-932300-09-3
Cate Swannell	No Ocean Deep	978-1-932300-36-9

About the Author:

Sky was born and raised in England. From a young age writing has been her greatest joy, and she likes nothing more than to immerse herself in whatever story she is working on. She also has a passion for the outdoors, and enjoys long walks at the beach or in the countryside. Ideas for several more stories are rattling around inside her head, all of which are just waiting to be written.

VISIT US ONLINE AT
www.regalcrest.biz

At the Regal Crest Website You'll Find

- The latest news about forthcoming titles and new releases

- Our complete backlist of romance, mystery, thriller, adventure, drama, young adult and non-fiction titles

- Information about your favorite authors

- Current bestsellers

- Media tearsheets to print and take with you when you shop

- Which books are also available as eBooks.

Regal Crest print titles are available from all progressive booksellers including numerous sources online. Our distributors are Bella Distribution and Ingram.

Lightning Source UK Ltd.
Milton Keynes UK
UKOW04f1531160315

247947UK00002B/382/P